UNDER CONTRACT

JEFFE KENNEDY

Under Contract was first published by Carina Press in July 2015.

Thank you for reading!

Credits
Cover: Ravven (www.ravven.com)

Celestina Sala is so far underwater, she can't remember what it's like to breathe. Grief-stricken by her identical twin's death, parenting her orphaned nieces, abandoned by the husband who never wanted to raise children, in debt past her eyeballs, and now just one more laid-off landscape-designer in drought-stricken Los Angeles—it's all Celestina can do to get through the day. Running into her former wealthy—and devastatingly attractive—client, Ryan Black, when she looks and feels her worst is just the cherry on the crap sundae her life has become.

When Ryan offers Celestina a way to pay off her debt, by submitting to whatever he asks of her, she's appalled. And tempted.

His colleagues and competitors describe Ryan as ruthless in business. It's true. And that no-holds-barred attitude is how he built himself from less than nothing to the immense wealth he enjoys today. So, when he has the opportunity to finally get his hands on Celestina's voluptuous body, Ryan employs every enticement at his disposal. He's wanted her for years—and respected the fact that she wasn't available—and now that she's practically dropped into his lap, he's taking advantage of the opportunity. He'll play fair, however, offering her a contract where she can choose, down to the tiniest details, what she's willing to let him do to her, for what price.

He plans to pay very well to be able to indulge his darkest desires with her.

DEDICATION

To Margaret
who gave me permission

ACKNOWLEDGEMENTS

Huge thanks to my longtime CPA-extraordinaire, Pam Dunnuck. She not only keeps *me* on the up and up with the IRS, but she took time during tax season to vet the finances in this book. She also turned out to be an amazing source of ideas for additional plot twists related to debt and taxes. If only I could have used them all. Any errors are mine. Which is what we'd tell the IRS, too, ironically enough.

Special thanks to Madhu Ahuja Zierath, Gamma Phi Beta sister from way back, who generously answered questions about dance teams. Her talented daughter, Rani Zierath, is a graduating senior with the varsity Plano West Royales.

Thanks to Sandy James, a wealth of information on snarking up teacher names; Jodi Griffin for the gazelle joke; Lynda Ryba, Lorelie Brown and Mermaid Sharon for advice on Los Angeles places and logistics.

This is apparently a book influenced by old college friends. Thanks to Lesley Malin for the incredibly self-indulgent and expensive coffeemaker information and Scott Malin for giving me the best cup of coffee I've had in my life.

Thanks to the lovely gentleman at the Getty Villa who answered my questions with some bemusement, then enthusiastically debated whether guests could likely cross PCH at night.

Thanks to Lynn Spencer for suggesting "meaner than a striped snake" and "useless as tits on a bull."

Also thanks to my own fabulous Larry, Larry Redlin, for

consulting on Tina's hairstyle.

As always, deep gratitude to my crit partners—Marcella Burnard, Anne Calhoun, Carolyn Crane and Anna Philpot— who keep me grounded and always say such smart things about my stories, even when they're a mess.

Thanks to brilliant and supportive editor Deb Nemeth, Angela James, and all the Carina Press team. Our tenth book together—amazing!

Special thanks to Dana Almos, for being awesome, generous and working her magic as a favor.

And, of course, a big thank-you to David, for passing food and wine under the door, and saying all the right things at exactly the right time.

UNDER CONTRACT

JEFFE KENNEDY

CHAPTER ONE

"I'M SORRY TO tell you, Tina, but this is it." Linda's gaze skittered away.

Another ending. Not the worst blow, but the one that might finally drop her into the abyss. Tina tensed. She'd be panicking if she didn't feel so numb.

"It's obviously bad for all of us." Linda put her cold Diet Coke against her forehead. "Losing this account is the final straw. I can eke out a few weeks' severance for you, but not anything more. If I waited another week, I couldn't get that much past the forensic accountants. I'm really sorry."

"I could stay and keep working. Maybe—"

"You know I'd tell you if I thought there was a chance." Linda set the Coke down without drinking. "We're tanked. It's just not common knowledge. I'm letting you and a few other people go now so you can at least start looking for other jobs. With your particular niche, I know it might take a while."

Another understatement. Tina had chosen landscape design as a profession—and specialized in water-focused features—with all the idealism of the naïve. Back then she'd believed in studying what you loved. Follow your passion and the money will follow. That's what all her guidance counselors said. What her parents, God rest their souls, had affectionately encouraged

1

her to do. The perfect complement to Arabella's degrees in civil engineering. They'd had such dreams, she and her twin sister, of working together, always in tandem.

So many endings.

"I'm really sorry," Linda repeated. "I feel like I failed you. You know you have a tremendous reputation and I wrote you the most amazing reference letter I could dream up. It's not enough, but…"

"It is what it is." Nothing like having that tremendous reputation in a niche specialty like water design in a freaking desert during the worst drought in recorded history. The land had dried up, year by year, echoed by the devastation in Tina's life.

"I know you're like a third-generation Los Angeleno, but maybe you should consider moving? Take the girls, make a fresh start."

Tina gave Linda a reassuring smile, at least the best one she could muster. Her boss had tried her best. She took the envelope Linda handed her. Three weeks' severance wouldn't last more than a few days against the mountain of debt threatening to crush her in a landslide of unopened bills and haranguing voice mails from creditors. "We might have to do that. Guess I'd better go start the job search."

She knew there was nothing to find in the city, for sure. She'd been killing herself, tagging past clients, trying to drum up new business. The slow collapse of Delaney Landscape Design had followed the crash of the California construction industry, drawing ever closer to the edge, then falling into that ever-expanding crater. No one had thought the downturn would last so long, but with every year the firm had lost money and clients. Even with new xeriscaping jobs, they hadn't held steady. No sense keeping their star water feature artist in the face of a city ban against fountains.

Now the ground had crumbled beneath her feet and, like a disaster-movie heroine who'd been too stupid to run, she was clinging to the edge of the abyss, screaming. Except no hero would suddenly appear to haul her to safety.

"You know what they say." Linda produced a weak smile. "When a door closes, a window opens."

So you could throw yourself out of it. A slow burn of anger began to penetrate the numbness.

It must have showed on her face because Linda's smile faded. "Take the rest of the day off," she suggested. "Carly and Josie don't get home until after four, right?"

"Later today, with dance team after school. And then Carly has some science club meeting."

"Take some time then." Linda pulled two twenties out of her billfold. "Buy yourself lunch in some little place overlooking the ocean and rest your brain."

"I don't want your money." Beneath the numbness, her pride stirred. She had that much still.

Her boss blinked rapidly and pressed her lips together. "I have Bill's salary to fall back on. Let me do this for you. When was the last time you did something nice, just for you?"

She knew the exact date. Twice now she, Carly and Josie had taken sick days to light candles at the cathedral and toss the ashes of letters into the surf to commemorate the day that changed all their lives. How would she support them now?

They had no idea how bad things were—Tina had managed to shelter them from that fear, at least—but there would be no hiding this. So she took the forty dollars, for her nieces. Not to squander on lunch, but to buy groceries.

Linda knew they had it bad. But she had no idea how bad. Even Tina didn't really know, because she couldn't bear to look.

"Thank you for everything. You know I loved this job." Tina stood and Linda did likewise, coming around the desk to hug her.

"We loved having you here. You know how many projects came in because of your gift for fountains. I'll be expecting a deluge of phone calls checking your references. And anything you need—just ask."

"I will." Tina choked the words out, acutely aware of the lie in them. She wouldn't be asking for help because there was none to be had. When people offered that, they meant well, but they didn't expect the kind of price tag hanging over her head. Tina had stopped keeping track of anything but the general number, so overwhelmingly huge it overshadowed everything else.

Only money—huge amounts of money—would help at this point. And, like the rain that vanished before it ever hit the ground, money didn't fall from the sky.

Blindly, unable to muster motivation for anything, she cleared her desk, stowed her things in her crappy car and started walking down Figueroa. Rush hour had subsided in the Financial District, with everyone busily tucked into their offices, but traffic never stopped in LA. So many busy people with places to be. Maybe something would occur to her, some way out of the crater of debt and desert of unrelenting grief. Not for the first time, she vaguely contemplated suicide. Not the deliberate kind, but the sort where she might just trip and fall in front of a bus. Except that would solve only her own despair and leave her nieces even worse off without her.

Stopping at the *Salmon Run* sculpture by the Manulife Plaza, she let the fluid lines soothe her soul. The artist, Christopher Keene, had crafted the bronze to look like water. The scent, the sweet life-giving essence of it, almost wafted up from the sunbaked metal. The mother bear and her twin cubs feasting on the bounty of salmon. Both ferociously powerful and joyful, it reminded her of Ara, and how fiercely she'd loved and protected her precious daughters.

Tina couldn't fail to do less than that.

RYAN CHECKED HIS phone, noted he had plenty of time before his next meeting, and indulged in an extended appraisal of the woman studying the bear sculpture. Though the heels were low enough to qualify as dowdy, excellent legs rose up to a deliciously formed ass. She'd look amazing in stilettos. Perhaps four-, even five-inch heels with some training.

As he drew nearer, he caught the edge of her profile and recognized Celestina Sala with a start of surprise and an increased surge of lust. Odd to see her here and now, after all these years. He might not have recognized her out of context, if he hadn't spent so much time surreptitiously studying her lush figure. She'd designed the garden pools at his offices three—no, four—years before, and she'd been married and therefore off-limits, even for someone of his questionable mores.

Hell, who was he kidding? Morals had nothing to do with it. He hated complications and she had never seemed like the type to cheerfully commit adultery. That had stopped him from suggesting anything, but not from enjoying her easy sensuality, the swing of her hips that made him think of salsa dancing, tequila, hot nights and hotter sex.

Or from the occasional fantasy of dragging her across the conference table, baring those mouthwatering breasts and taking her with brutal savagery while their colleagues watched in titillated horror.

He knew how to behave in polite society, how to cover his baser nature with the gloss he'd developed as painstakingly as his identity, and he'd made sure she never suspected his interest. They'd kept things strictly professional and he hadn't laid eyes on her since the project ended. Barring the occasional starring role in his sexual fantasies.

She looked different. She'd cut her hair short—a pity, as he'd entertained himself with visions of releasing the gleaming black coil of it, seeing her naked framed by the glorious waves, of winding his fist in it to hold her still while he watched her suck him off. Now he'd never see that and he was not a man who graciously gave up what he wanted. Still...what if serendipity had handed him a new opportunity to make some of it come true? With her left side to him, hand wrapped around the strap of her bag, the telltale gold gleam of her wedding band should have been visible in the bright sunshine. Had fate put her back in his path, this time as a free woman?

Gifts from the universe such as this should never be taken

lightly. People made their own luck. He'd made up for poor beginnings in life by courting serendipity as his favorite mistress, fickle though she might be. No one had ever accused him of bypassing an opportunity. It knocked, he answered—and dragged it inside before it could escape. If the lovely Celestina happened to be available, he owed it to himself—and to fate—to do his utmost to capture her as well.

All right then. If she was free, he'd talk her into lunch. And then into bed.

The decision firm in his mind, he tucked his smartphone into the inside pocket of his suit jacket and eased up beside her.

"Celestina Sala?" he purred, going for charming and sensual, beginning the seduction immediately. Women responded well to sound.

Celestina, however, nearly jumped out of her skin, shoulders spiking to her ears in a reflexive flinch. She spun, eyes hidden behind her sunglasses but dismay clear in her body language.

"Remember me—Ryan Black? I'm sorry I startled you."

She relaxed, though not by much. Rather, she took on the studied demeanor of a woman who recognized a valued business client and pulled herself together. Assuming that careful poise she'd always carried, that regal bearing that begged to be stripped away. Giving him a smile, polite, not the warm, unconsciously sensual one he recalled, she held out a slim hand. "Mr. Black, of course! Forgive me—I was deep in thought. How has the pool series worked out for you?"

They hadn't been happy thoughts, by the look of her. She'd changed more than her hair. She looked tired and tense.

The shorter length could work for her, framing her high cheekbones and emphasizing the fullness of her lips, but the cut hadn't been high quality and now looked a bit unkempt, grown out too far. She tucked a lock of hair behind her ear as she spoke, a nervous gesture that revealed she no longer had the perfectly glossy manicure she'd always kept in the past but, more important than any of it—that she indeed no longer wore a wedding band.

His lust rose up like the beast it was and salivated at the prospect of having her. Lull her with small talk and shared business, yes.

"It was very well received and the plantings have grown up quite a bit. Of course, we've had to empty the pools, change out some of the more water-dependent shrubs and flowers for some xeriscaping. The drought continues to plague us all."

Her mouth flattened unhappily—not the direction he'd meant to take with her—so he added, "But I think the design carries it well. You should come see it."

"I'd like that. And maybe we could discuss other projects you might be interested in starting?"

He shook his head, then caught the keen edge of desperation from her. He could have strung her along with that bait, but business was business. Even if he could get any kind of new landscaping past his board—and good luck with that—the ban on water use meant he had nothing for Celestina's signature water-focused designs. It would be true for all of her clientele and she couldn't be a stranger to that disappointment. Better to deliver that sort of pain decisively.

It wasn't personal, just business. As in, once they dispensed with business, they could move on to personal. Besides, he knew how desperation motivated people—used it ruthlessly to his advantage—and this could be the opening with her that he needed.

"Unfortunately, no. You'd be the first I'd call, but with the ban on new water installations we—"

"Yes." She cut him off with a flash of impatient anger, the fire he recalled. Then she held up a hand and smiled in apology. A glint of her eyes from behind the polarized lenses showed she'd rolled them dramatically. "Again I apologize. The lack of work has been rough."

Her voice had a ragged tone, one he knew well from negotiations. Not just desperation but the sound of a person on the edge. Hating himself for the impulse, as it went directly opposite his desires, he suggested, "You might do better to relocate. Pacific Northwest, perhaps. Or New England."

She laughed, not the rich, sultry one he recalled, but slightly hysterical. That turned into a sob. Her lush mouth crumpled and she covered it with her hand, ducking her face but not before she hid the fat tears rolling down her cheeks.

"Celestina." He took her by the shoulders, bracing her, keeping her from taking off. "What's wrong? Can I help?" Perhaps his instincts had led him true after all, to the words that cracked her composure and made her vulnerable.

"No," she gasped, clearly lying and trying to make up for it by shaking her head vigorously. "Just…having a bad day. I'm so sorry for this. So embarrassed. I should—"

"You should come sit down and catch your breath." Firmly he steered her to the umbrella tables nearby, deserted at this time of day. "Tell me what's going on."

She dragged off her sunglasses and furiously swiped at her eyes. "Look, I appreciate your concern. Really I do, but I'm fine."

Patently untrue. Giving her a moment to reassemble the shreds of her dignity—breaking down in front of a client you'd hoped to be pitching work to could hardly be a comfortable experience—he reevaluated the situation. And ruefully discarded his plans to immediately seduce her. Wooing a woman in a shattered emotional state never paid off. He steered clear of boggy emotional ground for good reasons, not only because he knew his limitations. Besides, he might be a determined businessman and a ruthless opportunist, but he wasn't a monster. At least, not that sort.

Still, he'd made the decision to have her and he never went back, once he'd set his mind. Failure was one thing. Failing to persist despite obstacles another thing entirely. Solve her problem, then seduction.

"I can't help you unless you tell me about it." He tried to make the demand coaxing, but he wasn't letting her get away this time. No matter what.

CHAPTER TWO

A N ESPECIALLY CRUEL twist of fate to put Ryan Black—one of her best and most high-profile clients, the man who could afford anything—in her path and then snatch even that thin hope away.

For a breathlessly optimistic moment, she'd imagined that a window really had opened, that Black would offer her some lucrative design job that would at least keep her going another year. Even a few months. But no. His brusque dismissal of the possibility—which, if she'd been thinking clearly, she would have known would be the case—had been the penultimate straw.

The ultimate one being, of course, his blithe suggestion that she simply move. That's what people did, wasn't it? As if her problems could be solved as easily as he waved his dismissive hand in the air. The Pacific Northwest or New England. He might as well have suggested Saturn. Really, it had been the frustration that undid her. Always her Achilles heel.

When they were eight, she and Ara had been moved into a different math class where they were asked to perform fractions. It immediately became clear to their teachers that she and her sister had somehow skipped over the multiplication tables and they were sent home with a note. Their father, chagrined that any of his family might fail to pass muster, had taken it as a personal slight and taught them their tables in two evenings after dinner.

Ara, always far better at math, easily memorized the numbers, placidly correcting her errors. But Tina hated making mistakes, being wrong. Numbers never made sense to her. When she tripped over seven times eight for the third time and her father snapped "Fifty-six!" at her, she'd burst into tears and refused to do more. It had taken her mother's intervention to extract her and an extra evening with her father to get them all down. Though Ara hadn't needed to, she'd sat with her, pretending to hesitate here and there, even making a few mistakes, just to make her twin feel better.

To this day Tina had to think twice about seven times eight.

A thought that did nothing to help dry the onslaught of shameful tears in front of the intimidating and charismatic Black, who'd sat her at the table and looked at her as if he'd considered calling an ambulance—or a mental health crisis team. Then calmly offered to fix her problems.

Apparently the day could get worse. What next— earthquake? Immediately regretting the thought, she sent a quick prayer that, if so, at least Carly and Josie's school would not be hit. She even braced herself for it and Black frowned.

"Afraid I'll knock you off your chair?"

She managed a fake laugh and released her grip on the iron armrests. "Bracing for the six-point-nine earthquake that would make my day complete."

He smiled slightly, softening his somewhat craggy face. With his boxer's nose and personal intensity, even in his expensively tailored suits he had a tendency to look like a brute. More like the bodyguard behind the mafia boss. Until he smiled and pulled out that urbane charm. He covered her hand with his. "Tell me about it," he invited again.

Oh God. Was there anything more difficult than trying to stay tough in the face of someone else's sympathy? And then for it to be a business client…in the middle of what was no doubt a very busy day for him. He must think her bad off indeed, to be wasting his time this way. She lifted her chin, pulling her composure together. *Be professional, dammit.* "Thank you, but I couldn't possibly burden you with my minor troubles. I'm sure you're very busy and—"

"Actually, I'm not. I just finished an early meeting where we signed off on a major acquisition and I thought to take part of the day off to celebrate. I am at my leisure."

She sighed, appalled at how uneven it sounded. How perilously close to losing it again she still was. Time to escape, while she had some of her dignity. "Thank you for the offer, but I should go."

"Sometimes an objective ear makes all the difference. Maybe I can help. Tell me."

Maybe it was the habit of pleasing her clients, going along with what they wanted, but something about the way he demanded her story made her unable to resist any longer. "I lost my job today. Got another for me?" She shouldn't have snapped at him, but he shouldn't have pushed her.

Instead of getting angry, he regarded her thoughtfully.

"Rough place to be. Linda can't have fired you. Or did you screw up?"

"No." Her pride stung by that implication, she pulled the envelope out of her jacket pocket and held it up. "Severance and references—glowing, she promised, though I haven't looked. The firm is closing, for exactly the same reasons you pointed out earlier."

"The construction market collapse has taken bigger firms under. A testament, really, that Delaney lasted this long. May I?"

She waved a hand in permission, not that she expected him to give her a job, but because she just couldn't find it in herself to refuse him. Before today she'd wondered if the unending numbness meant depression and she'd barely resisted research-ing the symptoms on the internet. What would she do about it, anyway? She couldn't afford counseling or medication. Now, though Black had always been a bit larger than life, with his commanding presence and didactic ways, it seemed something other than the inability to act drove her.

"Not very generous," Black commented and she belatedly realized the check and terms would be in there, too.

"It was probably more than she could afford to do." She took the papers back, feeling the prick of guilt for putting Linda in a bad light, and folded them without looking. "I didn't mean for you to see that and feel…" She stopped herself from making it worse.

"Sorry for you?" He gazed at her steadily. "I wouldn't. It is what it is. Now you make of it what you can. Find another job. Move if you have to."

She set her teeth against the desire to snap at him again. "It's not that easy."

"Sure it is." He sounded brusque, as he had in meetings when someone suggested what he wanted might not be possible. "You don't even have to pack. Have an estate company sell your things, recover some cash that way, start fresh with low overhead in a friendlier market and build yourself up again. You wouldn't be doing anything countless millionaires haven't gone through before you. One company crashes and burns—you extract yourself and make a new one. One thing ends, another begins."

She glared at him, anger rising at his terse instructions and pat advice, curling her hands into fists. "You have no fucking clue what I'm dealing with."

His flinty gray eyes went stern, face settling into harder lines. Not angry, but intently interested. Something of a challenge in it. "Then explain."

"So you can solve my problems for me?"

"Yes. I'm a problem-solver. That's what I do—and I'm damn good at it. I could nod and smile and pat your hand, but is that going to help you with whatever has you this distraught? It's not just the job, I think."

"Isn't that enough?"

He cocked his head, pursing his lips as if considering. "My instincts say no. For some people it would be, but you always struck me as more resilient than that. So what else—the divorce?"

That sucker-punched her. "How do you know I got divorced?"

He dipped his chin toward her hands, knotted in her lap. "You used to wear a gold wedding band, chased with a design of interlocking ovals."

"How could you have possibly noticed that?" *And remembered.*

"I noticed a lot of things about you, Celestina." Not a man who hesitated to say what he thought. Still the gentleman, but that essential toughness ran under it, a glimmer of something else, too. Beneath the polished veneer, the affable charm, the effortless style of the very wealthy, something predatory showed itself. A chill ran through her, an atavistic warning of the wolf in the shadow of the trees, poised to spring and devour.

"That wedding band in particular presented an annoying barrier at the time," he continued. "When I saw you just now without it, I'd thought to ask you out to lunch." The way he said that carried a sexual intent she'd been blind to up until that very moment. A sensual intention that penetrated her haze and dug into her veins, quickening her heart with a sharp spur of desire she'd long thought herself dead to. How could it resurrect at this broken moment, with this man and his edge of contained violence? He wasn't handsome, necessarily, with the old acne scars and the nose that looked like it had been broken and badly set. But whatever erotic thoughts went on behind the sensual way he'd said those words transformed him, so all she noticed now were those burning gray eyes.

"I'm not in a place where I can date," she told him slowly, feeling much like the mouse under the raptor's circling shadow.

He looked irritated. "That much became clear in seconds. I said that's what I initially planned. It's not why I'm talking to you now."

"Then why are you?"

"You seem like you need…assistance—and an objective problem-solver. People pay me huge sums for my business advice and I'm offering it to you for free. You'd be foolish to bypass such an opportunity."

He had a point there. God knew she could use advice. Perhaps if she told him her troubles, he'd see what a mess she was and give up…whatever ideas he'd formed.

"Fine." She smoothed one eyebrow, then the other, willing the stress headache to ebb and the tears to stay locked away. "Six years ago, my parents died—no, don't say you're sorry or we'll be here all day if we have to stop every time for that. Cancer for both, ironically of two different varieties. After fighting it for years, my mother passed. Unfortunate timing, because my father might have survived his, but her death took away all his will and he died a month later. The hospital bills, even after insurance, were enormous and it turned out they'd second-mortgaged the house to pay them. They'd even canceled their life insurance and had less than nothing, so we had to front the money to bury both of them.

"Ar—" She choked on her sister's name and decided to skip it as an irrelevant detail. "My sister and I were handling it. We'd made inroads on our student loans, but we both had large mortgages and quite a bit of other debt when the economic downturn hit. With excruciatingly poor timing, my sister and her husband had recently started their own business, which required a fairly significant start-up cost." That she was supposed to have been part of, too. Big dreams. "They hadn't been able to qualify for a small business loan on their own."

"Tell me you didn't cosign the loan."

"Of course I did." She returned his exasperated look, refusing to be ashamed of it. That, at least, she'd never regretted, despite everything. "She was my sister. There's nothing I wouldn't have done for her. They would have been successful, too, in time."

"The past tense is giving me a bad feeling."

"In 2012, 2,857 people died in vehicular accidents in California. Two of them were my sister and brother-in-law. Please don't say anything." She took a deep breath. "They were in debt and upside-down on their mortgage."

"And as a signatory on the loans, the creditors came to you."

"Yes, along with my two ten-year-old nieces."

"Christ."

"Exactly. So, we've been forging on. One day at a time and all. But things keep getting worse instead of better."

"When was the divorce?"

She laughed. God, how tragic it all sounded. "He had me served three months after the accident, to the day, just to cement the date in my mind. The rest didn't take long."

"Spousal support?"

"I just wanted him gone. I signed the papers." *Couldn't have afforded a lawyer anyway.* She stared down his incredulity. She had her pride. "I didn't want what wasn't mine. I did get the house."

"Any equity?"

"Also upside-down. I can't even walk away from that. Another reason moving isn't feasible."

"Not even a short sale?"

"No. I've been to the financial counselors. I was fucked before today and now I'm unemployed."

"You're intelligent—you could get an education in a different field."

"Which takes more money on top of time that I could be earning at least something. There's nothing anyone can do." She willed him to listen, to stop reaching for a solution that didn't exist. To let her go on her way, to whatever dismal prospects awaited.

"Have you considered filing for bankruptcy? It's there for situations exactly like this."

She pressed a hand to the burning spot where her sternum ended and her ribs flared. Probably an ulcer or acid reflux, but she hadn't wanted to research *those* symptoms either. "I know. I probably have no other option. It goes against everything I believe in, everything our parents ever taught us about hard work and responsibility." She glanced at him. He regarded her with that same penetrating expression, weighing her. Like the wolf, still circling. Why? "Worst—though it seems ridiculous to say so, given everything—it stings my pride."

"There's a reason they say that pride goeth before a fall." His voice lingered over the words, putting her nerves on edge.

"Yes, well, I've fallen hard and yet my pride continues to hang on. Maybe it will take that crucial fatal blow as I apply to work at temp agencies and fast food joints." Though, who was she kidding? She'd been losing ground with her previous salary. Even working two, three or four lower-paying jobs, she might not be able to catch up. Not to mention the twins would be thirteen soon and showed signs of being gorgeous with it, turning the boys' heads. No way she could leave them unsupervised that much.

"I have plenty of money."

The bottom dropped out of her stomach, a turmoil of wild hope and crushing humiliation. The tears threatened again and she pressed her lips hard against them. How the mighty had fallen. She straightened her spine. "Thank you, Mr. Black, but I couldn't possibly."

"Don't decide until you've heard me out. How much is your total debt?"

She squirmed on the hard chair, the iron lattice cutting into her skin through her thin skirt, unable to meet his eye. "I'm not exactly sure," she muttered at her lap.

"How can you not know?" he demanded.

"Because once it gets huge enough, it hardly matters, does it?" she retorted, glaring at him.

A smile flashed across his face, lightning through a building storm. "Give me a ballpark figure—in the neighborhood of 850 K?"

She gaped at him, flabbergasted that he'd come so close, and he gave her a wry look. "I deal in this kind of thing a lot. I couldn't help doing the math as you described the various events."

"That's unreal."

"I like to think of it as a gift." He'd backed off the intensity, his teasing grin creating charming crinkles at the corners of his eyes. Surprisingly, it helped that he could say the numbers so matter-of-factly, as if he'd pulled the monster out of the closet and thrust it into the bright light of day, giving it a face.

"It might be closer to nine—" she tried to match his tone "—less a pretty much irrelevant few thousand."

He nodded, looking up and calculating in his head. "So, unless you have amazing interest rates, which people in your situation never do, the interest on the debt is accruing at between 100 and 200K each year."

Glancing at her for affirmation, he continued. "Given your miserable severance, your salary wasn't even enough to keep up with the interest, let alone allow you to cover expenses for you and two adolescent girls or make inroads on the debt principal."

"Your math is flawless. Which at least puts it all in black and white, but doesn't make my options any more appealing."

"Yes. It's not a pretty picture. Even if I could justify hiring you into some position not exactly suited for your qualifications, which would be problematic as I'm not the final word in such things even in my own companies, the salary wouldn't be enough to dig yourself out of this hole."

A crater, she wanted to correct him. An ever-expanding crater of disaster sucking her into its maw, the edges crumbling under her shredded fingertips.

"In your place I wouldn't want to file for bankruptcy either. It would be like admitting defeat."

She watched a group of pretty young women stroll by, carrying shopping bags and giggling, envying their carefree lives. Ryan didn't seem to notice them, keeping his unwavering, intent gaze on her. Looking away again, she picked up her purse. *Like admitting defeat. Yes.* "I'd better go and start working on solutions instead of dwelling on the problem. Thank you for talking me out of my tree." If nothing else, it had helped to back away from the roiling emotional pit and share the worst of it with someone outside the situation.

Well, to anyone at all. She hadn't discussed every financial detail of the whole ugly mess with anyone.

"Don't go yet." Black laid a hand over hers and gave her a long, somber look. "I'd like to propose an alternative."

CHAPTER THREE

H ER LIQUID DARK eyes narrowed with suspicion, for which he could hardly blame her. After all, even a part of himself stood back in shock at the audacity, the impropriety of the plan that had sprung full-blown into his mind. A stroke of inspiration, really. He'd never been the sort to let the implausibility of a new idea stop him. In fact, he credited much of his business success to the times he'd followed a path everyone else called insane.

This would be one of those.

Working Celestina around to seeing the logic of it would be the real challenge.

His concept was fraught with social implications and went against all sorts of traditional values. As with presenting any unlikely prospect to a board of directors—in this case, a board of one with total veto power—he'd have to tread carefully. He'd laid the groundwork painstakingly. Though he'd walked through the math with her—always good to verify that you fully understand the details—he'd done it mostly for her sake. In acquiring financially flailing companies, part of the job involved making them face just how dire their situations had become. People had an infinite capacity for hope and denial. In his position, he often represented the hoped-for rescue. As such, it fell to him to first crush their denial so they'd accept the help they so desperately needed.

Not that he intended to put it in those terms to Celestina.

That aspect, acquiring Celestina on his terms, played into making his proposal a tricky one. Also exhilarating. Nothing like a risky, and risqué, offer to fire a man's blood.

"You already made it clear that hiring me is not a viable option—either as a landscape designer or outside my expertise in one of your firms."

"I'm thinking of something more like contract work. Something you're uniquely qualified to do."

Cautious, nervous, she leaned away from him. She'd always been sensitive to nuance, her artist's sensibilities attuned to the world around her. When they'd worked on the landscape design, she'd seemed to read his mind, pulling the vision from his head. She read him well. Something to both capitalize on and be wary of. "I—I'm not sure what that would be."

"I'm asking you to hear me out. That's all."

"Fine. What is your proposal?" She held herself rigid, spine perfectly straight, clearly braced for it. She possessed a noble quality to her posture and he imagined Spanish queens in her ancestry, demanding an explanation in precisely that self-possessed tone.

"I've made it clear that I'm interested in you. Have been since the first time we—"

"Isn't the concept of a kept mistress a bit archaic?" she interrupted, color rising though she still didn't look at him, poised on the edge of her chair to flee.

"Yes, which is why I'm not suggesting that." The evenness

of his reply calmed her slightly, though she didn't exactly soften. He waited her out.

Finally she lifted her fingers in an irritable gesture. "Whatever. Go on."

He suppressed a smile at the California girl burr in "whatever"—something she'd surely picked up from her nieces. So different than the accents of his youth. Time to pare down to the bones of the idea, before she could cut him off again.

"Here's what I'm suggesting. I'd like to have a sexual affair with you." He put a hand over hers again, pressing a little to keep her from standing. "Don't run yet. Hear me out. We'd have very defined boundaries. A contract, as it were. I have certain interests that make it difficult to find willing partners with the right frame of mind and patience to explore them fully with me. You would have absolute power to choose what we engaged in together and I would compensate you accordingly."

She yanked her hand away and spun on him—not incidentally putting more space between them with a grate of iron on concrete—eyes black with sparking fury. "We've gone from archaic to the oldest profession. I can't imagine what about me *ever* made you think I'd prostitute myself."

"You're resorting to labels to make this black and white and it's not. You have something I need. I have something you need. This is a way for us meet in a mutually beneficial relationship." *Keep it in the realm of reason, not emotion.*

"Oh my God." She pressed her fingers to her temples and they trembled visibly. "I can't believe I'm hearing this."

"Stop reacting and take a moment to assimilate without the knee-jerk responses. Forget what other people would call it.

This would be a private agreement between us that would allow me to help you financially in a way that your pride can bear."

"I think I'd rather file for bankruptcy," she said to the air, sounding faint and horrified. "It's execrable that you'd attempt to take advantage of my desperate circumstances this way. I never suspected you would be so base and vile."

"Am I really?" he pressed, ignoring the stab of annoyance at the accusation. *Base. If she only knew.* Still, her reaction was predictable, not founded on any understanding of his history, and needed to be worked through. Much as he wanted to attack in return, he'd refuse to rise to the bait. A hard-won lesson from years past. "I'm willing to give you the money to get yourself out of a very deep hole with no strings attached. I'm also offering you a personal contract whereby you could earn that money—a great deal in a very short time, more than you could any other way—in scenarios that you choose to agree to or not."

"By doing something so wicked any decent person would be horrified to learn of it."

"Sometimes being wicked, going against social norms, is reason enough to do something. It's liberating."

"You make it sound so logical." Her full lips tightened and she leveled a betrayed look at him. "What does a good whore earn these days—fifty dollars for a blow job?"

"Quite a bit more," he replied, holding her gaze, "for the high-end call girls."

"Of course you'd know."

"Paying for sex is far less fraught than dealing with relationships. If I'd followed my first plan, I'd have enticed you into having lunch with me, and then worked my way around to sex, either quickly or slowly depending on how much seduction you needed. At that point, with trust sufficiently established, I'd have tested the waters for kinkier possibilities, all the while investing in the possibility of getting the kind of sex with you I'd most like to have. What I'm suggesting here gets me exactly what I want much faster, with greater certainty and less emotional entanglement, with the added benefit of saving your financial ass."

"You're a cold bastard, aren't you? You seem so charming on the surface, but this…"

She had no idea. He absorbed the insult and let it pass through. He'd rattled her, which gave him the advantage. One he pursued with all his cold and ruthless skills. "Let's say you're right about that. You're a beautiful, intelligent woman, Celestina, and I've long imagined you have the kind of passion I most enjoy in a lover. I wanted that with you when we met years ago and you weren't available. I didn't make any overtures to you then because of that. I think it's fair to say you never suspected my attraction."

"You're right. It never crossed my mind." She hurled it at him like an insult, but she couldn't know that it didn't surprise him in the least. Most women weren't attracted to him until he coaxed or lured them in that direction. Another lesson learned long ago.

"My point is, I hardly spent the last four years pining for you. If we part in the next few minutes and never see each other again, I won't suffer unrequited affection. Maybe that makes me cold, but you and I have had only a business relationship and are barely more than casual acquaintances. Neither of us owes the other anything. In my mind, I'm not taking advantage of you but rather offering you help that you obviously need."

"In return for sex."

"In a nutshell."

"Kinky sex."

"The kinkier, the more valuable to me. Supply and demand."

"And you would decide what I'm worth to you." She sounded mean as she said it, but his business instincts tingled with the certainty that they'd moved into negotiating. Though she might not realize it, she'd stopped rejecting the concept as a whole and had begun picking apart the details. Which meant that, on some level, she was considering at least aspects of the proposal.

Time to move delicately so as not to crash the deal before they hammered out an agreement. Controlling the zing of triumph at the prospect of both having her at his mercy and at winning such an audacious move, he kept his voice gentle and reasonable.

"I'm prepared to be generous as this would be a rare opportunity for me. What I have in mind is a living contract, whereby I would suggest the value to me of various sexual acts and scenarios. You could then sort through and choose what you'd be willing to try, according to your personal tolerance compared to the potential rewards—both financial and pleasurable, I should specify—and your sense of adventure."

"Adventure?" She cocked her head, startled out of her train

of thought by that. Good.

"Yes." He let himself lean in a little, looked at her lush mouth and thought of what he'd like her to do with it, willing her to feel his interest. "It would be a kind of game."

"A game," she echoed. Another excellent sign that they'd synchronized, falling into a harmony of understanding. His cock hardened at the prospect that she might actually agree to this.

"A private one." He spoke softly so she had to shift closer to hear. "To all appearances, we would be simply dating, as people do. Exclusively. We'd spend time together, with your nieces, if you like. All very aboveboard. You would be able to spend time with them, as I'm sure girls that age need, and you would be able to do what you liked—go back to school. Develop a new expertise. Write that novel you've always wanted to." She didn't smile at the joke, but she had definitely relaxed somewhat from her rigidly offended posture. "Meanwhile, you would be bringing in the money you need to extract yourself from this financial hell not of your own making, with everything totally under your control. You would decide what you will and will not do. You can choose only what you enjoy."

"What if I agreed to something, get into it and *don't* enjoy it?"

Did she realize she'd begun to seriously consider the proposal enough to be adding her own points of negotiation? "We would agree on a code where you could immediately stop something like that," he answered carefully. No sense triggering her with lingo.

"Like a safeword." Ah, but she went there herself. Promising.

"If you like," he agreed softly, deliberately caressing her with his voice and gaze. All part of the necessary seduction. "You can trust me to always treat you with great care. I would never want you to feel that you're in the position of doing something that makes you uncomfortable."

"Though I might—if the price tag were high enough."

"I think you're made of sterner stuff than that. But we could put in the contract that it's null and void at any time either of us wishes it to be and you can either accept a loan from me instead for whatever debt you have left or you can simply walk away, no harm, no foul."

"But we'd have penetrative sex."

"It would be on the menu, as it were, but you wouldn't have to agree to it. There's plenty else I'd love to explore with you without going there. Particularly to begin with. We could work our way up to it."

"It would be worth more."

"It would depend." The conversation alone was the most interesting one he'd had with a woman in months. Years. Maybe ever. A kind of sexual intercourse in its own way. "Very kinky non-penetration could be much higher on my list than vanilla penetration. Some things I'd price highly wouldn't even involve you taking off your clothes."

Her eyes flickered. "Like what?" she asked, reluctantly curious.

"Ropes bind a woman over her clothes just as effectively as with her naked."

She processed that, her sensual lips pursed against whatever she wanted to say, an aroused glint in her dark gaze. There she lurked, the passionate woman he'd glimpsed all those years ago, before grief and despair got their hooks into her. Scenting victory, he risked pressing just a bit more.

"You'd have fun, Celestina. When was the last time you had fun?"

She flinched, yanking herself back. Too much. Or an unexpected trigger. A risk and he'd nearly blown the deal. Not completely though. She hadn't walked away from the table.

CHAPTER FOUR

*W*HEN WAS THE *last time you had fun?*
When was the last time you did something nice, just for you?

She'd given up thinking the day couldn't get any worse, and settled on the decided possibility that it would go down in her personal history as, if not the most awful, then certainly the strangest day of her life. God only knew what the universe was trying to tell her with all this. But when she'd dropped the girls off at school this morning, she'd had no idea that, only hours later, she'd be unemployed and sitting with Ryan Black, semi-seriously considering the outlandish and outrageous possibility of having deviant sex with him for money.

Because that's what it came down to, right? He could dress it up in whatever phrasing he liked—because, no doubt he excelled at making the most appalling suggestions sound reasonable—but she'd be trading sex for profit and there were words for that.

Ugly words.

He regarded her steadily, gray eyes alert, though his stocky body assumed a relaxed, even indolent pose as he nearly slouched in his chair, hands folded on one knee. He didn't fool her for a moment. Lions looked lazy, too, until they sprang on the gazelle and gutted it with one swipe. He exuded sensuality the same way a predator communicated menace in the intensity of its gaze. Impossible that she'd totally missed this aspect of him before, as if he'd been undercover somehow, this savage sexuality cloaked under the casual charm of impeccable manners.

If she were honest with herself, she'd have to admit that this ghastly suggestion tempted her beyond the promise of money, piquing her prurient interest, too. What would be so very outré that he'd pay top dollar for? She'd question why he'd want to bind her with ropes even dressed, but the image of herself trussed like that had gone straight to her gut—but with warming fire instead of the anxiety that had plagued her. So surreal that she'd sat there and discussed penetrative sex with him when she hadn't had any since Noah and only with one other guy besides him. The wages of marrying young.

You'd have fun, Celestina.

Some part of her roused to it. A mischievous, vital part she thought had died with Ara. The young woman she'd been back before they each married, when they'd spent their time on the dance team, gossiping about cute boys and dreaming of their future. Naïve fantasies where they'd marry wealthy, handsome men and their lives would be full of travel, romance and tropical nights of breathtaking pleasure.

This was how the devil tempted you, with seduction and lies, right? He offers the answer to your prayers and darker desires, then consumes your immortal soul. They'd gradually stopped going to Mass after she and Ara were confirmed. Mostly they'd wanted the dresses and the party and she didn't really believe in a lot of the Church's policy, especially toward women. But those old lessons lingered in her mind, whispered in the dry, disapproving voices of the stern-faced nuns.

This was wrong, no matter how Black spun it. You could debate whether wives exchanged sex with their husbands for security or if all sexual interactions involved transfer of more than mutual pleasure—it all came down to that she would never condone Carly and Josie entering into such an arrangement. And she would be ashamed for them to know that she had. She owed it to Ara to take care of them.

That was the line in the sand.

"I can't," she whispered, too faintly, because he leaned in to hear her over the steady beat of traffic. "I can't do that." There, loud and firm.

His eyes darkened with irritated disappointment, though his expression remained calm as he nodded. He reached into his jacket pocket and pulled out a silver card case and one of those pens that people pay thousands for, writing something on the back. Handing it to her, he said, "That's my personal cell number. If you change your mind—about any of it—or if you just need a friendly ear, call me. Anytime."

She held on to the creamy cardstock dumbly, taken aback that he hadn't argued further. But his gaze fell again to her mouth, brushing against her lips in that way that felt as palpable as a kiss, in a way that made her think he hadn't given up at all.

Because she recklessly wanted to lean in, find out how an actual kiss would feel, she stood and made a show of putting the card in the special compartment of her phone wallet reserved for important clients. How call girls referred to their customers, too, right? *Don't think about that.* "Thank you."

She started to go. Felt bad about the chilly goodbye, despite everything. Turned back. "I'm sorry that things aren't different. That my life hadn't gone another way and you could have taken me to lunch and…"…*work our way around to sex…kinkier possibilities…investing in the possibility of getting the kind of sex with you I'd most like to have.* Other women had sexual adventures. Maybe she could have done that. If she'd become a different person.

He watched her intently, as if reading the direction of her thoughts, a small smile curving his mouth. "It's a standing offer, Celestina. It's never too late to make your life go another direction."

"Experience has taught me otherwise."

"Maybe serendipity guided us together to change that."

Yeah. Right. "Goodbye." She said it crisply and strode off, toward the parking lot and her car, without indulging in any backward glances. She'd meant that, because it had certainly proved true.

Though his words made her wonder.

SHE WONDERED EVEN more as the world and its realities came back. Sitting there with Ryan Black, of all people, had been like a bubble out of time where only the two of them existed, when she'd thought only about the ramifications of his extraordinary offer—and the illicit thrill of it. When she'd felt irritation and desire, bright emotions compared to the dusty fog of grief and despair.

That's the only reason she'd even pretended to entertain his outrageous proposal—because she'd been drawn in by the illicit and shocking intrigue of it all. By her reluctant fascination for the sensually cloaked savagery he'd let her glimpse. *Sometimes being wicked is reason enough to do something.* She'd always been the good girl, done the right thing, the expected thing—and look how her life had turned out. Some reward for good behavior.

Logically she knew that it wasn't about cause and effect, bad things happened to good people, correlation wasn't causation and yadda yadda yadda. Just because her life had turned out for shit despite doing the right thing didn't mean she should do bad things instead. Still, the part of her that had roused during her conversation with Black spun dark fantasies of what would have happened if she'd agreed. Along with it, unexpected emotions flooded her. Sexual yearning, yes. Regret. A certain deep frustration that felt like...

Anger.

So much anger.

Wow—how hadn't she known she carried this around? Odd that, when the numbing fog of grief and despair thinned, she mainly felt blinding rage. Initially she'd thought Black's insulting offer drew her ire—an obvious target.

But, driving home, she really began to wonder. Burning wrath kept bubbling up, popping and reforming like the twins' lava lamp, going acid green to angry orange to seething crimson.

Her parents, taking out that insane second mortgage.

Ara, dying like that, as if they didn't share the same life, the same heart.

Noah, after all the shit she'd put up with from him, bailing on her when things got bad. *We agreed we'd never have children.* He'd had the gall to say that when their nieces, the daughters of the people who'd treated him as family, had been orphaned. He'd accused her, more than once, of loving her twin more than him. When he left, she'd told him he was right, because Ara would never have left her on purpose.

Besides all of that, though, she raged at what she'd missed. That she'd somehow be turning thirty-three and had less than nothing to show for it. *A hell not of your own making.* Black had summed that up a little too succinctly—and too neatly. Everyone made their own hells, didn't they? And she'd contributed to this one sure enough. She wasn't letting herself off that hook.

She stopped at the store and spent Linda's forty dollars—all but a dollar twenty-three—on food that would last the three of them probably a day and a half, the way the girls ate. Sending a mental apology to Ara, who'd always fed her babies organic food and whole grains, Tina picked out the cheapest turkey meat and tried not to think about what all might be in it. She passed the liquor section and gazed longingly at the wine she couldn't afford, briefly indulging in the thought of drinking a bottle before the girls came home from school and soaking in her sorrows.

Except she wasn't sad. She was pissed. A pity party might turn into one of those deals where a person inexplicably decides to douse their house in gasoline and set fire to it, then drives off down the San Bernardino Freeway cackling madly.

Compared to that scenario, Black's salacious offer sounded

quite sane.

Which went to prove how unstable she really was.

She pulled into the driveway and glared at the house. Like an old lover who'd betrayed her, she hated it as much as she'd once loved the place. Their starter house, she'd thought. A charming bungalow in a pretty neighborhood, made far too expensive by proximity to the beach. She'd had to have that, pretty dreams of jogging on the beach every morning. When was the last time she'd taken that walk? Years. When the twins went to hang with their friends, she drove and dropped them off with their coolers, umbrellas and beach blankets. Exercise had gone the way of everything else nonessential in her life.

Like decent grooming. Black had noticed her Super Cheap Cuts hairstyle. A man like him would and his gaze had brushed over it. She hadn't imagined that. She should have kept her hair long. Then she could have trimmed the ends herself and put it in a bun every day. But that day she'd caught her reflection in the mirror and thought with a wild stab of hope that Ara had walked into the room...well, she hadn't been thinking at all clearly. She'd just been deranged in her desperation to never make that error again, sawing through the thick mass with her grandmother's sewing shears.

Making herself get out of the car, she retrieved her paltry bags and carried them into the house. It, too, had gone downhill, with its dead lawn and chaos of clutter. The girls were supposed to clean as part of their chores, but they usually blew it off and she rarely mustered the energy to nag them about it. Especially when it felt like putting brass polish on a turd, as her grandmother would have said, since she'd deferred all the big maintenance, even before everything had happened.

Of course she'd thought about setting fire to it.

Probably everyone in her position did. All those movies where the arson detectives investigate. The damning evidence of a desperate bid for insurance to end the eternal cycle of dealing with creditors, the endless messages and accusations.

Speaking of which, oh joy, bills in the pile of mail scattered inside the door. And an envelope with the insignia of the private school the girls attended. Her gut clenched and she stepped over it, carrying the bags into the kitchen. She'd missed the deadline for their tuition payment. The dean had been polite, understanding—to a point—and, unlike the others dunning her for payments, the dean could trap her in person. They'd be making decisions soon for fall enrollment and anyone not paid up would relinquish their legacy position.

The school cost way too much, but she'd managed the past two years by putting the tuition payments on credit cards. Ungodly interest, of course—Black would no doubt be aghast. But the girls had attended that school since first grade and she couldn't bear to wrest that, too, away from them. It had been their one constant in the chaos of being orphaned and moving in with their aunt. At least they'd had the same friends, same teachers, the same excellent counselor who knew their heads inside and out, from way back.

If she couldn't find a way to pay, they'd have to enter the public school system as eighth graders, with all the social pressures that entailed. Innocent and lovely lambs to be fleeced by the street-savvy boys, the gangs and drug dealers. Because she and Noah never intended to have children, she hadn't looked at the schools local to the neighborhood. They hadn't been great to begin with and had only gotten worse with the rampant foreclosures and squatters living in empty houses. Even if Steve's family hadn't convinced her that taking a short-sale on Ara and Steve's house made more sense, their public schools hadn't been much better. She might as well move cross-country as send her nieces to the local high school—it wouldn't be any less wrenching for them.

She put the groceries away, decided to skip lunch as a cost-saving measure and since her stomach hurt too much to eat anyway. Instead she made herself open the latest round of bills and look at them instead of just shoving them in the box in her closet. Black had been so matter-of-fact about the numbers. He wouldn't hide away unopened bills as she had, hoping they'd somehow vanish. *How can you not know?* Maybe, just maybe, she could find a card with enough credit, or consolidate a couple to free up room on another to eke out one more year of school. They'd be getting the financial aid check and she had the severance money, which was—God! Not much at all. Was Black right about every damned thing?

Hours later, she faced the dire reality that, even if she ignored all her other bills, she simply could not pay the tuition.

Maybe burning down the house and driving with the twins to some low-cost-of-living town in New England wasn't such a bad idea after all. They could change their names and live in a rustic farmhouse. It had a certain appeal, the fresh start. Not like she had any family left to lecture her about failing their legacy.

After a Google search for "landscape design jobs New England"—the Pacific Northwest would be way too expensive—she settled into surveying the various job postings. Several asked for experience with the harsh weather and wide temperature changes, making her shiver reflexively. Frozen fountains—how did that work? But she could learn. She had to do *something*.

The thud of the front door and the high pitch of voices startled her. Dusk had fallen, so she turned on the desk lamp, listening for the twins' mood. As usual, Josie and Carly were arguing with each other. On one hand she didn't get it, as Ara had always been like the other side of herself. They'd fought occasionally, but not the near-constant sparring Carly and Josie engaged in, as if they'd taken all their initial shock and grief and turned it on each other. Reflexively, she closed the laptop and shoved the tuition letter and other bills under some junk mail.

"Antina!" Carly yelled, feet pounding down the short hall. "Stop it, Jo! Antina, I need a new cell phone. This battery won't hold a charge and it's so old it doesn't even have Siri. *Everybody* has Siri!"

"You don't get a new phone unless I get one," Josie insisted, turning to her aunt to back her up. "Besides, I get new shoes, first. It's my turn. We agreed, right? I've been waiting a whole *month*."

"It's a stupid rule. Why can't we get new shoes at the same time?" Carly demanded, hands on hips. "Mom never did that."

No, Ara had never had to. The fire of anger burned anew.

"*Antina.*" Carly turned on her with a stern expression. "There's no way around it, I *have* to have a new phone. This dinosaur is practically dead."

"Because you text too much." Josie wrinkled her nose. "Maybe you killed its techno-brain with your bad spelling."

Carly grabbed one of Josie's blond curls and yanked viciously. "Shut up!"

"You shut up," Josie sneered, "whiny little beyatch."

Not a straw. Not a camel's back breaking, but gasoline to the fire burning in her stomach, the anger Black had somehow awakened now blazed without restraint. She found herself standing slowly, her face hot. Something in it alerted the twins, because they ceased all sound and motion, pretty brown eyes going wide, mouths staying open on the insults that dried in their mouths.

"Shut. The. Fuck. Up. Both. Of. You."

CHAPTER FIVE

U NDER OTHER CIRCUMSTANCES, it might have been funny. Maybe someday she'd look back on this moment—the image would surely be forever etched in her brain— of the almost cartoonish way they gaped at her.

She'd never spoken to them in anger. Not once, before or after Ara died. Before that she hadn't needed to, had been the indulgent auntie. After…well, who would yell at girls who'd suffered what they had?

In the clarity of her rage, however, this mistake also made itself clear. Always so lovely, having won the genetic jackpot with their father's blondness but their mother's thick hair, and the bitter-chocolate brown eyes exactly like Ara's and her own, the girls had left the gangly preteens behind and glowed with the early bloom unique to adolescent girls.

Not to mention the bitchy selfishness of it.

"Antina?" Josie ventured.

Tina wrestled down the words that wanted to rage at them, horrified at herself, yet also desperate to say more and worse. It wasn't their fault that she'd hidden the worst of the financial situation from them. That not only would Carly not get a new phone or Josie new shoes, but that it wouldn't matter because they faced true, disastrous poverty.

Hell, she'd be lucky if they had a roof over their heads by summer.

"C'mon, Carly," a much quieter Josie said. "Let's go make supper."

"But—"

"Come on." Josie tugged her sister out of the room and they went down the hall, whispering furiously at each other. For once on the same team.

Tina stood rigid, replaying the scene in her mind, their aghast faces superimposed over the afterimages of the huge numbers on the bills. Her anger ebbed in the face of grinding shame. The twins hadn't deserved that. They were selfish and self-absorbed—and so was every other twelve-year-old on the face of the earth. They deserved a real mother to help them through these years. Never mind an actual father. Even-keeled parents, who kept track of the bills and didn't lose their only source of income.

People who weren't failures.

Like admitting defeat.

She sank back into the chair, her legs abruptly weak. What the hell was she going to do?

A tapping on the door, Josie poked her head in, followed by a bowl of instant macaroni and cheese. Of course that's what they'd made, of the things she'd bought. Absurdly it made her sad, the faux neon orange of the zero-nutrition sauce coating the cardboard noodles. She'd meant to make them turkey burgers, before her little meltdown.

"Hungry?" Josie asked, taking her measure, then slid into the room before she responded, closing the door behind her and setting the bowl on the desk. Hitching her butt onto the desk, Josie cocked her head. "Bad day, huh."

Tina's laugh came out watery and she shoved a spoonful of the mac and cheese into her mouth to keep it from turning into a sob. "I'm sorry," she said, once she'd swallowed. The stuff felt warm in her stomach. Maybe not eating all day had contributed to her upset, the "hangry" the twins always joked about. "I shouldn't have yelled like that."

Josie lifted a shoulder and stuck out her lower lip. "I dunno about that. Sure shut Carly up."

"I'll apologize to her, too."

"Don't. She deserved it." Josie gave a self-deprecating smile. "I probably did, too. We dump our shiz on you and never ask how your day was. So—" she raised her eyebrows expectantly "—how was your day, Antina?"

"I lost my job today." She hadn't expected to confess it so soon, but it was a relief to say so. "You, Carly and I need to talk about what we can do."

"Wow." Instead of looking like a flower about to bloom, Josie abruptly seemed six again and afraid of the monster under the bed. "Can you find another one?"

"I'm going to look, but…" She poked a noodle with her spoon. How much to tell them?

"Eat your dinner. Don't play with it," Josie said, and grinned when Tina coughed out a laugh. "Remember how Mom used to say that?"

"Yes." It hurt to remember that, but in an oddly good way. "Your grandmother used to say it to us, too. And your great-grandmother."

"You know, I've been thinking." Josie kicked her feet back and forth, eyes on her ragged sneakers. She really did need new ones. "Mom was your twin sister like Carly is mine. We were talking about genetics in school, and how twins run in families and funky stuff about identicals. Some of the kids were asking me and Carly if we were like that—had twinspeak and psychic connections and stuff."

"You had your own language, when you were really little. You grew out of it."

"I kinda remember that. But I was thinking—even though Carls drives me crazy sometimes, she's always been there. There was a story about these twins that felt when the other one got hurt and, even though they weren't together, they died on the same day."

Tina's chest tightened. She hadn't known when Ara died. Not for hours. She hadn't felt a thing when the other half of her heart vanished from the face of the earth. "I've heard some of those stories, too. I'm not sure how true they are."

"Yeah, and I thought, 'That's how Carls and I will be, if she dies, I'll die, too.' But then I realized that Mom—don't cry, Antina."

"I'm not." She wiped away the tears as if to make it true. "No, I didn't feel it when Ar—your mom died, if that's what you're asking."

"I'm not. I mean—I didn't mean to, if it sounded like it. That's private. Just, with all this thinking, it kinda hit me that your life has pretty much sucked since…everything happened. Losing your twin and getting stuck with us. And you never let on. Before today."

"Josie." She took her niece's hand, sorry to see her eyes well with tears also. "I did not get stuck with you two. You've been the only bright light for me. Sometimes I think I wouldn't have lived, if you and Carly hadn't needed me."

Josie gave her a watery smile and that one-shoulder shrug. "I guess that's good, huh?"

"It's very good."

The door creaked open and Carly peeked in with one wide brown eye. "Are you guys talking about me?"

Josie ostentatiously rolled her eyes. "Seriously, Carls, the world does *not* revolve around you."

Carly stepped in, scowling, and folded her arms. "Then what—why are you guys crying?"

"Oh God!" Tina wiped her cheeks again. "There. I'm not, okay?"

Josie shook her head. "We were talking about Mom. You know."

"Oh. Yeah." Carly glanced at her twin and back again. "So, Jo says I should apologize so I am. Kasey Pearlman can suck it with her criticism."

"Now Kasey is the major beyatch," Josie chimed in and she and Carly touched fingertips, then fluttered them away, their gesture of solidarity, grief set aside for the time being. "She was totally picking on Carls's footwork at dance team."

"Isn't that the coach's job?"

Both girls rolled their eyes in perfect harmony, a synchronized sarcasm team.

"Ms. Atwater?"

"Ms. Passwater, you mean?"

They giggled. Sarcastic young women one second, silly girls the next. She was doomed. Better that than dwelling on what they'd lost, though.

"Ms. Atwater," Josie said in a prim tone, "was otherwise occupied with Mr. Bates."

"Master Bates," Carly whispered and snickered.

"Carly!"

The girl opened her eyes wide in faked innocence.

"You should come volunteer," Josie jumped in to rescue her sister. "Now that you don't have a job, you have time. You're a way better dancer than Passwater."

"You quit your job?" Carly demanded. "We thought it was PMS."

"No." Tina shook her head, then couldn't help laughing a little. They thought nothing of it. So exuberant, so preoccupied with their own lives, which was as it should be. They didn't know how bad it was and they never should. This was her problem and they deserved to be shielded from the ugliness of their situation. "Just a really bad day."

"Can you get another one?"

"Maybe. What if…what if we had to move?"

"Move?" Josie said it like she'd never heard the word.

"To where?" Carly demanded.

"I don't know yet. I'm looking into some things. New England, maybe?"

"Don't people, like, freeze to death there?" Josie looked panicked.

"No," Carly scoffed at her. "But it is practically Canada."

"Oh, it is not Canada and they have central heat. We'd

adapt. Or Seattle. It's not as cold there."

"It's not exactly sunny either," Josie said.

"Do they even have dance teams there?" Carly asked.

"We'd find out these things. It could be an adventure." *A poor choice of words.* Both girls gazed at her unhappily, disturbed in a way she understood. As with her, all of their changes had been bad ones. "Those are just options," she reassured them. "Probably not very likely ones at all. We don't have to talk about it. Let's do something fun."

"Want to build a blanket fort and watch *Pitch Perfect?*" Carly said and Josie jumped off the desk.

"Yes!"

Her lovely, wonderful nieces. They'd been through so much. Would she have made it without them? Hard to say. But there wasn't anything she wouldn't do for them, wouldn't try to spare them, if she could. She had a chance to dig them out of this hole. They'd never have to know how close things had come. She'd keep looking for another job, but in the meantime, she did have a way to make sure they could stay at the school they loved. They were worth it.

"I'd love to."

After they were asleep, she'd call the number Black gave her. The thought gave her the jitters.

Or was that a shiver of dreadful anticipation?

HIS CELL VIBRATED and Ryan surreptitiously slipped it out of his pocket to glance at it under the tablecloth. An LA area code, but unfamiliar number. *Yes.* His blood surged in his favorite blend of sex and triumph. She'd called. And much sooner than he thought she would. Though it could be just to talk, he cautioned himself. If that was all, he wouldn't push.

Much.

"I'm sorry," he interrupted his dinner companion, holding up his blinking phone, "I have to take this call." *Absolutely have to.*

The man nodded curtly, offended. Good. Double duty if he got to chat with a beautiful and fascinating woman, hopefully about sex, while delivering a mild insult to a pompous ass.

He popped the Bluetooth into his ear and accepted the call, to stop it from going to voice mail, but waited until he'd moved a few paces before saying, "Celestina. How delightful to hear from you."

Her startled pause nearly echoed through the phone, then a little intake of breath. A lovely sound he craved to hear more of. "How did you know it was me?"

"Only a few people have this number and all are pro-grammed in. Process of elimination. Of course, now I have you, also."

She hesitated and he pictured her dark eyes firing with annoyance, though she spoke evenly. "You do not *have* me."

"As a contact in my phone, I meant," he replied, smiling at the pleasure of the back-and-forth, and stepped out a side door onto a little balcony. The ocean gleamed in the moonlight, a shimmering contrast to the sharp glitter of the city. "How are you—did your day get better?"

A small laugh, a private, self-conscious one that made him wonder what she'd been doing. "Actually I guess it did."

"Good. I'm glad." He nearly said something more, but thought better of it, reining in his impatience. Let her say it.

"So..." She dragged out the word, took a breath at the end. Let it out again. Charmingly nervous. Tempting to rescue her. More rewarding to hear what she might say. "About your...offer."

"Yes?"

"You're not going to make this easy, are you?"

"What would be the fun of that?"

She huffed out an impatient sound. That got her. Something about the concept of fun triggered her, probably because her life had seriously lacked any for far too long. He planned to change that. No reason they couldn't both enjoy what he longed to do to her.

"I'd like to discuss it more. If it still stands."

"For you, Celestina?" He loved the sound of her name, sensual and elegant at once. "Always."

"All right then." A tapping sound. Her nails on the table? "We should...meet?"

"Now? We could have drinks." And he could ditch out on this dinner. The possibility of seeing her, perhaps even having her tonight, had his cock hardening in delicious anticipation.

"My nieces are asleep. I can't."

"Ah. Thoughtless of me." *Thinking with the little head there.* "Tomorrow—will they be at school?"

"So soon? I mean, yes, that works. What time? My schedule is obviously flexible." An ironic tone to her voice. She sounded more certain than she had that afternoon. Less lost.

He scrolled through his calendar, mentally juggling. He

was booked, but this took priority. "Ten thirty? My house. We can discuss terms and then…have lunch."

She didn't reply immediately, effectively confirming a direct hit from the way he'd spoken the innocuous phrase. Was she blushing? He wished he could see her face.

"That would be fine." Formally phrased, with a faintness beneath. God, she would be a brilliantly responsive lover.

"I'll text you the address."

"Okay." She paused. A breath in and out. "Good night then."

"Celestina? Sweet dreams."

She clicked off, but not before he caught the whisper of her laugh.

CHAPTER SIX

H E CALLED HIS go-to tech innovator, not caring if he woke her. Though of course he didn't—Cat answered on the second ring.

"Yo, boss! Please do not tell me the server crashed again." In the background, keys clicked and he envisioned her fingers flying over the keyboard as she brought up the server status.

"Not to my knowledge. But wouldn't you know if it did?"

She made a disgusted noise. "Do I have alarms rigged to tell me if it does? Yes. Do either of us believe they couldn't fail? Ha! But yeah—Baby is humming along. What's up?"

"I have an emergency job for you, if you can handle it."

"I can handle anything. That's why I deserve the big bucks you pay me."

"I couldn't agree more. It's time-sensitive and confidential."

"Shoot."

"My idea is this—a tablet or mini, with a special program. The user would be able to select from a menu of options, with drill-down to specific details, not unlike the online sites that let a customer choose the components for a computer. So each component would be associated with a price, with a final summation of the total. Could you do that quickly?"

"Piece of cake. The content?"

He looked thoughtfully over the water, leaned his hands on the stone balustrade. "That's the rub. Is there a way to set it up so I can enter the content and pricing? Some sort of idiot-proof data-entry fields?"

"That shouldn't be difficult."

"Then another step—could it link to one other tablet? Encrypted so only those two could read the current status, but it could be continually updated."

"I can do that," Cat answered, more slowly, thinking it through. "Tougher to QA. Could you enter content and bounce it to me for a cross-check?"

"No—this would have to be private."

"In-ter-es-ting." She drew out the syllables, clearly dying to ask more, far too accustomed to working for him to do so. "So, the user is also private. We're not looking at commercializing the product down the road?"

He laughed, imagining Celestina's shock even as his business intuition pinged. Probably he *could* sell something like it. Married couples could bargain sexual favors for chores. Hook-up sites like Grindr would no doubt go crazy over it. And, inevitably, pimps and other exploiters of prostitutes would jump on it also.

"No. I would never take this public." *Probably.*

"Okey-dokey. How sensitive is time-sensitive?"

He gave it a beat. Not that Cat—and many other employees—hadn't pulled all-nighters at his behest on many occasions. As she noted, that's why he paid them well. Money provided the best of motivations. Never before had it been for something personal, however. Certainly not to do with his sex life, which he'd always kept assiduously separate from his work life. "I need them by early morning. I have a ten thirty meet and I'd need time to enter content."

"Yeah. Might not be perfect, but I'll set it up so you can wipe content and hand it back to me to fix any bugs if they crop up. I'll drop them by your house. What's too early?"

Given how revved he felt, he might not sleep at all. "Don't worry about it. Come by when you're done and I'll make sure I'm available. I'll pay you privately—at twice your usual rate—and approve you to take a paid day off tomorrow. Fair?"

"More than!" She sounded cheerful but distracted, already working through the details. "I have to head in to the office to pull a couple of fresh tablets from the inventory. Check them out to you, I take it—any code you want on that?"

"No. Personal use."

"You got it."

"I don't want to hear any gossip about this."

"Can't spill what I don't know. I got you a couple of tablets for personal use. Story stops there." He almost heard her shrug. "Who knows what you eccentric tycoon types get up to?"

He laughed. "You might be overstating."

"Don't say that—then I can't pick up boys in the bar by saying I work for an eccentric tycoon. See you around dawn, I'm guessing. I'm totally expensing the caffeine I intend to pound, by the way."

"Bring me the receipt, you mercenary."

"Music to my ears, boss."

SHE FRETTED OVER what to wear. Like an idiot.

But, seriously—what did one wear to an occasion that was half first date, half job interview, not to mention mostly illegal. And 100 percent crazy. In the bright light of morning, she almost regretted making that call. It had taken her a full hour to press the green phone button, staring at his number sitting there innocuously. And then he'd answered so fast. She'd prepared a voice mail message, something breezily professional, along the lines of "Let's talk!" But he'd picked up, practically purring her name in that goose-bump-raising way of his.

Then he'd toyed with her, teasing her into saying what she wanted. This was what it would be like with him, that much was clear. He liked getting her worked up and off-balance, which would no doubt be part of these games he had in mind.

What the hell was she getting herself into?

She really, really wanted to chicken out, even as she picked out a sexy wrap dress and put on her best lingerie. *Going for first date then, huh, chica?* To shore up her resolve, she reread the tuition letter and looked at the pile of bills, making herself absorb the damning numbers. Definitely helped incentivize her.

Rather than the lesser of two evils, she'd opted for the lesser of two fears.

As she carefully curled the ends of her hair, wishing she'd had time to get it shaped properly, she had to be honest with herself that she wasn't fussing with her appearance due to the numbers. In fact, she needed to think about them more, focus on this as a business arrangement, to forestall the uneasy anticipation of seeing Ryan Black again, with all his potent sexuality. *We can discuss terms and then…have lunch.* How did he *do* that—make a phone conversation feel like a physical caress?

No, this was not about romance. Even if she did have a different life and they'd met in the park and he'd invited her to *lunch*, what followed would have been a sexual affair also. Adults—not her, but everyone but her, apparently—did this kind of thing all the time. The stuff she tried to keep the girls from watching, even on free network TV, was full of the hookups and booty calls and God knew what else. Her tween nieces probably knew more about it than she did. At least this affair—nice euphemism, that—would give her a better education to guide the girls with.

Look at her—coming up with brilliant rationalizations right and left.

After she completed her makeup, she took final stock of the finished product. *Good to keep in mind, chica. Don't forget what you're selling.* Funny how her internal voice sounded an awful lot like Ara. Would she have been horrified or egged her on? She didn't know. Ara had always been bolder, more adventurous and flirtatious. She'd been the one to fall in love and get engaged first. Tina studied her face for signs of her sister. More than the hair, the image in the mirror no longer looked like Ara, who would never be older than thirty. Tina would age without her, which seemed tragically unfair to them both.

Shaking off the sudden melancholy, she banished Ara's voice. Her twin couldn't go with her on this journey. Or any adventure, ever again.

She had to do this on her own.

Pulling up to the gates of the cliffside estate in her patched-up Volvo, she had to clamp down on the sense of shame. Josie and Carly hated the car with a passion, insisting on being picked up and dropped off at least a block away from where anyone might see. Given how much they avoided walking anywhere, that was saying something.

Job interview with wealthy client. That's all this is.

No good thinking about what might happen to her between this moment and when she drove out of the gates again.

The gates swung open soundlessly before she even hit the intercom button. Watching for her arrival then. Feeling like she should pull around the side to the servants' entrance, if only to hide the shabbiness of her car, she instead stopped her car in the circular drive at the foot of the grand front steps with a flare of defiant pride. A fountain that looked like it might have been relocated from Barcelona stood dry in the center island. Water would have changed the drab lines of the stone, brought out the color in the mosaic tiles, but they were dull with the dust of the drought slowly killing the entire region, not just her bank accounts. It hurt her heart to see it.

The front doors opened and Ryan Black strolled out, wearing a thousand-dollar suit with no tie, the shirt unbuttoned a couple of notches. Just your typical, casual, at-home look. He gave her a smile of welcome that carried a possessive kind of triumph that sent a warning trill over her nerves, and trotted down the steps to meet her at her car. With the door open, keys in hand, she hesitated, then lifted her chin, defying him to comment on it. "I wasn't sure where I should park?"

"Here is fine." He waited for her to shut the door and drop

the keys in her bag, then took her hand. "You look beautiful."

She tried to make it a business-meeting-style handclasp, but his mouth quirked with wicked mischief and he held on, tugging her closer and brushing her cheek with a kiss. She never quite knew what to do with the cheek-kissers, so she did her usual trick of waiting it out. He prolonged the moment, however, staying close with his lips near her ear.

"I'm really glad you're here," he whispered in a tone that took her mind straight to sex, not even remotely on business at all.

With a laugh that quavered instead of sounding polite, she drew away. "Well." She held out her hands. "Here I am."

What an idiot. *Kill me now.* She waved a hand at the center island, then knotted her fingers together because they visibly shook from nerves. "You let your fountain go dry."

"Water restrictions apply to everyone."

"A lot of wealthy people in your position wouldn't agree."

"I suppose that's true, but now you know not to paint me with that same brush."

"I'm sorry. I didn't mean to offend."

"You didn't." He raised an eyebrow at her. "Nervous?"

She blew out a breath and indulged in closing her eyes for a moment. "Extraordinarily."

"I know ways to work off that energy." He appraised her intently. "Unless you need more time before you commit."

"No," she said, too hastily, and wanted to kick herself. "The thing is—and this sounds really terrible—but I…I need money. Right away. A lot."

"Why would that be terrible? We both know that's why

you're here. I'm very much looking forward to giving you a lot of money—and to what you'll do for it."

She swallowed down the sense of panic at that and his gaze went to her throat, the wolf sensing fear.

"Only what you agree to, Celestina," he said softly. "But once you commit, there's only one way to back out."

"I know." She steeled her spine. *Only sex.* "I don't want to back out."

"All right then." He directed her to the steps, then opened the door for her, gesturing her to go through, his gaze like a heat lamp on her back as she walked.

"Through here," he indicated, guiding her with a light impersonal hand at her back. Mostly gentleman at the moment, the client she'd worked with, genial, polite, non-threatening, just a whiff of that brooding sexuality. Already she found herself keeping a finger on the pulse of it, tracking his shifting moods, subtly bracing for when he dropped all pretense and let that darker nature loose. She distracted herself from it by taking in the graceful home with its classic Spanish design. It had been extensively rehabbed, as it had to be at least 150 years old, but much of the original architectural elements remained, though rearranged to allow much bigger windows than would have been traditional. He'd furnished it with an eclectic mix of modern and period pieces, all carrying the flavor of Espanola and the early settlers in the region.

"You have a beautiful home." Small talk to stave off the inevitable.

"Thank you." He showed her into an office, spacious and much more modern, with huge windows that overlooked the ocean open to the welcome breeze. "I love the Hacienda style and tried to honor it."

She cocked her head at the wall of glass and he grinned.

"Within reason, of course. No sense suffering because some Spanish nobleman didn't have access to good glaziers."

"More of your 'enjoy life' philosophy?"

"Absolutely." He stopped in the middle of the room, gestured toward the glossy desk with the visitors' chairs before it, then toward a cozier sitting area. "What's your preference?"

Ever the gracious host. She sat in one of the visitors' chairs in front of the desk, set her purse down and crossed her legs. "This is business, right?"

He settled himself behind the desk and leaned his elbows on it. "I made a bet with myself that you'd choose this."

"Are you a gambling man?"

He looked faintly surprised at the question but considered it thoughtfully. "I wouldn't say so. In fact, I'd say I dislike risk for risk's sake. I prefer to arrange situations so negotiations work in my favor whenever possible."

"And is this situation in your favor?"

His gaze sharpened, a glint of that sexuality showing through. "You are on my territory, which naturally gives me an advantage. I was somewhat surprised you agreed to it."

She mentally sighed. Stupid of her. That would have made sense—ask to meet in a neutral place. Probably giving her the choice of seating was another negotiation tactic of his. But, really, she was out of her depth in this arena and that would have only forestalled the inevitable. "I shouldn't say this, but I imagine it's obvious. I'm not a good negotiator. And, as you said, we both know why I'm here and that I'm desperate with no other options. We might as well set the terms and acknowledge that the advantage here is entirely yours, no matter where we discuss it."

Sitting back, he considered her, tapping the tips of his fingers lightly on the desk blotter. "I won't lie and say I don't savor having the advantage in any negotiation, and particularly with you, but it's important that we *both* agree on whatever terms we set. I won't have anything but your full compliance—on record."

Though he'd assumed a politely neutral expression again, something under it seethed. It seemed unlikely that she could even scratch the confidence of a man like him, so better to be brutally honest.

"I won't lie either—I wouldn't be here if I didn't need the money so badly," she told him, meeting his gaze and trying to be unapologetic about it.

"I can live with that, but not with you vacillating." Impatient now, the lines of his face settling into that expression that reminded her of a boxer or street fighter, he started to rise.

"No!" She startled him enough that he paused and sat back. *Dammit.* She was doing this all wrong. "Please. I made this choice with full knowledge, being of sound mind and body." She forged on when he didn't smile at the feeble joke. "My pride won't let me do otherwise, ironic as that sounds."

"Because you feel like you're swallowing your pride by agreeing to a sexual relationship with me?"

Her throat went as tight as if she indeed had that pride lodged there. "A...particular sort of sexual relationship." *The prostitution kind.*

"I see." He went quiet, looking at his fingers tapping on the blotter. Notes and doodles ranged over the paper, numbers in columns and cubes stacking on each other in blue ink. He raised his gaze to hers. His gray eyes had a darker ring at the outside, making the lighter part almost silvery in this light. "I would very much hate the thought that my touch revolted you, Celestina. I can't do this if that's true. If you're only here because I've manipulated you into a corner."

An unexpected, even raw glimpse of honesty from him. One that took her aback, given everything else. "I'm not," she reassured him, not at all sure if that was true or what she was arguing for. "I mean, your touch isn't revolting, that is, I don't think it would be, and I'm intrigued by..."

She trailed off at his slow smile.

"You're blushing," he said. "I love that you're someone who can."

She clapped her hands over her cheeks. "I hate it."

"Don't." He came around the desk and sat in the other chair, held out his hands and waited for her to take them, a challenge in his gaze.

"Look at me, Celestina," he urged. "I only want these things if you want them, too. I won't have you unwilling. I mean it."

"I know," she said, without real sound, and cleared her throat, forcing herself to meet his gaze. "I'm willing."

"Are you?" His silvery eyes roved over her face, studying her. "Let's consider today a test then. A pilot."

Tentatively, steadying herself, she gave him her hands. His

felt warm and smooth, much larger with his knotted knuckles, strong in a way that both reassured and intimidated her. Could she really put herself in the power of a man with hands like this?

"Let's get this out of the way. You said you need money right away. How much?"

CHAPTER SEVEN

H ER MOUTH WENT dry over confessing the amount and she might have tugged back if his hands hadn't tightened on hers, patiently holding on. "It's just a number, Celestina. I already know the big one."

"Easy for you to say." But he was right. She took a breath and held it. "Forty thousand."

He nodded, as if she'd asked to borrow a five, and picked up a tablet, keyed in a security code. "Have you got a checkbook in that voluminous bag of yours?"

She frowned at him but picked up the bag, digging out her checkbook. "Why do men always have to criticize women's purses?"

"It's in the Man Book. We have to tease you about certain things or our membership gets revoked." He raised inquiring brows. "I assume direct transfer to your checking account works for you?" At her nod, he keyed in her routing numbers.

"Yes." Her gut unknotted with the relief that at least the tuition would be handled. "Aren't you going to ask what it's for?"

He paused, watching the screen. "It's none of my business. I'm not giving you a grant where you have to provide reports to me on how you spend this money. You could have a hankering for a new convertible, for all I know."

"It's not anything like that," she protested, stung. "I have to pay tuition, for the girls. To keep their place for fall."

"You've been paying 40K in tuition on your salary? How the hell did you pay your daily expenses?"

"Well, obviously, I didn't," she snapped, more comfortable with being irritated with him.

"Generous of you. I hope your nieces appreciate it. I made it fifty thousand, as you must have other bills that need immediate attention. It might take a couple of hours for my bank to confirm the routing numbers, but it will be there." He handed her checkbook back.

"I'm grateful." She tried to compose herself with the busy-work of putting it away again and settling the bag at her feet. Though she immediately missed the meager protection it had provided.

"They don't know," she said, not sure why she wanted to explain or why she felt like she'd been unfair to him. "My nieces. They don't know how bad it is. After Ar—their mother died, I couldn't bear to pull them out of their school on top of everything. Maybe I should have, but they were so devastated, so sad. And at least they had their school, a different kind of family. But maybe it would have been better for their whole lives to change at once because now it would be even more wrenching and they're *so* pretty and their counselor says they're emotionally vulnerable and they have zero experience dealing with boys and if they went to public school now, well, you know how guys are, they're—"

She cut her babbling off to find him watching her coolly,

with something that appeared to be amusement but wasn't.

"Predatory," he finished.

She refused to flinch. "Well…yes."

"On that note, let's continue this pilot project of ours and discuss what you'll do in exchange for the fifty grand."

"What do you want?" she asked in a small voice, almost afraid to hear the answer, though she knew. She knew.

"What do I want?" His hands were on the armrests of her chair—thick hands, like a fighter's, despite the gentleman's manicure—and he turned it so she faced him, though she didn't look up. Her heart stuttered, with fear or anticipation she wasn't sure, except that she'd gone wet, which only confused her further. What would be worth fifty thousand dollars to him?

He spoke quietly, the sound part caress, part scraping over her nerves. "I want you, Celestina. I want the feel of your skin under my hands, to see your spectacular body naked and feel you writhing under me. I want to hear you out of breath from ecstasy instead of nervousness, for you to gasp my name in my ear as you come. I want to push you past every boundary you ever thought you had and for you to go there because I made you. I want you to do things you think are wicked and discover how much you like them. Most of all, I want to be there with you, so I can savor your scent, the hot clasp of your body, lick up your sweat and tears, drink in every small sound you make as you lose yourself to the pleasure I can give you."

He was only inches away. Her face blazed and blood thudded in her ears, her palms slick with sweat.

"But, I'm willing to start with something less than that.

Let's discuss terms."

He rose and went back around the desk, putting the tablet into a drawer, then locking it. Taking out a notepad, he picked up one of his expensive pens from a holder on the desk and looked at her expectantly. She tensed further, half expecting him to demand sex at that moment. "For a start, I'd like you to change your shoes to a pair I've picked."

Not what she'd expected. Too easy? She nodded and he wrote it down.

"A kiss." He offered.

Still easy. "All right."

He noted it on the pad and made bullets beneath, in his crisp, linear style. "As long as I want it, openmouthed, including tongues."

Bemused at the level of detail, she agreed.

"That can be with you clothed. After that, however, I want to see what I've bought. I want you to strip and let me look at you in only the shoes. I won't touch you intimately, but I will ask you to do as I say, so I can look my fill. Unless you'd like to allow me to touch you?"

Ah, upping the ante. Could she strip for this man she barely knew? She'd have to. "I'd rather not. Just looking for now."

He wrote that down, cocked an eyebrow at her. "Blow job?"

She'd gotten decent at those, a quick way to make Noah happy without having to go to greater lengths. *What does a good whore earn these days—fifty dollars for a blow job?* No, fifty grand, it turned out. Mutely, she nodded.

Giving her a nod of satisfaction, he noted it, then glanced

up. "Do you swallow?"

Absurdly, given the baldness of the rest of the conversation, her face grew hotter. "I—I'd rather not."

"Fine. What's your counter offer?" His gray eyes intent, but with a glitter that hinted at how much he enjoyed this back and forth, he waited.

"Do…do you have a second-best choice?"

"I'd like to come on your naked tits."

Oh God. Had her face felt hot? It blazed now. She stared down at her knotted fingers. "Agreed," she said quietly, wondering how the hell she'd get through this. Except that her heartbeat thudded in her ears, not only from nerves.

"Are you all right with kneeling for it?"

She nodded. She'd figured on that anyway.

"Can I restrain you? Tie you up in some way?"

Her heart skipped a beat, a stutter of real panic. "Not yet for that?"

"Fine. That should do it then."

A shudder of relieved breath escaped her. She'd gotten off lightly indeed.

"Your safeword?"

Puzzled, she met his inquiring gaze. "Do I need one? I mean, this isn't…"

His thick lips quirked. "Yes. It is. Pick a safeword."

Mind racing, she couldn't think of a thing.

"Shall I pick one for you?"

Gratefully, she nodded.

"Angel. That work for you?"

"Yes."

"All right then." He spun the pad on the desk and slid it toward her, offering the pen with a glint of aroused challenge.

"That's it?" She stared at the pen, the silver glitter almost menacing, the neat list of what she'd promised to do. "That's not worth fifty grand."

"It is from where I'm sitting." His gaze drifted down to her breasts, heating as if she were already naked in front of him. "Besides, recall that one of the rules is *I* decide how much something is worth to me."

"Then you have an arcane system of measurement," she retorted, losing sight of what she argued for.

"Exactly. Highly personal to me. Which is why I get to decide. Nonnegotiable."

"And, since you're in the position of power, you get to decide everything."

"Not quite. Once you sign, yes."

That moment of standing on the high-dive platform, the decision point. Go back and climb down the ladder or jump, not knowing how the long fall, the cold, sometimes cruel slap of water would be? As it did in those moments, the decision evaporated into inevitability. She jumped without consciously crossing the line from no to yes.

She signed.

His smile turned triumphant, even feral, and he locked the pad in a drawer and put a finger on the intercom. "Mrs. Matthews? I need a pair of shoes. Size?"

Startled, she blinked at him, abruptly on the spot. Seven times eight is…what? She didn't know.

He cocked his head, face going stern as if he were about to

accuse her of backing out.

"Six and a half," she blurted.

"Did you hear that? The red Manolos should be that size. If not, anything red." He clicked off and studied her. The predator savoring its prey. "Do you need to use the facilities?"

"No." She wasn't sure she could walk that far, weak as her legs felt.

A woman came into the room, silver-haired and formal. How much did she know about what Black did, that he kept women's shoes to be delivered to his office for female visitors? She set the shoes on his desk. "Anything else, Mr. Black?"

"No," he replied, watching Tina, not her. "Close the door on your way out."

The door closed with a click and he smiled at the sound, a twist of his mouth both cruel and teasing. Picking up the shoes, he came around the desk and, with a lift of his brows at her flinch, settled at her feet.

"No hose, good," he commented, sliding his big hands over her calf. Pulling off the heels she'd worn, and setting them aside, he slid on the very high crimson heels, working carefully and seeming to enjoy it. "Perfect fit." He grinned at her, that odd combination of lethal charm and sexual intent. "Like Cinderella."

"I don't think this is how the fairytale went," she answered, breath brittle in her lungs.

"This will be better."

He stood and she half-expected him to pull her to her feet, but he braced himself on the arms of her chair and lowered his mouth toward her, slowly, so slowly that she thought she might scream with the tension. He paused a breath away, stayed there. Waiting for her to close the distance, she realized. Waiting for her to prove her compliance.

She touched her lips to his, tentative, feeling like she might be the one testing him. He answered the question almost tenderly, returning the kiss with the same pressure, which was barely at all. So odd to experience a man's mouth again after so long. Even with such light contact, he kissed nothing like Noah had. If she could even remember. Before him it had been high school boys, too hard, too hesitant, too sloppy.

But Ryan—wow. As he took control of the kiss, coaxing her into opening up, letting him touch the tip of his tongue inside her mouth, his scent and taste filling her senses, his expertise became clear. He didn't touch her, still braced on the arms of the chair, but she'd lifted her hands to his shoulders, aware of the expensive fabric of his suit jacket, the crisp brush of his lapel, and his sensual lips stroking hers.

Something in her unfurled, making her sigh at the almost-pain of it, as if her heart were breaking in reverse. How long since she'd touched a man so intimately? Or anyone besides her nieces? Since a man had kissed her like she tasted delicious. A soft moan arose out of her depths and he made a sound in return, of agreement, and deepened the kiss so she had to tip her head back until it hit the high wooden edge of the chair. He pursued, the kiss going from gently sensual to fiercely sexual.

Rather than frightening her, the increasing demand released some of her nerves, much as he'd promised. As if the power of the kiss broke through her barriers, the careful shell of numbness she'd wrapped herself in. Her personal blanket fort against the world. For the moment, all that mattered was the connection of the kiss and she gave herself up to it, sinking into the swirling desire that boomed through her blood.

This would be okay. It could work. She clung to his shoulders, arching her back, aching now to be touched. Maybe he'd change his mind and open her dress, fondle her breasts and maybe throw her to the floor or bend her over the desk. More the usual thing.

But he ended the kiss.

Not abruptly, but a gradual lessening of intensity. Decreasing the speed and pressure, an airplane banking, going into final descent. He backed it out the way he'd gone in, slowly withdrawing until their lips just brushed, a nearly chaste farewell before he drew back completely, looking down at her upturned face with slumberous silver eyes, full of leashed hunger.

Standing and adjusting his jacket, he touched her on the cheek, then sat behind his desk. Giving her the go-ahead with a negligent gesture that belied the heat in his gaze, he waited. "Time to show me what I bought," he said in a soft tone, both expectant and taunting.

Rattled, both by that devastating kiss and the prospect of stripping for him, she eased to her feet, oddly grateful for the distraction of having to concentrate on balancing in the sky-high heels. Then she steeled her spine and fumbled with the ties of the wrap dress, glad at least that it would be easy to remove. Opening it, she looked anywhere but at him. She didn't need to as his eyes raked her as viscerally as claws.

Unsure where else to put it, she dropped the dress on the chair, then undid the clasp of her bra, easing the straps down her arms, inadvertently glancing at him. He'd turned his chair slightly sideways, a man at his leisure, watching her with obvious pleasure and perhaps a hint of amusement at her hesitation.

Blowing out a breath, she dropped the bra on the chair and stripped off her panties, too, fast, before she lost her nerve. Then stood there, uncertain what to do next.

"Walk to the door and back," he told her, smooth and calm.

It had been a while since she'd walked in heels so high, but she found the rhythm after a few steps, acutely conscious of her naked bottom swaying and his rapacious gaze on her. She'd thought her legs weak from nerves, but as she walked, moisture slicked her thighs. That kiss, it must have been. Not this. This putting herself on display. *I want to see what I've bought.* She shuddered at the possibility that it was this part that aroused her so. When she turned to walk back, seeing him in his suit behind the desk, fingers steepled, watching her every move, she felt owned.

And was oddly transported by the sensation.

"Come to the desk, set your palms on the blotter and lean over," he ordered.

She complied, feeling her heavy breasts hang down, nipples aching as he savored the view.

He sat there a long while, then rose and walked behind her. Her ears went hot from the raging of her heart.

"Spread your legs."

Her arms shook as she did, feeling torn between weeping and begging him to...what? She didn't know. Thoughts fragmenting at the loss of control, she couldn't seem to muster any reaction but this state of heightened, unnamable and keenly edged emotion. *You're in the position of power.* Her own words echoed in her head. Until this moment, she hadn't understood how profound that statement could be.

"You're wet, Celestina," he said and she nearly moaned at the realization that he could see it, that he stood behind her, studying her open sex. "Most gratifying. Stand up and face me."

She did, moving slowly, taking her time before meeting his gaze, finding him watching her with interest. "You're very beautiful. Now kneel down."

He leaned back against the desk, his erection obvious in the clean line of his perfectly tailored trousers, and she knelt at his feet, part of her standing back astonished at what she was about to do, but most of her cruising on the tide of helpless desire. Better to lose herself in that.

"Proceed," he whispered, face set in almost harsh lines, his voice rough.

Fingers trembling, she undid the clasp and lowered his zipper. Then freed his cock from the black silk boxers beneath, gratified at the hitch of his breath. Her own little bit of power. He was as big as his hands and with the same thick brutality, veins standing out and the head dark and knoblike. Glad she'd bargained not to swallow, as she'd have had trouble with his girth, she licked him. He groaned, knuckles whitening with his grip on the desk, but he didn't grab her head as Noah had done from time to time.

Instead he let her find her rhythm, taking in the broad head, hot against her tongue, wrapping her mouth around him and relaxing to draw him deeper, digging her hands into his muscular thighs for purchase. He smelled of spicy soap and she found herself strangely exulting in the moment, thrilled in an unreasonable way to be kneeling naked at his feet while this powerful man moved in her mouth, hips flexing and breath going to harsh grunts.

He touched her cheek and she looked up into his fierce expression, releasing him and then unable to tear her gaze away as he fisted his cock in his big hand and stroked it in rapid pumps, far rougher than she'd handled him. Veins bulged at his temples as they had on his shaft, and his jaw flexed as, his avid gaze fixed on her breasts, he pointed his cock at them.

The semen hit her skin and she gasped at the sensation, both shocked and further aroused by it. Rapt by the shifting expressions on his face, she watched him go from that brutal ferocity to a relieved, nearly peaceful smile. A different man than she'd seen so far. He finished milking himself, then pulled a silk handkerchief from his pocket and handed it to her. A gentleman's gesture, as if she weren't the bought woman at his feet.

"Ready for lunch?" he asked.

CHAPTER EIGHT

S HE LOOKED SO incredulous he was hard-pressed not to laugh. God how he loved piercing that regal poise and putting her off-balance. She'd be a brilliant lover, responding so ardently to the mild games they'd played so far. Not to mention the way she'd kissed him back—with real need, with passion and vulnerability and he had no intention of letting her pretend otherwise.

She seemed to realize she was still holding on to his thighs and let go, brushing her hair back from her face and briefly glancing at her naked breasts, holding the handkerchief as if unwilling to clean herself while he watched. He'd have to change into another suit before he went into his afternoon meetings, which he'd do with great pleasure, recalling how she looked in this moment, all flustered, lips wet from sucking his cock, nipples hard and dark in the centers of her spectacular tits.

He wanted to touch them, but he wouldn't. Not yet. Everything from here would be in their contract, captured by the tablet program so she'd have to see that she opted in. He couldn't wait to see what she picked first. Because she would. She was all in and they both knew it.

"There's a bathroom through there, if you'd like to clean

up and dress in private."

Not meeting his eyes, she nodded and rose, picking up her pile of clothes and reaching to pull off the heels. A pity, as she'd looked beyond gorgeous in them. But he'd keep to the terms. Once she disappeared, closing the door behind her, he cleaned himself with wipes from his desk drawer, tucking his cock away and replaying the scene in his mind with relish. Celestina had shattered his expectations in every way. He'd loved every moment and it gratified him that she had also, whether she was ready to admit to that or not. It had worked out well, that she'd agreed to a scenario that left her unfulfilled. She likely thought she was protecting herself, but that would play into his favor. Good for her to want him, to be restless and needy. He could use that to keep her coming back for more.

She emerged, cool and composed again in that sinfully clingy dress that emphasized her lush curves. Giving him an uncertain glance, she raised her chin. "I think I should probably go."

"After lunch." He held out a hand to her, amused that she regarded it with suspicion.

"What is with you and lunch?"

"My favorite meal of the day."

She finally took his hand, tentative, as if she hadn't just stripped for him, knelt and taken his cock between her lush lips. "Nobody likes lunch best. Brunch maybe, but lunch is what you grab at your desk or suggest for a business meeting because you can kill two birds with one stone."

Keeping her hand, he unlocked the desk drawer and withdrew his tablet and hers, which was wrapped in gold foil with an elegant bow. Bringing them, he led her out to one of the patios overlooking the water. "My contention is that you are doing it wrong."

"Excuse me?"

Ah, that arch pride. Her regal nature—reviving again as she pulled her composure around her like a cloak—appealed to him as much as her hot mouth and voluptuous figure.

"Lunch," he clarified, with an extra smile to let her know he'd seen through her, enjoying how a faint rose was still kissing the arches of her high cheekbones. She had an amazing blush, a lovely tell that betrayed the emotions she didn't otherwise reveal. Leading her down the cliffside walk, he studied her as she took in the setup. As he'd arranged, a table waited for them on one of the patios set into the steep hillside, one of the several along the stone steps that eventually led to the beach. A bottle of white wine sat in ice, and silver domes covered the plates. A bright triangle of canvas had been arranged to cut the offshore breeze instead of catching it, and would give them shade. They'd serve themselves as Celestina would no doubt be more comfortable without eavesdroppers.

He held the chair out for her and she sat, taking an immediate sip of her ice water.

"You see, the Europeans have it all over us with lunch," he continued, pretending not to notice her continued state of arousal, savoring it surreptitiously. "They eat in the early afternoon and can spend hours at it, drinking wine, savoring the food and company." He removed the stopper from the uncorked wine.

"I don't want wine," she protested.

"Because you have an important appointment in an hour?"

"Well, no, of course not, but—" She sighed when he poured and pressed her lips together on the rest.

"Breakfast—" he made sure not to smile at her capitulation, lest she take it the wrong way "—may be the most important meal of the day, but that's about fueling the body. We're not awake enough to enjoy it. At least, I'm not." He held up his glass, waiting for her to lift hers. "What shall we toast to—new beginnings?"

She eyed him darkly. "To paying tuition."

"An excellent reason to celebrate," he agreed. Let her pretend that she had felt nothing, didn't still seethe with the need he'd instilled in her. That worked for him. "Would you like some bread? House made. Now, dinner or supper—most people pick that, but without really thinking about it. Did you know people in more rural or agrarian regions are more likely to say 'supper' whereas urbanites will say 'dinner'? And the rural folks often say dinner for what you and I call lunch."

"I did not know that," she replied, applying butter to her roll with a neutral expression, but a lilt of suppressed laughter gave her away.

"Most people don't, which is exactly my point."

"You have a point?" Her eyes sparkled with irritation and amusement as she glanced at him. Good. Better.

"I do. For people who work with their bodies, supper is the snack before they retire. Whereas lunch—or their dinner—is the hearty meal that sustains them through the day. Same for the Europeans, which includes your ancestors, if I'm not mistaken. Spanish?"

"Close. Most of my family is Catalan."

"Ah. Very much part of the Mediterranean lifestyle. They enjoy a long, leisurely and hearty midday meal, then have a light supper later in the evening. Again, when one is tired from the day and ready to wind down." He reached over and took the dome from her plate, did the same with his own, and set them aside. "Lunch is meant to be savored and enjoyed at the peak of alertness."

She divided her bemused stare between the plate and him. "I can't possibly eat this much."

"You have to, to soak up the wine." The crust of the seafood cassoulet broke under his fork, steaming fragrantly with the fresh whitefish, scallops and squid. "The sauce you can soak up with the bread."

Shaking her head, she sampled her salad, trying to look unimpressed at the delicate citrus taste of his chef's special dressing. "And to think last night I ate mac and cheese."

"Tell me it was at least real cheese and not the powdered variety."

"Generic, even." Celestina gave him her own cheeky smile, relaxing more. "You, my friend, are a snob."

Ridiculous that her calling him a friend got to him so much. Finding his way through her maze of prickly defenses wasn't easy, but the small victories were oh-so rewarding.

"I prefer to think of it as having excellent taste. Part of the point of being able to afford the best is actually enjoying it."

"A theme with you."

"Very true." Catching the thought behind her expression—he began to read her better now—he allowed her to see the satisfaction in his smile. "I'm very pleased with my most recent expensive acquisition."

Flags of color brightened her cheeks and she closed her mouth over some retort.

Quiet for a moment, she ate more of her cassoulet, using the bread to catch the gravy, and then sipped her wine with obvious pleasure. When she relaxed into it, more of her sensual side showed through. The trick seemed to be getting her to relent enough to do so.

"I'm surprised you didn't ask for more today," she said, much too casually, though she had to know the sally reopened negotiations.

His blood quickened, both at the promise of wrangling the deal and at the confirmation that she had wanted more. "Why—did you have a fantasy of what else I might do to you?"

She shook her hair, probably hoping it would cover her expression, likely regretting she'd brought that up. But then she met his gaze squarely. "That's what we're discussing here, isn't it? The kinkier, the more valuable, you said. Not my fantasies, but yours."

"But you enjoyed today," he countered.

Meeting his gaze squarely, she glared at him. "Does that matter?"

Considering her, he turned his wineglass, admiring how the color glowed like late afternoon light. "I don't know if it matters, but I like seeing you come apart, lose yourself in the moment and become aroused by being in my power. I want more."

That got to her. She sipped her wine, poked at her food

with her fork. "Like what?"

"Whatever kink you'll agree to."

"Like…" she took a breath "…spankings?"

"A spanking barely qualifies as kink in this day and age."

"So you wouldn't value that highly."

"I never said that."

"But it would be on the—what did you call it?—the menu."

"It might. It would depend."

Her lips flattened a bit with frustration. "What would it depend on?" She used a tone of exaggerated patience that didn't bother him in the least.

To convey that, he shrugged elaborately, affecting a careless attitude. "On my mood."

"Is that so?" She sounded dangerous, her temper rising. "Don't toy with me."

"Oh, but you're so much fun to toy with, Celestina."

She gritted her teeth. "You're trying to get a rise out of me."

"It's working, too," he pointed out. Then had to laugh at her expression of combined anger and chagrin, compounded by frustrated desire. "Eat your lunch and let me explain what I have in mind."

He handed her the wrapped box containing her version of the mini-tablets Cat had brought by just before dawn, as promised. He'd sent one of his assistants out to find a case for it and she'd found a lovely, discreet one, then wrapped the gift for him. One that Celestina glowered at as if it were covered in greasy newspaper.

"What is it?"

"Not a poisonous snake. Open it."

She held it in her hands, staring at the package, then set it on the table and pressed the tip of her finger to the corner of her eye, the way women did to check their makeup. The glimmer on her lashes, however, made him realize she brushed away a tear. He reached out and took her hand. "What's the problem?"

"Nothing." She shook back her thick hair, which had started rioting in the ocean breeze, then pinched the bridge of her nose between her fingers. "I'm sorry. I know I'm all over the place emotionally."

"It's fine. You're charming. What about the gift got to you? One, I might point out, you still haven't opened."

She laughed a little and pulled her hand out of his grip, working off the bow. "It's dumb. It's just been a long time since anyone gave me something. It's…so pretty."

That grated on him. "What about your nieces?"

"Well, I can't afford to give them an allowance, so I told them not to waste what little spending money they do have on me. Linda, my other friends—I asked them not to, since I couldn't reciprocate."

"Fuck them for that."

She paused in lifting the lid off the box and gave him a strange look. "They respected my wishes."

"They took the easy way out. A gift is a gift, Celestina. Not an equivalent market exchange."

Almost she said something back to that, which he would have accepted as he'd opened himself up to it, with their particular version of bartering. But she let it go and finished opening the box, drawing out the folio and reflexively stroking the smooth leather with appreciative fingers. He soothed himself by indulging in a flash fantasy of those fingers stroking him the same way. Today hadn't been anywhere nearly enough.

"It's lovely," she said, finding the snap and opening it. "A tablet? You can't give me this."

He sighed. "We'll pretend you stopped at 'lovely.' Besides, I can because you'll need it. Go ahead and swipe it on. It will ask you to establish a security code. Pick a good one. One your curious nieces won't be able to guess."

"So no using my birthday."

"Speaking of which, when is your birthday?" He withdrew his phone from his inside jacket pocket and opened the calendar.

"Soon, actually." She frowned at the tablet, at least taking the code seriously.

"The date, Celestina."

She glanced up to see him poised to enter it. "You don't need to do that."

He stared her down until she threw up one hand in a dramatic gesture. "Whatever. March 9." She grimaced as he keyed it in. "Don't make a deal about my birthday, okay?"

"Are you instructing me as you did your friends and family?"

"No. I mean, yes—in a way. I'm saying I don't need that. I don't want you to feel…obligated or anything—now I've made you angry."

"You reckon so?"

"You know." She set down the tablet. "You're very interesting. You seem all polished and polite, charming even. Then you go zero to sixty, from relaxed to totally pissed. Yes, it's obvious. Fine. Make a deal of my birthday. Though I don't get why you'd want to."

"Then let me make something clear to you. I thought I had, but apparently not. No matter how we've come to this point, to this deal we're cementing—" he tapped the tablet cover meaningfully and she eyed it with speculation "—you and I are entering an exclusive relationship. We will be open about seeing each other. You'll accompany me to functions. I will 'make a deal' of your birthday if I wish to because I'm not a cad who ignores such things."

"You do make speeches." She measured him, looking into him with that insightful way of hers, then seemed satisfied. "I suppose I'd better ask when yours is then."

"You just missed it, so you're safe. January 18."

"You're a Capricorn then. That explains a great deal."

"Surely you don't believe that stuff."

She tilted her head a little and gave him a shrewd look. "Shall I tell you the characteristics of a Capricorn and prove it to you?"

"Now I'm afraid." But she'd regained her color, so he was willing to go along, amused that she seemed to be finding her way into teasing him in return. "Let's hear it."

"Pragmatic. Forthright. Ambitious, but with integrity. Disciplined. Driven to excel. Easygoing and deals with irascible people well. Willing to listen to others pour out their woes.

Satirical, even dark sense of humor. Likes to be in control."

With that last, her gaze dropped to his hands and then flicked to the tablet she had yet to explore. The sexual tension suddenly crackled in the air, thick, intensely exciting. Not just his, but emanating from her as well. Meeting and winding together.

"You made all that up," he baited her, to see what she'd say, "tailored to suit what you know of me."

"Think so? You could research it easily enough." She avoided his gaze by entering the code into her tablet, swiping it on. "I assume this has internet access?"

"Actually it's set only to communicate with mine."

She looked up then, eyes darkening with something. Intrigue? Desire? But she only said, "How interesting."

"More private that way."

"I'm all for privacy."

"There's only one program on it—take a look."

She dabbed at her mouth with her napkin and folded it on the table, then studied the tablet without touching it. Back to the poisonous snake.

"Nervous?" he asked her for the second time. He liked that she'd owned up to it, that she offered up that level of emotional openness and trust. In many ways, exploring a woman's emotional responses excited him as much as discovering her sexual ones—not only because the two were so profoundly intertwined.

"I don't think I ever stopped being nervous, except—" She stopped herself, actually biting her lip to hold the words back. Too late.

"Except when?" He held her gaze, demanding the answer.

She stared back in consternation and seemed torn about how much to reveal.

"Shall I hazard a guess?"

"Fine. From the kiss on. I wasn't nervous then. Until…after."

"There is something to be said for getting swept up."

"Yes." She gave him a long look that made him wonder what she was thinking. Then, with the air of someone facing an onerous chore, she reentered her code into the tablet that had locked itself as they talked. "This…what? Very formal agreement thing is about *not* getting swept up."

"There's something to be said for ritual and formality, too."

"I'm not sure about that."

"It's part of the discovery, isn't it? Maybe you'll find that going about things with deliberation and forethought changes how you experience it."

She opened the program and scanned the screen. "I think I'm finding that you're a very unusual man."

"And you're a perceptive and sensitive woman." Perhaps more so than any he'd been privileged to know.

He waited as she looked through it, watching the flags of color deepen on her cheeks, itching to see exactly what made her catch her breath here or widen her eyes there. A form of discipline for himself, not to look. To sip his wine and savor the anticipation of seeing what she'd pick for their first planned encounter.

"Wow," she finally said. Then took a long drink of her wine. He helpfully poured more for her, reining himself back from interrogating her about what exactly put the shine of excited desire in her eyes. He would find out soon enough. "So—you put all this stuff in there?"

"Yes. That's just a start—what I had time for. You'll see that there's a section where I wrote out the basics of our agreement, ground rules. Let me know if you have questions or want to negotiate. Then there are specifics for elements of scenarios. I can continue to add to it from my end. As we try the scenarios and so forth that you pick and we discover how they go, what works and what doesn't, I might add or subtract various menu items. My imagination will no doubt be inspired as we go forward. There's also a messaging function, if we care to use it. It should have a calendar option, too."

"I see the dollar values and we already had this conversation, so I'm not going to argue about how inflated they are."

"Good. When you choose a scenario, you'll see the final total. Then the program will send me your list, I'll route you the sum, we can agree on a place and time and..." He loved the way she squirmed at the prospect. "And go from there."

"I shouldn't get the money until afterward."

"No. You get it when you sign on the dotted line, as it were. I don't want you hesitant to slow or stop a scenario because you're thinking about the paycheck."

"I can't believe we're discussing this. I'm thinking now that you might be very warped."

He laughed, delighted with her. "Fun, isn't it?"

She shook her head. "Okay. So nothing more today, I take it."

"For me, anyway." He pulled out his phone, unpleasantly surprised by the time, seriously tempted to cancel the afternoon's meetings. But he'd stacked them up to carve out this more than half day already. Filling out the initial menu of all the ways he'd like to have, pleasure and torment Celestina had taken hours. Delicious, absorbing hours—but the time had to be paid for. "You, of course, can spend the time as you like. You're welcome to stay here. Swim in the pool. Use the exercise room, if you like. Take a nap. Watch movies. Read. I have an extensive library, too."

Of course you do," she murmured, still with that odd look on her face.

It moved him to pick up her hand and kiss the back of it, a gesture that took her by surprise. "What is that look for?"

"I don't have a look."

"No, it's gone now. What were you thinking?"

"I don't have to tell you everything I think." She stood, tugging her hand away as she did. "You know what I want to do?"

"Hopefully something to treat yourself."

She laughed, as if at some private joke. "Actually, yes. I think I'll get a haircut. A good one. And a pedicure."

"Let me make you an appointment at the Oro Salon—you could spend the afternoon."

She hesitated and he thought she might be stubborn about it. "All right, since I'm sure you have a way to wave your magic wand and make that happen. I'm paying for it myself, though."

"What if I add something to the menu and pay for the visit if you agree to that?"

She picked up the tablet, fastened the folio closure and slipped it into her bag. Then put on her sunglasses, hiding her eyes behind the dark lenses. "I'll think about it."

CHAPTER NINE

S HE COULDN'T QUITE decide how she felt about the—did she call it a date? Ryan would probably say so—coming to an end. Relief warred with a vague sense of disappointment. Also more than a bit of shame at not having her own meetings demanding her attention. Her mother and father both, God rest their souls, would not approve of her squandering hours having lunch—with wine no less!—and whiling away the rest of the afternoon at an outrageously expensive spa.

This is your job now, she told herself firmly. Ryan might enjoy the pretense that he wasn't hiring her to perform sexual services, and she appreciated the lengths he'd gone to with the exquisite lunch, being charming and flirtatious, but neither of them could forget her real status. No being in denial about that. She'd seen that and it wasn't pretty.

She'd once been a bridesmaid to a woman who, once the ring was on her finger, informed her husband she would only have sex with him when he bought her what she asked for. So far as Tina knew, he went along with it. She'd let the friendship quietly fade away.

At least she and Ryan knew up front what the expectations would be—he had a good point there. And going to the salon pretty much counted as job preparation, right? Being in his elegant home, surrounded by perfect things, not to mention the sleekly groomed man himself, made her strongly self-conscious of her untended cuticles and grown-out cheap haircut—not to mention the lack of pedicure in those sinfully sexy shoes. If he intended to parade her about as his plus-one at society functions, then she didn't want his associates wondering if he'd lost his mind or was slumming it.

Though neither of those possibilities would be far from the truth.

In fact, she should probably be aware of his preferences for her appearance. Just another part of the job. Who was she kidding? If he put something in that diabolical menu of kink that he wanted her to have done at the salon, she'd do it. The illusion of free will here was just that—an illusion. So, as he walked with her back up the spectacular stone steps and escorted her to her car, she made herself ask, "Any other suggestions for my salon visit—hairstyle, nail color, anything?"

He glanced down at her, taking her elbow as they paused next to her car, his expression a mixture of amusement and aggravation as it had been since she arrived. Except the once she'd really pissed him off. Ostensibly over her birthday, too, which she hadn't quite processed. Probably the insult that he'd do anything less than check all the correct boxes.

"Celestina," he said, as always using her full name and lingering over it, even when he spoke with more exasperation than pleasure, "you might have me fairly pegged as someone who likes to be in control, but I am not a micro-manager. You are a beautiful woman who I've never seen be anything less than polished and put-together. I'm sure whatever you choose will be delightful."

Absurdly, she wanted to argue, but that would get them nowhere.

"What about you—what does your birthdate say about you?"

Surprised at the rapid switch of topic, she had to think. "Pisces? Not pragmatic or driven or disciplined at all."

"What you are, not what you're not."

"We're the dreamers." She waited for him to comment on that, but he only nodded, as if filing it away mentally.

"Fine. Then I guess, well…" She'd have to sit down, silence the nuns in her head, and pick some things off the tablet menu. "I'll, ah, be in touch."

"I look forward to hearing from you with great anticipation." He nearly purred the words, sending a thrill of renewed arousal through her system. When he leaned in, she reflexively lifted her lips, braced for—and to be brutally honest, hungry for—another of his sensual assaults. But he only brushed her cheek with a kiss as chaste and gentlemanly as when she arrived. "Until then, Celestina."

She got in her car and drove away, aware that he stood and watched her go. In a few miles she'd stop and search for the address to Oro, plug the directions into her phone. Like she'd have any idea where it was, or even what it would be like except that it would be insanely expensive.

It felt good to laugh. To have a light wine buzz, more than a little of which came from having lunch in that gorgeous spot with a compellingly attractive man. And that list of sexual activities—she'd thought the top of her head might come off and she'd barely been able to form coherent thoughts. It hadn't helped that she'd been so keenly aware of his attention on her, observing, even savoring her reactions.

Ryan might be solicitous of her comfort, a good listener and as charming as one could wish, but he definitely enjoyed toying with her. That would be a huge part of the thrill for him in this relationship. What she'd absorbed from his diabolical app made that very clear.

She would look at it tonight, after the twins were asleep, and find *something* in there that she could handle. For the time being, she had an afternoon to spend pampering herself and the sweet, sweet knowledge that the money would be there to pay the girls' tuition. Tonight she'd send that check and pay some of the most pressing of the other bills.

For the first time in years, the grinding pressure of hopelessness had lifted, leaving her almost giddy with the surcease. Maybe people with chronic pain felt this way when they found a medication that worked. It would be worth it to put the debts behind her. She could play Ryan's sex games and, if how she'd felt today was any indication, maybe even enjoy some of it. If nothing else, that kiss had proven to her that her sexual self had only been hibernating, not killed during those years with Noah. They'd play it through and she'd maybe get the debts to a manageable enough level to start over. From what she'd seen of Ryan so far, they'd part politely and she could go on with rebuilding her life.

Or, failing that, building a decent one for her nieces.

NO SURPRISE, THE spa was incredible—luxurious, gorgeous.

Like stepping through the looking glass into all that was La La Land. Josie had texted asking if they could go to a friend's house after dance team to work on a project, and so they wouldn't be home until after seven. That gave Tina time to go for the full package—the ironically named Top Shelf Menu—that Mr. Black had suggested. So said the elegant blonde who'd met her and said she was Tiffany, Tina's personal concierge for the "experience." Body polish, wrap, facial, waxing, mani/pedi and hair. Tina made a valiant effort not to wince at the reminder of menus or extortionate prices. She nearly asked if they had a Fixer-Upper Special, but decided Tiffany would not be amused.

In settling on the specifics, she went ahead and checked the tablet to see what Ryan added. She had a pretty good idea what it would be. Sure enough, a new content message alerted her to a menu addition under Miscellaneous for a Brazilian wax, valued at "Full Cost of Top Shelf Menu + gratuities."

Sneaky bastard. Though that verified her suspicions. She had to hand it to his business sense. He'd have figured the salon prices would soften her up enough to tempt her into that deal. Back in the day, when hanging on the beach had formed the bulk of the summer for her and Ara, and sexy swimsuits their uniforms, she'd gotten regular bikini waxes. She'd never gotten the full Monty because, well, nice girls didn't do that. After a while, self-conscious that she wasn't as slender as she used to be—something Noah pointed out more than once—she'd stopped wearing swimsuits at all, so waxing went by the wayside.

Funny that she'd been so hyped this morning that she

hadn't thought about any of that, though Ryan had clearly made a note of it.

She'd seen enough of the sex menu to know that, as promised, she'd never have to be naked again if she didn't, as he said, "opt in." Why he'd treat her just for getting the wax he might never see, she didn't know. Except…

I want you to have fun, to do things you think are wicked and discover how much you like them.

Could that be his motivation? She mulled it over as she relaxed into the treatments. He probably hoped to get to see it—and more, given some of what she'd skimmed in the menu—but all of this had another feel to it. This sense that he was goading her on for some nefarious purpose of his own. Like that thrill he said he got out of pushing her envelope. From getting her to drink wine at lunch to enticing her into a full Brazilian to, well, some of the more startling scenarios on his menu.

Judging by how easily he'd gotten her to agree to strip, she likely would again.

She went for it. He wanted to pay for this ridiculously expensive salon visit? Let him. Pulling out the tablet during a rest between treatments, she opened the program and clicked in the box. Choosing her first opt-in. The fact that he'd see it on his tablet gave her an odd and prurient thrill. That he'd know something so intimate about her. And so strangely sexual to know she'd agreed because he asked it of her. *I want to push you past every boundary you ever thought you had and for you to go there because I made you.* She'd never thought of herself as a particularly submissive person, but neither was she, as she'd told him, very disciplined or driven. In this context it felt…erotic to do as he suggested, entirely because he wanted it. When she saw him next, no matter what she wore, no matter what she took off, they'd both be aware that she'd made herself naked in that very private way. For him.

Wicked, indeed.

TINA MADE IT home just before the girls did. "Hey!" she called out, hearing them rocket in the door. "Did you eat yet?"

"No." Carly dropped her bag on the kitchen table. "And I'm starving. What's for dinner?"

"Wow!" Josie made an astonished face. "You got a haircut. You look like Catherine Zeta-Jones' character in *Chicago.*"

"Velma," Carly supplied.

Tina self-consciously ran a hand over the shining bob that left the back of her neck bare and came to points just below her jaw. "What do you think?"

"Thumbs up," Josie replied, then elbowed Carly.

Carly had pounced on the folio containing the tablet. "What's this—you got a new tablet? Not fair! Is this cover Kate Spade?"

"It's for my new job. It's on loan." She'd decided to be upfront about that, as they'd spot it eventually.

"What's the security code?" Carly asked, when Tina's usual one—her birthday, of course—didn't work.

"Secret. I bought steaks—sound good?"

"Oh, come on, I just want to play with it a little."

"Nope." Tina withdrew it from her hands. "It's a high-security thing. I swore not to let anyone but me use it."

Josie, sitting at the table, chin in hands, watched the exchange. "Must be a good job, if we get steaks and you got a haircut. That's not from Super Cheap Cuts."

"Can we go where you went, too?" Carly wanted to know, her gaze still on the denied tablet.

No way in hell. "You can pick a place and I'll treat you to new styles. We can go shopping, too—new shoes and some clothes."

"What about my phone?" Carly demanded.

"If you're good."

The girls hooted and touched fingers, fluttering them away, then chattering happily about highlights and debating the merits of various hairstyles and smartphones. Tina set to cooking, relieved that their self-absorption had worked in her favor and neither had thought to ask what the new job involved.

Much later, after the twins were asleep—or at least whispering to each other quietly enough behind their closed door that she couldn't hear them—Tina poured herself a glass of the wine she'd treated herself to, and curled up in bed with the tablet.

You don't have to pick anything tonight. Just look.

As soon as she logged in, a message request came up. He'd left it an hour ago, so might not be online now. Maybe she shouldn't accept. She could pretend she hadn't looked. Or simply decline, as he'd said she could. Except, with her intimate skin clean and sensitive because of this man, not to mention what happened that day, he occupied her thoughts. And she wanted to talk to him with a surprising amount of hunger. Why not? She could always sign out again. With a sense of vibrating anticipation, she accepted the message and waited, telling herself she wouldn't be disappointed if he was no longer online.

A message popped up immediately.

Good evening, Celestina. I've been thinking about you.

She hesitated. Then went for it. Me too.

How was the salon?

Amazing. Over the top. Thank you.

Thank YOU. I liked thinking of you, getting naked for me.

Blushing hotly, she messaged back. You might not ever see it!

I have a vivid imagination. It's enough to know.

What all would he be imagining about her? Plenty, no doubt.

I got a haircut, too.

Show me? I think you can send a photo via the tablet.

Hang on.

The girls did selfies all the time, so she had an idea how to do it. The stylist at the salon—Larry the fabulous—had redone her makeup, too. "Gratis, honey. Can't have you looking like an escapee from the '90s."

The first couple of shots came out unflattering and she deleted them immediately in case he could somehow connect to them. When she had one she liked, she sent it.

You look beautiful. Sexy. How about a photo of the other haircut?

She laughed, scandalized, and quickly smothered the sound in case the twins heard it.

I don't THINK so!

Just as well, I might lose my mind at the sight and frighten my companions.

You're not alone???

Business dinner. Awful. You've made it much more interesting.

I can't believe you're sexting me while at a business dinner!

They think I'm running numbers. Gives them the illusion that I'm considering their ridiculous offer before I destroy their hopes. I'm also terribly important and busy. ;-)

Flirting with me.

I like flirting with you. Would you touch yourself for me?

Already wet, her bare pussy clenched at that. So illicit to be doing this. She'd always wondered, when women did phone sex, if they did those things or just lied. Maybe it didn't matter to the listener, but it mattered to her. Keeping an eye on her closed bedroom door, she slipped her left hand into her PJ bottoms and caressed the smooth, slick, somewhat stinging skin. Very different without any hair. More defined and exposed. She messaged back, typing with her right hand.

I am.

How does it feel?

Soft. Naked. How far should she go? Something mischievous in her took the next step. Wet.

For me.

Yes.

When I can I see you again?

She stroked herself, enjoying the shiver of sensation and the power of teasing him for a change.

I haven't decided. Watch your tablet.

I have been. Impatiently. Don't you have homework to do?

I was going to when I got distracted.

Mea culpa. Don't let me distract you. Pick something. Anything. Tomorrow?

She didn't know about that. Maybe.

Your choice of course. Until I have you.

I know.

Good night. Sweet dreams.

Good night.

She sent the message and closed the window, thinking of him in the business dinner, pretending to run numbers while daring her to take nude pictures and send them, coaxing her into touching herself like this. Such a different man than she'd ever known. Unpredictable in some ways. He liked the secrecy of their tablets, seeming to do one thing while engaging in another. An interesting insight.

Aroused again by the conversation, she perused the intimidating menu with more interest and less trepidation. Some of it didn't look quite so alarming after all. The night after next was Friday and the girls might be out late again. If that happened, she could see Ryan. Or something during the day?

He had a section for Public Events, which gave her pause until she saw it included options such as dinner out or attending a cocktail reception with him. They seemed innocuous enough until she drilled down and discovered the more salacious options she could choose to include. The cocktail reception tomorrow evening was priced at $20K—ridiculous, but it would make a solid inroad on what she owed on one credit card—and then letting him choose what she wore added on to it, with top dollar for letting him provide the clothes from lingerie up.

Various add-ons included "jewelry," which made her laugh that he thought of nipple clamps that way—especially when they came in mild, moderate, tight and painful—with ascending values for each, doubled if he put them on instead of self-applied.

It seemed she could, as he'd promised, get away with agreeing to a great many things he'd never actually see or touch. Even yesterday she would have questioned why that worked for him, but she began to understand him better now. He liked to imagine what he couldn't see—especially now that he'd gotten a long, intimate look at her—and indulge in the secrecy of only the two of them knowing. Enjoy the thrill of getting her to do something at his instruction. Oddly, it gave her a thrill, too.

Fine, she would be his date for the party. A good trial run. Perusing the various drop-down menus, she selected the parameters of their next encounter.

CHAPTER TEN

RYAN USED THE motion of locking and stowing the mini-tablet to adjust the somewhat painful pinch of his hardened cock. That helped—though he'd better cool his thoughts if he hoped for the erection to subside soon.

Turning his mind back to the business at hand certainly helped cool his ardor. Even with the fascinatingly sexual and yet enigmatic Celestina filling his brain, as if she'd been in the room and departed, leaving only the florid scent of her perfume, the expectant expressions of his hosts irritated him. Another reason he preferred lunches. Dinners always seemed to be when his associates foolishly pressed for concessions. They should know he never signed off on anything at night—only in the bright light of day.

Pretending to listen to their arguments, he thought of Celestina in her bed, touching herself because he asked it. He'd glimpsed the headboard behind her in the photo, the cheesy powder-blue padded kind that had seen better years. She looked phenomenal, the haircut emphasizing her thickly lashed dark eyes and lush red mouth. Hopefully she'd choose to see him soon or he'd have to...what? No. No, he wouldn't press her more than he had already. No matter how much he craved to possess her immediately, in every way.

Ending the evening as quickly as possible, which meant agreeing to an early morning meeting to set the final numbers—which would *not* be what they hoped for—he waited until his driver had pulled away from the restaurant to pull out the tablet again. He told himself he wouldn't be disappointed if she hadn't agreed on their next encounter yet. For the time being, he'd exercise patience.

But luck was with him. With a renewed surge of lust and curiosity—excellent combination—he opened the packet to see what she'd selected. Conservative choices to begin with—no surprise there—with a few surprising twists. More daring of her than he'd predicted, but not necessarily the highest dollar options. Fascinating woman. The following evening promised to be one of the most entertaining in ages.

Taking out his phone, he began making notes of supplies to acquire and have ready for her.

Good morning Celestina.

The text awaited her, blinking there on her phone when she thumbed the alarm off. Sent at 5:00 a.m. Good lord, did the man ever sleep? She probably didn't want to know the answer to that.

Good morning, she sent back, her heart tripping a little over what he might want, and headed to the kitchen to start the coffee. Good coffee, not the cheapie brand. Soon she'd have to go back to shopping on a budget, but it had been so much fun the night before to be frivolous and squander some of the money. She'd have more already, having agreed to the "date" that night. She should get serious about making a plan of which bills to pay first. Maybe tomorrow. It seemed wrong to be looking forward to the evening, but she was and she wouldn't think about it too much beyond that.

I have a few questions, when you can look. Logistics. Looking forward to tonight.

Down the hall, the girls argued about who got the shower first. K. Gotta go.

He didn't reply, so she deleted the conversation and went to mediate the shower argument. Then she made breakfast, sliding the organic eggs with spinach and feta, turkey bacon on the side, in front of a wet-headed Josie, whose turn it had been to go first. She would start feeding the girls the way Ara would have wanted, to the best of her ability.

"Where's my cereal?" she pouted.

"Too much sugar in that crap. With my new job we can afford to eat healthier and we're going to."

"Oh joy. Sprouted bread and alfalfa juice."

"We'll make a good California girl out of you yet."

She grumbled but ate with enthusiasm. "Antina?"

"Yes?"

"Since you got a new job already—does that mean you can't help with the dance team coaching?"

Tina turned back from making Carly's eggs. "You were serious about that?"

Josie nodded, mouth full. "You'd be great. I've seen the vids of you and Mom. You two were awesome. You'd be hella better than Ms. Passwater."

"You shouldn't call her that and 'hella' is more swearing than not."

"She's not here to hear me. Besides, she's not a real teacher."

"Yes, but she's a human being and deserves your respect. I'll think about it. The new job is flexible, which means I'll have different hours. I won't be home until about eight tonight. I'll ask Mrs. Henderson to come over."

"Noooo," Carly wailed from the doorway. "We can stay by ourselves."

Tina pointed at her chair and put the plate in front of her. They were borderline age for it and she wouldn't be out late. She and Ara had started staying home alone when they were eleven, but...

"Please, Antina." Josie straightened her shoulders. "We'll be responsible. We'll even cook a healthy dinner." She kicked Carly, who was poking at the eggs.

Okay, they were all trying new things and she needed to trust them more than she had. They'd grown up so much. "No friends while I'm not here. Doors stay locked. Homework before TV. Healthy food."

They nodded along with enthusiasm, attempting to look like the angels they weren't. Time to take a page from Ryan's book and sweeten the deal. "If you two can stay alone while I'm doing my job *without incident* for the rest of the month, you can have new phones."

That got them. They jumped up and hugged her as they hadn't in forever. They chattered happily as she drove them to school, full of sincere resolve to make it easy for her to do her new job that brought them such unexpected riches. Both girls even turned and waved before they rounded the corner, after she dropped them the requisite block away from their school.

Instead of driving home—Ryan's ideals were permeating

her life—she went to a coffee shop, ordered a large, decadent latte and sat outside in the sun to drink it. Checking the tablet, she found a private message from him, sent at nearly midnight. That answered the question about whether the man slept.

Logistics: I can either send the clothing, etc., to your house and send a car for you to meet me, in which case I need your address. Or you can be at my house an hour before the reception, change, then my driver can bring you to meet me. Also, remember from the moment we meet, the rules are in effect. Use your safeword if necessary. Respond ASAP.

It made her smile, despite her irritation at his didactic ways, all he put under the umbrella of "logistics." While it would be more comfortable to change at home, there would be the risk of running into the girls if they got in early or having one of the neighbors notice the car picking her up. Better to keep it all as separate as possible.

As for the safeword…it gave her a little shiver to contemplate. She hadn't thought about using it the day before—had been frankly too swept up. Not much that she'd chosen for the evening should stray into dicey territory that she might feel the need to bail on. But, despite the level of detail on the specifics, there would be quite a bit of room for Ryan to tease and toy with her as he seemed to like to do. The contract part had made that clear. He wouldn't ask her to do anything she hadn't opted into, but within that, he'd have quite a bit of control. She either had to do as he said or safeword out.

They'd be at a public party and she hadn't opted in for actual sexual contact or nudity for it, but she'd allowed kissing, touching of exposed skin and what he'd called "discreet restraint." Dipping her toe in with that last. She might not be a top negotiator, but she suspected he'd factored in any number of loopholes and would happily take advantage of them.

Those she might need to get out of. She messaged back that she'd be at his house at four.

Finishing her latte, she went to run errands and pay some bills, telling herself the tremors in her gut were nerves, not excitement.

Just in it for the money.

When she arrived at Ryan's, the tremors had gone to full-blown jitters. The gates swung open and, for a moment, those gothic romance book covers flashed in her mind. Always with the woman running away from the house. And here she was, going in. The surreal sense of foreboding increased when the older woman who'd brought the shoes met her at the door. With a stern face, she assessed Tina and gave her a nod.

"Ms. Sala. I'm Mrs. Matthews. I'll show you to your suite and be available to assist you with anything you might need. The corset, in particular, may require another set of hands to lace up."

The corset? *Good God.* She took a deep breath. Then another, just in case she didn't get to breathe for the rest of the evening.

She followed the woman upstairs to a guest suite with a large attached dressing room, walk-in closet and bathroom, like a suite at the Four Seasons she'd stayed at for a swank conference, back when she worked in a lucrative field. An outfit lay on the bed, all in shades of crimson and scarlet, silk and lace. She didn't look too closely yet.

"Mr. Black says you're to regard these rooms as yours.

Make yourself at home. There's a shower through there, if you care to rinse off. The driver will be ready to take you in forty minutes."

"Thank you, I think I will."

"Press the intercom button, should you need me."

The woman, who Tina really tried not to think of as the psycho housekeeper from *Rebecca*, left and pulled the door closed behind her. She went in to run the shower. On an elaborate vanity table, an array of expensive cosmetics awaited. The very brands and shades Larry had used on her. Clearly in cahoots there. A crystal glass and a bottle of Pinord cava sat nearby. Nice touch. The closed jewelry box must contain her other accessories.

She hung her clothes on the hangers thoughtfully provided and rinsed off, using the one shower gel in evidence, which smelled rich and floral, like a tropical night. After toweling off and using lotion from the vanity, perfumed with the same scent, she put on a filmy robe draped over the back of the chair. Then poured herself a glass of wine, did her makeup the Larry way and opened the jewelry box.

Not so bad. A gorgeous gold torque necklace and matching bracelets. The nipple clamps didn't look like much—more like thin gold circles—but then she'd picked "mild" for a reason. No telling what that would be like. She slipped on the torque and the bracelets, the metal cool against her skin. Beautifully formed, they fit her closely. No doubt why she'd had to enter all of her measurements into the program. And no wonder he'd been up so late arranging for these things. The torque was heavy and rigid enough to sit in a tight curve against the base of her neck, then draped over her collarbone, coming to a pair of asymmetrical points.

Opening her robe, she bared her breasts and slipped the circles over her nipples. With a slight spring action, they tightened just enough not to come off easily, not enough to really pinch. They made her much more aware of her breasts, however, and made her nipples taut. Hopefully they wouldn't drive her crazy, though that was probably what Ryan hoped for.

Time to finish the outfit. She went into the bedroom and surveyed the items, which seemed to be laid out in order of assembly. Panties first—red and scandalously tiny—then the corset, which hooked in front and pushed up her breasts while barely covering them. Or would, if it fit right. Much as she didn't want to, she called Mrs. Matthews on the intercom and slipped the robe on for whatever modesty it might provide.

She answered the discreet knock and the woman came in, no nonsense. "Those laces are always difficult, aren't they?" she commented. "Drop your robe, turn around and hold the bedpost, please."

She did, though not in that order, turning her back first so the woman wouldn't see the nipple clamps. Feeling both exposed and a bit like Scarlett O'Hara preparing for an erotic barbeque, she gripped the upright post. With almost brusque efficiency, the woman adjusted the corset's position, then systematically adjusted the laces. The corset cups tightened over her breasts, making her even more aware of the gold circles on her nipples, and gradually the boned fabric sealed over her rib cage.

"There you go, Ms. Sala."

"I think it's too tight."

"It has to be that way or it will fall off. Anything else?"

"No—I think I can get the rest."

"Yes, ma'am. I'll expect you downstairs in ten minutes."

Tina glared balefully at the door Mrs. Matthews closed behind her. "Yes, General Matthews," she muttered. Moving quickly, though, she smoothed on the silk stockings and attached them to the corset garters. Then came the dress of a deep crimson with classic lines. The strapless top made of a heavy brocade fitted smoothly over the corset, clearly made to go together. It dipped slightly between her breasts, came to graceful points over them and clung to just below her hips, where the smooth silk skirt flared out into a full circle. A short jacket with a high collar went over that, closing narrowly over her waist with two gold buttons.

Finally, she pulled on the heels—the same ones she'd worn for him the day before. Very high, arched confections of red and gold. She might have to use a safeword if Ryan expected her to stand around in those for long. Taking one last swallow of wine, she refreshed her lipstick, put the tube and her phone in the little gold clutch that matched the outfit, and went downstairs.

Feeling a little breathless to find out what would happen next.

CHAPTER ELEVEN

RYAN CHECKED THE time, his anticipation spiking when he saw that Celestina should arrive soon. Leaving his office, he said goodbye for the day and took the elevator down. He arrived at street level exactly as his car pulled up. Waving Ernesto off, he let himself in to find Celestina, fragrant as a Mediterranean night, smiling at him hesitantly.

Absolutely gorgeous.

He brushed her cheek with his lips, more to inhale her scent and savor a brief taste of her satin skin than to kiss her. As she always seemed to, she stiffened a little. Both boldly assertive in some arenas and timid in others, she never quite responded how he thought she might.

"You look lovely," he told her, taking her in as the car pulled into traffic. "The dress fits perfectly." It fit her like the proverbial glove, in fact, with the lines of the bodice enhanced by the corset she wore beneath. It lifted her amazing breasts and shaped them, showing off her neat waist below. The torque necklace—not quite a collar but evocative enough to rattle his brain with fantasies of her in actual chains—gleamed against her skin, the curves a perfect echo of her bosom and winged collarbones.

"It should." She shifted her gaze away and smoothed the

skirt. "All those measurements you wanted. I had to dig out my grandmother's tape measure from her old sewing kit."

"For me, at least, the effort was well worth it. And the nipple rings—do they fit well also?"

She flushed, fingers twitching as if she resisted touching her breasts, and glanced at the window separating them from the driver.

"Ernesto can't hear us." Had she thought he wouldn't ask about the clamps? She might not have agreed to let him see— yet—but the knowledge she wore them for him seared his imagination. Her nipples were beautifully dark, like her mouth, and would be distended now from even that light pressure. In the tight corset, they had to be throbbing. "Tell me how they feel."

She gave him an oblique look. "I don't recall opting into that."

"No?" He opened the bottle of red wine waiting and offered her a glass. "It's not against the rules either. In fact there are no rules against me asking anything I'd like to know, but there *is* a rule that you have to do what I say, within the parameters of the scenario, unless you use your safeword."

Sighing out a short, aggravated breath, she sipped the wine. "I just knew there would be loopholes."

He laughed and indulged in trailing a finger over the upper curve of her breast revealed by the parting of the jacket lapels, the sharp lines perfectly setting off her ripe cleavage. She started under the caress, and her scarlet-painted lips parted, eyes flying to his, as if she wanted to ask a question. Really he hadn't expected her to agree to intimate touching yet, even if she'd granted over the clothes or what her outfit exposed. That said, he planned to take ruthless advantage of even the tiniest liberty she granted. Her breasts rose and fell in a tremor of response, revealing her quickening arousal.

"You should know something, Celestina." He bent over and pressed a kiss to the spot he'd just touched, licking her lightly, the satiny skin sweet under his tongue. Her breath hitched and she suppressed a sound, a quiet, closed-lipped moan. He smiled against her skin, tempted to nip, just a little, but not wanting to leave a mark on her just yet. The idiots at this particular party didn't merit such a sight. "I have a tremendous fondness for loopholes. Now, tell me how the nipple rings feel."

She stared at her wineglass and he caressed the spot he'd kissed, moistened now and the more sensitive for it. "They, ah, feel tight. Distracting." Her voice had gone throaty.

"Do they hurt?"

"Not exactly."

"More detail please."

She shifted, uncomfortable. "They're just sensitive and when I move, the fabric…"

"Yes?"

"Kind of chafes them." She glanced at him, dark eyes full of some new vulnerability, so he pressed a light kiss to her mouth, gratified when she softened and warmed to it. "You'll get lipstick on you," she said when he pulled back.

"Very much worth it. Take off your jacket, please." He took her wineglass from her to free up her hands, but she didn't move.

"I *know* I did not opt in for nudity tonight."

"You're fully clothed under the jacket, yes?"

She muttered something about loopholes, undid the buttons and set the jacket aside. Ignoring her questioning look, he took out the length of gold chain he'd put in his jacket pocket, and clipped it over the thin bracelet she wore, watching her expression.

Seeming shocked, she stared at it. "What's this for?"

"Discreet restraint," he reminded her. "Turn your back."

Steadying herself with a hand that shook slightly on the seat, she pivoted away from him, showing him her lovely bare shoulders and the nape of her neck so exquisitely exposed by the new haircut. Threading the chain up through the torque, he looped it once, then ran his hand down her arm and clipped the end to the other bracelet. It made a stirring sight, the graceful drape of the chains from the collar down to her wrists. She breathed unevenly. Clearly rocked by this but also aroused, as he'd hoped she would be. He pressed another kiss to her shoulder and she shivered.

"You can put your jacket back on," he murmured and, since it wouldn't show there, nipped her shoulder so she jumped and arched her back, taking in a long breath. She reminded him of those tea roses that slowly unfurl in hot water, going from closed and brittle to ravishingly lovely. He'd make things even hotter for her and they'd find out just how she'd bloom. It surprised him that she hadn't opted in for any sexual satisfaction. She had to be wanting it, judging by how he'd left her the day before. Intriguing, really, that she held out on that, which gave him food for thought. And only made him want to tease her even more, to find her breaking point.

Frowning a little, she eased the long sleeves up her arms again, her expression shifting with her realization that the chains would be hidden underneath the stiff material. He helped her adjust the high collar of the jacket and enjoyed the rise and fall of her cleavage as she fastened the buttons. Then she cocked her head, accepting the wine he handed her again.

"What's the point? They don't actually restrain me."

"But you feel them there."

"True."

"And I know they're there." He picked up her hand and slid his finger along the velvety texture of her inner wrist until he found the bracelet, then hooked his finger in the chain just enough to tug on it. She pressed her lips together, perhaps holding back another of those sensual moans. "It's symbolic. You're wearing chains I put on you. When I look at you tonight, I'll be savoring that thought—and that you'll be aware I'm picturing you like that, remembering how you trembled when I locked them on you, how you went hot and soft under my hands and mouth. You'll feel a catch now and again, the slide of metal on your skin, and you'll think of how you let me put my chains on you. When that happens, I'll be watching."

She stared at him, rapt, desire and trepidation giving her a seductive fragility, one that made his hands crave more. So tempting to strip her of the jacket and fasten her hands together with the chains, wrap his fist in them to hold her still and helpless while he filled his mouth with her.

"What are you thinking?" she whispered.

"Dark things." He tugged the chain, watching her register

the pull of it, then leaned in to kiss her under the point of her jaw, gratified that she yielded, dropping her head back. "Does that frighten you?"

"Some." She breathed unevenly. "I'm thinking it doesn't frighten me as much as it should."

"There's nothing real to fear. It's all part of the trip."

Her confined waist formed a perfect arc, one he couldn't help following up to the lush swell of her breast. The brocade jacket and heavy boning of her corset prevented him from feeling the thrust of her nipple or the metal trapping it, but he squeezed and her ragged moan, the shudder of her pulse under his lips, told him she felt it just fine.

"Are you ready?"

She stilled and he smiled against her skin. Not what she thought at all, but he loved where her mind had obviously gone.

"To go inside," he clarified. "We're here."

TINA NEARLY ASKED where, but her mind cleared in time to prevent her from making a complete idiot of herself. Ryan with his sex tricks had a way of shattering her grip on reality and weaving a spell around her that took her into another world entirely. An intimidating universe where she became somehow infinitely vulnerable—answering his intrusive questions, giving herself over to his hands and mouth in a way she never recalled doing with a man. Responding with wild arousal to the smallest gesture.

For the first time she wondered if she'd entirely miscalculated the real danger here. Not losing herself to sin and immorality, to the illicit lure of his kinky games, but surrendering something far more precious.

Ryan adjusted her sleeve, making sure the chain remained discreetly tucked inside, then opened the car door and held out a hand to help her out. Scooting across the leather seat, she experienced anew the grip of the corset and the light but relentless pinch of the rings on her nipples—all the more extreme with the way her breasts had swollen in response to his extraordinary words and teasing caresses. Even the slide of the garters on her thighs had become more titillating, and she'd gone wet enough that she wanted to check the back of her skirt to make sure she hadn't soaked through.

When she subtly reached to run a hand over her bottom, however, under the guise of adjusting the fall of the dress, her hand caught, the chain snagging on the torque collar and reminding her of its presence. Though the symbolic attaching of the chains had gotten to her exactly as he'd described, she hadn't quite processed that they would restrict her movements in small ways. Ryan, missing nothing, sharp gray eyes on her exactly as he'd promised, smiled ever so slightly.

You'll think of how you let me put my chains on you. When that happens, I'll be watching.

He smoothed his hand over her bottom and brushed her cheek with one of his gentlemanly kisses that weren't that at all, but rather an excuse to murmur darkly suggestive things to her. "That's why you should always lift your skirt and sit bare-bottomed. Just imagine if you hadn't been wearing panties. When you agree to let me take them away from you that will be something to keep in mind. Shall we?" He offered his arm as if he hadn't completely rattled her, and escorted her into the busy bar.

The reception took place in a private room, people in cocktail attire having quiet conversations, holding drinks in sparkling glasses. A gazelle-like blonde, her hair swept up into a flawless chignon, Hollywood-thin body encased in a black sheath, swanned up to them with a smooth smile.

"Ryan!" She took his hands and leaned in gracefully for his cheek kiss, accepting it with far more suave confidence than Tina had ever mustered. Though, at least theoretically, he wasn't using the opportunity to whisper diabolically arousing suggestions to her. Likely that trick of his would ruin any chance Tina would ever be able to receive those social kisses with aplomb. She'd forever think of him.

"Sarah, this is Celestina Sala." Ryan set his hand at the small of her back as he introduced her. "Celestina, Sarah Prescott—our hostess for the evening."

Sarah's slim, cool hand barely touched hers, though her crystal-blue eyes raked her thoroughly. Hadn't expected Ryan to bring a date and didn't like it. "Love the dress," she said. "So…dramatic."

"Celestina is a landscape designer," Ryan informed her. "Her work does have a certain drama. I think you're familiar— the series of pools at my downtown offices?"

"Ah yes. Pity we have no water for them." She laughed, not kindly.

"And what do you do?" Tina asked, as she would not have normally.

Sarah waved an airy hand. "I lunch. I shop. I throw parties.

I'd be a total parasite if not for my charitable work." She rolled her eyes dramatically and slid her arm possessively through Ryan's, snugging up to him enough that her elegantly slim breast pressed into his arm. "Ryan is one of my best benefactors. I'd be lost without him."

Tina smiled easily, finding an odd sense of freedom from the woman's needling. Had she been Ryan's actual date, she might have been uncomfortably jealous or threatened by all that Sara insinuated. But the woman couldn't know how much Ryan had paid her to be there, to wear his chains and participate in his secret sex games. It added another level to the prickly, tedious social interactions, and she suddenly understood more of why he enjoyed this subterfuge.

She toyed with the torque, catching Ryan's keen-eyed glance. "I can just imagine. Ryan's an incredibly generous man."

Sarah narrowed her pretty eyes and opened her mouth, but Ryan smoothly cut her off. "Would you care for a drink, Celestina? I see the bar over there. We won't monopolize our hostess."

Just as smoothly, he extracted himself from the woman's grip and guided Tina toward the bar. "Well played," he said for her ears alone.

"She'd like to have you, I believe."

"Oh yes—she's made that more than clear. I, however, am not interested in being had."

"Because you like to be the one doing the having," Tina said, before she processed how bold it would sound. He drew a certain frankness out of her that she'd have to be careful of.

Ryan slipped his hand up to the back of her neck, brushing his fingers under the jacket collar to touch the torque, eyes caressing her face with appreciative desire. "See how well you understand me? That, and for a number of other reasons. Shall I describe them in more detail?"

"No." But her nipples, though it seemed impossible, hardened further and she had trouble drawing a deep breath. The corset, far too tight. "I don't think I can take much more."

"Oh, my pet. We've barely scratched the surface of what you can take. What would you like to drink?"

"I'll stick with wine."

She only sipped as they mingled, Ryan's heady effect on her enough to keep her somewhat buzzed. People kissed up to him endlessly, a behavior he deflected politely, occasionally dismissively, turning conversation to her and her work. He touched her often, socially correct yet intimate reminders that they both knew what was going on under her clothes, keeping her on such a sexual simmer that she forgot to be nervous. Didn't realize he talked her up to potential clients until several people expressed interest in vague, but definitely possible future projects.

"Thank you," she told him quietly, as they moved to another conversation. "I didn't expect you to drum up clients for me."

He slid an arm around her waist and brushed her cheek with a kiss, warning her. "Only as a landscape designer, however," he said into her ear. "I shall be the only client for your other services."

She couldn't help the shiver of response and he laughed,

soft and warm. "On that note, I believe we can safely say our goodbyes. And there are things I want to do to you yet, before we must part for the night."

That was enough to put her into a haze of mingled dread and anticipation, so that she barely registered the farewells. With the exception of Sarah, who was not at all happy to see them leave, gazing after Ryan with such a wounded expression that Tina suspected the woman might have it worse for him than her social flirtation suggested. Something in the way she'd dismissed the shallowness of her own life elicited Tina's sympathy. She couldn't be that, a woman with nothing to do all day. The car met them at the curb and Ryan held the door for her, handing her in. Once inside he checked the time.

"By my count, I have about thirty minutes until we reach the house, which gives us plenty of time to find out how much more you can take within the current parameters. Let's see how deeply we can scratch your surface."

CHAPTER TWELVE

IN A STATE of near panic, she processed his words, frantically trying to recall what all the parameters had been. The apprehension made no sense, because she trusted him to abide by his promises. And yet a sense of acute vulnerability sent her brain spinning, counter-intuitively expressing itself in an elevated state of arousal. Everything in her—physical and emotional—ratcheted up to a new alert level, making her hypersensitive to the least bit of stimulation.

"Better fix your skirt," he said with a meaningful smile that made her face go hot.

Somehow that seemed too much. "I don't think I—"

"Do as I say, Celestina." He said it with a note of warning, but gently enough that it contained the reminder that she could use a safeword. She might feel trapped with him, at his command in the back of this fancy car, to be enjoyed as he did the wine and other luxuries, but it was fundamentally an illusion.

There's nothing real to fear. It's all part of the trip.

And yet, it didn't feel that way. Some profound part of her whispered that she'd been captured and was in terrible danger, but that only added to her heightened state. Pinned by his demanding gaze, his face taking on that contained violence of the fighter, she gathered the skirt up, fumbling a bit as the chains tightened, then set her bottom on the seat. The skimpy panties covered so little that she might as well have been naked, the smooth leather a cool reminder against her skin.

"Thank you," he said. "Now remove the jacket."

Trembling a little, she did, placing it in the hand he held out. If he told her to take off anything else, would she? But she hadn't opted in for that. No nudity. She was pretty sure not even a loophole could change that. Next time—hard to think of what *that* would bring—she would study his "parameters" more and firmly fix in her mind where the boundaries lay, what they included or excluded. Never mind the damn loopholes. He had a way of making her forget, of wanting to offer more than she'd opted into when her brain wasn't drunk on the sensual haze he created, when he wasn't there to give those casual orders she seemed unable to resist.

He set the jacket behind him and arranged the chains so they draped forward over her breasts, his gaze intent. "You are gorgeous in my chains. I very much look forward to when you agree to wearing nothing but."

She searched for breath to reply. "I might never do that."

His eyes, shadowed in the dim light, traveled up to hers, and he cupped her breasts, squeezing enough that the nipple rings tightened, making her gasp. "Your choice, of course. But I think you will. I think you like this as much as I do. Maybe even crave it. Are you wet for me again, Celestina?"

She didn't want to answer that, not while he watched her, hands massaging her breasts, making her want to beg him to release her from the corset, to make her as naked as he'd described. He stared her down, however, and she had to look away, down to his grip on her, the golden chains glinting. A mesmerizingly erotic sight.

"Yes." It felt like a confession.

"Good." He murmured. "Good," not that he was pleased, but to praise that she'd told him. "So here's another loophole. You agreed that I can touch you over your clothes and on any exposed skin. I'd like to point out that your panties count as clothes. You're going to part your thighs so I can touch you over them."

Her pussy spasmed as if he already had. Impossible to allow that. "Ryan…" Her voice broke on his name and his hands moved over her breasts, up to her throat and collarbones, stroking with obvious pleasure.

"I love how you say my name like that," he confided. "That pleading sound. Beg as much as you like, but it won't save you." He tugged on her chains. "Do as I say."

With a low sound, half sighed breath, half moan of despair, she obeyed, not quite believing she was, parting her legs, the red silk whispering over her skin, the fabric riding to just over her knees.

"Wider." He kept one hand wrapped in the chains, tugging her hands up to the level of her breasts, and set the other on her knee, just under the hem. She couldn't tear her gaze from it, those blunt fingers that would touch her so intimately. Feeling a bit faint, she opened wider, her thighs separating so that air hit the soaked crotch of her panties. His hand disappeared under her skirt, out of sight, but maintaining contact with her skin, tracing along her inner thigh.

She nearly clamped her thighs closed, trembling with the

effort to keep them open. The bracelets bit into her wrists, and she realized she'd tugged against the chains he was using to keep her hands high and out of the way.

"You're more than wet, my dear," he observed, finding the damp skin near her crotch. "I'd say you're slick with arousal and have been for hours. But it's escalating now, isn't it? You're panting. Very close to begging for more. Spread wider for me."

With an incoherent sound, she complied, tensing as his hand moved invisibly up, her breasts aching with need, suddenly desperate for him to touch her there. *Very close to begging for more.* Yes. His fingers brushed up, rounding over the top of her thigh, a ripple under the silk, tracing the thin strap at her hip, then in to the center, caressing the lace confection stretched taut over her mound, moving inevitably down. Her skirt had ridden higher with the movement of his hand, the tops of the stockings coming into view, fancifully erotic.

"I'm curious." He stroked the silk and lace just above where her nether lips parted. "When we texted and I asked you to touch yourself—did you make yourself come?"

More words, seeking to open up her private moments as resolutely as he'd ordered her to open her thighs. "No," she whispered.

"No? I'm surprised. Look at me."

She dragged her gaze up to his, feeling unutterably shy with his fingers hovering so near her clit, knowing he felt the heat and moisture there, how much she wanted and dreaded more. He studied her face and she let her head fall back against the seat, giving up what little resistance she'd mustered. Who was she kidding? She'd let him do whatever he wanted to at this point.

"Why didn't you? You said you were wet."

"I don't know. I had things to do—pick from the menu, input the measurements. All of that."

He pressed his fingers more firmly against her and she strained not to lift her hips, to writhe shamefully. "Is that the real reason? Too busy to rub one out?"

"It's not like that for women." Though she felt close now, as if the bite of the bracelets, the strength of his grip, and the exposure of having her thighs wide because he commanded it released some fundamental inhibition. That, rather than her usual striving to climax, she wouldn't be able to restrain it.

"Isn't it? Tell me what it's like." The note of demand in his voice penetrated her. At the same time his fingers pushed down, bracketing her clit, the tips pressing against her vulva. The thin silk was so wet she might as well be naked. The sensation panicked her and she reflexively closed her thighs around his hand, tugging on the chains that held hers fast, whimpering. "Look at me, Celestina," he urged and she did, not realizing she'd torn her gaze away.

He met her eyes for several long moments, then began rocking his hand against her, her closed thighs making no difference now that he had his fingers buried in her intimate folds. "Tell me what it's like," he insisted.

"Not easy." Her hips moved with the rhythm of his hand, the burning arousal circling up.

"Have you ever orgasmed? Don't look away or I'll impose a punishment."

Making a helpless sound, she wound her fingers around the chains in his grip, holding on, face burning at how he touched her, how she responded and that he watched her so intently. "Please don't," she gasped.

"Don't what? Ask you probing questions?" He flexed his fingers, pushing the silk inside her, an intense invasion that made her thighs relax apart. "Punish you? Touch you like this? You know how to make it stop if you really want to."

"I can't talk while you're doing that."

"You seem to be doing fine. Answer my questions."

"I've had orgasms." Only twice with Noah, before he declared it too much work for too little reward, and she'd agreed with a sense of reprieve. Reaching for those orgasms he'd so diligently attempted to deliver had begun to feel like training for a marathon. It had been a relief to them both to stop trying for it. Before that, there had been unexpected ones that snuck up on her in the backseats of cars after very long make-out sessions. No rhyme or reason to them.

"It sounds like you can count them on one hand." He changed his grip on the chains, moving her wrists so the bracelets scraped against her breasts, right over her hypersensitive clamped nipples. She groaned and ground her pussy against his hand, losing herself in the need. So close. "Is that right, Celestina?"

Groping for what he'd asked her, she stared at him, his pale gray eyes glowing like moonlight in the soft gleam of the car interior. "It takes me a long time. I don't know why."

"The why doesn't matter. I'm going to make this both easier and harder. You are forbidden to climax. By my hand, your own or anyone else's, until I decide otherwise."

Yet still he touched her, the hard edge of the bracelets apparent through the layers of cloth that compressed and chafed her, catching the metal rings of the clamps, his fingers buried between her legs, one pushing the silk inside her aching channel and his thumb on her clit. Suddenly, an orgasm seemed inevitable, as if by forbidding it, he'd triggered some contrary part of her into insisting on the climax that usually eluded her. She shuddered with the first tremors of one. "I can't stop it," she panted.

"You can. And you will. Or the next scenario will be only punishments for you to choose from. Don't do it."

That thought only made her wilder. She'd only glanced at those sections, daunted and scandalized. Spankings, whippings, belts—in various positions, bound and not. "You wouldn't, would you?"

He bent closer, lightening the pressure of his fingers, holding her chained wrists still and brushing her cheek with his lips. "I would love to, Celestina. The thought of you under my power that way fills me with excitement. You could love it, too. I intend to see to it that you do."

Groaning, she arched her hips, pressing hard against his fingers, the orgasm close. "Don't do it, Celestina," he ordered. Then he drew his hand away and used it to hold her thighs open as his mouth took hers, kissing her hard and deep. Unable to muster the will to resist, the threat of climax receding, she relaxed under it, savoring the skill of his clever mouth and the sensual sweep of it, carrying her past thought.

When he pulled away, she blinked at him, caught in his

web and without will, waiting for whatever he'd do to her next. With a smile he stroked her cheek. "We're home."

With surprise, she looked to the lights of the house. He opened the car door and held out a hand for her. Still dazed, she took it and let him lead her up the steps, still holding her hand. Mrs. Matthews opened the doors and welcomed them in. With a flush of shame, Tina realized Ryan carried her jacket over his arm, and the chains were clearly in evidence, draped over her bosom.

He turned to her. "I know you need to get home. Would you prefer that I or Mrs. Matthews help you out of the corset?"

Knowing her face flamed red, and also aware she'd never be able to undo the knots herself, she stared at the tips of her gorgeous shoes. "If you would loosen them, yes," she muttered.

"Of course. As you were, Mrs. Matthews."

He escorted her up the stairs with a hand on her back. Had he done this on purpose, a new level of exposure? She risked a glance at him and found him observing her as always. Oh yes. Yes he had.

Once in the room, with the door closed, she turned on him. "That wasn't in the rules, letting her see that."

He nudged her closer to the bed. "Lift your hands over your head."

Confused, she seized the bedpost as she had before and he moved them higher, looping the bracelets over a hook there. It put her on tiptoe and she strained against them, discovering she couldn't easily unhook herself.

Ryan ran his hands down her arms, over her breasts in front and down the boning defining her waist. "Discreet restraint, remember. Mrs. Matthews is very discreet. She's also aware of my more eclectic activities and is quite experienced in assisting." He unzipped her dress just to the waist and began unknotting the laces.

"What does that mean?" Her breath wouldn't quite steady, her body resonating with both distress and unrealized arousal. She couldn't decide how she felt about that. "I don't want to have sex with her."

"No, no. I thought I made it clear you will have sex only with me, and then only if you opt in." The laces gradually loosened, easing her breathing but not the fluttering demand for oxygen. "But exposing you to other people who understand, taking you farther on the trip by putting you into another's power, however chastely, can be profoundly exciting. Discreet restraint means that. In a public or semi-public scenario, it's impossible to guarantee no one will see what I put on you.

"Beyond that," he continued, "I'm finding that I greatly enjoy the idea that I own you, if only for the few hours you put yourself in my power. Having my housekeeper deliver you to me would be especially delicious and I'll be adding it to the scenarios."

The corset gave, sagging away from her breasts, her nipples singing with bright pain. She pulled against the hook holding her arms above her head, feeling desperate. He quietly zipped up her dress, covering her again, then kissed the nape of her neck. "As always, your choice, Celestina. Read your options carefully and decide from there." He cupped her breasts, thumbs brushing her trapped nipples through the brocaded silk, and she writhed, uncertain if she tried to escape or press closer. "You struggle so beautifully. And you continue to exceed my every expectation. I hope you'll come back. Remember the rule. No orgasms. I will ask and you will have no choice but to give me an honest answer. Check your tablet and you'll find I'll have a selection of punishments for you to choose from if you do. Including allowing someone else to punish you while I watch. Mrs. Matthews, perhaps."

He stepped back, unhooking her wrists. "I'll be in my office if you'd like to stop in and say goodbye before you go." The door closed softly behind him.

CHAPTER THIRTEEN

ROCKED EMOTIONALLY AND physically, Tina barely managed to stagger to the bathroom and undress. Her nipples had gone very dark, and taking off the rings brought a rush of pain as the blood returned to the compressed and sensitive flesh. Along with the sting came a sharper arousal, her clit throbbing in time with her nipples, as if somehow indelibly linked. To her utter mortification, prominent on the vanity sat a jar of numbing cream. No doubt placed there by Mrs. Matthews, who obviously knew far too much about this wild sexual journey she'd unwisely engaged in.

The cream felt like heaven, however, numbing and cooling the fiery flesh, and she considered putting it on her overstimulated clit, too. That would fend off any of the now-forbidden orgasms. Why did he get to demand that? Where she'd felt nothing but relief when Noah said he wouldn't put them both through trying for it anymore, this pissed her off. All of it did. How he'd teased her and promised punishments if she disobeyed. Making her want so desperately and then withholding it.

Or the next scenario will be only punishments for you to choose from.

He thought he had her. That he could financially blackmail her into agreeing to be punished for something as trivial and natural as having an orgasm—which she wasn't likely to have in the first place.

Uncertain of the exact source of her anger, except that it seemed to be her default response of late and that this new sexual frustration didn't help, she dressed in her street clothes, which seemed drab after the fabulous dress. *Just a costume. Dress up and pretend to be a man's fancy sex slave.*

What the hell had she been thinking?

One thing she knew, she would not be visiting Ryan's office for a cheerful good-night and the pretense that they enjoyed a friendly relationship. Fuck him. And not in the literal sense.

RYAN WATCHED HER car pull out of the drive, wincing as she nearly clipped the gate. Well and truly pissed off then. Tamping down the disappointment, he sipped the whiskey he'd poured in an attempt to distract himself from the burning desire—no, more like an inferno of need—that had begged him to go back upstairs and devour her instead. Even this angry, maybe because of it, she'd probably let him seduce her fully. He could have had her in the car, the way she'd yielded so sweetly to him.

But that wouldn't have been fair.

Not just because of the semi-arbitrary rules he'd created, though he wanted to be scrupulous about bending those too much. Celestina possessed a sharp mind and she'd be on the lookout for loopholes going forward.

If there would be a going forward.

Truly, he'd forgotten about the chains or that it would

mean anything to someone else that Mrs. Matthews had witnessed them. Sloppy and stupid of him. A mark, perhaps, of how far he'd gone down the rabbit hole of deviant sex, that it hadn't occurred to him to cover her up. If she gave him another opportunity, he'd be more mindful of her relative inexperience. Of course, it could also have been that he'd been so enthralled with her and their combined need that he'd simply lost his head. He frowned at the whiskey. Unlike him.

Though it had been a cover story—couldn't have her knowing he'd screwed up, after all—he hadn't lied about the charge it gave him. He'd never been that much into the concept of owning slaves as some sexual dominants were, much as he loved the collars, chains and ropes. Nor did he want Celestina as a slave. Not exactly. Something, however, about buying her time, a gambit that had begun primarily as a way to get her to both take his money and allow him to seduce her to the dark side of sex, had taken on a more powerful meaning for him.

He'd loved feeling as if she belonged to him. His alone to torment and savor. Though it wouldn't help resolve the nearly painful erection that showed no sign of abating on its own, he entertained the captivating vision of Celestina, naked, collared and chained, being led by the leash into his study. How her dark, startled gaze would find him and she'd wait, wherever she'd been tethered, obedient and full of that aroused trepidation that so moved him.

He wanted her beyond reason.

At the stifling reception, juxtaposed against the skinny heiresses and fashionably pale society butterflies of Sarah

Prescott's ilk, Celestina had looked like a fervid red rose among fragile orchids. The dress, the light chains, the way she responded to his teasing, all conspired to set off her luxuriant and lavish sensuality.

For a few hours, she'd forgotten her worries. Had left behind the despair that trailed her like an oppressive cloud. She'd opened up to him, if only sensually, her lips and thighs parting at his least caress, lustrous eyes seeking him out, revealing her growing hunger.

No, she wouldn't be able to stay away. She couldn't.

Even if he'd frightened her, though she might be angry at him, she'd calm down. She'd wake tomorrow—or perhaps cool off on the drive home—and realize that she wanted him as much as he wanted her. That, deep inside, she craved the same things he did.

"What are you thinking?" she'd asked. And when he told her *"Dark things,"* the words had blasted right through her, cracking through her shell to the violently passionate woman he sensed beneath. Absurd that she thought it took her too long to reach orgasm. Some man had told her that. Her ex-husband, no doubt. Ryan blew out a breath to cool the burn of a too-large gulp of whiskey. Fucking idiots. Too anxious to get back to their beer and ball games to devote the time and attention to pleasuring a woman. Probably set it up like an athletic event, servicing the standard spots, drumming on her clit with all the finesse of a file clerk hoping to finish the paperwork by closing time. Exhorting her to deliver her climax like they'd urge a racehorse over the finish line.

She hadn't liked talking about it, regarding it as a failing, most likely, and with a shade of the impatient exhaustion the topic had brought her in the past. Tensing even through her arousal, she'd begun to resist him and the orgasm she'd been on the verge of, reflexively shying away from what should have been pleasurable and had become a chore.

It might have pissed her off, that he'd impulsively imposed the rule that she shouldn't climax, but she'd come to understand in time. The lure of the forbidden overcame many barriers. Life had worn away at her fiery brilliance, burying her under layers of ash and old anger. She could dig her way out, given enough incentive. Thwarting him would channel her rage. He'd love to see her do it. When he gave her the pleasure that had eluded her, she'd be that much more bound to him.

If she'd let him do it.

If he hadn't run her off entirely.

If he hadn't fumbled the entire thing, forgetting in the delirium of her ardent responses that she hadn't played these games before, that she wasn't like any of the others. In any way.

Resigned—and unable to resist looking—he took his whiskey and sat at his desk to check the tablet. Nothing from Celestina, though she might not have made it home yet. He wasn't sure how far she had to go and, since she hadn't offered the information, he hadn't tried to look up her address. He would invade her privacy in other ways without remorse, even with remorseless delectation, but not her nonsexual life. Not until she trusted him enough to be part of her daily world instead of the hours he bought from her.

Because he felt certain she'd look for it, he added in his fantasy scenario of having Mrs. Matthews prepare and deliver her, tempted to put an insanely high value on it, reflecting how deeply the image had sunk its claws into him. He resisted that, too, lest she view it as additional pressure.

On impulse—maybe with a tinge of fear that she'd never contact him again—he added a few nonsexual encounters. Cat had set up that functionality, that he could make something a single a la carte item that could not be combined with anything else. Lunch. Coffee. Dinner. A walk on the cliffs. All very vanilla and an opportunity for them to talk, if she'd be willing. She hadn't been all that forthcoming about her private thoughts without sensual pressure, so it might not work. But the option should be there if she looked for it.

He hoped she'd look for it. They needed to talk.

How the mighty had fallen, that he could even think that tired phrase.

Taking out his phone, he sent her a text to say good-night. The ball was firmly in her court now. Resolving not to worry further, he went upstairs to take care of his persistent erection while he drowned his concerns in fantasies about the sybaritic Celestina.

Good night, Celestina. Sweet dreams.

The text flashed on her cell phone and she gritted her teeth, tempted to throw the damn thing out the car window. She needed to assign his messages a special tone. Like the theme from a serial killer movie. That might suffice to remind her of his predatory ways. He might have that polished veneer, the affable charm, the effortless style of the very wealthy—but under it all he was a monster. She couldn't forget it. The wolf who dressed in Armani and pretended to be solicitous, all the while circling, waiting for the moment of vulnerability to spring and devour with his sensually cloaked and contained violence.

God, she hated how vulnerable she'd been. After Ara died, she'd really thought nothing ever again would touch her. Even Noah's abrupt and heartless departure hadn't hurt, a sure sign that she'd gone numb. It hadn't bothered her that the twins had happily failed to acknowledge her birthday—she'd told the truth about that. Or her friends. She'd lost the one person she needed and that would leave her forever half-alive.

Or so she'd thought until tonight.

Something about Ryan Black got inside her, insinuating himself into her deepest thoughts as inevitably as he'd persuaded her to spread her thighs so he could stroke her intimately. Maybe the kinky games did it, circumventing her usual defenses, so he reached some fathomless part of her psyche where a different self lurked, still vital, naked, tender to the touch and violently sensitive to any overture.

It simmered still, churning with a hunger he'd awakened. She ached with unrealized desire as she never had before, not even after those youthful backseat make-out sessions. Those were the times that orgasms had slipped over her, stealthy, delicious in the quiet release they brought. Those had been so uncomplicated, full of furtive excitement, with no expectations of what would occur, better in many ways for both of them knowing it wouldn't culminate in sex, as if removing the all-important end goal let them luxuriate in the moment.

Not unlike what had happened with Ryan, come to think of it. Her nipples tightened with the memory, her clit and vulva starving for stimulation. With one hand on the steering wheel, she pressed the heel of her hand against her mound, a half-formed idea of calming herself in mind. It had the opposite effect and, seemingly unable to stop herself, she pulled up her skirt, the slide of cloth reminding her of Ryan's insistent caresses pushing the red silk up her thighs. Working her fingers under her panties, she almost gasped to find herself so slick and swollen.

Was that how she felt to him? So wantonly aroused, so obviously ready to be penetrated. No wonder he'd looked and behaved as he had, gripping her chains, gray eyes boring into hers. Of course he'd believed she'd loved every moment of it.

Hadn't she?

The heat built and she tried holding her hand still, just cupping herself for comfort.

No orgasms. I will ask and you will have no choice but to give me an honest answer.

He would, too, as it seemed there was nothing he wouldn't ask her. Another way of opening her. But she could always lie. He wasn't psychic or all-knowing. Maybe she'd never even see him again. She didn't have to ever go back. Never again subject herself to his restraints of any kind or his threats of punishment and *dark things.*

...a selection of punishments for you to choose from...including allowing someone else to punish you while I watch.

He probably meant that horrible Mrs. Matthews. Tina had been excruciatingly embarrassed—humiliated, even—that the woman had seen the chains, knew about the nipple clamps and had tied her so tightly into the corset. She'd looked at Tina with that cold expression, like a refugee from an English boarding school, the sort where the headmistress forces the schoolgirls to bend over her desk while she lifts their uniform skirts and paddles their behinds for minor infractions while they weep and squirm and—

The orgasm took her over in a rush, nearly blinding her with the red-black crush of it. She managed to guide the car to the shoulder of the fortunately dark and quiet street, riding out the climax by pressing her lips as tightly together as she pressed her fingers to her own slippery folds.

It left her wrung out, emotionally ragged. This wasn't her, acting like some sex-starved pervert fantasizing about being spanked by some strange matron while Ryan watched her, drinking in every plea and whimper, knowing she did it for him. Because he made her do it.

You struggle so beautifully.

Unable to dredge up the will to stop stroking herself, she turned over his words in her mind, all the things he'd said to her. She understood why he wanted this from her, that he got off on the power trip of owning her. That by placing chains on her she became subject to his will. Of course a man would love that. But why would she? Why had those images thrust her over the edge into a rare orgasm—possibly the most powerful she'd ever had?

It had taken the lure of money to get her to agree to all of this. She never would have otherwise. Money, though, didn't account for this urgent desire. She hadn't simply gone along with the program, she'd wanted to let him do his dark things to her. To chain her up, make her more wildly aroused than she'd ever been, to tell her she couldn't come and then punish her when she did.

As she'd just done.

The thought of you under my power that way fills me with excitement.

She'd never tell. Ridiculous to think she would. That she'd agree to be punished at all, let alone for something like that. No matter how the thought haunted her.

Good night, Celestina. Sweet dreams.

She'd think about it tomorrow. Resolutely removing her hand, she drove home to take care of her girls, the real reason for all of this.

The only reason, she told herself firmly.

Dark things.

CHAPTER FOURTEEN

Good morning Celestina.

She ignored the text as she had the one the night before, then deleted them both for good measure. Wishing everything else could be as easily erased. Focusing on getting the twins ready for school, she struggled to keep her brain clear of the erotic dreams that had taken over her sleep and the salacious thoughts that seemed all too ready to pick up the theme from there. Thank God for the twins' incessant chatter and supreme self-absorption. They were all excited for the oncoming weekend, going shopping and getting their hair done. They wanted to order pizza and rent a movie that night. And could they go out for pancakes before shopping the next day?

Once she dropped them off, however, nothing stopped the dream images from swarming up, hot, dark things rising from the cracks Ryan had pried open into her naked soul with the tantalizingly cryptic descriptions in his lurid program. Him putting her in chains while she knelt. The clap of a manacled collar around her throat, weighing on her with orgasmic intensity. His stern gray gaze on her from behind his desk while she bent over it, someone else lifting her skirt and she stayed riveted still, waiting to be punished however he demanded.

None of it made any sense. She'd never had those sorts of fantasies. Had regarded it all as vaguely ridiculous—the schoolgirls, the paddling, the women in prison. Now it seemed her fevered brain couldn't churn out enough of them. Her, behind bars, naked, sweaty and dirt-streaked, awaiting Ryan's pleasure. Or punishment.

Dark things.

Truer words were never spoken. And there she was, in the bright light of a sunny morning, craving more, the desire swelling her tissues and dampening a previously fresh pair of panties. Which only made her think of Ryan's admonition to lift her skirt and sit bare-bottomed. When she let him take away her panties altogether. That thought, like all of them, scandalized and titillated her. More than anything, she wanted to open the tablet and concoct some scenario to both stoke and cool this need. A Pandora's box of temptation and degradation, that luxuriously cloaked device. A hugely traitorous part of herself wanted to confess to her transgression of his rule— supposed transgression, as she still didn't agree with it—and subject herself to punishment for it.

Wanted to see if he could see her today. Perhaps even this morning.

Seduced by the devil, indeed.

Which was why she wouldn't do any of those things. Like an alcoholic giving up booze for a week, to prove to herself she could, she left the tablet closed away in her desk drawer, pulled on jogging clothes, pocketed her keys and walked to the beach. She needed to get back into shape and burn off some of this energy, both.

It felt good to be outside. Though it would be nicer if she could exorcise Ryan's voice from her head. Along with the feel of his hands on her body. And the way he looked at her, studying her responses to his more outrageous suggestions. Threatening to punish her, that glint of aroused cruelty in his eyes.

Reaching the boardwalk, she picked up her pace into a slow jog, joining the rollerbladers, skateboarders, bicyclists and other runners. All of them tanned and lean, bikini-clad and shirtless, human gazelles like Sarah Prescott. Once upon a time, in her heyday, she could have at least held her own, but not this first time out after such a long hiatus. People passed her on both sides, their polite "on your right" and "on the left" sounding an awful lot like "get out of the way, you pitiful loser." Far too quickly she was winded enough to have to slow to a walk—and suffer being passed by faster walkers.

All of it too much the story of her life.

Dark things. No, Ryan with his sunlit life and massive fortune had no idea how dark things could get.

She walked a while longer until her thighs began to ache and feel weak. Maybe she should take it easy for day one. Turning her feet back home, she contemplated the rest of her day. What bills she had money to pay were paid. They needed more groceries, but the checking account was already waning, especially with the twins wanting to splurge. Amazing how fast one could burn seventy grand by throwing it into the ever-growing crater of one's life.

Maybe she could pick out a small service to perform for Ryan. Pad the checking account and cement in her own head that all of this was about getting paid for a job. Nothing more. She wouldn't look at the punishment modules and she wouldn't tell him what she'd done. It almost seemed like it hadn't happened, that furtive orgasm on the shoulder of the road. Something else. God knows what he'd pay for maybe a blow job at work. The way Ryan threw money at her, she could maybe set up a scenario to earn the entire remaining $850 thousand. Maybe the girls would have an away performance with the dance team and she could give a weekend to letting him punish and violate her every way imaginable. Then she could walk away. Escape this sticky trap of desire before she couldn't muster the will to do so.

Telling herself it was only to see if it was possible according to the app, if not humanly possible for her body or psyche to withstand, she got out the tablet and tried adding absolutely everything. To her great annoyance, Ryan had—fully in character for him—been a step or two ahead of her and most of the menus would only let her select one kind of punishment at a time. She tried searching for the highest value scenario and found one worth two-hundred grand, but it was being displayed, touched and punished at a private party. The thought of which made her brain feel like it had swelled up and pressed against the inside of her skull.

No, she couldn't do that.

And, because she wasn't so certain of herself there, she did not read through the new scenario he'd proposed, except to note that it involved her being prepared and delivered to him, as he'd spoken of with such sexual roughness in his voice.

Among other new modules, he'd added ones simply called "coffee," "lunch" and "dinner." Curious to see if any of those involved a quick-cash BJ—look at her, learning to think like the prostitute she was—she tried selecting lunch and discovered it was not only worth $5,000, but she couldn't add "fellatio" to it. Not public or discreet—and who knew what "discreet" meant to him there. Not even "private" with one of the many possible positions he suggested. She couldn't even add a costume.

Just lunch. Him and his damn lunches.

He only had one to three open on his calendar, too, besides later in the evening, which she couldn't do. Irritated enough to message him, she did so through the tablet, though he would be working or in meetings and likely wouldn't see it for a while.

You can't pay me $5,000 just to have lunch with you.

She closed the tablet, deciding to make a grocery list. It pinged before she snapped the cover.

Don't worry, I can afford it.

She glared at the message, last night's anger rising again. I didn't opt in yet.

But you're thinking about it. Say yes. I want to see you. Talk to you.

Why? She typed the question, but didn't send. Erased it. It won't let me add anything else.

No. Nothing sexual to this. Lunch. So we can talk.

Feeling petulant she nearly typed that she didn't want to talk, but that seemed too petty. At a loss for anything better to text him, she closed the message window, clicked on "lunch" and saw him accept it immediately. He messaged an address but said nothing more.

Almost disappointed that he didn't, and not understanding herself at all anymore, if she ever had, she decided she'd better get showered and dressed if she wanted to hit the grocery store before her fancy lunch.

RYAN CLOSED THE tablet once it became clear that she wouldn't say anything more, and returned his attention to the meeting. Part of his attention, anyway, as Celestina occupied most of it. Difficult to discern tone in texts, of course, but people revealed more subtext in them than the common wisdom dictated. Terse messages, even for her. Nearly belligerent. Still angry with him, then. Or with herself. And yet she'd contacted him and opted to see him, which was more than he'd hoped for so soon. He'd resigned himself to the possibility of not hearing from her again for quite a while, if ever. Everybody had a different cooling period and he'd pegged her for a brooder, which could mean she'd seethe for days. He hadn't wanted to contemplate that she'd resolved to shake free of him entirely.

But then, she needed the money, didn't she? That $70K would have spent fast, given her dire financial straits, particularly with the tuition chunk. The dual feelings of self-congratulation at having a method to bring her back to him and the consternation that the money might be the only reason she would pricked at him. It had never much concerned him, that women might be interested in him solely for his wealth. In fact, he relied on it. He liked the money, too, after all—along with the comforts it could buy. He could personally attest that women were far more receptive to overtures from a wealthy man than a poor one, especially one as unhandsome as he. The romantic ideal that spouted about the best things in life being free was just that—idealized nonsense.

He should know.

There was absolutely nothing romantic about being hungry, or so cold your hands and feet ached, or not even having enough change to take the damn bus to your miserable job. Worst of all, the anxiety, the fear and the dread worked on you, putting a person in a perpetual state of stress. Each small setback becomes a calamity that threatens to pull you under because you're barely treading water as it is. That monotonous state of alarm had been apparent in Celestina, so much so that it grabbed him. He would have done much more to get her to take the money.

It had just worked in his favor that he'd been able to use it to seduce her and then possess her. She'd been at least a little attracted to him, much as she tried to act otherwise. She would not, however, have dated or slept with him without it. Certainly he couldn't have coaxed her into these games so quickly otherwise.

Wasn't that part of his original rationale? At last a woman he could be up-front with about his kink from the beginning. A clear and mutual understanding of what they both wanted from the arrangement, no strings, no confusions.

So it shouldn't bother him, that she kept treating this like business. Shouldn't rankle as if she intended it as some sort of personal insult. And he shouldn't be daydreaming about seeing her in just a couple of hours. Or worrying that she might be looking for a way out.

Well, he wouldn't let her out. There. Decision made before the meeting. Only the execution remained. They'd talk and he'd say whatever she needed to hear.

He arrived at the restaurant early, having cut the last interminable conference call short. Though the lunch crowd jammed the place, the reserved table on the quiet balcony awaited just as he'd specified. Another useful aspect of having plenty of money to throw around. A vase of bloodred roses in full, luxuriant bloom graced the table, and wine of the same color sat breathing in the bottle. Learning the Spanish wines had made an excellent substitute for learning Celestina's body in the late or small hours, when obsessive thoughts about her kept him from sleeping.

While he waited, he added the five thousand to her account, so she'd have it as soon as possible. A little hedge against fate, daring the universe to prove him wrong by having her not show.

She arrived late and flustered, speaking to the maître d' as she scanned the room, hesitant, as if she expected to be thrown out. The man led her across the room and Ryan caught the moment she spotted him, that enticing blush heightening her aristocratic cheekbones even as she kept her spine erect and head high. He'd expected something considerably farther south of his heart to ping at the sight of her and her unique combination of pride and timidity. She drew a sort of affectionate protectiveness out of him. The other face of wanting to possess her entirely, perhaps.

He stood as she reached the table, took her warm hands— damp from nerves?—and brushed her cheek with a kiss, which made her blush harder. "You look beautiful," he murmured, wondering what discomfited her so about the gesture.

Nodding away the maître d', he seated Celestina himself, enjoying the glimpse of the dip between her breasts as the boat neck of her black sheath dress sagged when she scooted the chair forward. He sat across from her and poured them both wine. At least she didn't argue this time, though she frowned at it ever so slightly.

"I haven't been here before," she said. "Lunch must cost as much as you're paying me."

"Not quite." He kept his voice smooth, refusing to rise to her bait just yet. Holding up his wineglass, he waited for her to lift hers. "To a delicious meal on a beautiful day with scintillating company," he said, before she could suggest toasting to whatever bill she intended to pay with today's fee.

Though she clinked her glass to his and sipped, she regarded him with suspicion over the rim. When he reached over the table to take her hand, she startled enough that he lost some of his patience. She'd better not be planning to break up with him. "Good Lord! I'm not going to yank you over the table and turn you over my knee—why are you so tense?"

She fired at that. Better than looking like a cat about to take off running. "I don't understand what I'm doing here."

He didn't grind his teeth, through great force of will. "I wanted to see you. Talk to you. It occurred to me that it's not balanced to see each other only when we're enacting a scene, because you might not communicate with me freely under those circumstances. Don't worry—" he added when she looked askance at the other diners "—no one can overhear, that's why I asked for this table. So I added in opportunities for us to spend time talking. Besides which, I enjoy your company."

If he hoped to hear her offer the same, she disappointed him. Instead of replying, she picked up the menu and studied it as if it were the most fascinating thing she'd ever seen. A complex and layered woman, his Celestina. Skittish and going to lengths to protect herself. Perhaps the ex had treated her worse than she let on. He liked that option—not about him in that case.

Giving her the time to decide—on her menu selection and what tack she'd take next—he soothed himself by savoring how lovely she looked, with the sun glinting off her shining dark hair, just a hint of red in the black. The simple dress should have been demure, but on her lush curves became as voluptuous as the red dress had been. An orderly soul, she'd likely be wearing black lingerie under it. Maybe thong panties, to prevent a line in the closely clinging material.

"When you look at me like that," she muttered at the menu, "I feel like I'm the one being served up for lunch."

He relaxed at her words, relieved of a worry he hadn't fully formed. It shouldn't matter that she was as aware of him as he was of her, but it did. More, it meant something that she offered the observation. A kind of gift, telling him how she felt without him dragging it out of her.

"Yes. I could devour you whole," he said softly.

She set the menu aside and met his gaze. Then she shook her head, as if clearing it, and sighed out a sharp breath. "And then you say things like that...I really can't decide how I feel about any of this, Ryan."

She'd called him by his name—the only other time since

he'd had his hand buried in her and she'd been nearly beyond reason. Offering him another kind of intimacy. Or signaling her intent to break it off with him. He marshaled the many arguments he'd prepared to convince her otherwise. "Tell me about it."

She glanced around at the other diners again, all too far away and too involved in their own loud conversations to overhear, but still hesitated. "I don't know how to handle things like...what happened last night."

"Be more specific. Was there one part you found it more difficult to handle than another?"

She tilted her head, the precise wing of hair brushing the similar line of her jaw, giving him a bemused look. "It's amazing to me the way you just discuss this stuff. At a public restaurant." She gestured to the other diners, as if he might have forgotten their presence.

"We'll have our food boxed up and go somewhere more private to talk."

"No," she said, hastily enough to make him raise his eyebrows. "That is, it's better for me to be in public with you for now."

That irked him. "I would never do anything with you that you don't agree to. That's why you have a safeword and everything is spelled out in the tablet."

"It's not that—though I could argue the Mrs. Matthews thing crossed that line—it's more that..." She trailed off, looking so distressed he wanted to pull her across the table, indeed, but to kiss and caress her senseless so she'd stop thinking so damn much.

The waiter arrived to take their order and she had to fumble with her menu, seeming to have forgotten what she'd chosen, if she'd truly picked anything before. After the waiter left, Ryan reached for her hand again and this time she at least let him take it. "It's more—" he prompted.

She wouldn't look at him, though she squeezed his fingers. "I don't think I trust myself to stop you."

Her voice had gone quiet enough that he had to strain to hear her, then the import of her words sank in. Not attempting to break it off at all. Instead acknowledging her submission to his will. The tremendous sense of relief nearly made him smile, which would be all wrong. Manfully, he swallowed it down, along with the surge of lust her confession caused.

"Celestina—that's why we set the parameters ahead of time. So you don't have to worry about stopping me in the throes of passion. We won't go past what you decide ahead of time."

She narrowed her eyes, darkly accusing. "One word— loopholes."

CHAPTER FIFTEEN

S HE HAD HIM there. Kind of. But he could see her point. "Okay—what's the solution? More specificity in the app. I can be more detailed, take more time with it."

The waiter set her meal in front of her and she thanked him with a flash of a gracious smile, one that lingered on her lips when she turned her gaze back to him, making him realize she'd never bestowed a look like that on him. It faded quickly as she assessed what he'd said. "You'd be willing to do that— give up the loopholes you enjoy so much?"

"I'm not sure there's much I wouldn't give up to have you the way I want to." *Or to earn a smile like that.*

"The Mrs. Matthews thing, that—"

"Was a mistake," he interrupted, enjoying at least her surprise at his admission. As if she knew he rarely admitted to them. Hated acknowledging mistakes almost as much as he hated making them in the first place. Though she had that knack of seeing through him, so maybe she did know. "I apologize for that. I…got carried away and lost my head. I promise never to let it happen again. Not without your prior agreement."

"That's not what you said last night."

"I know." He drank his wine, kicking himself for it.

"Why?" She asked it flatly, a kind of challenge. The queen, demanding an accounting.

"Why did I say otherwise?" How to explain this to her? He gave himself a moment to assemble his thoughts by sampling his meal, vaguely surprised by the prawns as he didn't recall ordering them and they certainly didn't go with the wine.

"Are you stalling?" She sounded amused and, when he risked looking at her, a small smile played on her lush mouth.

"I hate making mistakes," he admitted, hoping he wouldn't choke on it. "Being less than perfectly in control."

"So you lied to cover it up?"

Trust her to put it so baldly. "Yes. That sounds reprehensible, doesn't it?"

"A bit. But it also makes you more human. I hate making mistakes, too."

He didn't much like her saying that, seeing that in him, except that she seemed easier now, smiling a touch more. "I'm not...I mean, I understand that."

She cocked her head, as if listening intently to a sound beyond his hearing. "That wasn't what you started to say. What aren't you?"

"I stopped saying it for a reason." Damn her and her insights anyway.

"And now you're defensive. This is fascinating." She folded her arms on the table, dark eyes sparkling, and leaned in. "You're not what—human?"

"Funny girl. No, I'm human, which I'd be delighted to demonstrate to you in any number of ways as soon as you select one of the penetration options."

"Trying to rattle me. Taking the upper hand and using sexual taunts to distract me."

He put down his fork. "What are you after, Celestina?"

Unintimidated, she narrowed her eyes. "For the moment I want to know what you were about to say that you're not."

Feeling absurdly cornered, he cast about for a likely answer, but she discerned that, too.

"Don't lie to me. I'll know."

An echo of his words from last night. He shoved his plate aside and leaned in also. "Did you have an orgasm?"

She gave nothing away, not even a flicker. "We're not talking about me. Stop dodging the answer. Every time you do just makes me more determined to find out what you're trying so hard to hide."

A totally new face of her, this dogged interrogator. Having fun, too, by the glint in her dark eyes. Unfortunately at his expense. "All I was going to say is that I'm not..." He had to pause for a breath. Ridiculous. "I'm not comfortable with being flawed."

She eyed him with interest and perhaps a hint of compassion. "Why was that so difficult to say? We're all flawed in some way."

"Yes, well—I don't care to be. I've worked assiduously to eliminate my flaws and become a better person."

"Better than what?"

He dragged his plate back and took another bite, gave her an annoyed look that did nothing to change her expression of determined interest. "Than I used to be. Is this inquisition over?"

"You use a lot of five-star words. Why is that—English major?"

Apparently not over. "Why all these questions?"

"It occurs to me that I might feel better talking with you frankly—which was your suggestion, by the way—and doing…these things with you if I know you better."

"And knowing why I have an extensive vocabulary will do that?"

She lifted a shoulder and smiled, this one very nearly as dazzling as the one she'd bestowed on the waiter. As he grew more tense, she relaxed. Wonderful.

"Yes. This whole conversation is helping. It's kind of nice to see you not in perfect control."

"I like perfect control."

"I've noticed." Her voice tinged with the huskiness of the night before, when she'd pleaded with him.

"Better, I like being in control of you. I'm waiting for an answer to *my* question."

She started to lick her bottom lip, picked up her wine, sipping to cover it. Or to wet a mouth gone dry. "Then tell me this one thing and we can get to that."

What could it hurt to tell her? He rarely—okay, never—discussed his youth with anyone, but if this was what she needed to reestablish the trust he'd cracked with his carelessness…"I read the dictionary."

She laughed and abruptly sobered. "Seriously?"

Oh right—this reaction was why he hadn't wanted to say. "Yes. At the library. I grew up in a very small town with a miniscule library, where I spent hours every day. I read all the books they had, many of them several times. Including the set of ancient Oxford English Dictionaries."

Lips parted, she gazed at him. Clearly reassessing her ideas of who he was. Uncomfortable, he focused on eating the prawns. A meal his younger self couldn't have imagined, much less afforded. Extraordinary that he'd told her that much.

"Why did you have so many hours to spend there?"

"No." Resolute, he pinned her with his most dominating stare. "Your turn. Answer my question."

She flushed. "Which question?"

"Now who's dodging? Did you have an orgasm, Celestina?"

"I don't see why I have to tell you that either way."

"So that's a yes."

"No, that's an 'I don't think I have to share that with you.'"

"Afraid?" He drew the word out, taunting her with it. Definitely better to be the one in control of the conversation.

She glared at him. "Should I be?"

"If you disobeyed me, then yes. Because you know what's next."

JUST LIKE THAT, he had her in an emotional puddle again. Completely flustered and, ridiculously, given the context, totally aroused. Why this got to her made no sense at all. Her brain fought against the absurdity of him ordering her to tell him such a private thing, one that he had no business knowing or controlling. Every other organ, however, thrilled to each bit of it. Her skin tingled with anticipation, her breasts swelling and nipples hardening. Her heart thrummed, pulsing blood to her groin, where she'd gone wet.

Where the early tremors of a climax lurked, an impossibility as nothing could stimulate her. Still, he watched her with those penetrating silvery eyes, the harshness of his face giving him a stern look that made her want to beg him to punish her. What he'd confided to her had been astounding, the puzzle pieces of him reassembling in her head. The scars might be from chicken pox, not acne. The badly set nose a sign of a poor childhood. Hours in the library—a free and safe place for a child to go.

"I'm going to assume that your lack of denial is a confession and make any punishment you choose twice as severe because you failed to admit it," he said in a soft, warning tone.

If he'd intended to yank her attention away from thinking about his history—a distinct possibility, given how uncomfortable he'd been talking about it—that worked. Her face had gone hot and she squirmed on her chair, then stopped herself when a smile flickered over his firm lips. A cruel smile, full of anticipation that made her thickening desire even worse.

"Are you done with your salad? Would you like dessert?" He made the offer cordially, but the danger lurked beneath his silky tone.

"N-no." Dammit that she stammered in her nerves. "I'm fine."

"Let's go then. We can finish this conversation in private." He stood and held out a hand, commanding her obedience. Which absolutely worked, to her chagrin, as she took it and stood.

"Don't you have to pay?"

"I run a tab here."

Of course he did.

They entered the elevator and he pressed the button for the lobby. Before they'd gone a few floors, however, he pressed the stop button. And turned on her. Before she realized what he was about, he'd taken her wrists and raised them above her head, holding them in a tight grip and staring into her eyes, his gone sharp as silver knives.

"Tell me, Celestina."

She pressed her lips firmly on the admission. Wanting to press her aching breasts against his hard chest, needing to part her legs and beg him to fuck her. Where this person, this completely wanton slut version of herself had come from, she had no idea. But Ryan seemed to be able to reach into her soul and drag this woman out with a flick of one demanding finger, one casually uttered order.

The alarm began to shriek.

"Tell me," he demanded.

"People will come," she said, struggling to free herself. A mistake, as his face hardened with desire. *You struggle so beautifully.*

"Yes, they will. Shall I strip you out of this dress and pet you so they'll find you naked and panting with desire?"

"You can't. I haven't opted in."

"Maybe I won't follow the rules, since you aren't. Tell me or I'll do it. You know I can."

Despite her struggles, he easily transferred her wrists to grip them in one big hand. Reached for the zipper of her dress with the other and began tugging it down.

"Yes!" she shouted at him. "Okay? Yes, I had a stupid orgasm."

He stopped pulling down the zipper, but kept his finger on the tab. "When?"

"On the drive home," she admitted, feeling terribly exposed.

"Did you put your hand inside your panties?"

"Yes." She focused on his shoulder, the triangle of red silk in his suit jacket pocket. Just like the one he'd handed her to clean his semen from her naked breasts. Not a sight to calm herself with. "Please turn off the alarm."

"Of course." He let her go and started the elevator again, all urbane gentleman, as if she had but to ask and he'd grant her least desire.

The elevator opened on the building lobby and she stepped out, feeling more than a little wobbly. He stopped her with a hand on her arm. "Just a moment. Your zipper seems to have slipped." Sliding it back up the couple of inches, he then offered her his arm. "Come sit in my car with me for a moment. I imagine you drove here?"

Mute, she nodded. She should run screaming, not get into the car with this man who seemed to be able to make her do anything. He held the door for her, told the driver just to circle the neighborhood, and settled himself beside her. Then took her hand, studying her face.

"Tell me the rest."

"There isn't anything else to tell. I didn't mean to do it. I was driving and—"

"Not that. Engrossing as it is to imagine you unable to

restrain yourself. Tell me what had you so upset about all of this. You said you don't know how to handle things like what we did last night. You were going to be more specific about it."

She nearly laughed at the way he rearranged the conversation to suit his interpretation. "No, you told me to be more specific and I hadn't yet decided on what or how much to tell you."

"Tell me everything. I want to know everything about you."

"Just like you'll tell me everything about yourself?"

His jaw hardened at that, a flicker of the cornered vulnerability he'd shown before in his eyes before he chased it off. "That's not how this works, Celestina."

"Why do you always call me by my full name? Everyone else shortens to Tina."

"Because I love your name. It perfectly embodies you. Heavenly. Now, stop this eternal dodging and explain to me what you're having difficulty handling so we can address it and move forward."

She blew out a long breath, which shook and rattled as it left her lungs. "These things aren't easy for me to talk about."

"Sex?"

"In a nutshell, yes. But…especially your kind."

"Take your time then. Close your eyes and tell me, if that helps."

Oddly, it did help. But the nervous wings still beat in her stomach. "Would you…would you kiss me?"

With a low hum of assent, he gathered her into his arms and his mouth brushed over hers, the sensation both more acute and dreamier for having her eyes closed. He kissed her long, with thorough gentleness, the frantic wings slowing into a deeper, sensual beating.

"Better?" he asked, drawing away, but still holding her.

"Better." Without opening her eyes, she felt her way through it. "The things that happened last night—I liked them. A lot. Since then I haven't been able to stop thinking about wanting more. The things you said to me, wanting to see me struggle, wanting to punish me. Chains and having me delivered to you. I want it, too. Not because of the money, but because something about it makes me..." A tremor rattled her, throat going dry. He didn't say anything. Just held her loosely, rubbing her back. "I want them—the dark things. And I don't understand why."

"Do you have to understand?"

"Shouldn't I? These aren't normal, healthy things to want."

"People do, though. Who gets to say what's healthy and normal? Going most of your life not enjoying sex is hardly normal and healthy."

She opened her eyes to find his face close, gray eyes thoughtful. Not laughing at her as she'd expected. "I enjoyed sex." *Sometimes.*

"Like you did last night?"

"No. That's what concerns me. Those things...it's like I want them in a harder way, a craving." Uncertain, she lifted her hands to his chest, needing the contact. His chest hair crinkled under his crisp dress shirt, skin hot beneath.

"Craving isn't a bad thing, Celestina."

"I don't know. I don't think I've ever felt that strongly

about anything before. I'm not sure what to do with feeling this way." With feeling at all, after all the numbness. "I don't know why I find the idea of you punishing me so...titillating. How I can be both afraid and starving for it to happen."

CHAPTER SIXTEEN

H IS EYES GLITTERED, though he kept his hands gentle. Oh, he wanted that, all right. As if he starved for it also. "Being afraid of something is sometimes the reason we need to do it."

"I can see that, but it seems so…self-destructive." Which might be at the core of it. A part of her had stood back and recognized this trend in herself. The suicidal impulses. The depression. The insistent thought that she had been meant to die with Ara just as they'd been born together.

She was a mess. And this sojourn into perversion might be just another level of it. Another way of losing herself, with the money a convenient rationalization.

"I want you to listen to me." He stroked her cheek, waiting until she met his gaze. "It's the opposite of self-destructive because it's all part of the trip. It's not real, Celestina. Self-destruction is putting yourself in the way of real violence. This kind of punishment is pain, yes, but artfully, even lovingly applied. Some people think that we crave it to work out suffering we wouldn't be able to bear in real life. Perhaps you feel some sort of profound guilt and you believe, on a subconscious level, that you deserve to suffer for it. This lets you suffer in a way that's also cathartic, that won't cause you real, lasting harm. It could be that your subconscious self knows and understands this, and thus is the source of your craving."

Profound guilt. Oh yes. That hit home. "Pretty deep."

He smiled, a slight, wry twist. "I read more than the dictionary."

Letting the ideas he'd offered percolate, she searched his face in turn, contemplating the few hints he'd dropped. "And for you—it's the opportunity to be in control, to unleash violence without causing real harm?"

He looked unexpectedly stricken, a desperate shadow to him that she'd seen at the table when she goaded him into telling her about reading the dictionary. "Perhaps so," he finally acknowledged. "Besides the fact that having you entirely at my mercy is a fantasy I can't get out of my brain."

Evading her. Pulling back from the same boggy emotional territory he insisted she wade into. But she'd let him, for the time being. "All right then," she whispered, feeling the twin surges of elation and terror. "I came without permission. Punish me for it."

His hands flexed, a flare of triumph and hard-edged desire in his face. "I'll adjust the tablet accordingly. Tonight?"

She shook her head. "I can't. I'm spending the evening with the girls and taking them shopping tomorrow. I might…I thought I'd see if they wanted to stay with friends tomorrow night. Then I could…I wouldn't have to get home. If that's all right with you."

"Having you all night would almost make up for you making me wait for this. I'd have time to do so much more to you. To take you apart the way I crave to do."

"After the spankings, the oral sex?" she joked, trying to shake off the nerves at his electric intensity.

His mouth twitched, but he didn't smile in truth. Instead he stroked her lower lip with his thumb, making her think he envisioned her lips wrapped around his cock again. Inadvertently, she imagined it, too, how thick and blunt it had been, like his fingers. Filling her mouth. How it would feel filling her elsewhere. "Oh yes," he said, in an almost reverent tone. "And all the other kinds as well. Whatever you find the courage to give me permission to do."

With his thumb, he tugged her lower lip ever so slightly, sending an arrow of answering need to her groin. "But you'll see when you look—I can punish you fully clothed, without giving you any pleasure. This will be your punishment. Choose carefully."

"I'll consider that, but…" She hesitated yet again, not certain how much of her dark thoughts she should confide. Exceptionally silly as she sat here calmly discussing how she'd trust him with far more. He watched her with calm understanding, his savagery cloaked, his hands steadying. "I don't know how to say this."

"Just say it. You can't shock me."

A comfort in that to be sure. "I want all of it. I want to be…what you said. In your power and for you to, ah, well, possess me." Her cheeks flamed hot she felt sure, but he didn't mock her or even change expression so much except that his eyes went more heavy-lidded.

"I can do that," he murmured, his tone as caressing as his hands. "The difficulty will be waiting until tomorrow night."

"And it might not be tomorrow," she cautioned. "It depends on what the girls are up to."

"I could arrange something for them."

"No. I mean—thank you. But not yet. Let me see how it works out first. If—if it does work out tomorrow…can we be alone in the house?"

"Of course. I'll make sure that's explicitly part of the options from now on."

"Okay." She pressed a hand to her jittery stomach. "I'm nervous."

"What would help?"

"Can we—make out a little?" She laughed self-consciously when he smiled. "Being in the backseat of a car with you reminds me of being a teenager again. Oh, but you have to get back to work, never mind."

"Not so fast." He checked his phone, glanced out the window. "How about I have the driver drop me at the office and then bring you back to your car? That gives us a little time. About fifteen minutes, depending on traffic."

She'd caught the time on his phone. "That's fine. Either way, you're already late."

"It's good to be the boss." He gave her a cocky grin and the driver his instructions. "What are my limits—how much can I touch you?"

Oh, wow. A giddy thrill ran through her at the prospect. If she planned to have sex with him the next night, this might be the time to work up to that a bit. "As much as you want, short of intercourse?" she ventured.

"Done. Take off your dress. I want to see what I'm touching." Deftly he slid the zipper down her back and slipped the neckline down her shoulders before she'd quite processed his intention. So observant of permission, but once he obtained it, he took all leeway to the limits. Zero to sixty, as he did with all things. Something to remember, she scolded herself, as he coaxed her to lift her hips so he could slide the dress off her legs and set it behind him.

"I won a bet with myself," he commented, filling his hands with her as he studied her, clad only in black lace lingerie. "Come here." He didn't wait for her to move, but lifted her onto his lap and took her mouth in a kiss so swiftly devastating she never had a chance to ask what the bet had been.

ONCE AGAIN, HIS technique had worked. Making the decision that she would not shake free of him had taken the potential breakup lunch to this impromptu session with a mostly naked, delightfully hot Celestina moaning on his lap, all velvet skin and lush curves undulating in unspoken need. Along with the promise that she'd turn herself over to him entirely.

She looked incredible. Her full breasts strained against the black lace bra, round and taut. When he flicked the clasp open and it fell away, they remained high for their size. And Celestina gasped in such gratifying surprise at the feel of his hands on her naked skin, her nipples hard points against his palms, her mouth yielding so sweetly. She moved urgently against him, the dip of her waist enticing him to trace her curves lower, over her voluptuous hips, to squeeze one round globe of her ass.

With her hands running through his hair, she rubbed

against him like a cat starved for affection and he gave it to her, touching her everywhere, worshipping her with his hands and mouth while indulging himself in sating at least the need to feel her against him. She parted her thighs eagerly for him and he found her as wet as he'd expected, drinking in her moan as he cupped her through her panties. She trembled and pressed her ripe mound into his hand, but he had no intention of letting her come.

Much as she believed she craved punishment, it would go much easier on her with more sexual tension built up. He broke the kiss and moved his hand back up to her breast, loving how she overflowed his palm—and how she protested that he'd stopped. "It appears traffic was light for once," he told her as she blinked at him, dark eyes blurry with desire. "I should go in. Here."

He helped her wriggle into the sheath dress and zipped it up. "Wait," she said, her mind clearing. "My bra?"

Loving the way her brow creased in consternation, he pocketed it. "I thought I'd keep it, a souvenir to get me through a dull afternoon." Unable to keep his hands off her, he massaged her breasts through the light crepe, rolling her nipples so her head dropped back on a moan. "I'll put my hand in my pocket and remember how this felt, how you shuddered and moaned for me. And you, when your naked nipples brush against your dress, you'll remember this, too."

With reluctance he let her go, consoling himself with the thought of the following night. "One more thing, Celestina?" He waited for her to focus on him, suspicion entering her eyes. "The rule stands. No orgasms. I want to be clear on this. Not until I say so, and that won't happen until we're together again. Understand?"

She set her mouth, gloriously stubborn. "I still don't think I agreed to that rule."

"Agree to it now." He held her gaze, then wrapped his fingers around her slender wrist, to remind her of her admission that she wanted to be in his power. "I'm very serious. Promise me."

The gesture worked, or the note of command in his voice. She responded to both as sensuously as she did to his kisses and caresses. Amazing she hadn't explored her darker sexual nature before this. He wanted to believe she'd waited for him. A lovely delusion to indulge in.

Narrowing her eyes with sharp intelligence despite the extremity of her response, she looked at his hand on her wrist and back to his face, searching for something. "That's part of it? You taking control of that part of things?"

"Yes. For both of us."

She nodded thoughtfully. "All right. I don't like it, but I understand why it works. I promise."

"Say the words."

God how he loved to rattle her. She raised her chin, however, and held his gaze. "I promise not to have an orgasm until you say I can."

"Thank you."

"But it better be good when it does happen," she added, a flash of her imperious self. So distant from the woman who'd almost timidly explained that she rarely came at all.

"Ah, Celestina." He brushed her hair back from her jaw

and cupped it, holding her there for a sweet, hot kiss. "I plan to deliver on that."

He amused himself through the afternoon by first selecting all she'd allowed him to do to her in the car and transferring the appropriate funds. Then he tweaked the punishments, lending half an ear to his CFO's deadly dull assessment of cost-cutting measures he had no interest in implementing. His mama would have called the man meaner than a striped snake and just plain cheap to boot. He constantly asked to revisit the employee benefits he considered too generous. If he wasn't so savagely good at negotiating the labyrinth of California corporate taxes—Ryan drew the line at being more generous than he had to with that spendthrift government—he'd likely let the man go.

Funny to have his mama's voice come back just then. Celestina's influence, with her probing questions about the past.

Shaking it off—no good in going there—he played with the tablet while pretending, as he did every quarter, to dutifully consider the numbers before delivering the decision he'd made before he walked in the room. Not many people realized how key that was. He always knew his decision before any meeting started. If they could convince him otherwise, good on them. But the burden of proof rested on the person on the other side. As his CFO had yet to convince him of the need and continued to focus on the exact numbers, Ryan easily gave the lion's share of his attention to refining potential scenarios for the following evening. Just an extra spin that he might appear to be taking notes or running calculations on his tablet, as did the rest of his executive team.

Or, as they appeared to. How many of them did unrelated tasks? Judging by the studiously smooth faces ranging down the long table, most of them. They all knew him well and likely knew he wouldn't budge on this. He wouldn't hesitate to fire someone who didn't work hard for him, but while they did, he rewarded his employees lavishly.

No one should have to struggle to make a good living in such a wealthy society. It burned his gut that anyone thought they should. They didn't know what abject poverty felt like, what people like his mama had suffered. Maybe he should discreetly search for a new CFO. Surely knowledge of the tax laws and regulations could come with a more generous spirit. Poverty led only to misery, which people then cruelly shared with their supposed loved ones.

Once again shoving down those old memories that kept wanting to nudge into his thoughts long after Celestina had asked about them, he focused on making the details of her choices clear. In retrospect, he couldn't quite believe he'd answered her so honestly. He could have lied, as he usually did, since no one needed to know the dreary, very private details of his infelicitous youth. Reporters who asked about his rise from blue-collar kid to wealthy CEO always bought his story. Of course, it matched the truth on the surface well enough. You never knew what went on behind people's front doors. If he'd learned nothing else from life, he knew that.

Realizing everyone had turned polite faces to him, he pretended to finalize a figure, then swiped the tablet off and gave the decision he'd made before he walked in the room.

CHAPTER SEVENTEEN

TINA HAD REGISTERED the new deposit—and the attendant list of services rendered, which was what they were, even if Ryan didn't title it that way—with emotions so mixed she couldn't quite pick a predominant one. A hint of shame mixed in with the ever-simmering broth of her newly discovered rage, heavily flavored with the desire that accompanied the reminder of those magical minutes in the car. But soured with a sense of betrayal. Finally, a slap of pragmatic reality chilled it all. An excellent reminder, this, that everything she and Ryan did together, including lunch, came down to their business arrangement.

Itemized, recorded and paid for.

A very real problem for her that she kept forgetting it. That with his hands and mouth on her, with his penetrating insights and avid gaze, and those speeches that turned her inside out, though he affected her more than any man she'd ever known, theirs was not a romance by any stretch. He'd been clear about it from the beginning and it would be her own damn fault if she let herself feel more than that. Being solicitous, charming and seductive came naturally to Ryan—tools he wielded as competently as he used his business savvy. For him, the ardent interlude that afternoon had been enjoyable—extremely so, by the dollar value he placed on it—but he hadn't been swept up in emotion. Not like she'd let herself be. He'd said that when he first proposed their bargain, that it would be a way for him to have the sex he desired without the mess of a romantic relationship.

She'd been an idiot to, even for a few daydreamy hours, romanticize it even a little. Deciding to cling to the emotions stirred by the cold slap of reality wakeup call, she set aside all her other responses as unreasonable. Like a dog that had been kicked and starved, she'd responded to the first hint of solicitude. Like millions of idiot girls before her, she'd mistaken sex for affection. Even in the face of clear, codified information that it was not and never would be.

Sitting herself down, she paid some bills, to cement the realization for herself. Ryan might speak insightfully about her subconscious needs and why she wanted what she did, but all of that came secondary to her real reason for all of it. She would thank him for reminding her of that, except she had no intention of ever mentioning it.

As it was, she'd made a tidy sum for the day's work and enjoyed doing it. She hadn't had a man's hands on her skin like that for a long time, and Ryan took her under his spell so swiftly all she'd wanted was for him to touch her even more. Clearly he liked her well enough to pay handsomely for the privilege, so that would be enough.

Josie and Carly, too, made it all worthwhile. Over the moon with their evening of what had once been common treats and now felt like luxuries, wild with glee at hip new haircuts and clothes, they delighted her. They even stopped bickering for the most part. Tina spent way more on clothes than she'd intended, but the spree made them so happy. The twins deserved some happiness.

Judging by the initial sum for all she'd recklessly opted into, she'd have plenty of money to work with for the next week. All that remained was to sign off and send. Ryan had sent his ritual good-night and good-morning, which she had politely returned. Over a late lunch at the food court, since the pancake breakfast had lasted them well into the afternoon, she brought up the girls staying with a friend that night.

Carly immediately texted the news to their best friends while Josie chewed on a French fry and studied her thoughtfully. "I thought you didn't like it when we did overnights."

"At Caitlyn's house, no. But at Leticia's or Madison's, that's fine."

"What's wrong with Caitlyn's house?" Carly demanded, as if they hadn't had this argument a hundred times already.

"Not enough supervision and no more discussion."

"You're so mean, Antina," Carly reflexively complained, but stopped when Josie kicked her. "Except thanks for all the clothes and hair and stuff."

"You're welcome."

Josie still stared with narrowed eyes, then pointed a French fry at her. "You have a date."

Carly gasped theatrically. "She does? Who with? Do we know him?"

Dammit. Should she call it a work thing? Except Ryan wanted to meet the girls and would no doubt get his way eventually, if they continued on for very long, given how lousy she'd proven to be so far at refusing him. And he'd insist on being known as her boyfriend, regardless of the reality, he'd made that clear. Might as well bite the bullet.

"Yes, I have a date. His name is Ryan and no, you don't know him."

"Are *you* doing an overnight?" Josie asked cannily.

"No." She told the lie easily enough. The last thing she needed was the girls sneaking back with their friends to take advantage of an empty house and total lack of supervision. Not to mention being a bad role model. "But I might be out late and I don't want you two home alone."

"What if everyone is busy?" Josie persisted.

"They're not." Carly waved her phone. "Madison wants us to come over. Caitlyn and Leticia are coming, too. Party!"

Just to be on the safe side, Tina got out her own phone to text Madison's mom and confirm that she knew about it and would be home. Fortunately—or not, now that Tina's nerves were gearing up again—Madison's mom cheerfully confirmed. Tina thanked her and said she'd send some cash with the girls to treat everyone, something she'd never had much room to do before.

She waited until the twins had ensconced themselves in yet another dressing room to get out the tablet and send her final choices to Ryan, confirming that she'd be over later. As always, he messaged her back immediately.

I shall make the appropriate preparations.

So odd that such a formal reply gave her a flutter. And aroused her, which happened easily as the frenzy of desire he'd brought her to the afternoon before had barely subsided below a low sizzle. Even during that flash of anger when she saw he'd paid her. She'd been hard-pressed not to touch herself at all, and would have, if her promise hadn't constrained her. If she'd started though, she might be unable to stop herself. Every time that pulse of need riffed through her system, which happened frequently, and how she'd been forbidden to do anything about it, she thought of him.

All part of his diabolical plan, no doubt.

After she dropped off the twins at Madison's, forcing herself to chat naturally with Lisa, Madison's very high society mother who waved off any need for more treats, saying their pantry overflowed with more than a hundred people could eat in a year, Tina went home and primped for the evening. Ryan would provide her outfit, described in the program simply as "penitent slave girl," giving her a salacious thrill as she selected it, so she dressed in casual clothes that would be the sort of thing she'd wear for Sunday morning at home, should she pull it close to the girls' return.

With her hair and makeup done, she surveyed herself one last time, locked up the house and went to face what the night would bring.

He must have been watching for her—or, more likely, he had some sort of alarm that notified the house when someone approached the gates, so they could be remotely opened—because he came down the steps as she pulled up, opening the car door for her as soon as she killed the engine. When he helped her out of the car, instead of his polite cheek-buss, he drew her into an embrace and a deep kiss that sent her head swimming. Nearly vibrating with contained energy that matched her own mounting tension, he fed on her lips with a hunger that communicated how much he wanted what lay ahead.

He finally seemed to have enough, because he released her and leaned his forehead against hers. "Hi," he said.

It made her laugh, dissipating the nerves the kiss hadn't. She pressed a hand to her stomach and smiled at him. "That's better."

He framed her face with his hands, searching her eyes in the fading sunset light. "Nervous?"

"I want to do what we agreed on."

His eyes lit with that cruel silvery fire, and his face took on that almost grim aspect of consuming desire. "All right, then." His smooth voice had gone slightly hoarse. "Once we go inside, then we're under terms of the contract. But you can always use your safeword, at any time, for any reason."

She shivered. Anticipation, dread, excitement, fear and arousal rising to a keen edge that made all the colors seem richer, details sharper. "Okay."

He took her hand, led her up the steps and opened the door. Locked it behind them.

"You'll find your costume in your same room. Take everything off and put on only what I've set out for you." Showing her to an open door across the hall, to a sort of library she hadn't been in before, he said, "I'll be waiting for you in here. Take your time. When you're ready, come in and kneel in front of me. I'll take it from there."

"Okay," she repeated, unable to think of much else with the high whine in her head.

He put a big hand around her throat, bracketing her jaw

and raising her slightly straighter, tilting her face so she had to meet his stern gaze. "You disappointed me with your disobedience and lack of control, so I expect you to behave perfectly tonight. I'll ensure that you do. You won't have any choice. It's out of your control now. Understand?"

Her brain went to total white noise and her thigh muscles melted. Only his hand on her throat seemed to hold her up and, while he wasn't restricting her breathing, he had to be able to feel her frantic pulse against his hand. An absurd desire to plead with him, to apologize and beg to appease him, seized her.

"Answer me," he told her, the warning clear.

"Yes, I understand."

"Yes, *Master.*"

"Yes, Master, I understand." She'd wondered about calling him that, if she'd feel silly, but in that moment it felt true. She steeled her traitorous heart at how profoundly true it felt.

"Better. Go prepare yourself for me and meet me as I told you."

In a haze, she climbed the stairs, the skin on her throat hot where he'd grasped her.

Prepare yourself for me.

You won't have any choice.

It's out of your control now.

His words chased around in her head and she seemed to be unable to think of anything else. A trip, he'd called it. If so, she'd left the runway and soared into the air, groundless, gaining altitude so rapidly that everything she thought she knew about herself stayed far behind.

She undressed, leaving everything on the bed, and surveyed the very little he'd left for her to put on. Penitent slave. The nearly transparent white robe went over her head, with a deep vee front and back, so the inner curves of her breasts were exposed. Though, with the cloth so sheer, her nipples showed through almost as clearly. It hung completely open on both sides. A heavy gold belt, as wide as the length of her hand, closed tightly around her waist, the only thing that kept the robe from flapping open at the sides, making long slits instead. It locked like a seatbelt, with a click ominous enough to make her look for the release. Unable to find one, she resigned herself to the likelihood that only he would be able to remove it.

It's out of your control now.

Several rings attached around the circumference hinted at how the belt would play a role in the upcoming restraint. She checked the rest of the room. Nothing else in evidence for her to put on. Apparently that was it. Anything else, he would put on her. Not a comforting thought.

Barefoot, she descended the grand staircase, acutely aware of her near-nudity, particularly with how the filmy robe flared as she walked. At the doorway to the library, she paused, feeling her nerves and exposure, searching the dim room lit mainly by soft lamps and a cheerful fire. Two freestanding posts framed the fireplace, going from the floor to the high ceiling, making it into an open-sided alcove.

"Were my instructions somehow unclear?" He grated out the question in a dangerous tone that spurred her heart back into accelerated response.

Picking him out in a chair by the fire, she hurried and knelt in front of him. His shadowed face had a cruel, even thuggish cast. "I'm sorry, Master."

"Save your apologies. Eyes on the floor. Give me your wrists."

Shuddering, she looked down. The hard points of her nipples strained against the sheer cloth. He wore shiny black shoes. Somehow both details seemed important. She held her hands out uncertainly. Metal clanked, fastened around one wrist, then the other, both dragged down by the weight of heavy chains. The manacles fit tightly, with some sort of padding inside. Her arm muscles trembled with the effort to keep her hands aloft.

"Lower your hands to your sides. Lift your chin and look at me now."

She obeyed, grateful for the reprieve, then drew in a breath at the sight of the collar he held in his hands. Like something out of a European dungeon, made of thick iron, like the manacles and chains on her wrists, it hinged on one side and met in matching rings at the open end, with crimson velvet like a wound on the inner surface.

"You lost the privilege of freedom. A disobedient slave must be chained and punished. Do you accept your master's collar?"

Swallowing against the tightness in her throat, she searched his face, so remote, seething violence beneath. "Yes, Master," she whispered.

"Ask me to do it."

"Please collar me, Master."

He smiled, ever so slightly, but it sent a rush of relief through her that she'd managed to please him that much.

Slipping the collar behind her neck, he matched the rings and put a padlock through them, clicking it into place. It fit more loosely than the cuffs, but snug enough to be a constant sensation. So heavy. He hung the key around his neck with another, so they lay in the open vee of his dark shirt—out of her reach, in his control. He studied her, then brushed her cheek.

"You are so beautiful to me like this." He picked up another chain and attached it to the collar, adding to its weight, then draped it over her shoulder, so it hung heavily down her back. "Kneel up."

Feeling the effort of it, with the weight of the chain around her neck and dragging her wrists down, she did. Holding her gaze, he tugged the robe off her shoulders, leaving it to slide down her arms, baring her breasts. He picked up something brightly glinting. "This is when the pain starts."

Wetting his fingers, he rolled her nipple, already taut but becoming more sensitive by the moment. Pleasure arrowing to her groin despite her peaking fear. Or perhaps because of it. Poising the clamp in front of her trapped nipple, he caught her gaze. "Do you deserve this punishment?"

"Yes, Master." Her throat clogged with apprehension and she braced herself. He moved his feet, using them to pin the chains at her wrists to the floor. Then slipped the toothed clamp onto her nipple. The light pressure quickly increasing to bright pain.

Moderate, she told herself. *Only moderate.* But it continued to build and, when similar pain flared on her other nipple, she realized she'd closed her eyes and he'd meanwhile attached the other clamp without her realizing. The cuffs bit into her wrists. She'd been trying to lift her hands to pull the clamps off. With his feet holding the chains to the floor, she could only struggle with increasing panic.

His hands cupped her face, steadying. "Breathe into it," he advised. "I'm in control of this and you can't escape it. You deserve this pain. Accept it."

CHAPTER EIGHTEEN

S HE CLUNG TO his gaze, dark eyes bottomless, breasts rising and falling frantically. So incredibly beautiful in her supplication. That singular combination of tenderness and cruelty coiled through him. The impulse to both comfort and further torment, to break her open and then anoint her with love. Nothing else he'd ever found compared to these moments.

And Celestina, fully immersed, powerfully involved, outshone every other and drew him in like no other woman had ever done.

Still shuddering, she calmed somewhat. When he stopped pinning her chains to the floor, she didn't try to raise her hands, yielding to the clamps, no longer fighting it. Taking her chain leash, he wrapped it around his hand and stood, drawing her to her feet with it. She rose obediently, without instruction, fully in sync with him now, hands by her sides and chains dragging on the floor.

He positioned her in front of the fireplace, the light silhouetting her lovely figure. Draping the heavy chain leash between her full breasts, careful not to bump the clamps and cause the pain to flare—not just yet for that—he let it dangle there. With her waist compressed by the belt, her breasts naked and clamped, and the iron chains against her golden skin, she moved him impossibly.

With a remote he lowered the hook from above. A big iron one, like those used for hanging meat. Her already huge eyes widened at the brutal sight of it, then she closed them as he looped the ends of her wrist chains over the point. He allowed her the reprieve as it seemed to let her give in more easily. She opened them again when he raised the hook, her arms tugged over her head, the white gown sliding back to her shoulders, but catching on the outsides of the globes of her golden breasts, framing them perfectly. Not watching the hook, though, she gazed at him. When she'd gone barely on tiptoe, just enough to put her on the balls of her feet and off-balance, not enough to suspend her, he stopped it.

Cupping her soft cheek, he soothed her, though she hadn't struggled. Focusing on his face, she seemed about to say something, but didn't.

"Kiss my hand," he told her. "Show me your gratitude."

Her lips parted, glossy red with her still-perfect lipstick, and she trembled visibly, then turned her face and pressed a fervent kiss into the palm of his hand. Totally in the moment.

Moving more quickly, as he could only keep her suspended even this much for a short time, he brought chains from their niches in the posts on either side, strong ones, firmly fixed to the floor for this express purpose, and attached them to her belt. The leash chain came off and more, lighter chains went from her collar to the same posts, the better to keep her still when she began thrashing in earnest.

She flinched a little when he went behind her and locked

cuffs on her slim ankles, then moaned when he spread her thighs and tethered her feet to the posts also. Not so wide that she couldn't bear some of her weight, but plenty enough to amplify her sense of helplessness. Moving back in front of her, he picked up a big-bladed knife, showed it to her, then sliced the shoulders of the robe. She struggled, making the chains clink, as he stripped away the pieces of it, leaving her gloriously naked except for her many restraining chains. His slave in truth, at last.

She stopped squirming when he stood in front of her, trailing a hand down her center, between her breasts and the confining belt, over the delightfully smooth skin of her mound. As if frozen, she stared into his eyes, going rigid as he slipped his fingers into her swollen, slick folds.

Oh yes.

"Don't you dare come," he warned her, just to see the flare of desperation in her face. "Or I'll double your punishment. See what's laid out on the table there? That's everything you gave me permission to use on you. Some hurt far more than others. Time to decide how much pain to start with. Tell me—did you orgasm again since yesterday?"

"No!" It came out sharply as her hips rocked against his teasing touch.

He flicked her nipple clamp and she cried out, tears welling anew. "No, what?"

"No, Master," she sobbed out, shaking her head in denial.

"But you wanted to." He took pity on her and backed off the touch, letting her gather herself. "You wanted to very badly."

"Yes, but…" Her voice broke and she bit her lip, visibly bracing for another reprimand.

"Tell me. You have no secrets from me, no way to resist or withhold anything. You belong utterly to me in this moment. Feel my chains on you? I've mastered you. Everything is out of your control, because you handed that power to me. Whether you come or not is up to me to decide tonight. Everything that happens is mine to decide. You have only to yield. And even that isn't up to you, because I'll make you do it. You already have."

A strong stand to take with her, but she responded to his words as much as anything. In some unspoken way she demanded that of him, needing that permission to be out of control. From what she had confided, she'd shouldered crushing responsibility for years, while struggling through grief that would have destroyed many people. She hadn't said directly, but she must have been close to her sister. She wanted something from this, from him, and he needed to give it to her, with a bone-deep driving desire as strong as his desire to possess her utterly.

"Tell me," he insisted, running his hands over her sweat-slickened skin. "How did you feel? But what?"

"I wanted to wait to be with you," she said fast, then gasped and struggled. "I can't—"

"It doesn't matter. No can or can't for you. You have no power. It's all mine now. You gave it to me, remember?"

"Yes," she breathed, calming. "Master."

"That's right. I'm going to punish you now. You can't stop or change anything."

She closed her eyes, relaxing into the bonds, indescribably beautiful. Entirely his. His to torment. His to possess. Ablaze with the headiness of it all, he moved behind her. Her smooth skin glowed in the soft light, unblemished and tantalizing.

Picking up a light strap, he set about changing that.

THE CHAINS CONFINED and stretched her, giving her a curiously weightless feeling, even as her body pulsed ever closer to the edge of some precipice. Not orgasm, necessarily. Though when he'd stroked her pussy, she'd nearly fallen over that edge. At some point she'd stopped questioning why the entire experience rocked her so profoundly. Even the ongoing pain of the nipple clamps seemed to feed directly to her engorged clit. She might have begged him to just fuck her already, but it would do no good. Restful, in an odd, alien way, to know that.

Everything that happens is mine to decide. You have only to yield.

Why that felt restful, she didn't know. But the pain changed when he reminded her that she couldn't do anything about it. As if some part of her that continued to hold on, to wish things different, that fought against the unfairness of life and all the sorrow it brought, finally abandoned the wasted effort and let go. Naked, her soul exposed as much as her body, utterly helpless with him, she gave in gladly, with a sense of sweetest relief.

The strap fell on her bottom with a light sting, quickly followed by another. Reflexively she shied away, but the extremity of her restraint prevented it. *You can't stop or change anything.* He covered her bottom with whipping blows, one on top of the last, then moving out to the backs of her thighs, her calves, her shoulders. Without warning, tears began to flow out of her in great shuddering sobs, something else out of her control, in a rhythm seemingly unconnected to where the strap landed and how painful it might be.

Her whole body thrummed to it, nerves singing in a different way, almost drinking in the stimulation. Bright pain so much better than the years of gray numbness. He moved in front of her, strapping her thighs here, her belly there. She writhed and pleaded, nonsense sounds and "Master," over and over. Though he watched her intently, he ignored her pleas, flicking the strap against the sensitive underside of her arm, lashing so it wrapped around her ribs. Letting the end of it sting her mound. His face had settled into those deep grooves that transformed him from gentleman to thug. All that controlled violence.

His silver eyes like steel, he caught her gaze, held it an endless moment, and flicked the strap on her exposed clit.

She shrieked, body clenching in a paroxysm somehow beyond orgasm. Before she fully processed it, he flicked the strap against one breast, then the other. The singing pain turned to ricocheting agony and she screamed with throat-scraping volume.

He took her jaw in a strong grip, forcing her to meet his unrelenting stare. "Are you sorry?" he demanded.

"Yes, Master," she sobbed out.

The strap hit her open pussy and she cried out brokenly.

"Tell me," he ordered. "Tell me how sorry you are."

"I'm sorry, Master!" She came apart as he strapped her

pussy again, sending her head into an explosion of red. "I'm sorry!" she shrieked it, his face gone blurry with her tears. "I'm so sorry, Ara. Oh, Arabella!"

She dissolved completely, hanging in the chains, losing herself in the great, shuddering black convulsions of grief.

HE ONLY KNEW she hadn't fainted completely because she continued to weep piteously, breaking his heart—one he hadn't known he still possessed—along with her own. Working quickly, he removed the cuffs and chains, pressing the remote to lower the hook as he held her, supporting her to the floor, where she collapsed bonelessly against him. Clinging to him but also far away in the paroxysms of the emotional earthquake she'd suffered.

Carrying her to the couch, he tucked her against him, managing to wrap her in the soft blanket he'd stowed there. She was pliant as a newborn kitten, not seeming to notice when he rubbed the numbing cream on her clamped nipples. Though he hated to hurt her at this point—not how he'd envisioned removing them—they needed to come off. He did it fast, holding her tight, hoping that it might feel comforting, but she barely whimpered, so far gone in her head that the pain of returning blood to the compressed tissues barely registered.

Glad that he'd kept the keys on him, he removed her collar and the slave belt. She let him shift her, her tears gone silent now. Hopefully the storm was subsiding. Nothing else to do for her then but lie back and cuddle her against him. At a loss for what else to do, he kissed her damp temple, murmuring words of comfort, anything he could think of to calm and soothe her, to let her know he wouldn't leave her alone and that everything would be okay.

He hoped.

Finally she took a long, wobbly breath. Let it out. Then another. Her weight on him changed, from the boneless drape to something with more awareness. She would lead with embarrassment, knowing her. The fingers she'd wrapped into his shirt flexed and slowly released. She shifted. Started to sit up, but he kept his arms wrapped around her and she subsided.

"Take a bit longer," he said, keeping his voice low. "There's no hurry. Nowhere for us to be. We have all night."

She turned her face more into his chest, breathing more evenly. Thinking of what to say, most likely. "I'm so sorry about this."

"You can't be. You had no choice. It wasn't under your control." He could give her that much.

Lifting her chin, she looked at him, bemused. She was a glorious mess, her makeup smeared, hair in disarray, her eyes red and swollen—and she pulled at his heart. More than anything he wanted to kiss her tears away, stroke and caress her until she again undulated with pleasure and sighed his name. But he restrained himself. Not his forte. *Stick with your strengths.*

She sighed out a little huff of breath, sounding more like herself. "I don't think that's exactly true."

He just raised an eyebrow in reminder, gratified when she blushed—a sexual blush this time, rather than from embarrassment.

"I mean, I know I didn't have physical control, because of

the, ah…"

"Collar and chains I put on you." Something in him enjoyed pushing her to admit that, to face what she'd let him do to her and not dance around it. That same something relished the way she wriggled a bit at his words, her naked body hot through the soft blanket. If nothing else, he'd had that much of her. Testing, needing more contact in a way he didn't care to examine, he reached under the covering to stroke her shoulder. She moved under the caress, accepting and softening with it, and the rush of relieved tension made him realize how much he'd worried that he'd lost her trust.

"Yes," she whispered. "I get that. But I don't understand why the rest happened."

"I wasn't surprised." He rubbed her back, smoothing the graceful arc of it. "Or, rather, I suspected you had a great deal of emotion bottled up, tied up with some kind of survivor's guilt, so I thought it might come out." Not so hugely and spectacularly, but then his Celestina never did anything by halves.

"Oh." She frowned, a faint knitting of her brows, and laid her head against his chest, saying nothing more.

"What?" he asked gently, but insistently. No way she'd stop the conversation there.

She sighed again, that whiff of impatience. With herself or with him? "I just don't see how you can know very much about me. Particularly something like that."

He caressed her waist, the endearing dip of it, her flesh slightly ridged where the slave belt had dug in so beautifully. "You told me some of it and you're not so difficult to read, especially as I get to know you better and you let me in more. You're a powerfully passionate woman and I could guess how some of what you've gone through would have affected you. We talked about it some yesterday, why you might crave punishment, and I suspected that once you didn't have to be the responsible one, that might give you the permission to let it all go."

"I guess I did that." She sounded wry.

"Which is all right." He waited, but she didn't reply to that. "Arabella was your sister?"

"Yes." She barely vocalized her answer, the affirmation audible mainly because of the hiss of her breath.

"Arabella and Celestina." Lovely names. A thought occurred to him. "Your twin?"

"Identical." Though she showed no sign that she'd begun weeping again, the moisture dampened the silk of his shirt.

"I'm so sorry. I can't imagine." He'd longed for a sibling, those long lonely years ago. A brother to throw a ball with. A little sister to take care of or a big sister to tease. Anyone at all, really. "You were close then?"

"Like two halves of one whole. When...when she died, it took me a long time to believe I hadn't died also."

"Maybe you felt like you did."

"Yes." Then she was quiet so long he nearly prodded her again, but she took a breath and spoke quietly. "I think I have been dead, in a way. Going through the motions. Not feeling much of anything. That's why I let the money thing get so bad, did nothing about my dissolving career."

"And now?"

"I don't know. It's hard to know much of anything at the moment, to think very clearly."

"Then don't think, just feel. We can talk it out, as you're ready."

"I thought this was about sex, not therapy."

"They're not so different. Good sex should liberate us, allow us to vent our emotions, let the healing in."

"Well, I'm sure this hardly counted as good sex for you."

"Don't say that." He felt a stirring of his own impatience. "I wouldn't be anywhere else."

"Yes, but you hardly got to use any of those whips on me and no sex at all, so you didn't get what you paid for and—"

She squeaked when he flipped her over, pressing her onto her back and holding her down. He'd moved out of annoyance with her, that she'd bring up money at that moment, but when her tearstained face shifted with surprise, desire edging out the dredges of grief in her eyes, it seemed to be the right move. Deliberately, watching her closely, he tugged at the blanket between them, pulling it away and then running his hand down the length of her lushly naked body.

"First, all of this is sex. Second, we're not done yet, are we?"

"We—we're not?" She stammered on the question when he found her wrists and pinned them over her head.

"I haven't heard your safeword, which means you still belong to me. Mine to do with as I wish to for the rest of the night." He stared her down, enjoying how she struggled a little, biting her lip in consternation. Grief swiftly fading. "Unless you have something to say?"

CHAPTER NINETEEN

H ER FRAGMENTED THOUGHTS scrambled to keep up—
not really possible with the sudden awareness of her
vulnerability, naked and pinned beneath this man who'd gone
from gently reassuring to ruthlessly demanding in a flash. Her
body, still stinging and throbbing in places from the way he'd
punished her, her heart wrenched open so that she felt even
more exposed, all of her flooded with building desire, impossibly craving more.

Maybe part of her had been dead, but if so, then another
part had recently surged into vivid, needy life.

Ryan stared into her eyes, his steel gray and sharp. Face
going into those stern ridges that so bizarrely made her want to
yield up whatever he demanded. "Who am I, Celestina?"

His voice whispered over her nerves and she wasn't sure
how to answer. She struggled against his grip, an unthinking
impulse to escape, but he held her easily.

"You have two possible answers," he informed her, that
note of warning in his tone. "You either use your safeword or
you acknowledge me as your master still."

Use her safeword? She could. Stop it all—she could go
home or they'd maybe talk more about her many and varied
emotional issues. Or she could call him her master and give

herself up to whatever he had in mind. All the things she'd checked off as permissible in her reckless lust and disconcerting pitch of emotion. She couldn't remember half of them but she had no doubt that he did.

"I'm giving you until the count of five," he continued, measured and reasonable, as if he didn't have her naked beneath him, the hard line of his cock hot against her groin. "One. Two."

She should just say "Angel" and they could discuss. That would be the easiest option.

"Three."

But she didn't want to talk, or even think. She wanted to lose herself as she had before, in the rush of dizzying desire and the plummeting sensation of giving up control.

"Four." He narrowed his eyes and lingered over the word. "Fi—"

"Master," she whispered.

His eyes flared with silver light and his hands tightened on her wrists. "Who am I?" he asked again.

"Master."

"Yes. And you are?"

She hesitated, slightly, and he growled in disapproval. Frightening and thrilling. "Yours?"

"Say it like you mean it," he demanded.

"I'm yours, Master," she breathed, the edges of her self beginning to dissolve in the truth of the moment.

"Who do you belong to?"

"You, Master."

"That's right. You're mine. Bought and paid for. I can do

whatever I wish to you and you can't stop me. So what does that make you?"

"Your slave." *Bought and paid for.*

"My naked, helpless slave." He transferred her wrists to one hand, stretching them higher, the leather of the couch cool against her skin, and trailed his other hand down her body, pushing it between her legs, into the slick heat that had resurged at his taking possession of her again. A moan escaped her and she strained against his hold, deliciously unable to free herself. "Tell me, did you have an orgasm before? Did my strap make you come?"

"I'm not sure, Master. Please don't punish me."

He studied her face, sliding a finger inside her and smiling in a cruel twist when she squirmed. "Why aren't you sure?"

"It—" She gasped as he pushed in deeper. "It all blurred together. I don't think I did."

"Well, that's a problem, isn't it?" He mused over the question, as if it held great import. "I think we need to work on that. This is something you should be able to definitively answer, don't you think?"

"I don't know." She answered without thinking, because she couldn't with his hand working her so relentlessly.

"Wrong answer, my pet." He removed his hand. "As my slave, you owe me anything I ask for, don't you?"

"Yes, Master." She writhed in misery now, not quite understanding why this worked on her as much as his hand had. *Don't think. Just feel.* "I want to please you," she burst out.

He smiled more genuinely then. "Better. We're getting somewhere. Taste yourself on me." He laid his fingers against her lips. Riveted, she opened her mouth, allowing him to push his fingers in, sucking on them, the sweetly salt taste of her own arousal filling her senses. "This pleases me," he told her. "We'll work on more."

Abruptly he stood, yanked away the rest of the blanket and surveyed her nakedness. Reflexively, she started to lower her hands, to cover herself. "Hands stay where I put them," he ordered in a cool tone. He continued to study her, from her face to her toes and back up again, his gaze as palpable as his caressing hand had been. Reaching over, he turned on a table lamp near her feet. "Spread your legs."

She did, then raised her knees when he demanded that, too, keeping her hands stretched above her head and looking into the shadows of the ceiling while he looked his fill of her. Oddly warming to be on display like this, to be doing it entirely to please him. *Master.*

"Yes," he replied, making her aware she'd whispered it. "Stand up."

Scrambling to her feet, she stood on the plush Oriental rug, uncertain what to do with her hands. "Like this," he told her, arranging her as he spoke. "When I tell you *Stand*, then arms at your sides, palms open and facing me, feet shoulder width apart, back straight, tits high, eyes cast down. Good."

She held that position as he circled her, a sense of that relinquishing of will suffusing her, as it had when he'd locked the collar on her.

"Hands behind your neck, feet spread wide, tits high, eyes down."

She followed the simple instructions, though her feet

weren't wide enough to please him. He coaxed her until she'd spread as wide as when he'd strapped her exposed pussy, the memory making her shudder and slicken both.

"This is *Present*," he said, trailing his hand down her spine, to cup her bottom, then into her cleft so she wriggled. He smacked her ass, quite hard, making her wobble. "All of these positions you must hold no matter what I do, unless I tell you otherwise. Understand?"

"Yes, Master," she replied, struggling for the calm that had evaporated with the sudden sting.

He came around in front of her. "Look at me."

When she raised her eyes to his shadowed face, he cupped her breasts, squeezing. Then he brushed her sore nipples with his thumbs, making them spark with pain so that she nearly pushed his hands away, belatedly remembering to keep her hands behind her neck, leaving her breasts vulnerable to him. His lips twisted in that cruel line and he deliberately repeated the motion, watching to see what she'd do.

"Do they hurt?" he asked, not unkindly, and she nodded. When he released her breasts, she thought he'd stop torment-ing them, but no. "Offer me your tits. That means to cup them in your hands and lift them up for me. Feet and eyes can stay wherever they are when I ask for this."

His eyes glittered with amused arousal as she tried to com-ply, blushing furiously as he rearranged her hold on her own breasts to maximize his viewing pleasure. "Just like that—but arch your back. Really offer them to me. Show me that I can do whatever I like to them."

She began to feel curiously out of her body with each passing moment, offering herself to him like this, acutely aware of her nakedness while he remained clothed. Holding her gaze, he slowly and deliberately took her proffered nipples and pinched them lightly, making her gasp.

"Shall I hurt them more?" he asked her.

Chewing on her lip in consternation, she searched his face for the right answer.

"If you want me to," he said, "then you say, 'Yes, Master.' If not, you say, 'Only if it pleases you, Master.' That way, you never deny my pleasure, even to save yourself, but you can let me know how you feel. That might not change anything." He grinned with his wicked charm. "But I'll know. So, my beautiful Celestina—more pain?" He rolled her nipples and she whimpered.

"Only if it pleases you, Master." She said it pleadingly, but he seemed all right with it, as he nodded and let go.

"Present."

With a sense of reprieve, she did. Funny, as she could still safeword anytime. But she forgot that for long stretches in this game of his, where he made her feel as much or even more under his control than when he had her chained to the pillars. Perhaps because she chose to obey his soft directives, rather than being coerced. Though it didn't feel like choosing. A different sort of coercion then.

"This one is more difficult," he said from behind her, setting his hand on her back and pushing her to bend over. "*Display.* Everything the same except you bend over with your back flat."

As she did, his hand moved over her hip, to slide familiarly into her folds again, one thick finger gliding into her so she moaned.

"*Full display* means to drop completely and grab your ankles, if you can. Ah yes—you're nicely flexible."

The blood rushed to her head, making it swim, the dizziness compounded when he added a second finger to the first, stretching her channel. "This is an excellent position for fucking," he said in a conversational tone, as if his fingers weren't doing exactly that. "Though it's more strenuous for you. Also good for paddling." He pulled his hand away and spanked her smartly, making her yip in surprise and struggle to keep her balance. Swiftly his fingers penetrated her again, three this time, by the feel. She groaned, the only protest available to her. "Or to alternate between the two," he added.

Feeling increasingly out of control, she panted for breath, and pushed against his hand. He pulled it out and delivered several rapid smacks to her ass before finger-fucking her again. What would he do if she fell over? Probably much worse.

"Stay just like that." He patted her bottom and moved away. Doing her best not to move, her palms slick where she clutched her ankles, ass high in the air and warmed by the fire, she felt on full display indeed. "Stand," he said, and she obeyed with relief, straightening and dropping her arms to her sides, remembering to lower her eyes at the last moment—though not before she glimpsed him sitting in the armchair he'd been in when she arrived, a collar in his hands, though a different one this time. "A close one, though I'll allow the error this once. Come over here and kneel.

"There are four kinds of kneeling. When I tell you *Kneel*,

you may keep knees together, sit on your heels, hands palm up on your thighs. *Kneel and present*, hands go behind your neck and—exactly. *Kneel up* means thighs perpendicular to the floor, yes, and *Kneel up and display* means to spread your thighs. Wider, Celestina. You're past being coy. Better. Kneel and display."

She struggled to keep her thighs open as she sat back on her heels, knowing he was looking straight into her open pussy. Silly, as he'd seen her from behind, and on the couch and draped over his desk. She felt more exposed this way, though, with her hands clasped behind her neck, kneeling in naked supplication because he demanded it, while her body churned with arousal.

"One more," he told her softly. "*Submit*. Exactly as you are, but with your head bowed, arms stretched toward me and wrists crossed." She did as he told her, then shivered at the feel of cuffs locking around her wrists again, followed by the collar around her throat. "Stay like that and listen." He ran a hand over her hair. "Any time we're in a scene, I might ask you to adopt one of these positions, and I expect you to obey immediately. I might tell you to strip first or not, as I wish. If you agree to any public scenarios, I expect you to follow these same rules, understand?"

She shivered at the prospect of assuming these positions in front of witnesses, possibly naked. Could she? Thrilling and terrifying. And only if she wanted to. She consoled herself with that reminder, though at that moment, feeling so thoroughly under his control, it didn't seem that way. *All part of the ride.* "Yes, Master," she whispered.

"Kneel up." He took up a length of chain, smaller than the first one. It clinked musically in his hands. Threading it through what must be a loop in the front of the collar—also a different, lighter one—he then attached it to her cuffs. The cool metal draped between her breasts and fell in a swoop before rising to her wrists, but when he ordered her to Present, the chain came up under her breasts, framing them. Not satisfied, he adjusted the length so the chain snugged more tightly under them, lifting her breasts a little. Grunting in satisfaction, he reached behind her head and clipped the cuffs together there, so she couldn't lower her hands.

Her thigh muscles began to tremble, both from the strain of the position and from her accelerating sense of profound helplessness. With her thighs open so wide, air currents stroked the engorged tissues there, so that they ached for more. It seemed she hadn't orgasmed before or, if she had, it had done little to take the edge off her need. Never before had it felt so imperative that she be able to come, or more impossible that she'd be allowed to. *Allowed to.* It made her crazy that this one thing had always been so difficult to wrestle, that being able to climax easily, let alone multiple times had always been such a remote possibility with so much effort for so little reward. And now it lay within her grasp for the first time in her life, and yet it remained out of her reach. Because of *his* whim.

As if divining some of her thoughts, he stroked her cheek with affection. "You look beautiful like this, bound by my chains and my rules. Suffering for me." He picked up another length of chain, longer and finer, also running it through the loop at the front of her collar and letting it fall loose. With a close-lipped, taunting smile that set her nerves more on edge, he rose and went behind her. The twin sides of the chain brushed her inner thighs, drawing a despairing sound out of her. Slowly, teasingly, he drew them higher, until the cool, rough texture slid into her labia, tightening to bracket her clit. She trembled in earnest at the sensation, especially as he threaded the chains up between her cheeks and then finished by attaching them to her cuffed hands.

Though she knew what it would do, she couldn't seem to help tugging at it—which caused the chain to pinch her clit with greater tension and to drag against her achingly empty vulva. Distressed sounds came out of her and she struggled against the chain, succeeding only in making it worse. Both excruciatingly arousing and not nearly enough to make her come, the bondage would only tear her apart with unrealized desire.

He stood in front of her again, she realized, though she'd missed him moving in her fugue state, watching her with avid intensity. *You struggle so beautifully.* She couldn't quite recall if she was allowed to beg for mercy. "Master," she gasped, by way of asking.

He smiled, stroking her cheek again. "Yes," he said, and opened his trousers.

CHAPTER TWENTY

H E HADN'T BEEN sure if she'd be able to get back into the right headspace after her meltdown, but Celestina seemed, if anything, even more pliable, diving into the role-playing with even greater abandon than before. Maybe that made sense, that she'd lost some of her defenses, which meant she'd be even more receptive to the whole trip.

Regardless, she sank into the slave role without reserve, calling him "Master" with a tone of such lustful amazement, with her dark eyes so wide and glistening that he thought the top of his head might blow off. Showing her the various positions had given him some breathing room to cool and control himself, but her subsequent surrender to the chains robbed him of the little leeway he'd gained.

He had to have her mouth on him or he might lose his mind completely. Might forget what she had and hadn't agreed to and instead plunder her as if she truly did belong to him, body and soul. The sheer lust to do so gave him pause—a cautionary sober note in the headlong sexual rush—so he took his time freeing his aching cock, though the sight of her pleading gaze and the way she writhed within the simple torment made his self-control teeter on the brink of madness.

A full catapult into sexual insanity when she closed her lush red lips over his cock. He'd thought to go slowly, ease her into it, but she destroyed those thoughts with the exquisitely eager use of her tongue and mouth. He should have had her bring him off earlier, because he couldn't possibly last at this point. In point of truth, his balls were already tightening with the sting of incipient orgasm, taking him like a teenage wet dream. And she hadn't wanted him to come in her mouth. She'd forgotten that in the wave of utter sensual need, most likely, the way she fed on him, drawing him into her mouth tight and deep. Oh yes—she even made a sound of protest when he used his grip in her hair to pull her forcibly off of him.

One, two, three strokes of his fist on his shaft and he released, spurting over her glorious tits, so perfectly raised and framed by his chains. Thank God she'd allowed that much though she looked as adorably shocked by it as the first time, gorgeous violated. His head abruptly swam with the intense release and he had to sit, feeling not at all masterful, but somehow enslaved to his voluptuous mistress. Even now she gazed at him, lips parted as if she wanted to ask a question, her hips moving in unthinking response to the stimulating chain pulling tight against her mound.

She should be hyped enough. He'd decided that she would orgasm tonight for him. More than once. A challenge, especially as it would likely kill any possibility of it happening if she knew how much he wanted it for her. For him.

She just needed to dissolve a tiny bit more. Some of his strength regained, he sat up and took her face in his hands, cupping her jaw and cheekbones. The movement drew her up slightly and she moaned in that erotically vulnerable way that went straight to his gut. Feeling as desperate, he kissed her, her mouth hot and sweet and somehow smoky with lust. She loved to be kissed as much as he loved to have her that way. When he dropped his hands to gently massage his semen into her breasts, she melted into his hold and met his tongue with hers. Yielding and demanding at once.

Yes, she wanted what he'd implicitly promised, and she might be rocked far enough outside her usual experience to get there.

Time to deliver on that.

Without breaking the kiss, he slid his hands to bracket her narrow waist and helped her to her feet. She swayed in his arms—no surprise, as long as he'd kept her kneeling like that—and he steadied her, then walked her backward toward the rug immediately in front of the fire.

He indulged in running his hands over her, tracing her rounded curves, her skin velvety to touch here, slick and sticky there, so available to him with her hands bound like that. She panted into his mouth, her kisses growing more frantic, pressing her nipples against him, their soreness clearly forgotten in the pitch of her desire. All for him. Heady stuff.

"Lie down," he muttered, urging her with his hands, forgetting in his own extremity to make her obey, just needing her to do so. She went more than willingly, stretching out on her back on the dark fur rug, her skin gleaming as golden as some exotic animal. One he'd captured and temporarily confined, but wild still, proud and untamed in the dark demand of her eyes. With hunger, she watched him strip off his clothes, rocking her hips against the golden chain that gleamed so enticingly in the folds of her swollen sex.

Falling on her, he pushed her knees wide and back, fastening his mouth on her distended clit without giving her warning. She cried out, a wordless sound of joy and agony, so on edge she came immediately, her fluids flowing salty into his mouth. Perfect that she'd gotten there already, without time to overthink it. Easier to keep her there now. Without relenting, he kept up the pressure, driving her up again, holding her hips down as she thrashed against him. She screamed, much as she had when he'd strapped her, going rigid and then shattering into a series of convulsions. Darkly pleased, he thrust two fingers into her tight, hot channel, curling them up and sucking hard on her clit, not letting her come down from it or think too hard.

She pistoned herself on his fingers, crying his name. Not "Master," but "Ryan"—something that grabbed at his heart with unexpected, even blinding pleasure. Him. He brought her to this. His cock was ready as before, swelling with his ego. Some men never figured this out, the ones who easily attracted a woman, but then missed the concept of pleasuring her enough to keep her. Money made up for poor looks, but pleasing a woman in bed captured her affection more surely than anything.

He pushed the chains aside to flank the outsides of her labia, making her struggle anew as they scraped over her sensitized tissues. Managing to roll on a condom, he positioned himself at her hungry entrance, bracing himself on his elbows over her, to find her mouth waiting for his. She arched her back, body begging for the penetration even as her lips pulled at his, pleading moans coming from deep in her throat.

He thrust into her, going momentarily blind with the searing sensation, both at the tight clasp of her body, like liquid fire, and her shuddering response. She wrenched her mouth away, gasping his name. And he answered, reverentially, "Celestina."

Without calculation now, without much control at all, he stroked in and out of her, overcome by the slick velvet of her skin against his, her lush breasts crushed against his chest and the occasional bright grind of the chains she wore. His chains. All for him. She gave herself totally to him as no one ever had, never so profoundly, so utterly without reserve. He took it all, demanding more with every thrust.

Her body gathered in tension, moving urgently, and she sobbed with rising need. He held off as best he could, increasing his rhythm, stroking deep until she suddenly shattered, coming apart in a flurry, like a firelog collapsing in a shower of sparks. With her sweet cries filling his ears, he let go of all control and flung himself after, burying himself in her and releasing everything he had to her keeping.

As the drugging lassitude faded, she became aware of the bite of the chains first, where the heavier ones dug into her ribs under Ryan's collapsed weight. Shifting to relieve the pressure, she couldn't help smiling when his hands flexed on her and he murmured a negation, then almost immediately recovered himself and levered up.

"My bad," he muttered, sat, scrubbed hands over his face, then crawled over to the chair to retrieve the keys, she supposed. His scrotum hung flushed and heavy between his muscular thighs, his masculine ass nicely hairy. When he returned and, bleary-eyed, began releasing her from the chains and cuffs, he gave her a bemused look. "What?"

"Nothing." Her voice came out throaty. Too much screaming, mostly in pleasure. Unreal. And she couldn't admit to ogling him. "Just kind of nice to see you rumpled, too."

"'Gutted' might be more accurate." He tossed aside the collar and massaged her arms as she gratefully lowered them. "Are you excessively sore anywhere?"

"I might be able to tell you when I regain feeling in my body. I think I came more times just now than all the times before this." A hitch of alarm grabbed her. "Oh God!"

"What's wrong?" He ran his hands over her. "Cramp?"

"No, I just—" Should she call it to his attention if he forgot?

"Tell me." He stroked her hair back from her face and kissed her softly.

"I forgot I wasn't supposed to come," she whispered, as if not saying it too loud would somehow mitigate it.

He met her eyes, his smile unutterably smug. "Then you'll just have to be punished again, won't you? But not tonight."

She narrowed her eyes at his good humor. "This could be an endless cycle then."

Stretching out beside her with a contented groan, he nodded. "In an ideal world, yes."

Would it be ideal? Never before had she experienced such intense pleasure, or this amazingly delicious languor after. With the few boys she'd fooled around with before Noah, she'd always felt buzzing with energy after, lying there while they softly snored. With her husband, well, for a long time she didn't mind that it had been the same with him. The time between Ara's wedding and hers had been the loneliest of her life back then—envying Ara the happiness she'd found and hating herself for begrudging her any of it.

She'd thought marrying Noah would remedy that and, for a while, it did. At first she'd loved the romance and comfort of sharing the marriage bed, feeling connected and in sync with her twin again. The time she lay awake while he slept became a special private moment for her, while she dreamed of what the future might bring, places they'd travel, maybe a house overlooking the ocean someday.

Looking back, she'd been naïve. Not just in not predicting how her future, instead of expanding and blossoming, would constrict with tragedy and despair, with no roads out, but in not recognizing the path of her own feelings. Realizing over time that Noah didn't really love her, not like Steve loved Ara. How she'd gradually grown angrier and more resentful, sometimes indulging in the fantasy of kicking him hard, to wake him up and watch his startled face when she yelled, *I am not happy!*

Odd to remember it now, those restless nights, the frustration and emptiness of being married to a man who didn't even seem to like her, the way he criticized her, much less cherish and love her as he'd vowed. Then it all got wiped away and covered over by real sorrow. And she'd discovered what lonely could truly mean.

While she hadn't quite processed all she'd submitted to that evening, some of it a kaleidoscope of images and sensation, the satiation of her body made a marked contrast. Ryan's heavy arm draped possessively over her did, too. She didn't quite like the idea that she might need this every time to feel this way, but knowing she could get there made a difference.

And maybe made her unwilling to settle for less again.

Though, if it turned out she did need this kind of extremity, then finding another with Ryan's brand of kink might be a challenge. Though this kind of sex seemed profoundly connected with the man himself, and she couldn't imagine doing this with anyone else.

But she'd cross that bridge later, after this burned out.

"You're thinking awfully hard for someone who should be exhausted," he commented.

"Sorry." She winced. She'd figured him for asleep.

He levered up on his elbow and propped his head on his fist, considering her. With the fire dimming and most of the lamps on the other side of the room, the shadows intensified the crooked line of his nose and highlighted a white scar under one eye she hadn't noticed. The face of a brute. Someone who'd been in more than boardroom fights. But his eyes held warmth and kindness, the pretty silver alight with keen intelligence.

"Don't be sorry." He brushed her hair back from her face. "Talk to me. Anything you want to ask about? I can't know if something didn't work for you if you don't say so."

So funny that he could treat her that ruthlessly, with the implicit cruelty and unrelenting demand he'd shown, and then ask about her feelings.

"Why is that funny?" He traced her lips with the tip of his finger. "You're laughing at me."

"No." She caught his hand and, on impulse, laced her fingers with his and drew him down for a kiss. He obliged her, kissing her with heartbreaking tenderness. Just sex and business between them, perhaps, but she'd been friends with clients. It wasn't wrong to revel in the care he gave her. "Is this part of it?" she asked when they separated. "I don't remember it in the program."

He gave her a curious look, with maybe a tinge of annoyance, but rubbed his thumb over the back of her hand. "It's not in the program, because this is what people do after they have sex. They enjoy the afterglow and have conversations. Especially after trying new things, they talk about how it worked for them." He raised his eyebrows significantly.

"My husband mainly fell asleep," she confided.

"I just knew it," he muttered, on his way to pissed off. "Guys like that are useless as tits on a bull."

That took her aback. "He was a good man."

"No, he wasn't. Look what he had in you—an intensely passionate and giving woman, in his bed every damn night, and he fell asleep, leaving you wanting."

"It wasn't like—"

"Didn't he?"

His anger sparked hers and she sat up, pulling her hand from his and raking both through her hair. She was sticky— God, she'd let him come on her breasts again and a bunch had dried there—and she probably looked like a wreck. "I didn't ask him for more than that," she snapped out. Angry maybe with herself, for being such a doormat that she hadn't. "I need to clean up and I should go."

"Why not?" Ryan put a hand on her knee, not gripping hard, but insistent.

It took her a moment to process that he hadn't asked about her leaving, but was still dwelling on the rest. "Because I was fine. He did his best by me. That was enough."

"Was it?"

No, it hadn't been. She shouldn't have married him, shouldn't have been so envious of Ara and eager to equalize them again that she'd rushed headlong into marriage, knowing even then that Noah didn't really love her. Another of her mistakes. Not something she wanted to think about. "At least he never told me I wasn't allowed to come!"

"No, he did worse. He made it be about him, didn't he? Made your pleasure be about whether he felt manly, and when he stopped bugging you about it, you were relieved to drop the subject entirely."

Astonishment robbed her of the retort she'd been mentally building.

"I'm right, aren't I?" He looked less angry now but no less determined.

"I don't know how you could possibly know that."

He made a snorting sound and smiled slightly. "I'm a man. Anyone who says men don't gossip is a liar. And their favorite topic is women and the bagging and pleasuring thereof."

"You know—I saw your face and you looked downright smug...after. You can't claim that pleasuring me didn't make you feel manly, too."

"Oh yes." He nodded, that selfsame smug smile spreading across his lips. "I'm feeling excessively manly at the moment. The difference is that I know what to do for you, even if it means pissing you off by forbidding you to come."

"You're a very unusual man. An arrogant one."

"Acknowledged. And thank you, Celestina. I was hoping you'd notice." He picked up her hand, turned it over and kissed the inside of her wrist. "What is this perfume? You smell like hothouse roses."

"It's called Rosamor." She watched, feeling increasingly befuddled as he sniffed and licked her pulse, then began kissing his way up her arm.

"Oscar de la Renta, right? A new purchase then?"

"No, my mother had tons of the stuff. I've been gradually using it up."

"Mmm." He reached her elbow, kissing the inside of that, too. "I like it. When you run out, I'll buy you more."

"What are you doing?"

He placed a kiss on her shoulder, then in the shallow between her neck and collarbone. "Persuading you not to go."

"I'm a sticky mess."

"Aha! Fortunately I'm a wealthy man and I had this fancy stuff installed—indoor plumbing. You'll love it. You can even make the water hot."

She couldn't help laughing and smacked him on the shoulder. "You're ridiculous."

He took the opportunity to snag her around the waist and pull her in for a deep, mind-fogging kiss. "Yes. I need your steadying influence. Please stay."

Helpless to refuse him that, as with everything, she agreed.

CHAPTER TWENTY-ONE

R YAN SAID HE'D clean up, put the fire out and bring wine while she went ahead to run a bath for them. With a side trip upstairs to check her phone for any messages from the girls, though there weren't any. It felt weird—particularly in a semi-strange house and after living with body-shy pre-adolescents the past years—to walk around naked. But the slave girl costume was in shreds and, when she mentioned having nothing to put on, Ryan just cocked his head and said that they were inside a fenced estate on a cliff. No one would be looking in the windows.

As if that would be the only reason for her to put on clothes. Which to him it clearly was.

When she found the master bedroom—"at the end of the hall" being more of a trek than it sounded—she goggled at it. Good thing she had a moment to recover, because it looked straight out of *Architectural Digest*. She'd been braced for slick, knowing Ryan's tastes, but this exceeded even her speculations. Really, the master suite formed its own ground-floor wing, an entirely modern addition to the original house on the far side from Ryan's office.

Like there, most of one side of this room was windows, but looking into a walled courtyard that rioted with vines and flowers, lit with soft lamps that showed their verdant colors and no doubt kept them tropically warmed. The attached bath, such a far cry from her yellowing tub and cracked linoleum, was a glory of Italian marble and glass. A clear-sided tub also looked into the garden, with a freestanding, violet-lit rainfall shower nearby.

"What do you think?" Ryan came in, carrying a bottle of white wine settled in a bucket of ice in the crook of one elbow and two crystal glasses by the stem in the other. He looked brawnier naked than he did in his well-cut suits, with his thick thighs and broad chest.

Faintly embarrassed that she'd been gawking—at him and reflexively estimating the cost of such luxury—she gestured at the garden. "You could use a water feature."

He grinned, set down the wine and glasses and reached over to run the tub. "I wanted one. I even had you in mind to design it, but then the restrictions hit."

"Does anyone ever see this but you? It's unlikely you'd get caught."

"No, but it would still be wrong. How's that temperature for you?"

"I'm sure it's fine. The, um, water closet?"

"Through there." He stepped in the tub and stretched, reaching his muscled arms over his head, body flexing and popping, a sight that had a mesmerizing effect, and settled himself into the water. Unfortunately he caught her out at that, too, and flashed her a dazzling smile. "Need help?"

She flushed and shook her head, more self-conscious around him now in his animal satiation that in all the previous hours of outrageous intimacy, which made absolutely no sense. In the private toilet room—twice as big as her whole bathroom at home—she gasped aloud at her reflection. *Dammit, Ryan!* How could he have said nothing about her smeared makeup and generally disheveled appearance? With her swollen mouth and nipples, along with some red marks and forming bruises, she looked like a circus clown dragged through a porn flick. Finding some soap and a washcloth, she scrubbed her face clean, wishing for Visine or some green tea bags to reduce the red puffiness of her eyes.

She peed, which stung like a bitch from the lashing, and used the washcloth to sponge herself off—sort of overkill as a full bath awaited her. But still. Deciding she'd procrastinated long enough and not wanting Ryan to come looking for her, she made herself leave the dubious refuge for the bath he clearly intended to share with her. What had she expected for the night? With his fixation on restraint, she'd kind of envisioned being tied up the whole time. Sleeping in the maid's room or something, or chained to the foot of his bed. Not this. Not conversation, wine and…seductive kisses.

Not romance, she reminded herself. *Think.* Particularly given the extreme sex they'd just engaged in. All part of his style, switching up his approach, keeping his opponents off-balance like he'd admitted to by sexting with her instead of paying attention to them. Giving her ruthlessness and then the charm that he used to beguile everyone into doing what he wanted. Something to keep firmly in mind, to guard against the softer emotions that kept wanting to tangle her up.

Which she nearly failed to do when she emerged and found

a red rose lying next to her full wineglass on a ledge by the tub. The smile he gave her with it seemed almost boyish.

"Where did this come from?"

He cocked his head at the glass. "The garden. I ran out there and picked one for you. You remind me of a rose, in more than the scent of your perfume."

Lowering herself into the water, she hissed a little at the sting. "A bruised and trampled rose. Why didn't you tell me how awful I looked?"

Sipping his wine, he frowned at her reprovingly. "Because you didn't, obviously. You looked gorgeously ravished—all of which I did to you, I might add—and I loved every bit of it. Both the doing it and seeing the proof upon you."

The wine tasted bright and cold—and gave her something else to do besides respond to that. But he watched her intently, with his predator's patience. There would be no ditching the conversation now. "Is it—I'm wondering if it's a humiliation thing."

Instead of protesting, he considered that. Which she appreciated. For all his brusque ways, he never dismissed what she said, but gave her reasoned answers. When he shook his head, it came after some thought. "I don't think so. It works for me to have you helpless, in my power, yes. But the rest…it's more about smudging you. About peeling away your shields and seeing you come apart in a way that you don't for anyone else. No perfect mask to hide behind. Only you—real, raw and true. Part of you that only I get to see. Does that make sense?"

"I don't know. Maybe. I'll have to think about that."

"Did you feel humiliated?" he asked carefully, in a way that made her think it was new for him, to wonder about that. Still, he wouldn't drop any of his questions on how she reacted to all they'd done. The problem was, she wasn't entirely sure of any of her answers.

"Not until I saw myself in the mirror," she joked, but he didn't crack a smile. Instead he held out a hand, leaving it there until she took it, lacing his fingers with hers so their palms sealed together.

"Celestina." He regarded her gravely. "I know it's been part of the game, the whole ride—me paying you, with the app on the tablets and all that goes with it—but tonight was intense and a lot of it new for you. Anything you didn't like can be off the table from now on. I mean that."

"You seemed to be into it."

He smiled, a wry twist that faded quickly. "Yes. Without reservation. But I don't want to bruise more than your gorgeous skin."

She caught her breath at that. *Bruised. Raw.* "I guess I do feel a little...raw." So many things to feel, both old and new.

"Why don't you come over here?" He tugged at her hand and she let him draw her over to that side of the tub, snug her up against his side with his arm around her. She gave up and dropped her head against his shoulder, taking refuge, his skin hot and damp. He kissed her hair, then leaned his cheek against the top of her head. "Maybe I shouldn't have said those things about your ex. That was out of line. I shouldn't have let it annoy me."

For some reason that made her smile. That he picked that thing. And that he still sounded annoyed, even as he apologized. Kind-of, sort-of apologized, with his qualifiers and lack of an actual "I'm sorry." So him.

"It's not that," she told him, realizing it was the truth. He'd been scarily on-target about Noah and she needed time to sort through her thoughts there. "It's—well, to start, did you know I haven't spoken Ara's name since she died? No, don't say anything yet. That's not the point so much as that I did. Everything tonight, and leading up to it, it was all so intense. I would kind of lose track of time or where I was or even who I was." Except she'd never lost track of him, the central figure in all those flashing images and sensations. "And everything felt so much *more* than it has for years, maybe ever. I don't know if it's…"

Because of the kink or because of him. Not something she wanted to say out loud.

RYAN SET HIS glass down and put his other arm around her, embracing her lightly, wanting to comfort—an unusual impulse for him, as was the sudden doubt that he wasn't sure how to go about it. She sounded so lost and forlorn. With her face clean of makeup, she looked younger, though her lush curves belied that.

"Tonight was intense for me, too," he told her. Hugely intense. Beyond the stratosphere intense. When she'd talked about going home, the disappointment had sliced at him. He wanted her with him, a vicious possessiveness demanding it, any way he could have her. Some primal part of him insisted that she belonged to him now and he tried to tread around that carefully. Keep that particular monster in its cage. All part of the game. Not real.

And yet.

Celestina tilted her chin up to search his face. "Why?"

He rapidly scrolled back his thoughts to find the one she'd asked about. "Why was it intense for me—are you kidding me? You, plus a number of my favorite fantasies, amazing sex. You." He took a chance and kissed her, pleased to see her full lips curve.

"I'm serious," she said, scooting away and reaching for her wine. "I mean—can I ask about this?"

"Ask me anything." With a hollow sensation, he realized he meant it entirely. There might not be much he wouldn't confide to the alluring, dark-eyed Celestina. An alarming thought, if he weren't so thoroughly saturated with her.

At least she'd lost some of that sad look, the one that reminded him of bruised petals.

"So, you're obviously experienced with this kind of sex, all the equipment. You know what you're doing. I've read your lists, all the details. You've done a lot of it."

Though she didn't phrase it as a question, that's what it was. Though maybe not what she really wanted to know. "I used to do more than I do these days," he told her, feeling his way through, around the dangerous edges. "I kind of stumbled upon the kink in my younger years, after college. It was…an outlet for me." For that rage and aggression that threatened to pop out at any time, that had gotten away with him the once, enough to get him thrown out of college and put his hapless victim in the hospital.

Maybe he wouldn't confess absolutely anything to her, after

all. A healthy sense of self-preservation seemed to be returning him to his senses. Revealing that would only frighten her. Perhaps even drive her away entirely. Who would trust a man who'd nearly killed someone with his fists? Besides, he'd gone to great lengths to bury that incident where it could never be unearthed. Beyond foolish to confide it to her. No reason to do it.

Except some part of him wanted to. He shrugged it all off as if it were irrelevant. Too late.

"An outlet—what do you mean by that?"

Trust her to latch onto that slip, the way she saw through him. This needed careful treading, a particular spin. "For sexual energy, of course. When you have a certain kink, though other kinds of sex might suffice, it seems to work that only the thing you're specially wired for—for whatever reason—only that *thing* fully exhausts the need. Otherwise it builds on itself, growing hotter and more intense until…" *Shut your mouth, already.* His mama's voice. Digging too close to the old memories. He shrugged again, then, annoyed with himself for the tell, poured them both more wine.

She watched him shrewdly, not drinking. "Until what?"

He tried his most winning smile. "I don't know—I've never gotten there."

She tilted her head slightly. "You're lying." When he coughed on his wine, she nodded to herself. "You're good at it, no doubt of that. But you've been dancing around something and right then, when I pushed for an answer, you outright lied."

Biting down on the surge of defensiveness, he wrestled back

a number of curt responses, chiefmost among them that maybe they'd done better together when she hadn't been paying so much attention. He didn't really mean that. Not exactly. He definitely didn't like being called out for lying.

"It's none of my business, of course." Her voice had cooled. She was drawing that cloak of pride around her again, walling him out, which only served to piss him off more. "When you said I could ask you anything, I took that to mean you'd give me an honest answer."

He set his teeth. "I did not lie."

She raised an eyebrow. "No?"

"No," he bit out. How had this conversation gotten away from him, once again?

"You're getting that look like you'd rather have me in chains again," she said, and smiled, clearly enjoying herself.

"You might discover that's what happens if you needle me too much."

"I'll safeword if you try it. You're always pushing me to tell you my thoughts. Does this mean I get to lie, too?"

"I didn't lie!" He set his glass down, taking care that the glass didn't even clink as it made contact with the marble ledge. Celestina sank deep in the hot water, eyeing him with alert interest, reminding him of a cat with a cornered mouse. Enjoying having turned the tables on him. It would be lovely to put his hands on her and transform her expression from smug to beseeching and helplessly needy, but he could read the truth of it in her face—she'd safeword and he didn't want her to have to. Not because of this. "I may have prevaricated," he offered.

"I might not have read the dictionary, but even I know that means the same thing as lying."

"It doesn't. The first definition is 'to quibble, to shift or turn aside from or evade the truth, to equivocate or speak evasively.'"

Her lips parted as she gave him an incredulous look. Then she tucked her hair behind her ears and sipped her wine. Finally she said, "I'm not sure which to comment on—that you have the definition memorized or that you think 'evading the truth' is different than lying."

"Why decide when you can speak to both in one sentence?"

"Why are you so angry? I thought you wanted to talk."

"About your feelings, yes."

"Ah, I see." She nodded to herself. "This is all part of your control thing. You manage me like you manage your business associates, your hands on the strings, manipulating so everything goes exactly the way you want it to."

He was glad he'd set the wine down because he might have snapped the stem, the way his fists ached to clench.

"What's interesting to contemplate is what made you so determined to be in control. Were you out of control at some point in your life?"

The remembered helpless rage bubbled in his chest. How easily she glimpsed what no one else had ever thought to look for, much less seen so clearly.

She tilted her head, thoughtful. "I can see how a person would do that. I've never been in control of anything that happened in my life—and look at the results of *that*—but you, you're a self-made man, aren't you? You created all of this." She gestured at the garden, the bathroom, and finished with a spiral to indicate the rest. "Everything rigidly controlled. Even your lovers."

"Do you have a point, Celestina?" he ground out.

"What is it an outlet for?" she asked again, softly, insistently.

"Do I get a reward if I tell you?" He'd tried to lighten it, but he seethed with the old memories, and a haunting fear that she'd turn her back on him. He wouldn't let her. He'd chain her up and keep her captive forever rather than let that happen. *Down, boy.*

Celestina's lips parted at whatever she saw in his face. She licked them, nervous now, but lifted her chin in that regal way of hers. "All right. What do you want?"

Her. All of her, totally his, forever.

The monster inside lunged against its choke chain and he throttled it back.

He groped for a way to satisfy it. To answer her just enough to keep her trust and not so much that he destroyed it utterly.

"I want you to promise me something."

CHAPTER TWENTY-TWO

H IS VOICE CAME out in a rasp, his face set into ridged lines, shoulder muscles bulging with the tension of his clenched fists. Boiling with a rage she curiously recognized as like her own. Odd to have this unexpected kinship. It couldn't be the same—they'd led such different lives and arrived in widely disparate endpoints.

"What promise?" she asked.

He seemed to be searching for the right words. "Two things, actually. First that you'll never tell another soul. Second that this won't change anything between us."

A rill of fear iced her despite the heat of the bathwater. Had he killed someone? She'd never felt in real, physical danger from him before, but now...

"That's exactly what I'm talking about. Don't look at me like you're afraid of me."

"You can't command my thoughts and emotions, Ryan," she said quietly, almost feeling sorry for him. "That's not something you can control."

He looked mean, on edge. "Don't tell me what I can and can't control."

"I think you'd better just tell me. This is out there now and I need to know what it is."

"Promise you'll at least stay the night."

"No."

He uncurled his fists and, for a moment, seemed about to lunge at her. He restrained himself, seizing his wine and draining it. She braced herself, expecting him to hurl it across the marble bathroom, but he set it down with exaggerated care, then glared at her.

"Stop looking like you're about to run. I won't hurt you. I've never hurt a woman in my life, outside of a scene."

"Who did you hurt?"

He scrubbed his hands over his face, kept them there. "Promise me, Celestina. Throw me a bone here."

Despite her uncertainty, the insidious fear, her heart ached for him. It made no sense, but she wanted to offer comfort. Something about that soul-deep recognition of his pain. Like and unlike her own. His was older, blacker, with roots back to that library and the little boy who read all the books—memorizing the dictionary definitions. God knew she had no compass, had made terrible choices and had seriously screwed up her life. Still, she needed to trust this. Give him what he asked for when he'd been so generous with her.

Following her instinct, she moved over to him and put her hand on his shoulder. "I promise to hear you out and to give you time to make promises to me in return, if I need them. I promise compassion. I promise not to tell anyone if keeping your secret doesn't compromise my morals."

He laughed soundlessly and dropped his hands, staring her down. "I could threaten to tell everyone about our arrangement if you do."

"Don't ruin this by being a pig. I'm making you the best offer I can."

Reaching out, he put his hands on her shoulders, going slowly as if he expected her to pull back. Then squeezed gently, as if to prove his self-control. "I'm sorry. That was a terrible thing to say. I would never do that to you."

"I actually knew that, which is why it didn't bother me. Now tell me the rest."

IMPOSSIBLE THAT HE would, but also inevitable. Such an unusual woman, his Celestina. Trusting in him even when the fear and uncertainty showed clearly in her eyes. And offering him compassion, of all things. Such a strange, even old-fashioned thing to say. Something his mama might have said—and it felt like a balm to that deeply buried, angry wound.

And he'd blown it already. Now that she knew he had a secret, she wouldn't trust him until he laid it out there. Staring into her probing gaze, he considered lying—or at least glossing. Too dangerous. Too much risk that she'd detect the lie. She wouldn't give him much more rope. Dangerous either way.

"You know," she said, lifting her hands to lay them against his cheeks, framing his face and searching for some answer, "you don't have to tell me this."

"But you'll go if I don't."

"I'd have to. But you and I don't know each other well. This…arrangement, the way you set it up, means that we don't owe each other these truths. If this were a real love affair, then I'd have a right to know who you are. As it is, you owe me nothing beyond the payment you promised."

"Harsh." Perhaps this had been a terrible idea, to go about it this way. He never second-guessed his decisions—what the hell?

"But true."

He wanted to argue that she was wrong. That he did owe her this and that she, by God, owed him far more, but he had no grounds to say so. "It seems I'm fucked either way—you'll leave if I don't tell you and, if I do, you might leave anyway."

"Yes. It wouldn't be a huge thing though. We'd both go on with our lives. No hearts broken or homes wrecked."

He slid his hands up the silken length of her arms to her wrists, holding her hands against his face. Not for her, perhaps. He was no longer certain it wouldn't cripple him to lose her. And, due to his own dismal lack of emotional control, he had but one path to make her stay.

He'd decided long ago that no one would ever know, and he'd stuck to that resolution. Telling her would be one of the very few times he'd ever changed his mind. Disaster or triumph? That remained to be seen. Despite the high stakes, the thrill of risking everything for the big prize fired his blood. The same thing that had driven him to get out and fight through those dark years spurred him on now. *Nothing risked, nothing gained.*

"Let me tell you a tale then." Grateful for the physical contact and moving cautiously so as not to spook her, he turned her so she sat sideways on his lap, cradled against him, a soothing weight. Staring out into the delicately lit garden, he saw only the wretched past.

"It happened a long time ago." In another life, it seemed.

To another person. "I was seventeen and working my way through college, getting my undergrad degree in business. There was…this guy in my class. Rich. Arrogant. Privileged. Total git. Should have been at an Ivy League school, but he'd flunked out of several and ended up at our state school.

"Man, I hated that guy."

Celestina stayed quiet, listening with her head on his chest and one hand stroking his shoulder, as if to soothe him. Oddly it worked, smoothing away some of that old rage.

"He made my life a living hell. I don't know why he picked me, except that I didn't fit in and was an easy target. I had a…well, a hick accent back then. My clothes were for shit. I lived in this awful apartment building where I shared one bathroom with ten other rooms on that floor. Junkies, crackheads. Someone was forever puking in there or shooting up, crapping on the floor. Even when the shower worked, I felt filthier coming out of there than when I went in. When I could, I snuck into the campus gym and showered there, but that was tricky—illegal as I couldn't pay the membership fee. I cared more about getting expelled than smelling bad. It wasn't like the girls wanted anything to do with me, which I figured then was the main reason to smell nice.

"But this guy, he hounded me about it. Called me the Redneck Hobo and always went on about how I was probably this homeless guy scamming the university. Well, he said it often enough and loudly enough that the proctor started giving me grief, sending letters. I didn't have a mailing address— nothing anyone sent to me would have survived where I lived—so I used this mailbox at a group house near campus.

Grad students and stuff. They'd just pull their own mail out and leave the rest for the other residents to get. I'd go by at night to check and it worked well enough."

Every night he could, which wasn't as often as he should have gone. One of a number of mistakes.

"Well, I missed a couple of letters from the school and then somehow it turns out this guy had started dating someone who lived in the house. He saw my name on a letter from the university—how's that for shit luck?—and he takes it to the proctor. I get called in and cops are there."

"Mail fraud," she whispered.

"Bingo. Stupidest law on the books, if you ask me. Worse—that address had been my dubious proof of residency so they not only wanted to nail me with various charges, they wanted me to cough up two years of out-of-state tuition."

"Were you a resident?"

"Fuck no. I'd split my home state when I was a teenager, got my GED and went as far as possible."

"So they had you."

"They had me, dead to rights."

"What did you do?"

"What could I do? The cops booked me, then found out I had a record. All juvie, but still. I was still technically a minor at that point so it wasn't sealed."

Celestina sighed, though he couldn't decipher the emotion behind it. All the ugliness of that time. At least she'd know it all, which would make her the one person in the world who did. A strange calmness filled him, an almost philosophical distance from that boy he'd been.

"They let me out on bail, mainly because they didn't have room to keep me overnight, and they didn't figure me for much of a flight risk. I was to report back for court the next day, but I knew what would happen. They'd slap me in a state-run school, barely a notch above prison. I wasn't going back to a hellhole like that."

"How did you make bail?"

"A buddy from one of my jobs. I offered him twice the amount to front it. Cleaned me out, but I knew I had a paycheck or two coming—my timing was at least that good. Problem was, they went to that same mailbox. Back before the blessed invention of direct deposit." Odd that he could laugh. Or maybe that was just buffering himself against the worst part. "I had to risk going to get the money. And guess who was watching for me?"

"Oh no."

"Oh yes. He sat there in his fucking Aston Martin and watched the mailbox on the off chance he could catch me. Then got out and held up that paycheck and dangled it in front of me." It came back so clearly, the quiet residential street, the greenish glow of the streetlights. The way Douglas Whit-taker—the *third*, thank you—had held up that envelope that represented his chance of escape and sneered at him. *Looking for this, Hobo Boy?*

"Tell me you didn't kill him," Celestina whispered.

"I came near. He didn't know punks like me. I knocked him down with the first punch. He saw me as some redneck derelict, but I had a stocky frame, more muscle. I'd grown up knowing how to fight dirty."

"Oh, Ryan…"

"Thing was—I couldn't stop. I kept punching him, whaling on that pretty face, his fucking privilege, loving the way it went to mush under my fists. He'd never sneer at me again. I wanted to kill him. I could have and walked away happy."

Celestina made a choked sound and he relaxed the grip he'd tightened on her. She pushed away from his chest, but surprised him by not pulling away entirely. Instead she stayed and searched his face. "What stopped you?"

"You'd like me to say I had some kind of crisis of conscience, that I looked at my bloody fists and realized I'd become just like my father and I needed to step away if I wanted to be a better man than that. That I thought of my mama and what she'd tried to teach me." He laughed at the thought, the sound scraping a throat that had gone tight, and Celestina flinched a little. Good. Better for her to know. "No, I stopped because a car came down the street and the headlights caught me. People jumped out and started screaming. I ran. And I took my goddamn paycheck with me."

She pursed her lips, thoughtful. "How'd you get away with it?"

"Got a shady shop to cash my check—even with blood spatter—for a hefty fee, got on the first bus out of town. Created a new identity, found a book at the library to get rid of my hick talk, got another GED, saved up some money, established real residency, and started over. Ponied up for a PO Box that time. I was lucky."

"Lucky?" She sounded astonished. Appalled, too. But she hadn't pulled away yet. "So your name isn't really Ryan Black."

"Yes, it *is*." Through blood and sweat, that name was more his than the one his miserable parents had bestowed on him.

Celestina seemed taken aback by his forceful tone, but brushed her fingers over his shoulders, thinking. "How do you know he didn't die? He could have, you know."

"Because I checked, of course."

She looked fully surprised by that. Of course she'd think that anyone who'd done what he did would have moved on and never looked back. "It wasn't difficult—the assault was in the papers. I knew his name and what hospital they took him to. I'd call his room—make sure I talked posh like he did—and ask whoever answered to put him on the phone. Later I could track him through the internet."

"Still?"

"Yes. I can't seem to help it, though I look less often now. A while back I arranged to transfer a large sum of money to his family—not him, but to his folks, who paid the hospital bills."

"From the sounds of it, they didn't need the money."

"No. I needed to do it. Make amends, though it hardly counts. For my own peace of mind."

"Did it work?"

"Yes and no. I don't think about it as much anymore."

She looked thoughtful. "You were a minor and this was—what?—twenty years ago?"

"Pretty much spot-on."

"So you can't be charged. Statute of limitations has to be up, even if they could have gone after you once you were an adult."

He lifted a shoulder, feeling restless. "Yes. I made sure to track when I was clear of that. But that just means I'll never be held truly accountable for what I did."

She frowned slightly. "I don't know about that. At what point do you let it go, I wonder?"

Never. He could never let it go, lest he forget and revert back to that. "I saw him once."

Her lovely dark eyes widened, gratifyingly shocked. "You didn't!"

"I did. At a conference." It had been so bizarre to lay eyes on the guy again, to recognize him and not be recognized in return. Whittaker had looked the same, only older, and Ryan—well he in no way resembled Hobo Boy. He'd felt the gut-punch of panic, followed by a surge of old guilt and even more profound rage. He'd gone to the hotel gym and spent hours sweating it out. Then managed to look the guy in the eye at a meeting later and even shake his hand. Back then he'd wished for someone to tell, who would understand what that moment meant.

Someone like Celestina.

So far she hadn't given her opinion, still thinking through all he'd told her. But he had to know. Couldn't wait a moment more to find out if he'd be forgiven or damned in her eyes. He set her apart from him, on pretext of pouring himself some wine, though mostly he wanted to spare himself from feeling her physically pull away.

"The point is, Celestina, that's who I am, at the core. It's who I was, who I always will be. I have violence in me and that's why I do what I do. Part of me likes hurting people. Having them in my control and suffering for me. It's ugly, but

I think I...I think I need it, to keep from ever exploding again like I did that night. I wouldn't blame you if you wanted to walk away. I'll transfer you all the money you need now. Consider it the price of your silence."

CHAPTER TWENTY-THREE

S HE TURNED OVER the whole ugly story in her head—
including the huge chunk he hadn't verbalized. Perhaps
that he hadn't even realized he'd revealed...*that I looked at my
bloody fists and realized I'd become just like my father...*It fit with
the rest, with what she'd suspected from his tale of hiding out
at the library.

And now he stared her down with that challenging glare,
daring her to condemn him as he'd so thoroughly judged
himself. Some people might think he should have to pay his
debt to society. What he'd put himself through, however,
seemed far worse than what the justice system would have
leveled upon him. Extraordinary that he had managed to do so
much, at such a young age.

That simmering rage, the contained sense of violence—all
channeled into building his fortune. And into sex. Oh yes, she
recognized that anger as another face of her own—the defiance
of fate and all the bad luck she'd thought life had dumped on
her. She'd done nothing with hers, though. Nothing like he
had. She'd just brooded on it, letting the edges crumble until
she lost her footing, while Ryan clawed his way out of one far
deeper and more perilous.

"Just tell me," he nearly growled. Then made an impatient

sound, climbed out of the tub and snatched up a towel. "Never mind. Don't. I know the answer already. How could you possibly trust me, knowing this? Any day, at any moment, I could lose my temper and beat you to death. There wouldn't be headlights to save you. Maybe you should go to the police, to the reporters and tell the story. It's no more than what I deserve."

Bemused, she let him spin, vent that resentful energy. *Dark things.* Oh yes, she understood him better now. Maybe better than he did himself. A tantalizing, empowering thought.

Finally he rounded on her. "Are you going to say nothing at all?"

With deliberate languidness, she lifted her wineglass and sipped. Set it down again. "I was waiting for you to let me get a word in edgewise. Are you done telling me how I feel?"

He opened his mouth to say something to that, a mean glitter in his eye, then deliberately closed it. Blowing out a long breath, he sat on the side of the tub, the towel clenched in his fists, looked at her and waited.

"Better. You're wrong. You are not the same person you were that night. I—"

"Yes, I am. Don't kid yourself that—" He bit off the interruption when she raised her eyebrows at him. "Sorry. I'll shut up."

"Do that."

He looked chagrined enough at her firm tone that she had to smile, even as part of her wept for that kid inside him that so feared rejection, who seemed to crave her forgiveness and understanding. She could at least give him that, in return for all he'd done to help her.

"As I was saying, you're not the same person. You couldn't be. Not with all you've done since. You're smarter now. Certainly wealthier. You created Ryan Black from the wrecked foundation of that poor kid who was only fighting for his life."

"I wasn't fighting for my life, Celestina. I was never in mortal danger from that git."

She stood, letting the water sheet from her body, distracting him immediately. His hot gaze raked her. Stepping out, she took a towel and began drying herself, dragging his gaze from one part of her body to another.

"If you hadn't gotten that paycheck and made your escape, what would have happened?"

"I told you. They'd likely have sent me back to the juvie home I broke out of in the first place."

"Why'd you break out?"

He glared at her. "Goddammit, Celestina—you have no fucking clue what those places are like! You'd break out, too."

"Do you have any lotion?" She kept her voice mild.

With a muttered curse, he wrapped the towel around his waist and stalked, tense and stiff-legged, to a cabinet. Flung it open and gestured. "Here. Take your pick. I'm going to find something stronger than wine."

"Sit." She pointed at the fainting couch—because what's a luxurious bathroom without one?—and gave him her best tween-quelling stare. "Stay."

For a moment he looked like he might tell her to fuck off, but he sat, fisting his hands together between his spread knees and fixing his gaze on them. She sorted through the lotions, taking her time.

"I want you to listen to me without interrupting." She found a rose-scented one, to please him, and started smoothing it on her arms. "This is my take. I think that place likely was horrible—I have some idea, though no experience—and you are obviously a tremendously strong-willed person. Like they show in documentaries sometimes, the people who live through plane wrecks because their will to survive is so strong. I saw this one where a woman felt guilty because she remembered climbing over people to get out. She had a major complex about it—felt like she'd been an animal instead of heroically helping others and that kind of thing."

"Celestina—"

"Hush. I'm not done." She put a foot on the couch next to him and dropped her towel, slowly rubbing lotion into her ankle and calf. Of course he looked. "The point of the show was that survival situations are different and we can't expect to apply lofty thinking. You felt like that juvie home was killing you, so you broke out and cobbled together a plan to better yourself." Thinking of him living in that awful apartment building, a teenager all alone and scared, only a few years older than her nieces, made her that much more glad that at least she'd managed to do something for Carly and Josie. At least they would never face that. No matter what. "When that bully—which is what he was, make no mistake—threatened your freedom, you did what you had to do to stay alive."

"Like an animal," he grated out, gaze flicking up and snagging on the movement of her hands on her naked thigh.

"Or like someone with a passionate will to survive who was

pushed past his limits. And then you went on to recreate yourself again, to channel all of that anger and need." Pulling his gaze with them, she moved her hands up to her breasts. Speaking of channeling, that black rage simmering in him shifted, steaming in another direction as his expression went hard with hunger. "You said you wouldn't blame me for not trusting you. I trust you more than ever now, because I know what you've mastered in yourself."

It took him a moment, but he transferred his gaze to her face, bemused and suspicious. "What are you saying?"

She knelt before him, spread her thighs and offered her breasts. "I'm saying I'm still bought and paid for, and there's a lot of the night left to do whatever you want to me. Master."

IT TOOK HIM a few moments to assimilate her words and actions. As if a streaming movie had gotten the soundtrack and video out of sync and she'd stopped matching the script in his head. Few people surprised him as she did—which explained why he'd changed the decision he'd made before he walked in the room. He'd barely gotten over the shock of that, telling the ugly story out loud for the first time ever, and his subsequent bitter regret at doing so, before it began to penetrate his head that she somehow didn't see what he'd done as an unforgivable crime.

And that she wasn't afraid of him.

…you did what you had to do to stay alive.

He wasn't sure he believed that. But she did, offering herself into his power, her dark eyes full of lustrous yielding. Compassion and desire.

"Why are you doing this?" He couldn't help asking—just as he couldn't seem to stop drinking in the sight of her, the scent of hothouse roses rising from her damp skin.

"This is what I have to give right now."

"You have more than your body—"

"Not my body," she interrupted. "My trust. Tie me up. Torment me. Do whatever you like. I know I'm safe with you."

The hunger rose in him, fervid, insatiable. Craving her and what she offered. The dregs of that stupid teenager he'd been clung to the edges of his mind. Working all those jobs, living in that place among the crackheads and junkies. He'd thought himself clever, above the system, but he'd brought about his own ruin. Amazing, really, that only Whittaker had gone after him, he'd been such a wretched hanger-on. But he'd learned, hadn't he?

And how amazed his seventeen-year-old self would have been to see this moment. He'd forgotten, over the years, that he hadn't always lived like this, until he'd conjured up those memories of the squalor and the edge of desperation to acquire enough money to survive. That kid hadn't been able to imagine this in his future—or the gorgeously sensual, naked woman kneeling at his feet, still offering him her breasts. And anything else he wanted of her.

He stroked her cheek and she leaned into the gesture, trembling slightly. Not with fear, however. "Are you sure you want to do this?" His voice came out rough, full of both ragged emotional uncertainty and potent need to take what she offered.

She held his gaze, then turned her face to press a kiss into the palm of his hand. "I'm your slave. Use me as you see fit."

Everything else—the dregs of memory, the raw anger of the boy he'd been, the terror of exposure—crumbled at the edges, like paper burning to ash in the face of the raging desire her words crystallized in him.

"My slave." He slid his hand to the slim column of her throat, her pulse thudding harder at the gesture. Moving slowly, he raised her to her feet, then to her toes, hand snugged under the fine line of her jaw for leverage. Her eyes darkened as her pupils dilated in the deep brown irises, but she remained totally pliant in his grip. Sliding his other hand between her thighs, he found her slick and ready for him.

She moaned, undulating a little, and he knew she meant it. All of it. For all the artifice that brought her here, whether either of them truly believed he'd bought her or not, she'd given herself over to his possession. And he planned to use her as such.

Ruthlessly.

CHAPTER TWENTY-FOUR

H E SET HER flat-footed. Then, enjoying her flash of shock, bent and tossed her over his shoulder in a fireman's carry.

"Ryan!" she gasped, and he smacked her naked bottom, silencing her protest.

"Quiet. You know the rules." He spanked her a few more times, just to hear her whimper, feel her wriggle against his grip, her full breasts bouncing against his back. Carrying her through the house, the power of possessing her filled him. He felt strong. Gloriously so, in a way his younger self never had.

In a way no other woman had inspired.

Taking her into the library again—so much more pleasant than a dungeon—he put her down on a padded table. Even with her dusky skin, she gleamed in contrast to the black surface.

"Spread yourself for me," he ordered, mostly for the satisfaction of observing her trembling obedience. She did, catching her breath when he assisted, brusquely pulling her wrists to the far corners and widening the spread of her thighs. She watched him in wide-eyed anticipation, not resisting but clearly wondering what he planned for her.

What he planned was to keep her in suspense for a while

yet.

He showed her a slim glass dildo, then slid it into her exposed pussy. Not enough to really do much for her besides keep her attention there. Moaning a little, she flexed her hips.

"No. Stay silent. Stay still. If you move too much, that will fall out and you'll suffer for it."

Using rope—red, for passion—he took his time binding her hands to the corners of the table above her head. Her fine-boned wrists showed the loops of rope nicely, so he brought her elbows out to the sides and bound those also. Though her breathing deepened in aroused distress and her lips parted as if she wanted to ask a question, she didn't break the silence he'd demanded of her. Staying true to her word to yield him whatever he wanted.

Looping more rope under the table, he made several passes and bound her tightly to it with a series above her lush breasts and then another below. For good measure, he took smaller lengths and circled the base of each tit, tightening them so they began to strain full and red. She whimpered and he let that pass.

His poor suffering slave.

Going to her ankle, he drew it up flush against her bottom, then wrapped the rope between and around her thigh and calf, so her knee remained deeply bent. He repeated the process with her other leg, then ran another length of rope under the table and attached it to the ones binding her thighs. Working meticulously, watching her face, he adjusted the tension on the ropes so her thighs were splayed as widely as she could bear.

She mostly stared up at the ceiling, bound breasts rising

and falling with her frantic breathing, likely concentrating on holding the slick glass dildo inside her. He pumped it in and out of her, loving how she shuddered but managed not to move her hips in response. Of course, the way he had her trussed up, she could barely move anyway.

Ready to show her his favorite trick of that particular table, he undid the latches beneath, then folded it down, so her bottom and exposed pussy hung helplessly in midair, suspended by the tension of the ropes. She gasped at the shock, her gaze flying to his. Pulling the dildo out, he set it aside and worked his fingers into her, one, then two, then three. A snug fit that made her squirm. Just enough to demonstrate how vulnerably open she was to him.

For fucking and worse.

Leaving her there, he picked out red candles from the sideboard and set them on the table around her, lighting them so her sweat-slick body glowed with their soft flames. Putting on a condom, he entered her without ceremony or warning, simply sheathing himself to the hilt in her as she dropped her head back, exposing her throat in the erotic realization she could deny him nothing.

He rocked inside her and a low moan fluttered from her lips. Ideal that he'd come twice already, or he'd never last for this particular game. Stroking her turgid breasts and pinching her already sore nipples, he reveled in the way her muscles flexed around his cock, squeezing him as he held still, attempting to draw him in.

"Celestina," he murmured, waiting for her to meet his eyes. "You've done very well. You're a good slave. You may thank me."

"Thank you, Master," she replied, throaty with desire and the strain.

"However, even good slaves receive punishment, if only because that's what a slave is for. You exist to please me and my pleasure is to give you pain. Understand?"

"Yes, Master." Her dark eyes filled with tears and she licked her lips.

"I don't think you do. But you will." He picked up a candle and held it poised over her naked belly, waiting for her to catch on.

She did, a rush of trepidation crumpling her face. "Please don't!" she cried.

He paused, listening for her to safeword, and she stared at him in realization. Perhaps she considered it, her full lips moving silently over the word, but at last she pressed her lips together. Then sighed. "As it pleases you, Master."

"That's right. For your reward, you may make as much noise as you wish. You may even struggle." He allowed himself to laugh, loving the way she responded to the dark sound. "If you can manage it."

A crimson drop of melted wax hit her abdomen and she hissed at the sting. Then another, larger one made her cry out. She started to struggle—inevitable, really. Asking her not to would have been too much. Besides, her writhing made her that much more beautiful to him. Methodically, he dripped the wax over her belly, exulting in her pleas and how her pussy, hotter than the candle flames, clenched and spasmed around his cock.

Tears ran down her face and, when he dripped some wax on her crimson breast, she screamed, her body convulsing. Taking that for his cue, he unchained the beast and set the candle aside, fucking her in earnest. The black and red wave overtook him and he pounded his hips against her in savage delight.

THE ORGASM RIPPED her apart, filling her veins like the melted wax burning her skin, her heart pounding frenetically to push her thickened blood to keep up with the rolling, slicing knives of pain and pleasure.

Like a madman, Ryan pounded his thick cock into her, stretching her unbelievably in her tightly restricted position, face clenched with black lust, his hands digging into her as if he wanted to tear her open. Bound as she was—as she'd invited him to do to her—she could only receive what he did, dragged from one exquisite peak to the next without surcease.

With a hoarse cry of triumph, he slammed home and held there, staring down at her with a ferocity that hollowed her out. Even at this moment, when he so utterly possessed her, had her totally in his control, he watched her face, searching out her every tear, her every gasp of pleasure.

His hands on her relaxed and he bent over her, breathing as raggedly as a man chased by demons. Which, no doubt, he was.

Then he pulled out of her, ditched the condom and came around to her head. He stood over her, his chest still pumping with his harsh breaths, then brushed her sweat-drenched hair back from her forehead. He pressed a finger against her mouth and she opened, drawing it in and sucking on it as he seemed to want. A smile of tenderness softened his face and he replaced the finger with his mouth, drawing on her with a greedy hunger.

Lifting his head, he caressed her throat, spanning it in one big hand.

"Mine," he whispered.

In that moment, it was utterly, obviously true. Nothing else existed but this, belonging to him. His slave. She could deny him nothing. Not even her shredded heart.

"Yours," she answered.

He kissed her again, softly. Then he began cutting her free of the ropes, loosening her aching breasts first, then going in reverse order of how he'd bound her. The blood rushed back into her limbs and she grew sleepy with the release of tension. Emptied, unable to even form a coherent thought, she simply let her limbs fall where he dropped them.

He took warm oil and rubbed it into her skin, dissolving what wax that still clung and soothing any lingering sting. Working his strong hands into her muscles, he massaged her from temples to toes, sending her into such a stupor that she barely noticed when he turned her over, repeating the lulling treatment on her back.

Blearily she noticed him moving around the room, turning off lights. Then he lifted her into his arms, murmuring reassurance when she protested, and tucking her securely against his wide chest. Gratefully she sank back into oblivion.

SHE WOKE TO bright sunlight and a roaring sound that took her a minute to place. The surf, rushing against the cliffs outside, the sound drifting in the open patio doors to the garden. A warm breeze scented with roses wafted over her face, followed by the brush of Ryan's fingers.

Turning her head to find him in bed beside her, she smiled. "Awake then?"

"Barely." A yawn overtook the words and she stretched, feeling her body protest in every joint and muscle. Rode hard and put up wet, her grandmother would have said. Uneasily accurate, in this particular circumstance.

"I wasn't sure when you needed to get back or I would have let you sleep longer," Ryan said.

Oh. Good point. Her nieces and the world outside Ryan's erotically compelling sphere of influence. How irresponsible was she? "I should check my phone."

He pointed his chin at the bedside table, where her purse sat. She'd left it upstairs when she'd stripped to play slave girl and after that last check before the bath and round two. Blushing at the recollection, and at the kaleidoscope of vivid sense memory of all that had happened since then, she picked it up, grateful for an excuse to reach for it, turn her back and look away for a moment.

A hell of a morning-after.

And, whoa, almost nine thirty already. No texts showed on her screen, but she unlocked the phone and checked anyway. Nothing. They were probably all shocked that she hadn't checked in as usual. *As she should have.*

She texted both girls at once, in their ongoing group conversation. And waited.

"Would you like coffee?" Ryan touched her shoulder. She

jumped at the contact and glanced back to see him frown a little.

"I should really go." Jesus—what if something had happened to the girls? What if they had gone home and found her not there? She made a terrible mother. Why weren't they answering? They could have died and she wouldn't have known. A final way to let Ara down.

"Of course, if you need to, but—"

Her text alert interrupted him. Josie. *Oh, thank God.*

Stayed up to 5 playing Dragon Age. Sleeping. Can we come home later?

Apparently it had been a night for it. She tried to quiet her heart. Think of something reasonable.

Do you have homework?

We'll do it 2nite. Promise.

OK. Be home by 4. Call if you need a ride.

K.

"Good," Ryan said. He'd been reading over her shoulder. "Then you can stay awhile."

She hesitated and he took the phone out of her hands, tossed it aside, and turned her to face him. "Regrets?"

It took her a moment to realize he meant about the night before, not about Ara's death or the way she still expected people to go out in the world and never come back. He looked composed this morning, with little sign of the tormented and tormenting man she'd come to know so thoroughly the night before. Back with that charming veneer of the gentleman. Something she now understood as exactly that—a façade he'd painstakingly developed in creating his new identity.

"No. I'm just not that awake yet."

"But you'll stay awhile longer."

"Well, I think I'm only paid up till sunrise," she joked. And instantly regretted it at the pained offense that flashed in his eyes and then disappeared.

"Is that how it is?" He shoveled off the covers and strode out of the room, gloriously naked body flexing in the morning light.

Good going, Tina. That seemed to be her cue to vamoose. With a resigned sigh—not quite understanding the mix of emotions jangling in her heart, which seemed to be the norm lately—she slid out of the delicious sheets also. Taking a moment, she sat on the edge of the bed, pushing her hair back from her forehead and wishing he'd brought down her clothes, too. She felt like she could sleep for hours yet. Maybe she'd treat herself to Starbucks on the drive home. After she made her discreet exit.

Ryan, however, came back in the room and it seemed the temperature went up a couple degrees or the barometric pressure dropped with his crackling energy. She flinched at the impact of it, ever so slightly, but he noted it, frown darkening. "Get out your tablet," he told her.

"What?" She felt three beats behind. Should have accepted the offer of immediate coffee.

Ryan held up his own tablet. "Yours is in your purse. Get it out."

Feeling a little jittery, she took the easiest course and turned it on. Catching up now, she wasn't surprised to see he'd added a number of activities, including coffee and brunch, only, no sex—along with a ludicrous dollar figure.

"You don't have to do that." Feeling guilty, she glanced up to find him staring fixedly at her.

"Accept it," he bit out.

"Ryan, I—"

"Here." He snatched it out of her hands and accepted it for her. Then tossed both tablets aside. "Now. How do you like your coffee?"

"Look, I'm sorry. I didn't mean to say that. I don't know what's wrong with me this morning."

"What's wrong is I scared the shit out of you last night and now you're skittish as a long-tailed cat in a roomful of rocking chairs." He had his fists on his hips, jaw set, still stark naked, his cock long and relaxed while the rest of him vibrated with tension.

Despite everything—or maybe because of the high emotional pitch of the moment—she giggled.

"It's not funny, Celestina."

"A long-tailed cat in a roomful of rocking chairs?"

He shook his head, his expression relaxing slightly. "My mama used to say it."

"Southern girl?"

"West Virginia." He blew out a breath, raked his hands through his hair. Then looked at her. "Where I grew up."

Okay. Apparently she wasn't the only one feeling jumbled up. "It comes out, you know, here and there—mainly when you're mad."

He stared at her, truly taken aback, as he so rarely was. "It does not."

She nodded. "I can safely say I've *never* heard 'useless as tits on a bull' before in my life. And you once used 'reckon,' too."

Setting his jaw, he shook his head, as if to negate what she'd said. "I should find that tutor I hired and get my money back."

"It's okay. It doesn't mean anything. It's part of who you are."

"Maybe." He looked unconvinced.

"Let's do this. I'm going to use the bathroom and put some clothes on. Why don't you start that coffee and I'll meet you in the kitchen?"

He continued giving her that long look, pressed his lips together, then nodded. "I'll grab your clothes from upstairs. Sorry I didn't think of it."

"It's okay," she said again. She stood up, still feeling wobbly, and put her hands on his shoulders, then gave him a light kiss. Because he seemed to need the reassurance, she repeated it. "Everything is okay."

In that moment, she even believed it herself.

CHAPTER TWENTY-FIVE

*E*VERYTHING IS OKAY.

He didn't know how they'd gotten to this place where Celestina soothed and cozened him instead of the reverse. Of course, he also had no idea what had come over him the night before. Why he'd confessed so much—and then why he'd given in to taking out those dark emotions on her tender, inexperienced body.

He didn't blame her for wanting to run this morning. He also had no intention of letting her do it. She'd had her chance the night before. For better or worse, now she belonged to him. It would just take some time for her to come to terms with that. Though he'd be careful not to put it in those words, outside of scenes.

You belong to me. The words echoed through his brain in his father's voice, accompanied by the sounds of fists on flesh and his mother's pleas.

Not like that.

As if speaking of that time had further unlocked some part of him that had been hidden behind a door, memories rose up in his mind, unwanted pop-up windows of his past, interfering with his thoughts. Appalling that he'd slipped and used those hick clichés of his mother's. Her West Virginia drawl, the one he'd worked so hard to excise from his own speech, trailed through his head, like lingering shreds of Appalachian fog.

When you find the girl for you—you treat her right, you hear? Don't you ever hit her. A real man doesn't do that. You be better than that or I'll haunt you. I swear I will.

Well, she'd never said anything about whipping a woman or burning her skin with candle wax and fucking her until she passed out, right? Or maybe she'd never haunted him before this because he hadn't found the right woman. Superstitiously, he crossed himself as he hadn't in decades, sending a prayer for her to stay in her grave. *I'll haunt you. I swear I will.*

"Coffee smells good."

His turn to jump, startled out of his morose thoughts by Celestina's smooth voice. She'd showered and combed her damp hair behind her ears. Wearing worn jeans—with holes in the knees that she'd no doubt come by honestly, not as a fashion statement—and a faded In-N-Out Burger T-shirt, she edged herself onto a stool at the kitchen island, giving him a cautious smile.

More than anything else, he hated that she acted spooked around him now. Though she should, being a smart woman.

"Do you take cream in it?"

"Yes, please."

He adjusted the machine, letting it brew the cup, uncertain what tack to take next. He'd been so determined to make her stay, to talk things out with him, but now he wasn't sure what to say.

"That has to be the most amazing coffeemaker I've ever seen."

Okay, small talk worked. "It's a Jura Capresso. Incredibly

self-indulgent and expensive. Totally worth every penny."

"It looks almost steampunk."

"What's that?"

"Oh." She waved a hand in the air. "The girls like it. Kind of Victorian-era, if technology continued as all steam-driven. Lots of shiny brass, cogs and wheels, that sort of thing."

He set the mug in front of her. "There. Tell me that's not the best cup of coffee you've had in your life."

She sipped. Hummed and sipped again, dark eyes widening at him over the rim. "Oh my God."

"Told you." He found himself grinning, the pop-up windows of memory still for a moment.

"No wonder the machine is so expensive."

"The best things are worth the price."

Her smile dimmed and he kicked himself for bringing up that reminder between them. Leaning his elbows on the counter, he stared down at his own mug. "Look, I'm sorry. I shouldn't have gotten pissy about paying you to stay."

"I'm sorry I made that terrible joke. I was just…"

He looked up when she didn't finish, to find her picking at the strings around one of the holes in her jeans.

"Afraid of me?"

Her gaze flew up to his, full of some emotion. "No. I think you need to get over that idea. I'm not afraid of you. I thought I proved that last night."

"I think I proved that you *should* be afraid of me. I have no excuse for what I did to you."

She cocked her head slightly. "It was all in the possible scenarios I agreed to. You can look."

"I know, but I didn't do it for the right reasons. It wasn't about you that last time. Last night was supposed to be about giving you release. Not about…"

She raised her eyebrows at his realization. "Not about giving you release from your own brand of survivor's guilt and pent-up emotions?"

Was that what they'd done? No wonder he felt like a wreck this morning. He took a long drink of coffee, grateful for the soothing burn of it, wishing he could pour some directly into his brain.

"I'm surprised you didn't know that already," she continued. "You explained it all so well to me—and it seems we're kind of alike that way, but for different reasons. Some pair we are."

"Apparently you're much smarter than I am." What an idiot he was.

"Or…" She cupped her mug, looking thoughtful. "I think sometimes it's just much easier to see someone else's issues. We kind of muck about in our own so we can't see them clearly, but someone else's are in focus, from the right distance."

"I don't have 'issues,' Celestina."

Her serious expression broke into a wide delighted grin. "Oh, Ryan, honey—you have serious issues. You just have a much higher gloss on top of them."

He glared at her, which didn't dim her smile the least bit. "A gloss?"

"Sure. All that charm, the manners, the suits and the sophistication. Glossy."

"I'm beginning to regret making you stay for coffee."

That worked to kill her delight at his discomfort. She set down her mug and slid off her stool. "I'll go then."

Shit. "No, wait." He went around the counter and stopped her by putting his hands on her hips and holding her there. She looked up at him, uncertain again. "I'm doing things all wrong this morning."

"Well, I guess we're a pair in that, also." She gave him a tentative smile. "It occurs to me that I haven't done a morning-after in pretty much forever. I've forgotten how."

"They usually aren't this…" Fraught. "Everything goes differently with you, Celestina. Never quite how I have planned."

"Good. That makes me feel better."

That surprised a laugh out of him. "It makes you happy to see me discombobulated?"

"Yes, actually. I like knowing I'm not the only one making things up as I go."

"I don't like making things up as I go."

"I can see that. You always have a plan, don't you? A strategy worked out ahead of time."

"It's a business skill. Always have your decision made before you walk in the room. That's how you keep other people from pushing you around."

"And I'm business." She said it not in a mean tone or like she was hurt or disappointed, but in acknowledgement of a bare fact. Which it was. He'd set this up as a business arrangement from the very beginning and it would be foolish to deny that. Even more foolish to contemplate that he'd been lying to himself all along. That this chemistry between them, his endless craving for her that seemed to extend far beyond sex, had nothing at all to do with something as cool-headed as business.

"It will make you no doubt happy to hear that I'm not at all sure what you are." He eased her against him, needing the contact, wanting to strip her naked and have her on the kitchen counter. Strictly against the rules. Talking. They were supposed to be talking. No sex. He'd put it in the damn tablet.

"Ryan…" His name came out throaty and she licked her lush lower lip.

With a groan, he threw the rules out the window and kissed her.

THE KISS TOOK her under, fast and unexpected. He tasted of coffee, cream and sugar, bitter and sweet together. This felt better, more like how they should have started the day, reconnecting physically instead of rehashing the emotional bog they both seemed to be wretched at navigating.

He ran his hands up her back under her T-shirt, stopping at the catch of her practical bra, then breaking the kiss. "I know it's not in the rules, but I have to have you. Say yes."

"Fuck the rules, Ryan." She pressed into him, fastening her mouth to his and coaxing him into more of his hypnotic kisses, then groaned as he unsnapped her bra and caressed her freed breasts. Slightly sore—just enough to make every touch drill straight to her groin—her nipples hardened delightfully.

He stripped her shirt and bra over her head, then sank to his knees, ripping open the button and zipper of her jeans and yanking them, along with her panties, down her thighs.

Holding on to his shoulders for balance, she still nearly fell over when he grasped her hips and drove his tongue into her pussy. With her jeans trapping her ankles, her thighs stayed pressed together, but that did little to stop him. He held her in a tight grip, finding and licking at her rapidly sensitizing clit.

"Celestina," he said against her, slowing now, curling his tongue against her intimate flesh with lascivious pleasure. "Celestina."

He kept crooning her name that way, making it a kind of chant in between licks and kisses, as if he worshiped at her sex and she were some kind of goddess he beseeched for mercy. Letting the warm rise of arousal flow through her, she ran her hands over his head, learning the shape of his skull and the texture of his hair as she hadn't been able to before this. Showing him with her touch that everything would be okay.

With a groan, he tightened his hands on her hips and lifted her onto the barstool, then tugged her jeans off entirely, leaving her naked. Lifting her ankles, he hooked her knees over the chrome arms of the stool and scooted her bottom forward, so she was spread open for him to kiss and ravage in his leisurely way. As with his mouth-to-mouth kisses, he tantalized her with his sweeping tongue and occasional nips and scrapes, seeming to enjoy the act for itself. He lavished attention on every fold and hollow of her pussy, drinking her in, apparently for the pure pleasure of doing so. No sense of him driving her toward orgasm, just a slow and sensual exploration.

As a result, the tension built in her gradually, rising like the sun filling the kitchen with light. She let her head fall back and the lapping rays of warm fill her. "Ryan," she breathed.

"Not yet. Wait for me."

He stood and pulled off his shirt over his head, making his hair stand up in tufts. Kicking off his jeans, he fished a condom out of his pocket and rolled it on. Instead of plunging into her, however, he paused before her splayed thighs, tracing the soft skin from her knees to where her inner thighs met her pelvis. Feeling languid, she lay back, loving the way he looked at her. His gaze roamed up her body until he met her eyes, his a darker gray than usual.

"You are so beautiful, Celestina. So perfect for me in so many ways. I want to do right by you."

"You are." She lifted her arms to him and he leaned into her until she caressed his muscular shoulders. With a slow slide, he pressed his heavy cock into her, stretching her gradually, deliciously, eyes locked on hers. His face softened as he did, taking on a sensual, heavy-lidded look. She lifted her hips to ease the way and let out a long, humming breath as he pushed all the way home.

"You feel so good," he murmured, holding there and dropping kisses on her upturned face, forehead, cheekbones. "So warm and lovely, soft."

"You do, too." She realized that made no sense as he was anything but soft, but he started moving inside her then, gently and sensually, as if caressing her from the inside out. This wasn't the soul-shattering ritualized violence of the night before, but rather a kind of intimate embrace, intensely moving in its own way, his hands stroking her skin, his cock rubbing her from within. He permeated her every sense, muscles flexing under her fingers, the scents of coffee and their heated bodies, the susurrus of the ocean, echoed by their panting breaths. His eyes searched hers, gray as evening fog, and then his mouth settled on hers, filling the last corner of her emptiness.

She unraveled, coming apart even as he gathered up the threads of her being, holding her together in his big hands, buoying her through the gentle waves of the climax that dismantled her piece by piece.

Clinging to the rock of his body, she tore her mouth away so she could cry out, releasing a long, keening breath.

"Celestina," he whispered and followed her over the edge.

CHAPTER TWENTY-SIX

CELESTINA'S HANDS SLIPPED from his shoulders, her head dropped back showing the long, graceful arc of her throat and the satisfied curve of her full lips. Her body clasped him, hot and slickly velvet, cradling him in her hips as if he belonged there.

He wanted to extend the moment, the golden feel of it all, but the back of the stool had to be digging into her shoulders and he'd resolved to take better care with her. She murmured a vague protest as he slipped out of her, but willingly wrapped her arms around his neck, snuggling up to him as he lifted her, and pressed a kiss to his throat. If he weren't far beyond such things, his heart would have stuttered at the gesture, the spontaneous and unguarded affection in her kiss.

Post-coital glow made up for a world of sins.

He carried her back to bed, laying her on the tumbled sheets and settling in beside her. With a sound like a purring kitten, she curled against him, falling asleep. As had happened when they'd made love in the kitchen, her fall became his, and he let himself drop into the balm of sleep.

This time she woke before him, waking him with lightly tracing fingers on his chest. Almost he didn't want to open his eyes. By the warmth of the room, it was already afternoon, which meant she'd have to leave soon. Ridiculous of him. He opened his eyes to find her leaning up on one elbow and smiling at him. She looked much more rested now, dark eyes sparkling with mischief as she tugged at his chest hair. He covered her hand with his, holding it trapped against his heart.

"Time for you to go?"

She nodded. "Almost three o'clock. We slept the day away."

"Fair enough, as I don't think we got more than three or four hours last night."

"True enough." She tugged her hand free. "I'm sorry to wake you, but I thought you might be annoyed if I left without saying goodbye."

He turned onto his side as she slid off the bed, aware now that she'd washed up and dressed again, all while he slept like the dead. Unlike him, when he usually wakened at the least stirring.

"So…" She gave him a little wave. "Bye."

"I don't get a kiss?" His voice sounded rough in his ears, though he'd meant to be teasing.

She hesitated, but came to him, crawling up onto the bed on her knees. "Just a kiss," she warned. "I really have to leave."

"There is no such thing as just a kiss." He cupped her neck and turned onto his back, drawing her with him so her lush mouth covered his, fitting perfectly and softening like warmed chocolate in the sun. Her breath sighed into him and he took that in, too.

Then, with resolved determination, let her go. For today. Time to set into motion a plan to make sure that would change. Getting out of bed, he found some jeans and tugged them on, to walk her to the door. *Treat her right.*

"Your birthday is soon. Tuesday."

She cast him a sideways glance. "Yes."

"Come over that evening. Bring the girls and we'll have a party."

"Ryan, I don't—"

"Do you have other plans?"

She huffed out an impatient sigh. "No. You know I don't."

"Is there a reason you don't want me to meet your nieces?"

There was, palpable in the way she occupied herself with digging her car keys out of her purse, but she didn't want to say so. "Okay, fine. But—all on the up and up, right? No funny business."

He nearly laughed, feeling his grin spread as her glare grew more pointed. "Funny business?"

"You know what I mean!"

"I do. Just a fun, normal birthday celebration with your beloved wards and the man you're dating."

"Ha to that," she muttered, then waved a hand in the direction of the library playroom. "You're going to have to hide some of that stuff, you know."

"Yes, I do know. I've sanitized for polite company before."

He opened the door for her and she stepped out into the bright afternoon sun. Stopping at the first step, she squared her shoulders and turned back to him. "Ryan?"

"Celestina?"

"Don't give me money for today, okay? Any more than you did. Not for the sex."

He hadn't expected that. Hadn't even thought about it yet. Though she was right, that he would have soon enough. "But that's not fair to—"

"Just…don't. Consider it a favor to me."

He tried to read her expression, but she'd put on those huge dark sunglasses and he couldn't quite make out her eyes. He should make it a rule she couldn't wear them. And that she had to tell him everything she was thinking. Restraining himself, he simply agreed. "All right, I won't."

"Or for the birthday party."

Holding on to his temper, he kept his tone even. "Will you explain to me why?"

"I'm not sure I can. It's just…important to me. Can we leave it at that?"

"Of course," he made himself say. He'd get it out of her later. "Will I see you before Tuesday?"

Her lips curved. "Maybe. I'll think about it."

He stood there on the steps, watching her drive off in that wreck of a car. Ridiculous that she hadn't used some of the money to buy something more reliable. He hated worrying about her driving the damn thing, hated that she had to leave at all. An easy decision to make, there in the bright light of day. She should be here, with him. Whatever that took.

The afternoon had grown quite warm, with a dryness that hinted of the baking summer to come. The fountain he'd imported from Barcelona needed to be cleaned, its colors dulled by a coating of dust. Maybe they could fill it and have it going for Celestina's birthday celebration, as a special treat. Appropriate for her and her love of water-informed landscapes.

They should eat out by the pool, maybe. The girls could bring their swimsuits and they could grill shish kebabs or something. And champagne would be a must—sparkling cider for the girls, but crystal flutes for everyone. At least he could plan for the party while he waited for her to make up her mind about their next encounter.

What she chose would tell him a great deal about how she truly felt about all he'd done to her. And whether his efforts at making it up to her today had helped.

You treat her right, you hear?

"Yes, Mama. I hear you. I'm doing the best I can. You can stay in your grave—no need to haunt me." Amused at himself for speaking to the empty air, he shook his head, fending off the sense of old sorrow that sifted down like ash from the sky.

Going back inside, he headed for his office, to get his head back in business again.

"Who is this guy again?" Carly wanted to know. "And why do we have to go to his house—we don't know him."

"His name is Ryan Black and he's the man I went out with last night." Quite the euphemism there. "You have to go because he invited you and I said you would. He'd like to meet you."

"Maybe we don't want to meet him," Carly muttered, poking her spinach salad with a fork.

"I think it's already dead, Carls. You don't have to keep stabbing it," Josie said.

"Ha-ha."

"Besides," Josie added, "it's Antina's birthday Tuesday.

That's why we're going. Right?"

"I'm surprised you remembered."

Both girls looked suddenly glum. "Well, it was Mom's birthday, too." Carly sighed a little and shoved spinach in her mouth.

"Yes. It was thoughtless of me to say that—or to ask you to do something frivolous on that day. I'm sorry. I wasn't thinking." All those birthdays she and Ara had shared—how hadn't it occurred to her the girls would of course know the day and mark it? That's why they'd never paid attention to hers. It hurt too much. She'd been so selfish. "I'll cancel."

"Don't do that." Josie set her fork down. "Mom's gone and you're alive. You deserve a birthday party. We'll go and it will be fun." She raised her eyebrows at Carly, who reluctantly nodded.

"Are you sure? You two really don't have to. This is my deal."

Josie kept staring expectantly at Carly until she glared back. "What? I said I'd go."

"We'd love to go, Antina." Josie assumed a gracious, lady-of-the-manor tone. "Thank you for the invitation."

Carly rolled her eyes. "Whatever," she said under her breath.

"And we're excited to meet Ryan." Josie paused, looking thoughtful. "It's probably really good that you're dating again. You haven't since Uncle Noah bailed."

"So, is this, like, serious?" Carly asked.

"No. We're just seeing each other. Having fun. A temporary thing."

"But he wants to meet us," Josie pointed out and Carly nodded wisely. "That's the equivalent of meeting the parents in your world."

"Ooh." Carly's eyes lit up. "Will he try to impress us? We can grill him with all kinds of questions about his intentions toward you."

"You will not grill him."

"Antina." Josie gave her a stern look. "That's our responsibility. You take care of us and we take care of you."

"Besides," Carly said through a mouthful of spinach, "if you marry him, then he'd be like our…"

"Step-uncle?" Josie pondered it. "Uncle-in-law?"

"I think plain uncle would work," Tina said dryly. "And you don't need to worry about it because I won't be marrying him."

"But you could," Carly persisted. "Don't you want to get married again?"

"Yeah, Uncle Noah was an asshole, but that doesn't mean all men are."

Tina gaped at Josie, shocked more that she'd said such a thing than at the language. "You thought Noah was an…"

"Major asshole," Carly agreed. "We hated him."

"We were sorry he ditched out on you, but it was a relief to know we wouldn't have to live with him."

"And we were really grateful you didn't kick us out." Carly chewed her lip. "I probably should have said that before."

"Because we know you could have and he wanted you to." Josie looked sad and Carly patted her hand.

Her stomach cooled. "You knew that?"

Josie snorted. "It was hard not to overhear."

"I'm sorry about that."

"It's not your fault." Josie shrugged it away. "But that's why it's cool Mr. Hottie wants to meet us. He knows you're a package deal and he's working the angles."

"Right?" Carly bounced in her chair. "He knows if he wants to bag you, he's got to go through us. This could be an awesome gig."

Tina rubbed her eyes. The nap had not made up for the night of all sex and no sleep. "Now I'm sure I should cancel."

"Too late," Josie sang out with a bright smile.

"Too bad," Carly chimed in.

"Soooo sad," they drawled together, then giggled and touched fingers.

Ryan didn't stand a chance.

CHAPTER TWENTY-SEVEN

Good morning Celestina. My bed was cold and lonely without you.

She smiled at the text message and set the phone aside.

"Is that him?" Josie raised her eyebrows significantly. "Cuz if that was him, then you gotta answer."

"Or they think you don't like them." Carly grabbed her backpack. "You have to reply. Boys get their feelings hurt easily."

"I think I can manage this on my own. Don't forget your book in the living room." Impossible to explain that her relationship with Ryan had nothing to do with feelings. That his good-morning messages were…what? Taunts, in a way. Teases to let her know he wasn't letting her off the hook.

"Sorry, Antina." Josie shook her head sadly. "But you are not exactly the queen of dating. Trust us on this."

"Fine." To shut them up, she started to text her standard "good morning" reply, reconsidered and typed, I missed you, too.

He immediately replied, which likely showed the twins were right and he'd been watching for it. I'm glad. Misery loves company. I miss yours.

Well you get all three of us tomorrow night. Be prepared for interrogation.

I cannot be broken.

She giggled at that, recalled herself and looked up to see the girls grinning at her.

"God, we're good." Carly touched fingers with Josie, their typical finger flutter finishing in her direction.

"Tina and Ryan, sittin' in a tree," Josie started singing as they headed out the door, Carly enthusiastically joining in.

"Are you two five again?"

"It's just nice to see you happy." They piled into the car, thankfully switching to conversation about the day ahead. And not sniping at each other. Miracles did happen.

Was she happier? Certainly relieved to have the crushing weight of money worries lightened. And she felt more alive, the sun brighter, her body still humming with all the varied pleasures Ryan had wreaked upon it. He'd called it cathartic and that seemed to be the case, as if she'd shed the sorrow and anger she'd been carrying. Which clearly had been affecting her nieces, too.

"Wait!" Carly shrieked. "You can't drive right up to the school."

"Did you forget?" Josie met her eyes in the rearview mirror, as it was Carly's turn to ride shotgun.

"No, I'm coming in with you. I'm going to see about volunteering to help with the dance team." Ryan had rebuilt himself from far worse circumstances than she faced. Time to stop moping and do something productive.

"Yes!" Carly pumped her fist in the air.

"Thanks, Antina." Josie, to her surprise, leaned over the seat and kissed her cheek. "You rock."

HE WAS ODDLY nervous. *Be prepared for interrogation*, Celestina had said. When was the last time he was around girls that age? Probably when he himself was twelve. But they were people, right? You talked to them like you would to any person.

More, he wanted the evening to be fun for Celestina, to make everything perfect. While he knew it wasn't reasonable, he had this urge to somehow make up for everything she'd missed, give her things that no one had. So she would recognize how much he could give her.

The fountain in the driveway splashed musically, glinting in the landscape lights and lowering sun. The colors gleamed in jewel tones. He'd forgotten how much difference it made, to have the water going, adding life-giving moisture to the air and all that went with it.

The gate alarm chimed and Celestina's car came around the bend of the house. The moment it stopped, two girls popped out, blond hair shining as they turned in circles, taking everything in. Other than the hair color, they looked uncannily like Celestina—a window into the girl she'd been. One of them fixed on him and gave him a long speculating look, then grinned. Celestina had to call the other away from examining the fountain and herded them both up the steps.

She gave him a wry, amused smile as if they shared a secret. It went through him like an electric shock that she'd never been so unguarded with him, smiling so naturally. Something had changed between them when he wasn't looking. The sex? No. He didn't think so.

"Ryan Black," she said, with a hand on each girl's shoulder, "I'd like you to meet Josie and Carly." She patted each as she spoke their names. Fortunately they wore their hair differently, so he memorized which was which, fairly certain he'd lose points if he mixed them up. They studied him much the way Celestina did, their dark brown eyes large and lustrous like hers, with a similar suspicious glint, that reflexive bracing against more grief.

"Ladies—delightful to welcome you to my home. Happy birthday, Celestina. You look beautiful."

"Why do you call her Celestina?" the one with the shorter curls—Carly—demanded. "Everyone calls her Tina."

"Duh," Josie snorted at her sister. "Because it's more romantic. Remember Dad always called Mom 'Arabella' and no one else did."

"And Celestina is a beautiful name," he told them. "Are yours nicknames?"

"I'm Josefina and she's Carlotta."

"Also beautiful names. Shall I use those instead? Beautiful names for beautiful young ladies."

They both giggled and Celestina laughed lightly. "I warned you he's charming." But she gave him a sideways glance as the girls went inside, exclaiming over the house, as if she weren't quite sure of him.

"Straight through to the pool patio, out the glass doors," he called out to them, then caught her hand, holding it as they followed the girls. "What?"

"Nothing. You put water in the fountain."

"It's a special occasion. I thought it might please you."

"It does," she acknowledged, but a frown lingered around the corners of her eyes.

"Something else," he prodded.

"Just…this is strange. I'm not sure how to do this. Explain to them who you are to me. And everything."

A pang of irritated hurt riffled through him, but he calmed it. "People do this all the time. They date and they meet each other's families."

"Oh yes? How many of the women you've dated—and we'll leave out the peculiarities of our relationship—have had kids?"

"None that I knew of," he admitted. "But I was never serious enough about any of them to find out."

Her easy pace hitched a bit at that, something he noticed mainly in the altered rhythm of her high heels on the tiled floor. She didn't reply to that, just gazed ahead, her expression studiously calm. "Is that what this is about?"

"This?"

"The birthday party thing, meeting the girls." She glanced at him obliquely now. "Are you changing the rules on me?"

"Tweaking. I always reserved the right to tweak the rules."

She looked undecided about that, then her face transformed as they stepped out onto the pool patio, taking on a look of dazzled wonder, exactly as he'd hoped.

He'd pulled out all the stops, and his people had transformed the place into a fantasy land of urns spilling with roses of all colors, intertwined with white fairy lights. Another fountain played in the center of the pool, lit with ever-changing colors and dancing to the music emanating from the various hidden speakers. An arbor, dripping with more potted roses and glittering with lights, held a table set for four. A waiter stood nearby, ready to serve the champagne and caviar, while another brought out a plate of Oysters Rockefeller from the chef in the kitchen.

"You had this catered?" She asked the question in a tone of faint astonishment.

"You didn't think I'd cook, did you?"

"Actually, yes. When you said 'eat by the pool,' I envisioned a barbeque grill and hot dogs."

"I wanted this to be special, but if you'd rather do that, I—"

"No." She shook her head, glossy hair swinging around her jaw. Turning, she put her hands on his chest and rose up to give him a light kiss. "I'm being ungrateful. This is beautiful. Extraordinary. Thank you."

"You're welcome. Happy birthday." He wanted to say more, but the time wasn't right. Not yet.

"Aren't you worried about scarring our young minds?" Carly asked, wrinkling her nose, but avidly interested, he thought.

"You've never seen a man and woman kiss before?" He gave her a mock astonished look and she giggled. "I'm astounded."

"Can we have champagne?" Josie asked her aunt, eyeing the bottle on ice longingly. "Just a taste?"

"I have sparkling cider for them," he told her and Celestina chewed her lip, thinking. It must be difficult for her, deciding not only on her own standards, but thinking about what her late sister would have wanted. A heavy burden she carried.

"A little bit," she decided, then winced slightly at the girls' squeals of delight. "Our parents let Ara and me have wine on special occasions by this age," she told him, sounding a bit defensive.

"You don't have to justify it to me." He signaled the waiter to pour champagne and distributed the crystal flutes. "Tonight is a very special occasion. To Celestina, whose presence on this earth and in our lives is a gift beyond price."

Carly and Josie raised their brows and exchanged a look, while Celestina blushed. The girls clinked glasses and sipped, then whispered to each other.

"Don't whisper in front of people," their aunt told them. "It's rude."

"Okay." Carly's smile brightened and she pinned him with a look of sparkling mischief that reminded him so exactly of Celestina's that he braced himself. "So, are you totally rich or what?"

"Carly!"

The girl gave her aunt a look of wide-eyed innocence that fooled no one. "What? You said not to whisper."

"You have better manners than that." She turned to him, painfully embarrassed. "I'm so sorry."

"Don't be." He put a hand on her back, soothing her. At least here he knew the answers. "Yes, I am totally rich."

"We're totally poor," Josie confided and Celestina groaned under her breath.

"I've been poor," he told them, catching Celestina's surprised glance from the corner of his eye. "Seriously poor. The kind where I didn't have a coat to wear to school in the winter. It sucked. I wanted to make sure never to be that poor again."

The girls exchanged a look, a mix of avid curiosity and guilt on their faces.

"We're not that poor," Josie said.

"We're not poor at all," Celestina corrected. "We get by just fine. We have a place to live and food to eat."

"And you go to an excellent school that is quite expensive," he added, though Celestina narrowed her eyes at him.

"How do you know about that?" Carly frowned.

"Duh, because they talk to each other. It's what you do when you date." Josie gave him a keen look. "You know a lot about us, huh?"

"Some." Boggy ground here. Not, however, unlike dealing with a forthright business associate who wanted to mine him for information.

Josie nodded. "So you know our mother died."

"Yes. I'm very sorry. My mother died when I was young, also. It's a grief that never quite fades."

Celestina shifted under his hand and sipped from her champagne. Likely wondering why he was telling them so much. Things he hadn't told her.

Twin expressions of sorrow dimmed the girls' faces. "Yeah." Carly sighed, darted a glance at her aunt and lifted her chin. "So we want you to know that Antina is all we've got in the world. We won't let you take her away from us."

"Oh my God—Carly!" Celestina gasped.

"He should know." Josie glared at him. "Even if he's rich and we're poor, we have rights, too."

Celestina rubbed her temple. "Okay, I—"

"Everything is all right," he interrupted her. "This is between me and Carlotta and Josefina." In truth, he'd anticipated something like this, knowing Celestina and her pride, along with her warning about the pending interrogation. He'd made several decisions going into this. He looked from one to the other, both clutching their empty flutes, chins lifted in regal defiance. So like their aunt. So easy to see where she'd come from. "I understand that you're a package deal with Celestina. Any decisions she and I make about a future together will absolutely involve you. I promise right now we'll consult with you and take your preferences into account. Is that acceptable?"

"This is not something we need to—"

"No, Celestina. Your nieces asked me and I'm answering."

Josie and Carly leaned their heads together. They touched fingertips, then fluttered their fingers away, like butterflies taking wing.

Celestina gave him a rueful smile. "It's a twin thing."

He could see it, in the way the girls seemed to have a kind of wordless communication, totally in sync with each other. A deeper insight into what Celestina had lost, with the death of her own twin. Amazing she'd held up as well as she had.

"That's acceptable," Carly informed him.

"Good. Then, as this is meant to be a birthday celebration, perhaps it's time for Celestina to open her gift."

CHAPTER TWENTY-EIGHT

E VERYTHING SEEMED TO be moving at extra speed. The girls dropping that bomb on Ryan—who'd responded in a way she had not at all expected. What was he up to? The amazing decorations, the champagne that tasted like scented air, the incredible food.

Everything.

He refilled her flute and pressed it into her hand, brushing her cheek with a kiss. "You're supposed to be having fun."

"I am having fun." She was just totally overwhelmed. Carly and Josie had happily ensconced themselves across the table, digging into the oysters with enthused gusto, their ultimatum forgotten. "Thank you for—" she tipped her head in their direction "—what you said. I guess they needed to hear it. Even if..." She trailed off, not certain how to say "even if everything between us is a sham" without the girls catching on.

"I think it's just as well you didn't finish that sentence." Ryan gave her a serious look. "I meant everything I said. Now—" he raised his voice, "—I know it's Celestina's birthday, but it's also a special occasion of getting to meet you both—so I thought you should have a little something, too."

He handed Carly and Josie gold-foil-wrapped boxes, with silver bows three times the size.

They squealed in delight. "Told you this could be an awesome gig!"

Celestina shook her head in dismay, but let it go, especially as Ryan seemed to be not only unoffended, but amused by the girls' antics. She'd never quite seen Carly and Josie act this way—or not in years. They were wide-eyed with excitement over the fabulous house and everything Ryan had come up with. And maybe even crushing on him a bit.

As for Ryan, he showed a genuine interest in the girls she hadn't anticipated. Oh, she'd known he could break out the charm, but he'd also seemed to know just what to say to them to gain their trust.

She should have known, as he'd done the same with her.

The girls oohed and ahhed as they opened the velvet jewelry boxes, the glittering flash of jewels catching the light. She narrowed her eyes at Ryan and he gave her a cheerful grin, patting her hand, though she hadn't said anything. They were matching earrings, one with pink stones and the other with pale green.

"Steampunk!" Josie exclaimed.

"These are totally cool," Carly agreed in the same breath.

"They're both set with tourmalines," Ryan explained. "I didn't know what colors you liked, but we can swap out the stones for different shades or something else entirely if you prefer."

Steampunk. Of course he'd remember that offhand remark.

The girls briefly discussed trading and Tina held her breath, waiting for the squabble to break out. Finally they decided to have both, each taking one of each color, happily fastening them to their ears where they dangled, delicate brass cogs and clockwork.

"Your turn, Antina." Josie beamed at her.

"Here's yours," Ryan told her, nodding at the remaining package on the table. Also jewelry-sized, but long.

With some trepidation, she took it up, wondering how much he'd spent and firmly setting that thought aside. He watched expectantly, almost boyishly hopeful, so she resolved to act delighted no matter what it was.

As she opened the box, the rainbow glitter of diamonds on black velvet took her breath away. "Oh, Ryan..."

"Don't say I shouldn't have," he warned, but he looked delighted.

She took it out, a tennis bracelet of diamonds set in platinum, a charm shaped like a small fish dangling off of it, with delicately chased script that said *Celestina*.

"Look on the back," he said quietly.

On the back side, in exactly the same script, it said *Arabella*.

For the second time in a few minutes, tears stung her eyes and she blinked them back.

"So you'll always be together." Ryan took it from her and fastened it on her wrist, the diamonds moving sinuously like light on water. "And so you won't be tempted to sell it," he said for her ears alone, making her laugh.

"That is really, really nice," Carly whispered and Josie nodded, looking a little weepy also. Then Josie dug around in her bag.

"We got you something, too. Though it's not anywhere

near as fancy," she said, handing over a shoebox wrapped in what looked like leftover Christmas paper.

Unbearably moved, she held it. Just happy to have something from them. "You guys didn't have to—"

"It's very thoughtful of them," Ryan corrected, slipping the girls a titch more champagne each.

"Not too much—they have school in the morning." But she said the reminder automatically, opening the box and finding the old photograph inside. Her and Ara, posing in their sparkly dance-team outfits, their hair identically long and brilliant carefree smiles on their faces. The twins had found an old frame and decorated it with glitter pen writing that scrolled around the edges, saying CelestinArabella, over and over, with little fishes in between. Just the way they'd written their names when they were girls. "This is amazing," she whispered.

"It was in some of Mom's stuff," Josie explained. "She used to keep it on her dresser."

"I remember—though I forgot all about it."

"We should probably go through the boxes," Carly said. "They're all just sitting in the basement."

"Yes." Tina wiped her tears away, thinking of those stacks of cardboard boxes someone—she couldn't even recall who—had brought over from Ara and Steve's house sometime after the funeral. "It's probably time for that."

"May I?" Ryan asked and she handed him the photo. He studied it. Then shook his head. "I'm not sure which one is you."

"We did that on purpose. Not like these two. Ara and I, we always dressed alike, wore our hair exactly the same. We pretended to be each other all the time." She laughed, feeling some of that old happiness they'd shared. Ara had delighted in tricking people.

"You never fooled us," Carly said, but she sounded uncertain.

"We never tried. You were the only people Ara never wanted to trick. She loved being your mom and she didn't want you for a moment to think anyone but she was your mother." She kind of faltered on that, given how things had worked out. From the owlish looks on the girls' faces, the same thought occurred to them.

Ryan lifted a glass. "A toast then. Happy birthday, Arabella. You were well loved and are fondly remembered."

Grateful for it, for his unexpected sensitivity and ability to say just the right thing, Tina murmured a "Hear, hear" and they all clinked glasses. Ryan suggested they eat, so they did, feasting on fresh lobster and exquisitely tender tournedos of beef. Then the waiter wheeled out a cake with fondant made to look like a streaming fountain—a close replica of the ones she'd designed for Ryan's offices downtown. Funny how she'd almost forgotten how beautiful they were—along with that self she'd been back then, that she'd lost when Linda sent her home. Almost as if she'd been on vacation from her real life.

CELESTINA BLEW OUT the candles and they all ate cake. Then the girls asked if they could swim and, grabbing their backpacks, went to change into their bathing suits.

"You're good with them." Ryan started to pour her some champagne.

She covered her glass with her hand. "No more—I have to drive still."

"I'll have Ernesto take you home. Unless you'd rather I don't know your address."

She tilted her head slightly, as if surprised. "I'm sure you could look it up easily enough."

"Yes, but I haven't." Needing to touch her, he tucked a wing of hair behind her ear. "I don't want anything from you that you haven't freely offered."

"What's all of this about, Ryan?"

"All what?"

"Don't play games. This wasn't for show, to prove anything to the world or keep up appearances."

He bit down on the irritation that kept wanting to rise up. This evening should be perfect for her and he wouldn't spoil it by starting a fight. "Maybe I'm proving something to you."

"What?"

"Myself, perhaps." He held up the champagne bottle in question. Waited. The girls came whooping out of the house and cannonballed into the pool. "Ernesto can bring you in the morning to get your car. You could use the gym here, whatever you like."

With a resigned shake of her head, she held out her glass and let him fill it. "I'm already buzzed, so I'll take that ride home. The girls will be over the moon at the treat."

"Like I said—you're good with them. Good to them. They're lucky to have you."

She gazed out at them splashing around in the pool and he turned his chair to watch also. Where they'd seemed disconcertingly grown up earlier, with their old eyes and party dresses—new, they'd confided with delight—now they looked and sounded like children. The transition from girl to young woman and back left him a little dizzy. Getting to know them and be part of their lives would make for an interesting challenge.

He liked challenges, particularly the ones Celestina brought into his life. One more reason to put the next phase of his plan into motion. *Treat her right.*

"I don't know that they're lucky to have me, but I'm all they've got." Celestina transferred her gaze to him. "It was good of you to put up with the inquisition, especially since we both know this isn't a long-term deal, like they're assuming."

"I don't know that at all. That wasn't in the rules anywhere."

Her lips parted and she looked confused—and maybe a little afraid. "You can't mean that. Don't muddy the waters now."

"They're already muddied. You and I are as muddy as people get. And, as you pointed out, we've been wading around in each other's emotional bogs already." He took her hand, toying with the bracelet. It looked incredible on her, reflective of all her liquid luster. "Maybe that's what I'm trying to prove—that we can have more than the sex and the games. We could have dinners with the girls and tease them about their boyfriends and nag them about their homework."

"What exactly are you suggesting, Ryan?" She didn't sound happy. More…aghast, if anything.

"You all could move in here. There's plenty of room. Sort

of a trial run. Another pilot, of a larger project."

She sat in stunned silence, her mouth opening slightly over words she didn't quite speak. "Um…what?"

"Move in. Then you wouldn't have to go back and forth. It would be more economical, too." There. Very logical and rational.

She shook her head slightly, as if clearing water from her ears, and frowned at him. "You want me to uproot my nieces and move them in here, with the sex room and everything. Upend their lives on a whim."

"It's not a whim." He kept a tight rein on his temper. "I considered all the parameters and I'm confident this can work."

"One of those decisions you made ahead of time."

"Yes. Exactly."

"What other decisions have you made about me, Ryan?" Now *she* sounded pissed. This was not at all going how he anticipated.

"You know, a lot of women would be perfectly happy to move in here and enjoy the money. I have more than enough to share."

"Fine then—go find one of them."

"I want you. Carly and Josie are great. We could make a good home for them. You said your neighborhood is crap. Don't give me the thing about uprooting them—they already go to a private school. All that will change is their address—for the better, I might add—along with plenty of people to look after them and take them where they need to go."

"Ryan." She turned her hand to grip his. "This is an incredible offer, but we barely know each other—"

"That's not true. You know me better than any other person alive. I haven't gotten where I am by being indecisive. I've weighed the odds and our options. This can work."

"The girls, they were on their best behavior tonight, if you can believe that. You have no idea what utter pills they can be, and it will only get worse as they become teenagers. Do you know anything at all about raising kids or having a normal family life?"

That hurt, but he carefully funneled off the rage. "Are you saying that because of what I told you? About my mother and father. What I come from?"

To her credit, she winced, appearing chagrined. "No. God, no. I'm sorry. I meant because you've lived alone all these years. You have your life exactly the way you want it. Having us here would turn everything upside-down. The sex, the elaborate scenarios—we couldn't do that with them in the house."

"I'll remodel so there's nothing to see. We do what we can when they have sleepovers. Lots of mature couples deal with this. I really don't see what the problem is."

She made a sound of frustration. "You can't just make this stuff up as you go along!"

"Why—because *you* had so much practice raising kids before the girls were yours?"

That stopped her, but she only bit down on her retort. "Touché," she admitted. "But I had no choice and you do."

"Isn't this better then—for me to choose to have the girls be part of my life along with you?"

"It's not that easy."

"I'll take parenting classes. I'm good at learning new

things."

"Ryan—" She cut herself off, floundering, and he pressed his advantage.

"Let's ask them. I bet they'd be into moving in here. They can pick their rooms—or I'll have two connected so they can have an adjoining suite. Decorate it however they like."

She choked out a laugh and tossed back her champagne. "You're talking about a commitment of at least six years until they go to college. Longer if they don't."

"I know how to plan long term. Of course they'll go to college—we'll make sure of it. I've committed to projects that took far longer than that."

"People aren't projects, Ryan."

"I disagree—with both you take risks in the hope of greater gain, you live with it day and night, putting energy into seeing it through whether it's going well or not. You don't give up on it. And, if you work at it hard enough, the results can be spectacular."

She stared at him, bemused now. "I must be drunker than I thought because you're actually starting to make sense."

"Good! Then—"

"No, no, no. I am not deciding anything tonight. Maybe not this week or this year. I know you're changing the rules, and in the cold light of day I'll be able to figure out how."

"Okay." He took advantage of her surprise at his easy capitulation by going in for a kiss. "At least you're thinking about it. You won't be able to resist me for long."

"I can resist you," she muttered against his mouth. "When I want to."

"Happy birthday, Celestina."

"Thank you." She pulled back and smiled at him, a real one, full of affection rather than gratitude. All of her annoyance thankfully gone. "It was. For the first time in forever, it seems. So thank you for that."

CHAPTER TWENTY-NINE

THE GIRLS WERE, naturally, beyond thrilled to ride home in the limo. They played with all the buttons, chattered to each other about the evening, the pool and what they should wear to school the next day to show off their new earrings. She'd thought they might plague her with questions about Ryan, but they thankfully left the topic alone.

Which was good because she had no idea what kind of answers she'd give. She couldn't quite account for Ryan's rapid change of intentions. The champagne had been so delicious that she'd had far too much, especially with Ryan forever topping off her glass in his charmingly solicitous way. So, even though she'd stuffed herself to groaning, plenty of the bubbles had gone to her head.

She toyed with the diamond bracelet. Never had she seen anything so lovely, let alone owned it. It had to be worth huge amounts of money. Hundreds of thousands? She had no sense of scale on that sort of thing. And here Ryan just went out and bought it, as he did with everything that took his fancy.

Including me, a little voice whispered.

Because that's what niggled at her. In some ways their arrangement, the electronic buying and selling of sexual favors, had felt more straightforward than this even more outrageous offer of his. What exactly was he purchasing now? If she moved in, she'd be dependent on him not only for shelter but for the girls' happiness, too. She had a responsibility there and moving in with some man she barely knew because he flashed a big wad of cash and some diamonds at her hardly counted as a responsible decision.

So very many ways this could go horribly wrong.

What if they moved in and she and Ryan found they didn't get along—where would she go then? She'd feel trapped into staying, at least until the girls grew up enough to leave home. Of course, that would be true of many people who were financially dependent on their spouses.

But they weren't talking about being spouses, were they? *A trial run.* Of what, exactly? Certainly he hadn't mentioned the M word. Which was a good thing or she might have freaked out entirely. *Don't you want to get married again?* She'd honestly never even contemplated the possibility. Of course, she also hadn't been able to look past scraping together enough money to make the minimum payment on the credit cards and still have food in the house.

She'd absolutely never imagined marrying someone like Ryan. His life was so beyond hers, it would be like a mouse dreaming after an elephant. No—a jungle cat that might find her temporarily tasty and then forget her existence after he swallowed her whole in one greedy bite.

Then again…it might be worth it to give the girls such an amazing leg up in life. Catching her studying them, Josie and Carly sent her sunny smiles, without breaking the flow of their conversation. They were really happy tonight. If Ryan meant it, they'd have every advantage, probably even college, the way he threw money around. He wouldn't want marriage, because of the risk to his financial empire, and she wasn't familiar with the cohabitation laws of California—though all those celebrity stories about palimony indicated the consequences were nearly as dire. They'd sign some kind of contract, like a pre-nup, and she could ask him to promise to support the girls through college.

It would be unforgivably mercenary of her—her parents would be beyond shocked—but she'd already been selling herself, in bits and pieces, each time she let him pay her to devastate her body. Why not just sell him the whole cow?

The girls were worth it. God knew she wouldn't be able to offer them what Ryan could, even if she paid off all the creditors and found another job, a whole other career. In six years' time, she couldn't have made enough headway to pay for college for them, even if they went in-state and took advantage of their residency discount. Something else that had seemed so far down the road she hadn't even considered it.

Ryan definitely had it all over her in long-term planning, not to mention decision-making.

Would it be so terrible? She liked him. More than she'd thought when she agreed to this arrangement. The sex was obviously incredible, even—or maybe especially—the dark kind. He seemed to enjoy spoiling her and she'd never lack for anything.

...a lot of women would be perfectly happy to move in here and enjoy the money.

She could just picture those women. The ones like Sarah

Prescott, angling for the next husband to fund her lifestyle of shopping, lunches and salon visits. Occupying herself with planning parties and charity work. Tina had never wanted to be one of them. She came from hard workers, immigrants who made their own way in the world. Not social climbers. She'd always seen herself as someone who married for love, not money.

Not that *that* had worked out so well.

And that was the crux of it. She'd be making the same mistake again. In the ruins of her heart, she could admit she was falling in love with Ryan, but she couldn't allow herself to continue taking refuge in denial. Ryan didn't love her. She knew that and had to remember it. They'd found some kind of intense connection in the crucible of hot sex. Their intimacy had been created like forced blooms—heat instead of cold carefully applied to bring something into flower that wouldn't have been otherwise. They connected, yes, and knew each other's deep pains, but that wasn't enough to build a commitment on.

Of course, she'd thought she'd loved Noah and married him because of it. So look how great *her* judgment was.

Her phone flashed and a text from Ryan popped up.

Good night, Celestina. Happy birthday dreams.

She texted back, then caught Josie watching her with a little smile. "He's a really nice guy, Antina."

"I'm glad you think so, too."

IN THE BRIGHT light of morning—though miraculously without a hangover—she kicked herself for her own poor planning. Without a car, she couldn't take the girls to school.

She'd definitely lost her head the night before. She was about to ask the girls to text their friends to see if they could get a ride, when Ryan's limo pulled up out front.

Of course he'd think of that and look up what time the twins had to be at school. The man didn't miss a step in organizing everyone's lives. She poured a cup of coffee and took it out to Ernesto.

"The girls will be out in five minutes," she told him when he gratefully accepted it.

"No hurry. I have daughters that age." He grinned at her. "They're never done primping."

"So true. I'm sure I was never that bad." She returned the smile.

"Do you want me to come back immediately to take you to the house, or would you like to call me when you're ready?"

"Oh, just come back immediately. I don't want you waiting on me."

He gave her a wink and another smile. "It's no trouble, Ms. Sala, that's what I do all day. It's my job. A good job, too."

"Ry—Mr. Black pays you well?"

"Best employer ever. Makes sure we all have health insurance. I even have a 401(k)."

Of course he did. The girls came bouncing out of the house and Ernesto handed her back the empty mug. "Thanks. That hit the spot. I'll be back in half an hour then?"

"That works just fine."

She packed a bag with Josie and Carly's shared old iPod, loaded with songs that they "borrowed" from their friends, along with her workout clothes. She might as well try out

Ryan's gym. Her own trial run of what it would be like to be in his house with him off at work and the girls at school. While she waited for Ernesto to return, she checked her email for the first time in a couple of days. To her shock, a firm in New Hampshire had replied to her query, asking for her references and a time to discuss options. Uncertain how she felt about it, she stared at the email, then was spared making a decision when the limo pulled up at the curb outside.

Ernesto put the window down between the front and back, so they chatted on the way. It made Ryan seem more human somehow, that he had people who liked working for him. Apparently he paid everyone well—not just her.

Mrs. Matthews opened the door for her. "Good morning, Ms. Sala," she said, perfectly polite and cheerful, as if she had no idea of Tina's sexual status in the household.

"Hi. I, um, thought I'd use the gym."

Mrs. Matthews tilted her head. "Mr. Black has made it clear his home is yours. You don't answer to me, Ms. Sala. Quite the reverse. Please let me know should you need anything."

With a polite smile and nod, Mrs. Matthews went off to attend to whatever she did. Going up to "her" room, Tina changed into her workout clothes. If they moved in, would she continue to use this as her bedroom? That would be weird, but not as strange as sharing the master suite with Ryan. And then there would be the whole business of explaining the morality of it to the girls. They'd know she was sleeping with him, no matter where she slept.

So many people cohabitated these days that the girls probably wouldn't give it a second thought, but it bugged her that Ara might mind.

Happy birthday, Arabella. You were well loved and are fondly remembered.

Uncanny how Ryan seemed to understand her connection to her late sister—particularly given his own lack of family. His mother dead. That must have happened right before he left his home, got his GED and went to the first college. Where was his father? She mulled over the possibilities as she wandered through the house, taking the time to explore the many rooms, happy to discover the gym on her own.

It was, naturally, state of the art. Ryan did nothing by halves, it seemed. Including her. Something she seemed to be continually cautioning herself about. Getting on the treadmill, she thumbed through the songs and found the soundtrack to *Pitch Perfect*. No surprise on that one. If their school had an a capella group, the twins would be the first in line to sign up. God knew they sang the songs from the movie enough—and sounded pretty decent, too, even with only the two of them. Josie kept talking about starting one. Maybe they should try to make that happen.

She started slowly, walking, then jogging. The boardwalk was prettier, but keeping an even pace on the treadmill was easier. She'd work up to beach jogging again. As a reward for getting back in shape. By the time she got to the Bellas Finals, she felt loose and limber, sweat rolling off of her in a satisfying way. Great to work out in private like this and not worry about being watched. She sang along, amping up her speed, dancing as she ran. When they got to the part about putting their hands up, she did, too. *Love, love you…*

Exhilarated, breathing hard, she slowed to a walk to cool down and pulled out the earbuds. Turning off the treadmill, she stepped off, turned.

Screamed.

Ryan stood leaning against the wall, arms folded, grinning at her.

"You scared me to death!" she scolded him, her heart going faster than it had while running. "What the hell are you doing here?"

His smile only widened. "Enjoying the sights. A whole new side of you. I like it."

Oh God. "I thought I was alone," she muttered. "How long were you watching?"

"Long enough." He pushed off the wall and slid his hands around her waist. "You're a great dancer, even while running. I liked seeing you just having fun, enjoying yourself. I should take you dancing." He snuck a kiss against the side of her neck, even as she tried to push him away.

"I'm all sweaty."

"I like you sweaty." He licked up the line of her throat, making a hmming sound like she tasted delicious. "All salty, hot woman. With roses beneath. And you look amazing in those little shorts."

"You'll get your suit stained."

"God, I hope so."

"I thought you were at the office."

"I ditched." He had a smile in his voice. "I heard you were here and took the chance that you might be able to spend some time with me."

She laughed, shaky from the adrenaline hit and the unaccustomed exercise. That's why her thighs had gone weak. Not Ryan's teeth scraping all the right spots. "Time? Doing what?"

He found her mouth, kissing her with rising hunger that tripped hers up another notch. "Whatever you like. My top choice is sex—it's been days and days without you—but I'll take whatever I can get."

"It's only been three days," she got out before he took her breath away by cupping her breast and thumbing her nipple through her jog bra. "Barely seventy-two hours."

"That's what I said—practically forever."

His hands roamed over her, skilled and seductive, making his top choice rapidly rise on her own charts. With a bit of shock, she realized this was the first time they'd seen each other that hadn't started out as a pre-planned script. How would this work? Would he drag out the tablets and make her agree first— or maybe insist on paying her afterward? If she did move in, would he want to pay her a salary to be available whenever? But no, she'd been the one to insist on trading services. It seemed deeply wrong to continue with this arrangement when she could maybe take that job and make a living honestly. All such a complex muddle.

He raised his head, the glitter of his gray eyes sobering. "What's wrong? You went all tense."

"I'm—I just have a lot on my mind."

"I have a few ideas for what might take your busy mind off your worries." He leaned in and nipped her earlobe, making her groan as the sensation arrowed straight to her groin.

Somehow he always managed to flip a switch deep inside her, turning her into this sexual creature willing to toss all considerations aside, just to be had by him again.

But it wasn't that easy.

Surveying her with a keen expression, he settled his hands back on her waist. "Is this about you moving in?"

How did he do that? She glared at him. "Maybe not everything is about you."

He smiled easily. "Not everything, but this is. Come on, let's talk." He seemed to catch himself. "Unless you want to work out more?"

"No, that's enough for now. I'm out of shape."

His hand passed familiarly over her bottom as he escorted her out of the gym. "You feel like the right shape to me."

"Thank you. But I have this fantasy that I could be like those girls that rollerblade in their bikinis on the boardwalk. They look like gazelles, all graceful and golden."

"Perhaps—but you've watched the nature shows. It never turns out so well for the gazelles."

She had to laugh at that. "An excellent point." He turned down the hall to the master suite. Sex still on the agenda, then? She sighed a little, uncertain how to voice her many concerns without sounding like a crazy woman. Especially when she *was* a crazy woman. He kept going, however, past the big bed and into the bathroom. "What are we doing?"

He raised an eyebrow at her. "I thought you were worried about being sweaty and wanted to take a shower?"

Oh. Oddly disappointed—see? crazy—she turned to the shower. Ryan caught her by the arm, searching her expression.

"Want company?"

She did, but…

"Talk to me, Celestina." He got that stern look that made her insides go more liquid. "I can't read your mind."

Though he sure seemed like he did at times. She sighed and sat on the fainting couch. "I'm not sure of the rules anymore."

He sat beside her, then bent down to unlace his black leather shoes. "What do you want them to be?"

"I don't know," she admitted. "Do you keep paying me for sex? If you show up spontaneously like this, will you decide on the price later and transfer it?"

"I didn't for Sunday morning or last night," he said quietly. "I abided by your wishes."

"I know. I appreciated it."

"But you haven't explained them to me yet."

She made herself look him in the eye. "Because those moments were…special to me."

"They were special to me, too." He stroked her cheek. "And?"

Taking a steadying breath. "Remember when we met for lunch? And we kissed in the car on the way back to your office."

"How could I forget? It's seared in my memory."

"Yeah. It was intense for me, too. And afterwards you paid me."

He regarded her soberly. "Yes."

Nothing more than that. Applying his negotiation skills, neatly putting the conversation back in her lap. "I was really angry at you about that."

Turning slightly on the couch, he faced her. "You never said so."

"I'm saying so now."

"Okay. Care to explain why it made you angry?"

She rubbed her temples, then buried her face in her palms, leaning her elbows on her knees, sorry she'd said anything, feeling ridiculous in her jogging shorts and bra. "I'm not making any sense."

"Then let's keep working at it." His hand soothed down her back. "Let me hazard a guess. Because you felt like what happened in the car was outside the arrangement, that it was about emotion and spontaneity whereas the rest of what we're doing sexually is business. That's why you didn't want me to give you money when we had vanilla sex in the kitchen or for the birthday party."

Sighing into her hands, she nodded. She was an idiot.

"Celestina." He stroked the back of her neck. "You're laboring under a false assumption. I've never paid you for sex. Not once."

She straightened at that, dropping her hands and facing him. "Yes you have—I have the bank account to prove it."

"No." He shook his head slowly. "I gave you money as a gift. Money I wanted to give you anyway. The rest was all a game. A kind of role-playing." *I'm finding that I greatly enjoy the idea that I own you, if only for the few hours you put yourself in my power.*

"But you like it. You said so—that you like the idea of feeling like you own me."

He smiled, feral and sharp, making her heart thud at the

sensual promise. "Oh yes. Yes, I do. The money, however, means nothing to me, other than a means to an end. I'd give whatever you wanted to let me possess you. You fill a hole in me. I'd like to own you and never let you go. And, my precious Celestina, that is *entirely* emotional and nothing to do with business."

As they always seemed to, his words rocked her, touching her primal self, arousing her basest emotions.

"I thought that you were getting a kick out of it, too. But if you aren't, we need to talk about it. This is why you have a safeword."

"I do like it. When I'm in it, but…maybe I overthink things."

"Once it stops being emotional and goes back into the world of the intellect."

"Yeah." She blew out a breath. "How I feel with you doesn't always make rational sense. I'm trying to get better about making responsible decisions, and this aspect of things doesn't fit neatly into any kind of logic."

"Forget logic for the moment," he said softly, pulling her close to brush a kiss to her temple. "Not every part of the human animal fits into a rational model. Maybe it's enough sometimes just to feel."

As always, it felt good to be lulled by his words, seduced into giving herself over to him.

"I think you like being mine," he whispered in her ear, that dark rasp that gutted her. "You love it when I take you over."

Her worries faded like so much mist—just as, a quiet part of her mind pointed out, he'd promised to do for her.

Observing her reaction, he took her wrists in each hand, bracketing them. The gesture melted her further.

God help her, she did. And he knew it.

"Stand and strip for me, Celestina."

CHAPTER THIRTY

T HE EROTIC HAZE pulling a shroud around her mind, she obeyed, stripping out of her running clothes and standing naked before his glittering gaze, remembering to take the pose he'd taught her. Though he was barefoot, he still wore his business suit. In the edges of her vision, he was unknotting his tie, and her breathing accelerated in anticipation.

"Turn around, wrists crossed behind your back."

Going gloriously wet, she obeyed, shuddering as he slid the diamond bracelet out of the way and the silk tie cinched her wrists tightly in place.

"Lay yourself over my lap."

Uncertain, she caught his eye as she turned and he stared her down, the message implicit. She could safeword or she could obey. Restful to obey, to trust that whatever he had in mind to do to her would pleasure them both. Would stop the endless circle of her thoughts.

He helped her into position, so she lay facedown on the fainting couch, the silk cool under her cheek, her bottom high, raised by his muscular thigh at the crease of her hips. Running a hand over her cheeks, much as he had as they walked out of the gym, he made a sound of appreciation. "You have a gorgeous ass, Celestina. Round and firm. It tempts me to all sorts of wicked ideas. I suspect a bit of a spanking will help you let go of your overthinking. Fortunately, I happen to be very interested in applying one."

She moaned and he traced his fingers down her cleft and into her folds. "So very wet. See? No thinking here, just responding." He stroked a finger into her and she wriggled. His other hand clamped on her bound wrists, holding her firmly. "Just so you know, you will not be allowed to orgasm today. I have a plan. A little demonstration. By the way, I assume you're amenable to whatever I decide—within the limits of what you've allowed so far—unless I hear one little word."

He withdrew his fingers and caressed her bottom again, stroking the moisture over her. Then his palm cracked against her skin and she gasped. Another followed, the sting sharper. She flinched, anticipating the next, but he held her in an unbreakable grip, raining a series of smacks that seemed to accelerate and build the pain. Her sharp cries morphed into a series of moans as her skin heated under his hand and the pain inexplicably turned into molten pleasure. Each slap of his hand felt like a stroke on her clit and she found herself grinding her mound against his thigh.

"No, you don't." The stern warning struck her heart and she wanted to plead with him, for something. For mercy. For more. He adjusted the drape of her hips so she couldn't rub against him and she pressed her face against the silk in utter frustration. Humiliating to be spanked like a little girl and yet mind-blowing.

He continued to spank her, lightly for a while, then a series of smacks that broke through the sensual delirium. Her nose and throat clogged with tears and she started sobbing. This time, however, the emotion felt unconnected to anything or anyone. She simply wept. A hapless slave spanked on her master's lap, because he wanted to.

"Better." Ryan's voice came from a distance and he smoothed a hand over her fiery skin. "Your ass is a gorgeous shade, sort of deep rose. You're supple and relaxed, as a good sex slave should be—don't you agree?"

"Yes, Master," she breathed, feeling it in her bones.

"Good. Stand."

He helped her to her feet and led her to a full-length mirror, letting her look at her backside with a hand mirror to see the reflection. Uncertain how to process that vision of herself, the knotted tie around her wrists and her bottom deeply red, she looked away and searched Ryan's face. He ran a hand down her waist and over her hip. "Beautiful," he murmured. "Mine."

Setting the hand mirror aside, he pulled her into his arms, kissing her in his leisurely and thorough way. She gave herself over to it, letting him hold her up and thankfully thinking of nothing at all.

"Time for your shower," he said and spun her around to remove the tie. "Go start it and get in. I'll be right behind you." He smacked her bottom to send her on her way and she yelped at the surprising sting on her sensitized skin.

It felt odd to continue to obey him, even after he'd left the room. To be unfettered and still do what he'd told her to. It was what she would have done anyway, but doing it at his command only deepened the sexual haze. The water hit her skin with a million minute caresses. Almost painful on her swollen breasts and taut nipples. Definitely so on her bottom, as if on a sunburn. Her pussy throbbed with need and she ran her hands over her body, fingers drifting in that direction.

Ryan stepped into the shower, naked and startlingly large in the confined space. He slapped her hands aside. "No."

He fastened a pair of cuffs around her wrists, then looped the chain connecting them above her head to a hook she hadn't noticed before. Dangling there helplessly, she could do nothing but squirm and mewl as he set to vigorously washing her. He used a loofah with rose-scented body wash, scrubbing every inch of her thoroughly, taking the opportunity to tease and torment her at every turn.

Grasping her ankle, he lifted her leg to prop her foot on a ledge inset in the wall, opening her folds to his gaze as he knelt at her feet and washed his way up her thighs. Enough sense parted the haze for her to say "Angel" for the first time. Another test.

Looking up in polite inquiry, he raised his eyebrows. "We need to stop?"

"No…just—no body wash in there, please. I'm sensitive to it. Or on my face."

He looked amused but set down the loofah and rinsed his hands. "All right. Is that all?"

"Yes."

"So, where don't you want me to put the body wash?"

"Down there."

"I'm not sure what you mean. Give it a name."

She tugged on the restraints enough that he put a hand on her ankle to hold her in place. His other hand parted her slippery folds, fingers stroking. "Here?"

"Yes."

"What's it called?"

Her face burned with embarrassment, absurdly given her current position and what had transpired thus far. "My...vagina."

"Nice, but a little clinical."

"My pussy." She felt naughty saying it and Ryan knew it, smile going wicked.

"Ask me to lick your pussy."

"Oh, Ryan..."

He slapped the side of her thigh. "Who am I?"

"Master!"

"Exactly. Do as I told you."

"Please lick my...pussy. Master."

Leaning closer, he opened her folds and breathed on her clit. The warm water from the several shower heads ran over the sensitized skin. "Ask me again. Politely."

She groaned, unable to tear her gaze away. "Would you please lick my pussy, Master?"

He smiled at her, cat in cream. "No." Taking up the loofah, he set her foot down, and turned her, so he could scrub her back. She fumed, feeling the ache of denial and his teasing games. He shampooed her hair, actually quite good at it, doing it twice and rinsing between.

"Foot back on the ledge as before," he instructed, then thoroughly soaped her bottom, scrubbing harder than he needed to over her tender flesh, holding her tight so she couldn't pull away. As he washed her, he explored her, fingers drifting over her anus. "You keep bypassing options for this. Have you ever?"

Moaning, she shook her head and pushed against his hand, tempted to tell him to do it now, if he'd let her come. He laughed and took his fingers away.

"Not until you opt in, but I suspect I'm wearing you down. Soon enough."

The crinkle of a condom wrapper warned her, then the broad head of his cock nudged her slick channel. "Instead I'll take my pleasure here." He used his polite and charming voice—the cultured tones taught by a tutor—pressing into her easily with her so open to him. Holding her hips, he pumped lazily in and out of her. It hit her that, in this position, she wouldn't be able to come. She growled in frustration, sounding totally unlike herself.

He laughed and slapped the side of her hip, fucking her leisurely. "Ah, my little slave figures it out. Perhaps if you're good, maybe one day I'll let you come."

SHE LOOKED SO sexual, so mind-blowingly gorgeous strung up in his shower, her ass reddened by his hand and thrashing against him, increasingly desperate for the orgasm she'd disdained in the past. He wanted to make the moment last forever, the exquisite clasp of her hot, aroused body. It got to her as he'd hoped, to be fucked without the rise to climax.

Gripping her hips hard, he sought his own, thrusting into her and grunting louder than he might have, to tease her that much more. He finished on a shout that made her groan in despair, then pulled out, ditching the condom and soaping himself off while she hung in the restraints, panting with frustration.

"Put your foot down."

She obeyed and he turned her, meeting her edgy glare. Not at all submissive but absolutely delightful. He kissed her on the forehead and turned off the water. "That was very nice. Wait here."

Pressing her lips together—no doubt containing a smart remark—she stared at him accusingly. He took his time gathering what he needed, letting her stew in her own juices, then returned to towel her off. Nice and slowly, letting her feel every inch of her skin. She wasn't thinking about anything but her need now. That would be the key to getting her to agree to living with him, having her want what he could offer so badly that she couldn't resist. Showing her that they could play these games in the privacy of a shower if need be, and discreetly in other locations, as he planned to demonstrate next.

Once she was dry, he held up what he'd brought in for her, and her eyes widened.

"This was on the list for that first night," he told her conversationally, "but I decided against it then, for various reasons. That said, you never unchecked it, so I consider it fair game." He caught and held her gaze. "After all, I already paid for it."

Her lips parted and she flushed. Yes, she still had an emotional charge about the money. They'd just keep working it until she got it out of her system. He fastened the chastity belt around her waist, adjusting it to fit snugly against the flare of her voluptuous hips, then drew the rigid mesh between her legs and up to lock at the back.

"You'll still be able to use the bathroom, in case you're worried, but nothing will touch this hungry pussy of yours. Not until I decide it's time. Not if you beg me. It won't have anything to do with how good you are or how pitiful. I'll take it off when I feel like it. Understand?"

"Yes, Master." She sounded miserable. And rebellious. Very nice.

He unhooked her and unlocked the cuffs. "I'll get your bag and bring your other clothes—give you some time to explore your new best friend."

Her glare practically lasered the back of his skull, making him more cheerful than ever. An excellent morning's work, all told. She wouldn't be fretting about responsible decisions for the rest of the day. When he returned, wearing a fresh suit, with the bag and clothes she'd left upstairs, she was rubbing lotion into her skin with furious sweeps of her hands. Snatching her clothes from him, she snapped, "You can't be serious about me wearing this thing."

"Dead serious. How does it fit?"

"Perfectly, of course." She fumed at his pleased smile. "What's the point of this?"

He sat on the couch and watched her dress, enjoying particularly when she figured out she wouldn't be able to wear her panties over the device. "The point is always the same, Celestina—pleasure and release."

"Easy for you to say when you got yours."

"True." *Well worth juggling his schedule, too.* "And you'll get yours. Eventually."

She made a growling sound and finished putting on her

clothes, checking in the mirror that the chastity belt didn't make lines under her cotton shorts, then started in on her makeup.

"Why did you use the room upstairs?" he asked. Might as well annoy her thoroughly, since she was already pissed.

Eyeing him in the mirror, she brushed on eye shadow. "That's the room Mrs. Matthews told me I should, that first night."

"Yes, but things have changed since then. You'll share the master suite with me. Leave whatever things you like here."

"All by way of easing me into living with you."

"Whatever works. I like to get my way."

"Pushy as hell," she muttered. But they'd come a long way since her agonized doubts earlier.

"So this is how we'd play it," he told her.

She smoothed on red lipstick and he hardened again already, tempted to order her to her knees to suck him off, just to see it smeared on his shaft. But he needed to get back to the office and he'd given her plenty to stew about for one day.

"What do you mean?"

"If you and the girls moved in. You asked about that earlier. We'd share this suite, which is quite removed from the rest of the house and soundproof. We could steal moments midday like this, to indulge. Play with toys like the chastity belt and other forms of discreet restraint."

"All the better to drive me crazy?"

He couldn't resist. Going up behind her, he reached around to cup her gorgeous breasts, massaging them through her light T-shirt and bra. Closing her eyes, she shuddered, clutching the vanity table, hot as lava in his hands. He kissed the side of her neck and she moaned, pressing her perfect round ass into his groin. "Yes," he murmured in her ear, the way that seemed to go right through her. He licked the delicate shell of it. "Meet me here later?"

"I...don't know. Depends on what the girls are doing. I'm going to help with dance team practice this afternoon. And Josie has a special art class."

"Oh?" Giving her delicious ass a last pat, he went and sat on the couch again, letting her finish her hair. "That's a new venture, isn't it?"

She shook herself, giving him a long look in the mirror, as if reevaluating him. Good. "Yes. Josie asked me to and, as I have quite a bit of free time these days, I said yes."

"I think that's great. You're obviously a talented dancer and you had all that experience when you were younger. Is that why you're wanting to get in shape?"

She turned and folded her arms. "Is this also how it would be—we engage in conversations about our mundane daily activities as if you didn't just turn me over your knee to spank me and then take your pleasure of me in the shower, making sure I'm so desperate for you that I'm close to begging?"

"How close?"

Her eyes snapped with frustration. "You already told me it wouldn't do any good if I did."

"True, but the idea of you prostrate at my feet, begging for release, is fairly enchanting."

She gazed at him, glossy red lips parted. "You just love to do that, don't you?"

"All part of the ride, my sweet bed slave. Come over later and we can see how far you'll go. Maybe you can persuade me."

Tempted, by the yearning in her eyes. But she shook her head slightly. "I'll see what the girls are up to, but I doubt it."

"If you all lived here, that wouldn't be a problem, I feel compelled to point out."

"But you'd keep me stewing until they were in bed for the night."

He grinned at her. "See? You know the rules just fine." He stood and took her hand, toying with the bracelet. "Sadly, I have to get back to the office. Do you want to ride along and have Ernesto drop you somewhere or will you take your own car?"

"I'll take my own." She followed his gaze to the bracelet. "I meant to ask—I couldn't figure out how to take it off."

He'd wondered when she'd notice that. "You'd have to have a jeweler do it. The clasp is designed to lock once engaged."

She narrowed her eyes. "Is this another of your chains?"

Still holding her hand, he traced the long line of her throat, loving the way her pulse fluttered in the soft blue spot under her jaw. "Yes. Symbolic, of course. I have an idea for a similar necklace, one that you'd wear all the time."

"A collar."

"Well a choker of a single strand of diamonds, but you and I would know what it means." *Mine.*

"You're pushing me awfully hard, Ryan."

He studied her, taking in every flicker of her expression, her body language, her simmering heat making the rich scent of roses fill his brain. "I know I am. But not, I think, more than you can take."

CHAPTER THIRTY-ONE

NOT MORE THAN she could take, indeed.

She wanted to kill him. She also wanted to tie *him* down and ride him until this burning need released. Once she'd realized his plan, to have his way with her and leave her unsatisfied, she'd nearly melted down. And the sight of the chastity belt...

How could she be wearing the damn thing?

Why hadn't she refused?

He was a master of the mind fuck, for sure. Playing into all those nights Noah had left her unsatisfied and putting his own twisted spin on it. Of course, she'd barely been aroused those times and they had never dug into her like this. Impossible that Ryan found exactly the right way to wind her up, screw her and send her away desperate for him. She pressed her fingers against the rigid mesh, wild to get some contact against her clit. To no avail. It curved around her like a guy's athletic cup, stranding her swollen tissues.

If possible, she felt more aroused now than before. If time away from Ryan's teasing touches didn't abate some of this need, she would be crawling back and begging. No doubt exactly what he had in mind.

The idea of you prostrate at my feet, begging for release, is fairly enchanting.

She could see it happening, too. What had happened to her cherished pride?

Shredded by one man's domineering sexual torments.

Focusing on the dance team practice helped distract her for a few hours. Fortunately, as it looked like she wouldn't be able to get away that evening. Angela Atwater certainly was a piece of work and within the first thirty minutes Tina got why the girls didn't love her. Not only had she never been on a dance team, she came from a classical ballet background and held the sport in obvious contempt. They might not be in varsity competitions yet at this grade, but the girls on this team would be woefully unprepared if they wanted to do that in high school. Angie didn't challenge the girls at all and, sadly, the team showed the lack. Tamping down the guilt at how little attention she'd paid to this, too, Tina threw herself into making notes on ideas to both improve the team and work around Angie Atwater.

Because it was the only thing with her, other than her phone, she used the sex tablet to record the information in the notes app. So she saw when Ryan added a new module. Determined to ignore that, she scooted up to the second row of the bleachers, drawing up her knees to keep the screen from view, just in case he decided to say something incriminating.

Sure enough, he sent a message.

Thinking of you. Is it soup yet?

All the need flared to life, instantly, possibly worse than before. Tempting to simply ignore that taunt, but the desire to play his own game and answer immediately for once won out.

Don't bug me—I'm busy.

She pictured his surprise at her rapid response and the way

his eyes would glitter at the challenge in it.

Oh, Celestina. I'm going to enjoy making you pay for that.

Feeling reckless, she replied: Promises promises.

He actually paused, a full minute passing before he answered. Tonight?

Can't. ☹

Ah, well. You know it hurts you far more than it hurts me.

She wanted to kick him for that. Trying to keep her attention on the routine the team fumbled through, with painful lack of coordination, she willed the rising arousal to fade again. After about ten minutes and zero progress on the routine, a new module notification popped up, along with a message.

As promised. Short-term offer. If you accept before midnight, I promise to let you come. If you decline, you'll receive another offer in the morning. No guarantees.

It gave her a shiver of delighted anticipation even as she scowled at the screen. Him and his negotiations. Curiosity raging to know, she still wouldn't look here. Not until she had some privacy. If only to keep her from melting down the bleachers in a puddle.

After supervising Carly's trigonometry homework—like she knew much about *that*—while Josie met with her sculpture project team, she drove the girls home, talking about ideas to improve the team. They enthusiastically offered their suggestions, and the car ride, dinner prep and evening flew by in what ended up being a fun time for all of them. Two nights in a row—a miracle.

Once in bed—with a good hour before her deadline, even with getting home so late—she opened the tablet, her body lighting up to an intense level of desire just at the sight of the screen. Talk about Pavlovian programming. Because she couldn't touch herself where she most wanted to, she rubbed her sore bottom against the sheets, indulging in the extraordinary memory of being draped over Ryan's lap and spanked. Unexpectedly, the sensation on her skin felt nearly as stimulating as touching her clit would be. Combined with the intimate image, the body-sense of being totally under his control, she felt almost as if she could orgasm anyway.

If one of his intents had been to induce her to miss him, to regret their separation, then he'd succeeded brilliantly. If only she could now be retiring to the master suite with him, shivering with excitement over what he might do to her, rather than sitting alone in her empty bed with no surcease in sight.

He hadn't sent any more messages, so she checked the module he'd added last. And moaned quietly at the contents. Upping the ante for sure. Another demonstration of how things could work between them, no doubt. She studied the components. Only one thing she hadn't already granted in the past, just altered—and far more intimidating—circumstances.

Daunting to contemplate, but the lure of the promised release overcame her trepidation. Also, no matter the apparent risk of discovery, she trusted him to take care of her. For all his cruel teasing, he'd set this up entirely to give her greater pleasure. Even as she enjoyed their game of pretending to fight each other, it warmed her that he put so much effort into her sexual fulfillment. That he placed so much focused attention on her. More than just his absorption in the game, on what would get under her skin and control and rock her world.

Even if he didn't love her, he cared enough to pay more

attention to her than Noah had ever mustered. Maybe that would be enough to compensate.

With a thrill of anticipation so intense her finger shook, she accepted the module. Then texted him a good-night. Of course he replied immediately.

Good night Celestina. This is going to be good.

As her mind blurred into sleep, it occurred to her that she hadn't seen any prices on tomorrow's session. Also, dammit, she'd forgotten to reply to that email. She'd have to look again in the morning.

THE GIRLS WERE beside themselves thrilled when Ernesto turned up to give them a ride to school again. Apparently their social stock had risen considerably when he'd dropped them off the day before. Not thrilling that such ostentatious displays of wealth so profoundly affected the adolescent social circles and esteem, but also a fact of life. Go to a fancy school and pay the price—beyond the tuition bill. Another consideration to factor into the decision about moving them all in with Ryan. The wealth could turn her nieces into spoiled snobs. Something her working-class parents would have hated. Maybe Ara, too?

Though she and Ara had always dreamed of being silly rich—they'd just thought they'd make the money themselves.

No time to dwell on it, with Ernesto returning soon to pick her up. Taking the sealed box he'd brought when he picked up the girls, she hurried to prepare herself according to Ryan's instructions. Probably another of his gambits to keep her from worrying about anything except what surprises he might spring on her.

The preparation didn't take much, as she'd already done

her hair and makeup. Opening the box, she scanned the contents, then set about putting everything on. The black lace garter belt fit over her hips, just meeting the edge of the diabolical chastity device, attaching to the nearly transparent black silk stockings with a seam up the back. The bra cupped her breasts, lifting and plumping them, but leaving the nipples bare.

It took her a moment to figure out the nipple clamps. As Ryan had promised, they hurt more than the others. So much so that her eyes watered and she nearly pulled them off again. She could safeword on that part. But, after a few minutes, the sting subsided even as the craving in her groin accelerated. If she could stand it, she wanted the full ride he'd contrived.

The clamps also had the added benefit of having an outer surface like a smooth metal shell. So when she put on the black silk wrap dress, it fit smoothly over her breasts as it never would with her nipples exposed. Crafty of him.

She slipped on the very high heels, gorgeously sexual all on their own, also black with scarlet soles that seemed to hint at what went on under her dress. The limo pulled up to the curb, so she grabbed her bag and tablet, locked up and went out to meet the car, hoping none of her inner turmoil showed on her face. Ernesto handed her in with his usual genial smile.

"Mr. Black mentioned you'd be working on your tablet, so I have the window up. Drive should take about twenty minutes. Just use the intercom if you need to stop anywhere."

At least that spared her idle chitchat while she struggled to keep herself from going crazy with need. Taking the remark about the tablet as a hint, she swiped it on and found Ryan had sent a number of pictures for her to look at. As if she needed more stimulation. However, he'd asked her to comment on each, at least a like or dislike. Remembering, she pulled her skirt out from under her, sitting on a hand towel thoughtfully left with the sparkling water and a red rose in full bloom, and dutifully looked through the images.

One showed a woman tied on her hands and knees with legs spread, a jewel-ended plug in her anus and a vivid red handprint on her white skin. It felt like fatally exposing herself, to click the heart on that and others. That he would no doubt keep a record and revisit them with her in person.

Or on her person.

They arrived at Ryan's offices before she knew it. Tucking the hand towel in her bag before Ernesto opened the door, she accepted his hand out and entered the lobby. She hadn't been in the building since they'd finished the project. The glass walls curved around the center courtyard, the pools dry and the fountains still. The shape of water remained, the sense of the concentric circles flowing one into the next, like ripples in a still pond hit by raindrops, but the circles had been filled in with crystalline bright stones and, of course, no fountains splashed. The overall effect had become more like a Japanese Zen garden—surprisingly beautiful and peaceful.

Just not hers anymore.

"Ms. Sala?" An efficient-looking young woman smiled at her. "I'm Anna, Mr. Black's admin. He sent me to escort you up."

"Thank you." The man had a serious thing for having her delivered to him. She followed along with Anna to the high-security elevators. They'd needed the escort years ago, too, when her team worked on the project, so it could be just her that this felt sexual. Somehow the man made every damn thing sexual.

"I understand you designed the water gardens." Anna gave her another friendly smile. "They're so beautiful. I don't know how you can imagine something like that and then make it real."

"They were more beautiful with actual water."

The woman's smile didn't dim. "Yes, they were. When I first started working for Mr. Black, I'd take my lunch out there every day and sit in a new spot. Every one gave me a different feeling, a changed perspective. It still does that, in a different way. You're quite a brilliant artist. I admit when Mr. Black said you were coming by for coffee today, I got all excited to meet you."

It had to be her own excited state that had her hearing the double entendres. Coming for coffee, was she? Interesting.

"Besides," Anna added, "Mr. Black made sure that we maintained the pumps and everything. As soon as the drought ends, we'll remove the rock and refill it."

"What if the drought doesn't end?"

"Everything comes to an end," Anna replied with confidence. "That's the one thing we can count on—change. One thing ends, another begins."

"Very Zen attitude."

Anna laughed. "All that time sitting in your water gardens maybe!"

The elevator reached the top floor and opened into a recep-

UNDER CONTRACT

tion area that Anna led her through. No signing in for this meeting.

"I'm also really happy to see Mr. Black dating someone seriously," Anna confided in a lowered voice. "In the four years I've worked with him, he's never had a woman visit. In fact, I had to run interference on a couple who tried." She rolled her eyes with good humor. "You wouldn't believe how some of these bimbos act when they scent money—worse than sharks on blood. Really nice that he's found someone interested in him for himself, you know?"

She rapped on the double doors of Ryan's office. Waited for his reply, then opened it and gestured Tina in. "Ms. Sala is here to see you."

Ryan rose from behind his glass desk, the Hollywood Hills beyond framing his impressive form. He came around the desk and took her hand, brushing her cheek with a kiss. "You look lovely, Celestina. Thank you, Anna."

"Of course. I'll hold your calls. Nice to meet you, Ms. Sala."

Tina managed to return the sentiment, not easy with Ryan's fingers caressing her wrist and Anna's words ringing in her head. *Really nice that he's found someone interested in him for himself. Worse than sharks on blood.* But she was one of those "bimbos," wasn't she? In it for the money. She turned to Ryan, opening her mouth to say something—she wasn't sure what—but he slid a strong arm around her waist and, giving her no option to resist, pulled her in for a long, completely devastating kiss. He blanked her brain as only he could do, and she found herself clinging to him, desperate for anything he'd give her, nipples throbbing and the rest of her melting rapidly.

Ryan broke the kiss, gazing into her eyes with a ferocity that made her heart hammer. Then he stepped back and slowly untied the sash of her dress, unwrapping her like a present and dropping the silk to the floor.

"So gorgeous. Turn around, palms flat on the door, legs spread," he told her and she obeyed, a fine trembling taking her over. A key snicked in a lock and the chastity belt, thank God, fell away also. He ran light fingers over her swollen pussy and she groaned, pressing her fingers into the wood of the doors. "Not yet," he said. "You have a bit of making up to do. Go bend over my desk."

She did, hoping none of those mirror-windows shining outside meant people looking in to see her stretch herself over Ryan's desk, the nipple shields clinking against the glass. He came around to sit in front of her, coaxing her up onto her elbows, so her breasts hung between her arms heavily, much as she'd been that first time. Drawing something out of his desk, he held it up. With a liquid silver shape, it looked far too big to go where he had planned, and he smiled wickedly when she widened her eyes.

"What? It's smaller than my cock. If you're going to let me have you there, too, then it's best to start preparing you. You want to please me, don't you—make up for your impertinence?"

She did. On a deeply desperate level, she wanted nothing more. She'd yield whatever he wanted. Which might be her ruin. *Don't think. Only respond.* "Yes, Master. Whatever pleases you."

His face softened and he caressed her cheek, kissing her softly. "You are infinitely precious to me, Celestina." His fingers brushed the diamond bracelet possessively, then he rose and moved behind her. She waited as he posed her, pressing her lips against a moan when the cool metal touched her swollen labia. He drew the thing through her folds, gliding slickly, too smooth to give her the orgasm she craved.

"The advantage of having you so deep into your craving," he said in a conversational tone, dipping his fingers into the juices pooled at her vulva and dragging them up, "is that I don't even need lubricant." He braced her hips, holding her tight against the desk, and touched the plug against her anus, pressing. She instinctively tensed and he smacked her smartly on her bottom.

"Don't resist. You can't anyway, so give it up. I'll get this into you one way or another, even if that means spanking you into exhaustion first." His thug voice. The one that inexplicably gutted her. She sobbed a little, overcome, dropped her head and did her best to yield.

"Much better. See how easy it is when you just give in?" The thing widened her unbearably, not quite painful but dreadfully invasive. It slid into her, then settled with a *pop.* "Beautiful. You're a natural." He patted her hip where he'd smacked her, stroking the hot skin, making her wonder if he'd left a handprint as there'd been in the image she'd liked. Already getting her in trouble. More trouble.

"Over to the conference table."

He didn't help her stand, letting her adjust to the plug holding her open. Thighs wobbly from the intense arousal, emotional and physical, she walked to the table, profoundly aware of how her hips swung in the high heels. She remembered it, that smooth black table, from their meetings on the project. Ryan pulled away a chair and had her sit on the edge. Instead of instructing her, he lifted her hands and put them behind her neck, then spread her knees widely. Naked except for the heels, stockings, garter and barely there bra, she held as still as she could for his inspection.

"Do you remember sitting at this table, all those years ago? You always called me Mr. Black, even after months of working together."

She took the cue. "Yes, Mr. Black."

He fondled her breast, the caress stretching into her clamped nipple. "I thought about you like this, more than once. Even though you were a married woman and off-limits. But you never knew, did you?"

"No," she breathed. He'd always seemed so remote then. Powerful and charming. Impossible then to have imagined she'd be like this with him, handing herself over to be his sexual plaything. That she'd love it so much.

"You're going to notice me today, Celestina." He sounded both playful and savagely determined. "First off, these offices are reasonably soundproof, but maybe not for loud screaming. Which I plan to make sure you do. So I'm going to gag you." Producing a strip of black silk, he made her open her mouth and take it deep between her teeth. He passed the ends behind her head and tied them inside her mouth at the front.

"Too tight?"

It was tight. More, it shook her to be gagged. *Screaming*.

Her brain scrambled at the loss of control, the helplessness.

"Celestina?" He lifted her chin, studying her eyes. "Is it too tight?"

With a sighed breath, she stopped fighting it and blinked back the tears that had sprung from nowhere. She shook her head. He folded her thumbs inside her fists. "Keep them like this. If you need me to stop for any reason, open your hands and put out your thumbs. Understand?"

Relieved, she nodded. He brushed her hair back with affection and placed a kiss on her forehead.

"Lie back."

He arranged her on the conference table, with her legs draped over one end and her open pussy and bottom hanging just over the edge. One of his favorite ways to have her. He tied her legs in place, then stretched her hands over her head, palms up, wrists together.

"Time to pay up, my saucy slave. Let's see how busy you are now."

CHAPTER THIRTY-TWO

NOTHING LIKE REALIZING a long-cherished fantasy—and with the woman of his dreams, to boot.

He'd tried to keep his mind off of it back then. Women had a way of sensing prurient thoughts and he never wanted any woman working with him to feel uncomfortable or threatened. Something else he'd promised to his mother, though not until after she'd passed. A way of making things up to her in retrospect.

But Celestina had turned his head—and best intentions— even then, and more than once he'd fantasized about stripping her out of her pretty dresses, making her take down that gloriously thick hair, and stretching her out on the conference table like this. Okay, maybe the darker scenarios included their colleagues watching him torment and plunder her lush body as she struggled and couldn't help crying out in her pleasure, the audience heightening her distress. She wasn't ready for that, but maybe someday, under the right conditions.

Maybe she'd grow her hair out for him, too.

It seemed possible, the way she gave herself over so utterly, so acutely involved and responsive to the least thing he suggested. Seeing which images she liked had given him great insights—and induced a craving to search out everything that might get under her skin, that she'd revel in as she was now. Fully his in these moments.

She moaned against the gag, fully engaged, her mascara wet with unshed tears as she wriggled against the tight ropes. The black lingerie set off her body starkly and she reflexively pumped her hips for him, starving for more. Exactly how he wanted her. In this state, she didn't worry, didn't get that cautious look, like the one that had flashed through her eyes when she first walked into the office. Whatever she'd been about to say, whatever regret or reservation about their relationship she harbored, he didn't want to hear it. In sex they connected, so he'd just wear her down with her own lust until she stopped resisting emotionally and intellectually, too.

He would win her in the end, no matter what it took.

Opening his trousers, he rolled a condom onto the erection that hadn't subsided all morning, it seemed, keenly anticipating Celestina. He slid his cock into her slick channel easily, her long arousal making her completely open. Being careful not to stimulate any points that would put her over the edge yet, he stroked in and out of her, savoring the hot clasp of her muscles and the way she tossed her head in frustration. He could fuck her and leave her wanting again. Tempting to do so, just to see her brilliant temper flare. But he'd promised her a screaming orgasm and he planned to deliver.

He could toy with her tolerance for denial in the future.

Withdrawing—and gratified by her cry of frustrated pro-test—he carefully applied the vibrator clamps to her clit. No good to set her off before he had her where he wanted her. She stilled at the unfamiliar touch, staring up at the ceiling, no doubt wondering what lay in store. He might never be able to hold meetings in his office again, at least not ones he needed to pay attention to, because he'd forever remember her like this.

Once he had the vibrator in place and securely strapped on, he entered her again, holding the control in one hand and one of the nipple clamps with the other. She shuddered, anticipating.

Simultaneously, he yanked off the clamp and flipped the switch to the highest setting. Celestina convulsed, screaming indeed, as her body shot into intense orgasm, bucking against his cock and milking him so hard that he nearly came with her. Holding on to his self-control by the fingernails, he took her tormented nipple into his mouth, sucking hard. She continued to climax, staying at that sustained peak as he'd hoped she might. Keeping her there, he yanked off the other clamp, savoring the sounds of her muffled screams, her body writhing around him, eyes blind with the transporting combination of pain and pleasure.

When she started to come down, he dialed back the intensity of the vibrator, fucking her in earnest, letting himself thrust harder than usual. Her dark eyes found his face and she gazed at him, rapt, her face full of some emotion. He didn't dare hope she loved him, but he did plan for her to fall for him completely someday. To look at him like that when he wasn't inside her, sending her on the best ride imaginable. Long-range plans.

She would be his. Was already. His.

The thought sent him over the edge, the climax driving in deep, wrenching him also. It took him so hard, his legs went weak and he had to brace himself on the conference table, panting for breath. As soon as he could, he grabbed the bandage scissors he'd set nearby, cutting away her gag in case she needed to speak. And for any red marks to fade before she had to leave. Her thumbs remained tucked, so all should be okay with her.

Reluctant to leave her body, he stayed inside her and watched her lick her lipstick-smeared lips. Her eyes found his again. And she smiled. That lovely, sensual smile that was pure Celestina.

"Some lesson," she murmured and he laughed.

Reassured in a way he hadn't known he needed, he withdrew, ditched the condom and set about freeing her. She moaned a little when he helped her sit up, the long sigh of satiation. He brushed her hair back and she tilted her head to look at him. "That was unreal."

"Good." He kissed her, needing to taste her mouth, and she opened to him, hot and sweet, giving him everything he could wish for. At least, of her body. Shaking himself clear of the unaccustomed wistfulness—he had never been one to mope over what he didn't have—he broke the kiss and helped her off the table. "There's a private bathroom there, if you want to clean up."

"Thank you." She walked over to her dress, lush ass framed by the garters, swaying in the heels, impossibly stirring his lust again. Picking it up, along with the purse she'd dropped by the door, she gave him an uncertain look. "Can I, um, take the...thing out?"

Utterly charming, how she went from savagely abandoned

lover to nearly prim. Tempting, too, to make her keep it in. But it had been an intense twenty-four hours for her and she needed a rest. "Go ahead. Rinse it off and leave it in there. I'll take care of it."

She smiled, a bit of wickedness in it. "I did wonder about your cleaning service."

Definitely a downside of office sex, if he didn't want to risk offending Anna or the cleaning service. While Celestina dressed, he set her coffee to brew and set about cleaning up the aftermath of the short, intense session. Her body had left marks on the conference table and his desk, and he was tempted to leave them there, so he could see them and remember the heat of her body and the succor of her embrace. She would be embarrassed though, so he used a damp towel from the bar to wipe them down.

When she emerged, hair and makeup restored to her usual sleek lines, looking cool, composed and regal again—except for the excited flush on her high cheekbones—he handed her the coffee and took up his own. She looked amused. "We're really having coffee?"

He indicated a chair in his sitting area and the low table with a tray of pastries. "If you have time. Anna went to the trouble of going to the bakery for you, so we should probably indulge, if only to preserve the cover story."

"True." She sat, sipped and her gaze sought out the Jura Capresso. "You have another of those fancy machines here?"

"I'm here as much as I'm home, if not more, so why not?"

She took a pastry, her laughing eyes going thoughtful. "How would that work, exactly, if the girls and I moved in with you?"

He tamped down the triumphant glee. They'd moved into negotiating. She had her rhythm of warming to an idea. Just as she had that first day they'd talked, she'd stopped rejecting the concept as a whole and had begun picking apart the details. He was a devil for the details. "How would you want it to work?" He bounced the decision ball back into her court. Frankly, he'd agree to anything to have her there, in his house with him, where she belonged. But he also knew better than to say so. *Don't scare her off when the prize is so near to hand.*

Narrowing her eyes at him, she shook her head, glossy points of hair swinging around her jaw. "No. Don't pull out your negotiating skills. What would I do all day if you're at the office more than your house?"

"Well, first of all, if you were there, I'd have a much greater incentive to be home more, also. But I also assume you would continue to live your life as you wanted to. You might get another job as a landscape designer, or devote yourself to coaching the dance team, if you want to do something new. Or get a new degree, if you like."

"The school wants me to," she said hesitantly, as if she expected him to be uninterested. "Coach the dance team. They'd even pay me. Not much, but a salary."

"That's fantastic! Congratulations. Why didn't you say so?"

"I only got the call this morning and I haven't exactly had the opportunity yet," she replied tartly. But she smiled, clearly happy about it.

"We should celebrate. With the girls, too."

"It's not that big of a deal," she demurred. "But my point

is, that will take up my time."

"So?"

"You wouldn't expect me to be…constantly available or something?"

He set down his coffee. "Celestina. The sex is one thing. Real life is another. No, I would not expect you to be at my beck and call. It's a house, not a seraglio."

"It made me kind of sad to see my water gardens," she admitted, surprising him by offering him an insight into her thoughts without being badgered into it. "Not only because they're dry. I don't like being this person who doesn't have a real job." Her jaw set as she lifted her chin, daring him to argue the point about her employment.

"You're hardly that person. You've been unemployed for barely two weeks and you've already found something new. In the current market, the typical person is out of work for an average of eight months before finding a new job."

Her full mouth twitched. "You just know that statistic off the top of your head."

Picking up his coffee again, he couldn't decide if her wry amusement at his expense charmed or left him chagrined. "It's not a number that changes dramatically—usually around thirty to thirty-six weeks."

"How do people do it—that long without a salary?"

"It's hard. But you don't have that pressure, not if you don't want to. I'm more than happy to support you and the girls however you choose."

She assessed him, considering. "You disappeared the prices from the tablet."

Ah. He'd wondered if she'd noticed. "Yes."

"Why?"

Learning from him, bouncing the responsibility for speaking right back at him. He sighed and held out his hand, worried when she hesitated, gratified when she scooted up in her chair to take it. "I don't want the money to come between us. I transferred a million to your account this morning."

Her lips parted and she paled. "You can't just give me a million dollars!"

He went for boyishly charming. "Sure I can. As long as I keep track of the zeros, I'm fine. That should be more than enough to pay all of your bills and keep you going for a while, even if you don't move in."

"But..." She shook her head slightly, as if trying to clear it, then squeezed his hand. "I'm grateful, of course, but I can't accept it."

"You don't have to. The money is already in your account. Done deal."

"Ryan." She sat forward more, a resolved look in her eye. "I don't want to be that person either—the woman who's with you for the money."

A funny pain settled in his gut. "Is that the only reason you're with me, still?"

"No. I mean—I don't know! It seems hard for me to know much of anything these days. Half the time I still feel like I've only just awakened from a long sleep." She raked her hand through her hair, then gave him a long, penetrating look. "Why did you decide to transfer that money?"

"Because I didn't want that to be a factor in whether you

JEFFE KENNEDY

decided to move in or not," he surprised himself by admitting. An instinctive choice. Sometimes a bald, honest statement would move a negotiation to the final phase faster than anything else. "Now you have enough money to stay where you are. If you decide to move in with me, it will be because you want to. No other reason."

"Besides that *you* want me to." She wrinkled her nose at him, but squeezed his hand.

He let out a breath, that she'd relaxed enough to tease him about his high-handed ways. Dropping his head, he pressed his forehead against her hand. "I know I'm pushy, Celestina. Particularly when I want something badly. Fortunately you're good at pushing back."

She ran a hand through his hair, soothing and maybe even affectionate. "Except when I submit and let you take over entirely."

He lifted his head and smiled at her, feeling wolfish. Pressing a kiss against her hand, he admitted, "I do like that part."

Laughing sensuously, she cupped his cheek with her other hand and leaned in to kiss him. "I like it, too. I'm not even questioning why anymore, but—being with you is…amazing."

Not what she'd been thinking when she started the sentence, but he'd take it. "It's amazing for me, too." He searched her face. "What else are you thinking about?"

She sighed, throwing up a hand. "I don't know why you even ask when you can clearly read my mind."

"Only that there's something, not what it is."

Taking a deep breath, she sipped her coffee, then held it in her lap, studying it. "I might have a chance at a landscape design job."

342

A chill of foreboding ran down his spine. "Here?"

"No." She met his gaze. "New Hampshire."

"Are you considering taking it?" he made himself ask neutrally.

She shrugged and laughed, self-conscious. "All I've done is send my references. But…the girls won't want to move and—I'm not sure I want to either."

Part of him unclenched in relief. "Good. Because I want you to stay. You have the money you need. Don't make any hasty decisions."

"Not even to move in with you?" she teased him.

"That one you should make immediately." He grinned at her, beyond glad that she seemed to have discarded the idea of the other job so easily. "I have a benefit to attend tomorrow night—would you go with me?"

"I don't know what the girls will be up to."

"I thought you could bring them over. They could watch movies in the theater or swim. Mrs. Matthews could keep an eye on them."

She considered, nodded. "Okay. That would be fun." Raising her eyebrows, she asked, "Any games?"

He allowed himself a wolfish grin. "We can negotiate."

She laughed. "I can't wait to see this one."

"Excellent." He glanced at his watch. "Unfortunately I have a meeting in a few minutes that I probably shouldn't cancel." Again. Since he'd canceled it already yesterday to take the chance to go home and see her.

"That's my cue to go then." She drank down the rest of her coffee and stood, smoothing the dress, casting a rueful glance at the way her nipples stood out against the silk. Catching him grinning at her, she scowled. "I should have put a regular backup bra in my bag for the ride home."

Delighted with her, giddy with the prospect that she might unbend on moving in, he pulled her close and kissed her, careful this time not to smudge her fresh lipstick. "Eh—fuck 'em if they can't take a joke."

She smiled, warm and radiant. "My dad used to say that."

"A wise man."

"Yes." She gathered her things, waited while he unlocked the door for her, considering him. "You know, I think he would have liked you."

"I'm flattered." More than she knew. It filled him with a strange emotion, to think of this man who might have been his father-in-law, approving of him. Trusting his daughter and grandchildren with him. Mentally, he added the man to the shelf with his mother, as people he needed to remember to honor. "Will I see you this evening? I should be home early— no other plans."

"We'll see how practice goes." She started to go. Turned back. "I'll talk to the girls, about maybe moving in, see what they think."

Words rose in his throat and he choked them back. She wasn't ready for that kind of declaration. Unable to get anything else past it, he gave her a wave and stood there by the open door, like a lovesick fool, just to hear her dulcet voice greet Anna on the way out, thanking her for the breakfast pastries.

He was a lucky son-of-a-bitch, no denying it.

CHAPTER THIRTY-THREE

S HE FELT NEARLY giddy. Between the dean's call offering her the coaching job, the utter release of that mind-blowing session, Ryan's heady charm—not to mention a hit of sugar and caffeine—and the knowledge that she had a million dollars in her bank account, however ill-gotten, she practically danced back through the lobby.

Funny how that thought had hit her, that her hardworking blue-collar father would have liked Ryan. Her dad would have respected him, too, for being a self-made man. For being a good man.

Really, that was all that mattered, wasn't it? Everything else they could solve as it came up. Ryan obviously believed in hard work and rewarding it fairly. They could talk about a deal with the girls where they'd be held to chores and other responsibilities. She could pay off the bills, start fresh and maybe...maybe build something real with Ryan. He might not love her, but he listened to her and treated her with affection. They were sexually compatible—putting it mildly. That was a hell of a lot more than she'd had with Noah those last few years. If ever.

At home, she paid some bills, at least the ones she had handy. Keeping track of all those zeros, indeed! She'd have to dig them all out from their various squirrel-holes. Now that she could pay them, she could bear to open them again. Enough with worrying. Her luck had finally turned and Ryan wanted to help her out. She'd take the help and be happy. And if she could make him happy in return, then that would help make it up to him.

It felt good, too, to have seen her water gardens, however dry, and remember the joy of creating them. It helped, having interest from the New Hampshire firm, knowing that they liked her portfolio. That design sense could be adapted. It didn't *have* to be water. She could respecialize—maybe in xeriscaping, God help her. Suddenly there seemed to be many more possibilities than before.

Angie Atwater had apparently taken the offered out with relief, happy to focus on her ballet students, so running dance team practice was up to Tina. Sticking to the theme of making things fun for people, she had the girls break out their iPods and improvise dance moves to their favorite songs. It worked amazingly well and the team forgot some of the squabbling and even began incorporating pieces into a new routine. A fresh start for them all.

Josie and Carly bounced into the car so psyched about the great practice that they didn't even complain about riding in it. Once she was sure her bills were paid, she'd buy a new car. Nothing showy, but something the girls wouldn't bitch about being seen in. More important, one she wouldn't have to hold her breath every time she turned the ignition, afraid this time it wouldn't start. Of course, if they moved in with Ryan, poor Ernesto would probably get the job of driving the twins hither and yon.

"So, you guys." Tina turned down the radio. "I have something to run by you."

"Are you and Ryan getting married?" Carly nearly shrieked the question. "Can we be bridesmaids?"

Tina nearly choked on her own spit. "No!" She scaled it back. "No," she said more normally. "Marriage is a huge commitment that takes a lot of thought and consideration. I haven't known him anywhere long enough to be thinking about that." Ha-ha—just committing to cohabitation and sexual slavery instead. *No worrying.*

"Then what?" Josie asked, her forehead creasing in a concerned frown. The girls hated change as much as she did, for much the same reasons. All their changes had been bad ones.

She patted Josie's knee. "Nothing bad. And you both get veto power, okay?"

"What is it?" Now Carly looked worried, too.

Probably could have handled this better, but she pushed the guilt aside. "Ryan did invite us to come live with him."

"Us?" Josie repeated. "You mean, we'd live there, too—with you?"

"In Ryan's house?" Carly added on. "The one we went to?"

Tina laughed. "Yes, of course that one." Though, for all she knew, he had others.

"So he would be like our step-uncle," Josie said.

"We would figure out rules of the household we all could live with, but yes. It's his house and we'd have to adapt." *Don't let your mind wander to the rules he'd have just for her.* "But he definitely included you on the deal. He would probably pay for college."

"What's the catch?" Carly sounded suspicious and Tina caught her puzzled expression in the rearview mirror.

"There is no catch." That she knew of. "He likes you two and it's a big house."

"And he's totally into you," Josie said, smiling at her aunt's blush.

"That's probably true," Tina admitted, feeling like she was acknowledging the truth of that to herself for the first time. "And I—I'm really into him. I think that, maybe this could work."

"Would Ernesto take us to school?" Of course the thing Carly most wanted to know.

"Yes, unless I did."

"Could we bring our stuff?" Josie asked.

"Of course! Ryan said you two could have your bedrooms redecorated however you like and he even offered to remodel so you could have adjoining rooms—like your own suite. I was thinking we could keep our house and rent it out. That way we would have a place to go if things didn't work out."

"So…" Josie said slowly, as if trying to work it out. "He'd really do all that for us, because of you?"

"Partly because of me, but also because he likes you two. He would like us to be—" wow, amazing to put it into words "—like a family. I think he's been lonely." Something else they recognized in each other.

"Being lonely sucks," Carly said. "His mom died, just like ours. We understand how that feels. We could keep him company."

That simple sentiment, especially from the usually careless, self-absorbed Carly, made her a little weepy. "Yes, we could. But we don't have to decide right away. Take your time."

"What's to decide?" Josie shrugged. "This is like the prince showing up with the glass slipper, right? Cinderella didn't say, oh, well, gee—lemme think about it."

"We're going to live in a mansion and have our own limo driver." Carly bounced in the backseat. "Wait until I tell Kasey Pearlman. Do you think Ryan would let us have a pool party? Maybe for our birthday?"

She laughed, going from sentimental to giddy again. "I'm pretty sure Ryan would do a great deal to make you guys happy, to make all of us happy. He's a really generous person. I'm very lucky."

Josie gave her a little punch on the arm. "So are we, Antina."

"Lucky!" Carly crowed and started singing the Pharrell Williams "Happy" song, but substituting "lucky" instead. They all chimed in, singing like crazy women.

In that supremely joyful moment, they seemed very much the same thing.

WHEN THEY WALKED in the house, the girls stepped over the mail as usual, tossing down their backpacks and heading to the kitchen, arguing gleefully over how to decorate the new bedrooms they didn't yet have. An angry-looking Certified Letter caught Tina's eye immediately and her happy mood curdled into icy dread. No, *two* of them.

It's okay. Whatever bill it is, I can pay it. The money is there.

With shaking hands, she made herself open the first immediately. No more being in denial. The letter didn't make any sense. She couldn't quite process the sentences. Her eyes kept jumping to words like *audit, penalty, criminal investigation*, as if they stood out in red ink. Sitting down at the kitchen table, because she felt too weak to stand, she forced herself to read it. It still made no sense. She hadn't paid taxes? Yes she had. They went with the mortgage on the house.

Whatever it was, she was clearly screwed and she knew of one person who could help her. Pulling out her phone, she texted Ryan.

Are you busy? Can I come see you?

Not thirty seconds before he replied.

I was hoping you would.

Not for that—I have a problem. I need help.

Want me to come to you, so you don't have to leave the girls?

No questions asked, just the immediate offer. It warmed her heart, even through her panic, that he seemed to be always there for her like this.

No. They'll be okay for a couple of hours. I don't want them to overhear anything.

I'll be waiting at home.

She took a deep steadying breath. Put the letter back in its accusing envelope and put it and its companion into her bag. The other one was probably more of the same.

Getting the girls to agree to make their own dinner and promise to do homework, she told them she had an errand to run and would be back soon. One thing about them being focused on moving, they cheerfully agreed to everything and asked no questions.

Driving to Ryan's, she fought the rush-hour traffic with the radio silent. She wouldn't let herself cry over this. Maybe it was just a blip, or overstated. The creditor letters always did that—made things sound like the end of the world was coming.

When Ryan opened the door as she pulled up, though, a look of concern on his face, the stupid tears spilled over and she ran up the steps into his embrace, burying her face against his shirt.

"Hey," he said, rubbing her back. "Whatever it is, we'll fix it, okay? No reason to cry."

"I'm sorry," she gasped. "I warned you I'm a mess."

"You're not a mess. Come on, let's go sit." With his arm around her, he guided her back to his office. He'd clearly been working, with the computer on and some papers on the desk.

"I interrupted you. I'm—"

"No more sorries. You're a welcome interruption." He handed her a glass of brandy and sat in the chair next to her, where they'd sat that first day she came to negotiate their contract. "Tell me what happened."

Instead, she pulled the certified letters out of her bag and handed them to him wordlessly. He frowned at them, then got up and went around his desk, to sit in the better light. Pulling a pair of glasses out of a drawer, he took out the one she'd opened already. The brass wire-rims should have been too light for his face, but instead they emphasized the strong lines of it. Her brilliant street-fighter.

He looked at her over the top of the glasses. "You haven't paid your taxes in three years?"

"Yes, I have! They go with the mortgage payment. Even I know that much."

"Not your property taxes," he said in a tone of strained patience. "Your income taxes. They say you haven't filed a 1040 since 2011—is that right?"

Her stomach iced, despite the warming brandy. Stupid. Unforgivably stupid. "I don't know, so probably not."

He looked incredulous. "Who doesn't know to pay their goddamn income tax?"

"Someone who never paid her own taxes her whole goddamn life!" she shouted at him, standing up in her fury and crawling shame. She tried to snatch the letter from him, but he whipped it back in time.

"Explain that to me. How could you be so foolish that you never paid income tax?"

"Because I never had an income until after I was married, and Noah always did it, okay? I'm an idiot. There. Are you happy?"

"I never called you an idiot, Celestina."

"Close enough. I'm clearly an idiot for not knowing this. But it's mine to deal with."

"How?" He regarded her calmly, but with a challenge in his gaze. "What's your plan?"

"I don't know. I'll hire somebody to fix it."

"You came to me. I'll handle it."

"I came to you as a friend. Not to have you rescue me from this, too." Not entirely true. He was the obvious choice. But she hated that he'd seen how stupid she'd been.

"What I think we should do is for you to gather all your bills and financial information and let me go through it. That way I can see if there are any other surprises lurking."

"You don't need to control my finances, too."

He took a long breath, which did little to smooth the annoyed lines around his mouth. "I'm not trying to control you or your finances—I'm trying to help you. Obviously you need it."

"I'm not helpless."

"In some arenas, you come pretty damn close. That's why you like submitting to me, because I handle things for you. You need that from me."

"Fuck you for saying that." She said it softly, but she might as well have slapped him, the way he flinched. Grabbing her bag, she held out a hand. "Give me back my letters."

His jaw set in a stubborn line. "No. Sit down and let me read the other one."

"It probably says the same thing."

He gave her a long, cool look, saying without words that this attitude was what got her into trouble in the first place. All those unopened bills and letters she'd shoved in the filing cabinet. The prospect of handing all of that over to him filled her with shame and dread. How could she possibly let him see just how badly she'd mucked everything up?

"Sit, Celestina," he said more gently. "Drink your brandy."

Her anger draining away, she did, the snifter a warm, smooth weight against her palms. He read the second letter, pulled off his glasses and rubbed his temples with thumb and forefinger. "And this one is my fault."

"What does it say?" She braced herself for the worst. Clearly not the same thing as the other letter.

"It's from your bank. They're questioning the large deposits to your account. It doesn't say directly, but they likely think you're laundering money."

"Like from drugs?"

"Or other illegal activities. This one I have to get my lawyers involved in, as the money came from my accounts and they'll be looking at me, too."

"Oh."

"Don't look so stricken. That's why I have lawyers. I should have realized that moving that kind of money into your account would send up a flag. It wouldn't for the accounts I'm used to dealing with, but yours was…" he trailed off, seeming to realize what he'd said.

"Pitifully small? Yes, I know that. You don't need to protect my feelings."

He folded his hands on the desk, the letters trapped beneath. "I'm sorry for what I said. I didn't mean it like that."

He meant about the submitting, not the size of her account. "Is that what you think of me? That I'm just some helpless female who needs you to take care of her?" It rankled badly, that he seemed to be so capable, so proficient at dealing with everything, and she'd so far been only good at playing sex slave. Or not even playing at it, but being that. Taken care of. *You need that from me.*

"I don't think you're helpless at all, but yes—I think, in this way, you do need me. Is that such a terrible thing?"

She didn't know. Maybe. She'd always thought of herself as a capable woman. Smart. Educated. She had a Masters in landscape design, after all. *Who doesn't know to pay their goddamn income tax?*

"Celestina?"

"I don't know, okay?" She stood again and picked up her bag. "I should get back to the girls."

He got up and put his hands on her shoulders. "I don't like leaving things between us this way."

"I just need some time. To think. Thank you for helping me with this." She lifted her chin. "I'm grateful." She said it because it would prick at him and it did, the annoyance settling in the lines around his mouth.

"All right. Go think. Are you okay to drive home?"

"I'm capable of driving a car, Ryan."

His jaw flexed. "That's not what I meant and you know it. You're obviously upset. Ernesto can—"

"I'm fine. Thank you."

"I'll see you tomorrow night then, if I don't talk you before."

Tomorrow night? Oh, the benefit. "I don't know if—"

"If you intend to keep your promise to go with me?"

Her turn to set her jaw. He would phrase it like that. "I'll keep my damn promise."

He smiled, though he didn't look happy. But he kissed her cheek and let her go. "Good night, Celestina. Sweet dreams."

Unable to muster a reply, she turned and left. Realizing as she got in the car that he hadn't walked her out.

CHAPTER THIRTY-FOUR

F OR A WHILE after Celestina left, Ryan sat at his desk and brooded. He reread the letters, shaking his head at both her foolishness and his own, then made some notes for his CPA and lawyer to look into first thing in the morning. It might take some doing, but they'd get it cleaned up.

Fixing things with Celestina might not be as easy.

She hadn't been happy with him when she left, that much was obvious. It seemed clear that he'd handled things incorrectly, but he wasn't sure how. She'd acted like he'd betrayed her trust somehow when all he'd done was offer to fix the problem. She'd brought it to him to fix, hadn't she? Ridiculous that she had looked at him with that wounded pride. Okay, he shouldn't have said that about her needing him to handle things for her, about her liking that. It might be true—he certainly wanted it to be true, that she at least needed and craved what he could give her, even if she didn't love him yet—but she hadn't liked hearing it.

What did he know about having a long-term relationship? His parents had been lousy examples. If he was honest with himself, as he should be if he wanted this thing with Celestina to work, he'd kept clear of all but the most shallow encounters for precisely this reason. Once the relationship progressed beyond casual fun and intense sex, he floundered. He lacked the skills and he needed to shore that up fast.

Clearly he was out of his depth. Any other time he had a problem he'd consult with an expert. But who could advise him on the twisted channels of a woman's heart?

Maybe another woman.

Picking up his phone, he hit the speed dial. Cat answered on the second ring.

"Hey, boss! How are those tablets working for you?"

The question of the hour, though not in the way she meant. "Fine. Perfect. I'm not calling about that." *Not exactly.*

"Shoot."

Now that he had her on the phone, he felt like an idiot. But Cat was a woman and she understood how he thought, so he'd followed the impulse. "Can I ask you a question? About women?"

The pause stretched out long and inauspicious. "You're asking me about your love life?"

"You're right. It's inappropriate. I'm sorry I bothered you."

"No, no—that's okay. Just color me surprised. I happen to be a woman, so I might know the answer. What's the question?"

"Hypothetical situation. A woman is upset and comes to her...boyfriend—" what an empty word, he needed a better one "—with a problem."

"What's the problem?"

"I'm not sure it's relevant, but let's say she made a big mistake, a foolish one, and he offers to fix it for her. But she gets mad at him."

"Uh-huh. Did this guy in any way imply that her big mistake was foolish?"

He rubbed his temples. "Yeah, he probably did."

Cat whistled, like a bomb dropping. "Guy is fucked then."

His heart sank. "Seriously?"

Cat's laugh rang through the connection. "Okay, okay—that was mean. Your hypothetical guy made several classically male errors. First of all, your boss can tell you that the mistake you made was foolish, but your boyfriend can't. Secondly, when a woman is upset, she wants comfort and sympathy, not to have the problem fixed."

"But she came to me to fix the problem."

"Of course she did. And I'm sure you will, as you're Mr. Fix-It. But what a woman wants most from the man she loves is for him to give her comfort. To tell her that she's not an idiot. To understand and forgive her when maybe it's hard for her to forgive herself."

Well, not love in this case. He didn't fool himself about that. But the principle still applied. "That hadn't occurred to me."

"She came to you first, right? All upset, you said?"

With tears streaming down her face, holding on to him with a total lack of reserve, as she hadn't before outside of sex. He was an idiot indeed. "Yes. She cried."

"Okay, the good news is she turned to you, so she trusts you. You probably just destabilized that trust a little. Maybe pissed her off."

"Yeah, she left angry."

"So, give her some time to stew and be angry. Meanwhile

you do your Mr. Fix-It thing and then you grovel."

"Excuse me?"

Cat's laugh came through almost as an evil cackle. "Yeah, probably not your forte. But it's what she needs. Tell her you know you screwed up, that you're sorry and you want to make it up to her."

"I should buy her something."

She paused. "I don't know her, but I advise against it."

"Why?"

"Okay—you're my boss. I need some kind of permission to speak freely here."

"You always can, Cat. You should know that."

"About work, sure. This is dicier territory. Personal." She heaved out a sigh. "So, you're a generous guy and God knows you're loaded, but you tend to use money to interact with people."

"I don't understand what you mean."

"Like instead of talking to me about what a good job I've done, you pay me double and give me perks."

"And this is a problem?"

"I was afraid that would piss you off. Let me make it clear—it's totally not a problem for me, because I work for you. You pay me to do my job and, sure, I'll happily take whatever bonuses you toss my way. That's how our relationship works. But with your girlfriend, it's a different dynamic. She does not work for you. If she really cares about you, which I'm hoping is the case because you should dump her otherwise, she's not in it for the money. Don't let making things right with her be about the money."

He wasn't sure about that. What else would she be in it for? Perhaps for the sex. He harbored no illusions otherwise. He'd learned to crush his own idealism and denial first and foremost. Too easy to let those get in the way of a more realistic goal. But he'd asked for expert advice and the principal rule of that was considering the answer carefully, no matter his own knee-jerk response. "What do I make it be about then?"

"The lurv, Boss. Give her that sweet, sweet lurv. It's all any of us really want. Also? In the end, keep in mind that she's a person just like you are. Don't worry about how a woman thinks. Figure how you'd want to be treated if you fucked up because you were foolish. Operate from there."

ERNESTO PICKED THE three of them up, the girls cheerfully greeting him by name. How quickly they'd fallen into a familiar routine of being chauffeured about. Tina hadn't said anything to them about the possible job or her second thoughts on moving in with Ryan. Probably fifth and sixth thoughts by this point. She'd known he wasn't Mr. Sensitivity, had gone into this with her eyes open, that though they shared an intense emotional connection, it had never been about...whatever she'd hoped for from him the night before.

Really, it was her fault for expecting otherwise.

Still, the argument with him, the way they'd left things, reminded her acutely of being married to Noah. Especially in those later years, when he grew more distant, uninterested in her woes—or anything she said at all. She'd learned to keep things to herself rather than facing his indifference.

She didn't think she could do that again. It had seemed

possible, that the riches and easy life Ryan offered, along with everything else, would compensate for his emotional shortcomings. That going in with her eyes open, knowing exactly what he offered and what he wanted from her, would keep her expectations under control. Clearly it hadn't worked that way. She'd unthinkingly run to him last night, expecting some of the same understanding comfort he showered on her when she broke down in scenes.

Foolish of her. As she'd been in so many things. Ryan had been right to call her on that.

The thing was, if she moved in with him, buried her pride and handed over the monumental mess of her finances, which would include everything from Ara and her parents, too—something they all would have hated, even if the dead can't feel shame—then Ryan would be handling things for her. She wouldn't learn to do things better. She'd be selling herself, after all. Giving herself to him in exchange for security and blissful ignorance. And she knew from experience that nothing had ever made her feel lonelier than being married to someone who didn't really respect her. Not even being alone.

She should have realized that by now. Noah hadn't left because of the girls or her grief over Ara. That had been a convenient excuse. He'd wanted out and took the opportunity. Something else she should have extracted a lesson from, if she was ever to grow up and be an adult in charge of her own life.

The adult, the honorable and independent decision would be to do whatever it took to land that job and start their lives over.

"You look really pretty, Antina," Josie said. Her voice held a bit of a question, sensing some of Tina's unhappiness.

Don't people freeze to death there?

"Thank you, sweetie." She'd checked the tablet, but Ryan hadn't added anything for the evening ahead. No salacious offers or instructions on how to dress. He might be pissed at her still. Or disgusted with her foolishness on the tax thing. She'd finally texted him to ask what she should wear and he simply replied anything cocktail and that he trusted her judgment. The whole exchange had been curiously formal, with none of his usual banter or pushy ways.

It might be a long evening.

She cleared her throat of the nerves. "Don't say anything to Ryan yet, either of you, about moving in, okay?"

Carly went from bouncing to suspicious immediately. "Why not? Did you change your mind?"

"I never made up my mind in the first place. All I did was ask how you two felt about it."

"But you sounded like you wanted to," Josie pointed out.

"I thought I did, but it's not that simple. I need to sort some things out first."

"Like what things?" Carly demanded.

"Grown-up things that are none of your business."

"You guys had a fight, huh?" Josie looked crestfallen. "I figured."

"Mom and Dad fought." Carly nodded at her aunt. "Not like you and Uncle Noah, with the silent-treatment thing, but they'd yell and then make up after."

"Yeah, Mom told me the making up was the best part." Josie snickered.

Tina remembered that, too, Ara praising the virtues of make-up sex as the best way to clear the air after a fight. She and Steve had always enjoyed a much more passionate relationship than Tina and Noah had. More like she had with Ryan—without the contracts and kink. And an actual relationship instead of a business contract.

"Maybe so," she allowed. "I just need time to think."

Judging by the rebellious tilt of Carly's chin, that was not going to happen. Sure enough, as soon as they climbed the steps, Ryan greeting them at the door, she said, "Hi, Ryan! Can we explore the house and pick out our rooms?"

Tina ground her teeth and clamped a hand on Carly's shoulder. "Good evening, Mr. Black. Thank you for inviting us over."

Carly glared at her and Josie actually giggled. Ryan, who'd been watching her intently with some unfathomable emotion behind his steely gaze, broke into a charming smile just for the girls. "I think calling me Ryan is just fine. And yes. Feel free to look around. We might have to do some remodeling, but see what you think."

"Surely they shouldn't have free rein…" She trailed off at Ryan's lifted brows. He'd promised to sanitize and didn't like her thinking he wouldn't have.

"Locked doors are locked for a reason. Anything unlocked is fair game—that reasonable, Carlotta and Josefina?"

They happily agreed and took off, not even bothering to tell her goodbye. Leaving her awkwardly alone with Ryan. If he always knew his decision before he walked in the room, she was his polar opposite—never sure what she'd decide until she was in the moment. Probably what made her a poor planner compared to him.

"How are you doing?" he asked, uncharacteristically tentative.

"Fine. Thanks. How are you?"

"I mean…how are you feeling?" He seemed to be searching for words. "Are you still…unhappy?"

What was this about? "I'm fine. I won't burst into tears and embarrass you at the benefit or anything."

His jaw flexed. "That's not what I meant. It occurred to me that you might rather stay in. We could watch a movie with the girls. I shouldn't have insisted on keeping this date tonight."

"Well, I got all dressed up."

"And you look beautiful."

She knew she didn't. The dark blue cocktail dress had to be ten years old, but it was the only thing she owned that would be fancy enough that he hadn't seen her in. "Thank you."

He was definitely behaving oddly. Not at all his usual charming and arrogantly confident self.

"Well." He offered her his arm. "Shall we go then?"

"All right."

The limo pulled smoothly away. Ryan poured her a glass of Spanish wine without asking and offered it to her, pouring another for himself. The silence stretched out a little too long. Maybe she should have taken him up on the offer to stay in and watch a movie. At least the girls would have covered the awkwardness with their chatter.

"You should know—" Ryan cleared his throat. "My lawyers and CPA are looking into both issues. We should be able to resolve things reasonably soon. I wouldn't have had time to report the monetary gifts to you, which I would have claimed on my own taxes, so the laundering suspicions should be laid to rest quickly. As for your income tax, my CPA says you are far from the first person to fail to file in the wake of a family's member's passing. She says it's quite common, in fact."

"Ah." She sipped her wine, not sure if that made her feel better, to be offered that excuse.

After she didn't say more, he continued, "I know you feel like it's a capitulation, but I'd like you to consider meeting with her. Take in all the paperwork you can find and let her sort it out. That's her job and she's the best."

Of course—Ryan always employed the best. "I thought you wanted me to give everything to you to handle."

With a bit of a sigh, he took her hand. "I would, if you wanted me to, but maybe it's better if Pam does it. She'll keep your confidence, if that concerns you. She won't share anything with me."

"Was that this Pam's idea?"

"No, mine. I thought about how I'd feel if I made a mistake in the business. I'd trust my lawyer or CPA to know—as they do on this fiasco—but they don't judge and they know what they need to in order to do their jobs. That's why professional confidentiality exists."

"Okay." She let out a breath, feeling slightly less hunted at that prospect. "I'll probably do that. Clearly I'm no good at dealing with this myself."

"You're a landscape designer, an artist, not a tax lawyer or CPA. That's why I surround myself with the best people, so they can help me do the things I'm not good at."

She managed a small smile for that. "I didn't think there was anything you're not good at."

He squeezed her hand, then laced their fingers together and examined them, seemingly fascinated by the interweaving. "I'm not good at this, Celestina." He held up their joined hands in demonstration. "I've never asked a woman to live with me before. Never wanted to. I know I did things wrong last night, but I want to get better. I want this to work between us."

"You didn't do things wrong."

"I did. I was supposed to be sympathetic and comfort you instead of moving immediately to problem-solving."

She nearly laughed, but he was totally in earnest. "Did someone tell you that?"

"Yes." He looked both sheepish and irritated. "I needed expert advice, so I asked a woman who works for me."

Unreal. "You told one of your employees about our fight and she gave you advice on how to talk me out of my tree."

"Yes. Without personal details, of course."

"Did you tell her the bit about me submitting sexually to you, which therefore means that I want you to be my sugar daddy and take care of me for the rest of my life?"

"Of course not!" he bit out. "And that is not what I meant by that ill-advised remark. If I could take it back I would."

"What did you mean by it?"

"That it's okay for you to need me—either sexually or financially. I want to be there for you, Celestina. I *want* you to need me."

Unsure how to process that, she tucked it away to think

about later. With him holding her hand, stroking the back of it with his thumb and idly toying with the diamond bracelet, she found herself falling under his sensual spell. He possessed so much forceful charisma that everything he said seemed true in the moment. Only later did her mind unfog enough to question his assertions.

"It sounds like you talked to the girls about moving in?" He made it a question, though that much had been obvious. She raised her gaze from their joined hands to study his face. He seemed to be deep in thought, turning the bracelet so the diamonds snaked over her skin.

"Last night, before I saw you." When she'd still been on the post-coital high of explosive sex. One of her many, repeated mistakes—making decisions for emotional reasons.

Something she had to change.

"Obviously they're thrilled, dazzled by the money and everything." She took a steadying breath. "But I've decided it's a bad idea. I'll talk to them again and we'll get things figured out. I'll work with your CPA because I clearly need the help desperately. Then I think I should talk to her about filing for bankruptcy and then take this job. I'll find a way to pay you back for everything."

CHAPTER THIRTY-FIVE

"Ah." He didn't look up at her, the wheels in his brain turning with the spin of the bracelet, dazzlingly bright on her dusky gold skin, crossing her fragile blue-veined wrist. She seemed so remote. Not angry with him anymore, but...resigned. Disappointed in him. Planning to run in the opposite direction. For someone who prided himself on seizing opportunities, he'd certainly blown the one she'd handed him. He could have cemented her trust in him and instead he'd shattered it. Maybe forever.

"Did they offer you the job?"

"They want to interview me and it sounds promising. This is the responsible thing to do."

"And staying here with me isn't responsible? You'd rather break up with me?" He'd meant the question as a way of throwing down the gauntlet, setting the stage for turning the negotiations in his favor. Instead of putting him in the position of power, the question made him feel crazily vulnerable. Worse when she didn't immediately deny it.

"Ryan..." She sounded exasperated. Sad. "Let's not kid ourselves. I can't break up with you because we've never had an actual relationship. It's more...severing a contract, right?"

She shifted on the seat, trying to catch his eye, so he made himself look at her. So lushly beautiful. The blue shouldn't have worked on her, but it did, bringing out an unexpected navy sheen in her hair. She wore overstated rhinestone earrings when she should be wearing more diamonds, worthy of her regal bearing and damnable pride. His heart clenched at the sense of impending loss.

"If that's how you feel, why are you here?" His voice came out harsh and she flinched. Cat had been wrong. He should have stuck with money. It had worked in the past with Celestina. It would have worked again. Certainly better than this floundering through showing her understanding.

"I promised," she said softly.

"That's the only reason?"

She pressed her lips together and lowered her eyes slightly. "That and because I thought I should tell you in person."

A bit of a tell there. Something she wasn't saying. Or outright lying about. At the very least, by seeing this through, she'd given him a few more hours to change her mind. He couldn't see himself groveling, but he could work on her insecurity over the finances. Give her the diamond choker he carried in his pocket. Whether she liked it or not, she instinctively responded to him taking charge—he could use that to his advantage, push her into committing to moving in. Use her guilt over disappointing the twins, over moving them across the country, away from their friends.

But that's what he'd been doing all along, his usual manipulations that had brought them to this impasse. He'd lost the game that way and could stand to lose again, only postponed. If she moved away, he might not withstand the blow.

Give her that sweet, sweet lurv. It's all any of us really want.

With nothing left to lose, he decided to give Cat's advice one last go.

They pulled up to the curb, the lights spilling brightly out of the Getty Villa, and he handed Celestina out of the car. She took in the streams of people heading into the building, the other women dressed far more formally, and she frowned, shaking her head slightly. A mistake then, not to have given her better instructions on what to wear. He'd been trying to give her what he'd want—to show her he trusted her judgment, but that, too, had been a mistake.

He was seriously on a roll.

"We don't have to go in," he offered, yet again.

Her dark eyes flashed with wounded pride. "Don't be silly. We've gone to this much effort. Unless you're embarrassed to be seen with me?"

The accusation cut through his self-pity, sparking his own anger. "Don't be ridiculous. You could be wearing a burlap sack and still be ten times more beautiful than any of these women."

She smiled a little, a bare hint of her gloriously radiant one. "That's sweet of you to say."

"I'm not sweet—that's the honest truth. You're the one wanting to break up with me, Celestina. Not the other way around."

Her smile faded and she searched his face uncertainly. Seemed about to say something, then tucked her arm through his. "Let's go in then."

RYAN ESCORTED HER into the gorgeous museum, amid the dazzling women and imposing men, the glittering jewels and expensive scents. He was in a mood, running hot and cold on her. One moment flattering, the next boiling with angry frustration. To be expected, really. He'd been clear from the beginning that he liked to win and she'd foiled him. He seemed so honestly hurt by her decision, however, that she very nearly reneged. Yet again.

Another failing of hers, that she couldn't seem to stick to her resolutions.

Still, so much of that had to do with his devastating effect on her. She'd lied about why she'd come tonight, but it hadn't seemed wise to tell him that she wanted to spend a few more hours with him, store up some memories to last her once she removed herself and the girls from his life. She'd even put condoms in her evening bag, planning to seduce him in the limo on the ride home. One last time to drown herself in his particular erotic magic.

And he was wrong about her wanting to break up with him. She hated making this decision. But she had to start making grown-up choices, which meant looking down the road and predicting outcomes. If she moved in and then had to leave, she might not recover. Her heart, maybe never very strong, had been weakened with Ara's death and Noah's negligence. She needed to get smarter and start guarding it like the fragile thing it was.

Ryan brought her a glass of wine and escorted her around the silent auction, gallantly bidding on the least thing that caught her eye, as if they had a future beyond the evening.

Though the gardens bloomed as ever, the lovely fountains and pools she remembered from visits in happier days all stood dry in obedience to the drought restrictions. As if she needed reminding that things had changed.

She hadn't appreciated the water then, so she made an effort to enjoy these last hours with Ryan. With a possessive hand on the small of her back, he introduced her to his colleagues, acquaintances and business rivals alike with the same pride he'd shown on their first outing.

The women might have looked her over with disdain for her too-poufy dress and costume jewelry—though their gazes fastened with avaricious interest on the tennis bracelet—but the men flirted with her graciously, much more interested in the cleavage the bodice displayed than anything else. One of Ryan's colleagues pulled him aside to discuss a point of business and she found herself temporarily adrift, immediately missing his reassuring presence.

Another good reason to extract herself before she became totally dependent on him.

Unfortunately, the moment also left her without an excuse to sidestep Sarah Prescott, who spotted her and bore down like a competition-seeking missile.

"Christina Sala, right?" She fake-smiled, allowing a look of amused disdain to cross her face as she took in Tina's dress.

Tina didn't bother to correct her as Sarah didn't strike her as someone who wouldn't remember names. Better not to react to the insult. "How nice to see you again, Sarah. Is this party also one of yours?"

Sarah made a moue and shrugged elaborately, almost spilling her champagne. "Caught! You know I love to rope in Ryan and his impressive...bank accounts whenever possible. I was surprised to see you as his plus-one."

"Oh?"

"He rarely brings the same woman twice," she explained, a line forming between her sculpted brows. Her gaze flicked over to where Ryan stood by the bar, that look of wounded longing darkening the pale blue. Then she scanned Tina again, lingering on the diamond bracelet. "Really, I never thought that Ryan would, well—you're not really his type."

"Type?" Tina repeated dumbly.

"*You* know." Sarah gave the words a pointed significance. Just girls sharing secrets, urging Tina to understand. "You're not really from the same worlds. I mean, we couldn't run the city without you people, but..." She trailed off with a rueful smile, shrugging helplessly, the silver straps of her sequined gown nearly sliding off her elegant shoulders. "You know what I mean."

"It's true. The Catalan people have played a pivotal role in world history."

Sarah's smile faded. "Cata—?"

"Barcelona. Between Spain and France? I'd think someone as cultured as you would be familiar."

"Oh! Of course, I adore Barcelona. I just didn't realize." Sarah sipped her champagne and eyed Tina. Clearly reassessing. "I hope I didn't offend you."

She probably meant that in all sincerity. Not the sharpest tool in the shed as her grandmother would have said. Still, the emotions of the sort-of fight with Ryan, her own doubts and restless irritation wouldn't let her drop it. "Why would you think so? Did you imagine calling me Mexican was an insult?"

"No. It's just that—well, your ethnicity doesn't matter, anyway. I feel like I should warn you, so you don't get your heart broken." Sarah's eyes wandered over to Ryan again, her own heartbreak showing clearly. "Better women than you have tried and failed to hook that fish. He won't ever love you. I'm not sure he's capable of it."

"Because he didn't fall for you?"

"Oh, he fell for me, all right. We shared a number of intimate evenings. And will again. He always returns to me."

"But he doesn't love you."

Sarah snapped her attention back to Tina. "Love is an illusion. A game we play with ourselves to justify getting what we want. He might not have fallen for me *yet*, but I've got years invested in him. And I'm a far better choice for a man of his status and lifestyle."

Fury boiled in her veins. Damn Ryan for dragging her into this. She knew perfectly well his social circles weren't hers. One more nail in the coffin of this misguided relationship. If she had moved in with him, this sort of thing would have greeted her at every event he badgered her into attending. It had never been her idea to reach for more than she was.

Sarah emptied her glass and gave Tina a sympathetic smile, daring her to argue the point.

"I'm afraid you're the one to be disappointed, Sarah, if you hoped for drama." She stared the woman down, calling on all her pride to straighten her spine. "I don't care about Ryan any more than he cares about me. I was in it for the money and sex.

You'll be happy to know that, after tonight, that too is over. I'm out of here. You won't have to tolerate my presence again."

With that triumphant response, she turned to make a dramatic exit.

And crashed right into Ryan, fury and devastation in his gaze.

IF HIS BRAINS weren't already leaking out of his ears, they would be in another moment. Sarah widened her eyes in pretend horror and covered her mouth, artfully letting out a sly giggle. "Ryan! What a terrible thing for you to overhear. I'm so, so sorry for you."

"Fuck off, Sarah," he snapped, taking Celestina's arm in a tight grip, preventing her from running as she seemed about to do. She'd paled at the sight of him and the knowledge that he'd overheard her. Halfheartedly, she tried to pull away, but he wouldn't let her. "Come with me." He scanned the ballroom for an exit, dragging her to it and out of the Villa. The walk sign across Pacific Coast Highway caught his eye, a fortuitous happenstance, and they crossed through the headlights of the waiting cars to the beach. The sound of the surf would suffice to cover the shouting argument he intended to have with her.

Enough of this dance. They would have this out once and for all.

She didn't protest or resist as he pulled her along, but her breathing had gone a little ragged. More upset than she let on, with her composed expression and lifted chin. For his part, he worked on channeling his temper.

They reached the sand and she stopped. "I have to take off

my shoes."

He let her pull away, but stayed close, in case she bolted. She read that in his posture, because her dark eyes glittered in the light from the boardwalk. "Are you planning to kill me and dump my body in the ocean?"

"The idea has merits," he tossed back at her. "But no—you yourself said I'm not that person anymore."

She winced. "I'm sorry. I didn't mean it that way."

Taking her arm, forcing himself to be gentler this time, he tugged her out to the sand. "We all say things the wrong way sometimes."

She threw down the shoes and pressed her fingers to her temples. Took a deep breath and folded her arms, staring at him defiantly. "What are we doing out here, Ryan? We're just going to keep digging this hole deeper."

"No—we're going to communicate honestly. Not something that either of us appears to excel at, but by God we are going to have this out. What in three blue hells made you say what you did to Sarah?"

"She pissed me off." Celestina snapped up her chin, daring him to disagree.

"Understandable, but hardly the most politic way to handle her."

"Oh, so sorry! Did I embarrass you in front of your society friends? That's what you get for dragging your blue-collar ethnic whore to the fancy party. Sometimes she piddles on the floor."

"That is such a wrong-headed idea. Don't you ever say anything like that to me again."

"You can't control what I say. Not anymore."

She made him absolutely crazy. With no other outlet, he clenched his fists and turned and roared incoherently at the uncaring surf.

When he turned back to Celestina, she'd taken a step back, watching him with wide, cautious eyes. "Don't look at me like that. I won't hurt you."

"I never thought you would. I'm—" Her voice cracked a little. "I'm just really sorry I upset you this much. I know you like to win and we had great sex, but I don't understand why you can't just let this go. There are other women for you—like Sarah."

"I never wanted Sarah. I want you."

"You slept with her."

He snorted. "Did she say so? She lied to get your goat. I'm surprised you fell for that."

She sagged a little, some of her temper bleeding away. "Ryan—the point is that I don't belong in your world and there are other women who do."

"Is that your problem? Because you know better than anyone that I tricked and scammed my way into this 'world,' even bought my way in. None of those people know what I come from, what I've done. And frankly none of them care. We're not living in feudal Europe. You're ten times classier than the Sarah Prescotts. She doesn't like you because she knows it—and she's jealous of you."

"I don't know why. You and I don't have any kind of real future."

He thought his teeth might crack from clenching his jaw so

hard. "I offered you a future. I offered you any God Almighty thing you want. What do I have to say to get that through your thick skull?" This was the opposite of groveling. Not following advice at all.

Her eyes glistened with unshed tears. "Look. I'm sorry. I'm really so, so sorry that I can't take you up on that offer. Your generosity is amazing and I thought about it. I really did. But I can't do it. I just can't."

"Because of last night? I screw up one fool time and you're ready to cut me loose?"

"No!" She actually stomped her bare foot and put her fists on her hips. "That was not nearly as big a deal as you're making it. It made me stop and think, like I should have been all along. I had a loveless relationship and I won't do it again. With Ara's death and everything that happened, I'd forgotten those years with Noah. But it's coming back now—maybe I have you to thank for waking me up again—and I can't be in that kind of situation again. It nearly broke me before and I'm more fragile now."

He nearly laughed at the thought of her as fragile, particularly at this moment, looking like an enraged Mediterranean sorceress, with the ocean breeze whipping her skirts around her, strands of glossy black hair sticking to her crimson lips.

Show her the lurv.

"Celestina," he sighed her name, searching for the words to convince her. "I know you don't love me. Maybe you never will. I don't delude myself about that. Still, I think I could make you happy. I don't know how to be in a relationship, but I'm willing to learn. Teach me what I need to do so that you feel cared for the way you need to. You know I'm good with long-term projects and I'm a quick study. We haven't known each other that long, but we can't change that if you leave. Please stay. If you can show me how to love you the right way, maybe one day you'll feel about me like I do about you."

She gazed at him, lips parted. Shocked and disbelieving.

"It's not that farfetched," he insisted. "We're good together and not just with the sex—with everything. Love can grow from that."

Holding up a hand, she stopped him. "Are you telling me that you love me?"

"Of course," he said with impatience. "You knew that."

"No." She shook her head slowly. "You never once saw fit to mention that."

"Why the hell would I ask you to move in with me? Why would I share my life, my fortune with you, offer to make your nieces my family, too, if I wasn't wildly in love with you?" He wanted to take her by the shoulders, to force the understanding into her stubborn brain, but he restrained himself. "I'm offering to spend the rest of my life with you, and you think I don't love you?"

"You did not offer the rest of your life."

"Of course I did!"

"No, Ryan. To me the rest of my life means marriage and you never said word one about that."

"I couldn't ask you to marry me—we've only been seeing each other a couple of weeks. Even I know you can't propose to a woman that quickly."

"But you can ask her to move in with you."

"I may have moved up that phase."

She threw her hands up in the air. "I suppose you had all this as milestones in one of your long-term plans. You have a date predicted for the optimal time to propose to me."

That did make him laugh, an odd feeling through the angry tightness of his chest. She at least knew him well. "I thought a year from the day we met by the bear sculpture would be nice. Maybe even in that same spot."

"You are unreal," she breathed. Softly enough that it seemed safe to try to touch her. He moved close enough and she didn't flinch away from him, so he ran his hands down her arms, the gooseflesh bumpy under his caress. Pulling off his dinner jacket, he draped it over her shoulders and held it there.

"I know I'm not good at this, Celestina. But I think I could be. I'll marry you tonight if you want that. Or I can wait. That's why I thought we'd start with you moving in, that maybe you'd get used to me, to being with me, and you might begin to at least care for me. If you never find it in your heart to love me, I'll let you go. I promise. Just give me some time to try."

CHAPTER THIRTY-SIX

TINA'S THOUGHTS WHIRLED and reassembled. Like the spray of a fountain jetting up and falling back into a still pool. All water, just scattered and recombined.

She hadn't seen this. Not at all. And now it seemed so obvious. Ryan wasn't like other men in any other way, so why would he be in this? Him with his fast and decisive plans. His strange past. Maybe he simply didn't know you had to tell people you loved them. Had anyone ever loved him, for him to be so certain she didn't care about him?

"Celestina." He groaned her name, his hands flexing on her shoulders with all that carefully controlled strength and viciously restrained temper. "Throw me a bone here. We don't have to decide anything tonight. Just tell me we're not over. Tell me you won't take that job just yet. If they want you badly enough, they'll wait."

"Can I ask you a question?"

"Anything."

"How did your mother die?"

Old grief creased his brow and he sighed, bending his head to touch his forehead to hers. "Do you have to know?"

"I think so."

He let her go and stepped away, shoving his hands in his

pockets. "My dad killed her."

He pronounced it like "kilt," a hint of that mountain boy he'd been leaking into his speech. She waited for him to go on, but he just stared at her, as if expecting something. So she nodded. "I figured that much. But how did it happen?"

Confusion coursed through his face. "You guessed that?"

"Well, the clues were all there."

"Why didn't you leave when you realized then?"

Her turn to be confused. He was right about one thing— they really sucked at communicating with each other. "Why would I have?"

He bounced on his toes impatiently. "Celestina. My father beat my mother to death. Over long, slow years he wore away at her until she was like a ghost, haunting that hellhole of our house. One day he broke her completely and she died." His voice broke, too, and he pinched at his eyes with one hand, forcing away the tears.

"I'm so sorry," she said, uncertain if she should comfort him, brittle as he looked. "Were you there?"

He barked out a bitter laugh. "No. I was at the library. When I got home—late, because I stayed away as long as I could in those days—she was dead. Lying in a pool of blood in the kitchen. The medical examiner from the city testified that she'd been dead for eight or nine hours."

Testified. "They prosecuted him?"

"Oh yeah. I was their key witness. He got life in prison."

"How old were you?"

He lifted his shoulders. "Thirteen. Did the foster home thing until the trial finished, then got in trouble. Fights. You know the rest."

"Why didn't you tell me this before?"

"I didn't want to scare you off. I thought that, maybe one day, if you came to care for me, I could tell you and you wouldn't judge me or leave me because of it."

That was enough. She went to him and put her arms around his waist. He stayed rigid, hands in pockets, watching her with what could only be suspicion. "Ryan. I would not leave you because your father was a monster."

"He's in me."

"No. You are in you. You're a self-made man, remember? Ryan Black."

He smiled, barely, a wry twist to it. "Didn't have much choice there. After Mama died, there was nothing left of me."

"She'd be so proud of you now." Tears pricked her own eyes.

He moved then, framing her face with his big hands. "Do you think so?" He sounded heartbreakingly hopeful, like the boy he'd been.

"I'm sure of it."

His expression crumpled and a tear leaked from one eye that he didn't seem to notice. "I wasn't there," he said hoarsely, so that she barely heard him over the surf and only because their faces were so close. "I could have been. It was a Saturday, but I stayed at the library all day. I let her down."

"Oh no." The last pieces of her heart shredded. Her same guilt, that she somehow could have saved Ara, if they'd only been together. "No—he might have killed you, too."

"I wasn't big then, but I would have tried. I wanted to kill him. Part of why I got into all those street fights. I figured I'd better learn how, in case he came after me, too."

"Oh, Ryan." She stood up on tiptoe, sliding her hands to the short, prickly hairs on the back of his neck, and reached up to kiss him. "I think she was glad you weren't there. She would have been happy to know that you escaped and were safe."

He stroked her cheek. "Just as Arabella would have wanted you happy. To live the life she didn't get to."

"Maybe so." She tasted salt on her lips, unsure if they were her tears, his, or spray from the ocean. "It's important to me, to do right by her memory."

"I know. Carlotta and Josefina—they remind me of being that age. I mean it when I say I'd like them to have what I didn't. A happy home. Plenty of money."

"Money isn't everything, Ryan."

"No, but it makes things a hell of a lot easier and more fun." He smiled, a hint of his wicked grin. "It let a coal-mine rat like me bag time with the most amazing woman I've ever known." He sobered. "If you say you won't leave me because of that, will you at least give us some time? We can forgo the kinky sex. Or sex at all, if you want. You don't have to move in, but I really want you to. You can teach me what a man is supposed to be like, to have a woman love him."

Apparently her heart hadn't shredded, because it clutched with aching for him. How badly she'd behaved, so wrapped up in her own issues, not realizing how much she'd shut him out, depriving him of the care and understanding he needed. "And you call me foolish," she said, kissing him again.

"I never said I wasn't a fool, but I am an optimist. I have

great hope that you could love me someday."

She bit his lower lip, just hard enough to punish him for his blindness. "You're a fool because you haven't seen I already love you."

His hands stilled on her and he cocked his head, studying her face. "No, you don't."

She burst out laughing. "Wrong response!"

He smiled uncertainly. "I told you I need to be taught."

"True. Let's try this again, with that open and honest communication you dragged us out here to have. Ryan, I love you."

"You don't have to say it now, just because you think I need to hear it."

She heaved out a sigh. "One more time. Ryan, I love you."

This time he caught on, a quirk on his lips. "I love you, Celestina."

"And now you kiss me."

"*That* I know how to do." He kissed her gently, a brush of lips that quickly heated into his trademark devastating technique. She gave herself over to it, head over heels into his erotic spell, letting it go all through her. So much to feel. Maybe her heart wasn't so fragile, because it seemed to be operating just fine—beating strong, hard, full of life.

Not broken at all.

They parted and Ryan brushed her hair back from her face. "Now what? I can call my jeweler and you can choose a ring. Is that what you want?"

"Not yet. We have all the time in the world for that. I'd like to do something else."

"Anything."

"I seem to recall you promising to dance with me."

He grinned. "My pleasure."

They walked back up to the boardwalk, pausing for her to brush the sand off her feet and put the strappy high heels on again. Ryan fingered something in his pocket, eyeing her.

"What?" she asked. "Remember we're both going to be better about saying what we're thinking."

"Okay then. I'd like to give you something. I wasn't sure if I should. I want to, but I don't want you to feel like you have to take it. Or wear it."

"Are you telling me you did *not* make this decision ahead of time?"

His mouth twisted in rueful humor at her teasing. "I didn't. And it's even nighttime. Two broken rules. See what you've done to me?"

"All right. Show me."

He drew the slim jewelry box out of his pocket. Opened it to the fiery stream of diamonds. The choker he'd mentioned. She brushed them with her finger.

"It locks on?"

"Yes."

She studied his face, the wistful yearning in it. "If I wear it, does it make you feel like I'm more fully yours?"

"It would." His voice had gone hoarse again. "But I don't have to have it. Not now, not ever, if you don't want to."

She probably shouldn't be making this decision in the heat of the moment, but she wanted to. Maybe they didn't have all the time in the world. So many people didn't. Ryan's mother.

Her parents. Ara.

And maybe she hadn't been doing all that badly, following the steps that brought her here. Most of all—she really, really didn't want to leave him. Impulsively, she turned, bowing her head and clasping her hands. "Yes, Master," she whispered.

He let out a breath—of tension or relief—and his hands shook slightly as he slid the cool jewels around her throat, snapping the lock into place and kissing the nape of her neck so she shivered. "Mine."

She turned in his arms and pressed her breasts into him, enjoying the slow ache, the burn of lust for him. It meant something to her, too, to feel possessed by him. Maybe even to let him handle some things for her. She'd been without someone to lean on for so long, that she'd convinced herself that was a weakness. But in this moment she felt stronger than ever.

"Ready for dancing?" he asked.

"Yes, I am." They started back to the Villa, glowing with lights. Beautiful even if the fountains were dry. "I'm sorry I was rude to Sarah."

He squeezed her waist. "It makes me feel better, not to be the only one whose temper gets away."

"Far from it."

It made her feel better, too, to be understood.

WHEN THEY GOT home, the girls were wide awake, ensconced in the home theater, on the third movie of a Johnny Depp binge. Naturally, they were also on their phones, texting with their friends. Carly turned around, kneeling up in the cushy seat, and folded her arms across the back. "Can we spend the night? We picked out bedrooms, but we thought we should try them out. Maybe test out a few to figure out which is our favorite."

"Carls!" Josie sent Tina an apologetic smile. "Give Antina a break—she said she hasn't decided."

"But they look all happy again! You said you thought it was a good idea."

Tina glanced up at Ryan, who wore the same hopeful expression as her nieces. "Yes, we can stay the night. And I did decide—we can start the process of moving in. But—" She had to raise her voice over the girls' cheers. "There will be new rules and Ryan gets final word on everything, understand?"

"No," Ryan corrected, caressing the small of her back. "*We* are the final word. We're doing this together."

"Okay." She smiled at him. Josie and Carly exchanged eyerolls and touched their fingers together, giggling as they fluttered them apart.

"Oh!" Carly jumped up, bringing her phone. "I almost forgot to show you this cool thing, Antina." She clicked something and handed it to her aunt.

An article from the *LA Times*. "California drought could end with storms known as atmospheric rivers." Tina squinted at it. "Atmospheric rivers?"

"What are those?" Ryan asked.

"I'll have to read more, but the gist is that they think conditions are right for the winter to bring huge rains. Enough to end the drought."

"Serendipity smiles," he said.

"Pretty cool, huh?" Carly took her phone back. "Then you can design fountains again. That made you happy."

She stroked Carly's shining hair, surprised at her unusual sensitivity. She was growing up. "That did make me happy. But so do you guys." She leaned into Ryan, enjoying his strength and heat. She looked up at him. "All of you do. I think this is going to be good."

Leaving the girls to their movies, she let Ryan take her to bed.

EPILOGUE

The following January

THE RAIN BATTERED hard on the windshield. Once they got out of the car, they'd be drenched. But they'd already lingered at the cathedral, lighting their candles, and now Ryan had driven them out to the beach.

He touched her hand. "Should I come with you or wait here?"

"If we're getting cold and wet, Uncle Ry, you have to also," Carly said.

"That's what family does," Josie agreed.

"You don't have to—" Tina started, but he squeezed her hand.

"I have a letter for Arabella, too," he surprised her by saying.

They all piled out and hurried to the water. Josie and Carly held hands and closed their eyes, then tossed their balled-up letters to their mother in their hands. Tina took a moment longer, thinking of her twin, forever frozen in time. *Love you, Ara.*

Ryan waited for her, while the twins jumped up and down, making shivering noises, then threw in his own letter. As soon as he did, the girls were off, racing each other back to the car. Seizing the moment, she wrapped her arms around him and hugged, reveling in the feel of his strong body.

"I'm glad you didn't mind us doing this, especially in this downpour."

"It's a good ritual. An important one. And I'll never complain about rain again. Did you see the city is lifting restrictions on fountains? It's official."

Giddiness bloomed in her heart despite the cold rain. Or because of it. "Linda called me today with the news. They've already had inquiries. Clients wanting to jump on projects while they can."

"Are you going to work for her again?"

"I'm thinking...No. I want to go into business for myself. If you would help me with the numbers part."

"I can do that." He took her hand. "I would love to do that."

"But I want you to teach me how to do it—no taking over and handling it for me. I need to learn."

"Not even a little bit of handling?"

She couldn't help smiling at that. "A little. Only because I know you won't be able to help yourself."

They walked back to the car, still holding hands.

"Can I ask what you wrote to Ara?"

"I thanked her for being part of your life, for giving us the girls, and told her we think of her daily. And I asked her to look after my mother, if she sees her."

Oh. Tina brushed a tear away, salt lost in the freshwater rain. "I'm sure she would. That's a lovely thing to think of."

"What did you write to her?"

She squeezed his hand. "Stuff about the girls, what they're

up to. That I'm happy and getting engaged in a few weeks."

He smiled down at her. "So sure, are you?"

"I have it on very good authority. Someone promised that and he always keeps his promises."

"Speaking of which, I believe you promised me something for tonight."

The prospect made her blood heat, despite the chill rain. "The girls are spending the night with friends, so you'll be able to have your way with me."

"My favorite thing."

Hers, too.

One thing ends, another begins.

Look for these other books in the Falling Under series by
Jeffe Kennedy
Going Under and *Under Contract*

Available now from Jeffe Kennedy,
Under His Touch

Amber Dolors has it bad for her boss. Tall, dark, and smexy, the man has a way of giving orders that... Well, she just melts inside. Even though he's older and getting involved at work isn't smart, especially in her very first job, Amber can't help fantasizing about the delicious Alec, with his English accent and commanding ways. What if he's the one she's been looking for, the man who can initiate her into those dreamy, sensual games she's only read about?

Alexander Knight has obviously noticed his hot young assistant. Amber is as adorably nubile as she is whip-smart. But he hasn't risen to the peak of his profession by indulging himself. Integrity and self-discipline are what he lives by—and those don't allow for seducing a sweet, young co-worker who's likely far too innocent for him. Still, he can't help fantasizing about what he'd do to her, especially when she bends over his desk just so...

When the simmering, repressed passion between Amber and Alec breaks free, they're both caught up in the tide of long-ing—and in sating their fierce desires. But they can't forget that they're engaged in a dangerous dance, one that can't be kept secret forever.

"4 1/2 stars! Kennedy's novel has all the addictive tension and high-stakes passion that fans crave. Her main couple's interactions are intense from the start, and she doesn't shy away from either realistic details or dreamy fantasies. Best of all, she moves beyond their overwhelming physical passion to the emotions that drive them both, including the achingly real fears that threaten their happiness. As a result, this book is as touching as it is torrid."

~RT Magazine

Read on for an excerpt from Jeffe Kennedy's
Under His Touch

CHAPTER ONE

Amber scratched her temple, but Kiki didn't see the signal. Probably on purpose.

Her roommate and bestie appeared to be wrapped up in her half of the pair of guys currently chatting them up over cocktails in the never-ending quest for sex, romance and happy ever after.

Pretty much in that order—from easy to impossible.

Kiki looked fully into her guy, flirting outrageously, if the vigorous swing of her blunt-cut Bettie Page bob gave any hint. With her black hair and exotically slanted black eyes, Kiki tended to draw attention. Amber often joked that, when she was out with her friend, all the guys made eye contact with her about a foot to the right—or wherever Kiki happened to be standing. Not that Amber couldn't hold her own, but more as girl-next-door than glam.

She tried catching Kiki's eye again as she sipped her second martini, but her friend gave no indication a mutual-bail might be in her future. And their pact prohibited Amber from leaving alone. Too much could happen. She was well and truly stuck.

"So what's it like working on Wall Street?" The guy gave her what he probably thought was a winning smile. What was his name again? Mark. Steve. Dave. Why did they all have to have monosyllabic names?

"Actually, we're in Midtown."

"But is everyone totally ruthless and cutthroat to make money?"

Resigning herself, Amber tried to return the expression and leaned in. "Totally. I carry a shiv to the office."

He didn't quite get the joke and frowned. "Really? I didn't think the neighborhood was that bad."

Kill me now. Bored senseless, she couldn't help toying with him a little. She widened her eyes and twirled a lock of hair around her finger. "Oh, it is! Just last week one of the partners went berserk and attacked her assistant for using the wrong account code. Blood everywhere."

"Wow, really—did you Vine it or anything?" Then he pointed a finger at her, flashing yacht-club white teeth. "A joke, right?"

"Caught me! You're way too clever for me."

He actually puffed up at that and in despair, she elbowed Kiki and scratched her temple pleadingly.

Kiki, with a resigned wrinkle of her nose, made a production of yawning. "I'm beat and I have to be up early. Sorry to break up the fun, but are you ready?"

"Too bad." Amber grabbed her phone case, stuck her sunglasses on her head and shrugged into her coat. "Thanks for the drinks…"

"Greg." Her guy held out his hand and shook hers with a wry smile. "Should I bother asking for your number?"

Ouch. "Well, I—"

Kiki grabbed her arm. "Own it." She lifted a shoulder at

the guys. "Happy hunting, gentlemen."

They made a quick escape, weaving through the busy bar crowded with young execs of all genders, all remarkably the same in their sharp suits and expensive haircuts. Amber sagged dramatically against Kiki. "I so owe you."

"No, you don't. Not this time anyway."

"Color me surprised. I thought you were into yours."

Kiki rolled her eyes. "Works at a bookstore. Makes nothing and wanted to talk about how YA is failing to serve boys. I nearly stabbed him in the eye with my olive pick."

"Did you tell him you're an editorial assistant at the biggest YA publisher in New York?"

She slid a cagey glance at Amber. "No. I went with shampooer at a salon this time. As a test. A regrettable one, as he wasn't worth the lie. At least I discovered I need some realistic details to shore that one up. Do you think most shampooers are working their way up to stylist—or is it a dead-end job?"

"Sounds dead end to me. Why did you stick so long if you weren't into him? I'd been trying to give you the signal for fifteen minutes."

She huffed with impatience. "So you would give yours a chance! He was cute. And into buying and selling, like you are."

"Boring."

"You think they're all boring."

"Because they *are*. White-bread boy with promising career seeking same, but female, for flavorless sex, possible marriage and production of next generation to feed the prep school his entire family graduated from."

"Seeing as how you meet those criteria, I don't think you can cast aspersions."

"But I don't want to. I don't want a Hamptons wedding to a nice guy who comes with a nicely planned life."

"You know, there's nothing wrong with a nice guy."

"Never said there was. I've dated nice guys. It was very nice."

Of course it wasn't tanned Greg's fault that everything he said sounded like blah, blah, blah to her. Not entirely his fault that she wanted something different than what the Gregs of the world offered.

"I want a guy with more…presence." *Mastery.* A man like her boss.

"Does that mean kinkier?"

"Maybe. Probably. I'm young, unattached, living in the city. What if this is my window of opportunity?"

"Then you're doing it wrong because you're not going to find Mr. Kink at the Z Bar happy hour."

"Clearly I'm not going to find him anywhere at all."

"Normal people probably get in a relationship first, then suggest the kinky sex stuff."

"Maybe. So far that hasn't worked for me."

"There, there, darling." Kiki dropped her head on Amber's shoulder. "You'll find Prince Fetish someday. Probably will have a thing for fucking his horse though."

Amber snorted out a giggle and waved down a cab. "At least he sounds interesting."

"Yeah, well, don't be stupid." Kiki held out her crooked pinky and Amber linked hers with it.

"Don't worry."

But she did worry. At least, the problem remained on her mind as she dressed for work, buttoning up her favorite pink blouse and trying to think about the day ahead and not the several disappointments of the night before. First boring Greg and then the erotic book she'd saved as a treat had taken a bad turn. It had been decent until the heroine decided to quit her job, turn over all her money to her dom and become a 24/7 slave.

Why did these fictional doms have to be such assholes? Surely there was a real-world balance out there, a man who could fulfill the sex fantasies and see a woman as an actual person with career ambitions. Because the kitchen-cleaning porn? Not even remotely appealing.

As a palate cleanser, Amber had pulled out her box set of *Sandman*, losing herself in the painful and sometimes horrific journey of dark and brooding Morpheus, the King of Dreams.

Totally different from the world of high finance.

She did love her job. The rush of it, the huge stakes. Even the routine stuff got her revved every morning. Like walking through the steel-and-glass lobby of her office building, the satisfyingly sharp clack of her high heels on the marble floors, even having to show her ID to the security guard. It was all so shiny and exciting.

So was working for Alexander Knight.

She'd landed in clover with this job. Barely above an intern's salary, but with rich potential.

She was working it. Following the business mantra—make your boss look good. A man like Alexander Knight made for excellent inspiration that way, since he already looked pretty damn good. He had a similar vibe as Morpheus, especially at the end of a hectic day, with his dark hair ruffled from scraping his hand through it, snapping out orders to manage his empire.

If being around him gave an extra sparkle to things, well, all the better.

She could—and would—sublimate her sexual energy into the job. Prince Fetish would be nice, but apprenticing to the King of Dreams...priceless.

SHE'D WORN PINK again. That ruffled cotton-candy silk blouse under the severe lapels of her black suit. The one with the tight skirt that showed off her trim young ass. Absolutely appropriate, modest workplace attire. Not that you'd know it from the prurient direction of his thoughts.

If only he could stop thinking about popping her full breasts out of her bra, letting them be squeezed there amidst the pink, framed in black, while he pulled up her skirt and laid her back across his desk.

Bloody hell.

Alec rubbed a hand over his eyes to erase the image and to avoid watching her sashay down the hall, perfect bum twitching, slim calves like cream under her smooth hose, flashing through the demure back slit of the skirt. Though his computer pinged, announcing the arrival of yet another email, he waited a beat to be sure she'd moved out of sight. If he could figure out a way to transfer sweet young Amber Dolors off his team without unfairly impacting her blossoming career, he would in a heartbeat.

Not her fault she tripped his particular trigger, however. As part of senior management, he knew better than to make a pass at her—or do anything to put a smudge on her fresh and shiny reputation. Sending her out in under six months with no reason? It would look bad.

She was too bright and ambitious for some dirty old man to knock down, just because he couldn't control himself.

Because he *could* control himself. Prided himself on it. Iron self-discipline to govern the baser urges that sometimes threatened to overtake him. Stainless integrity. If he'd caught a whiff that anyone in the company—male or female— entertained thoughts about the junior staff of the variety that plagued him with this girl...well, he'd have them called out on the carpet. Had done so in the past.

Rightfully so. He could and would keep himself leashed.

Safe from temptation until the next time she made a trip down the hall, he focused on his overflowing inbox and gulped his tea. Too hot, but the burn helped him to concentrate. Not to think about whether her nipples would be the same color as her blouse or if he spread her slim, creamy thighs—

"No," he said. Inadvertently aloud, and clearly a little too loudly, because the devil herself popped her head round the doorframe. At times such as this he greatly regretted the firm's open-door policy. He needed a closed door. A solid one. And no windows.

Possibly a blindfold. For himself. *Don't think about how her mouth would look under a black silk blindfold.*

"Mr. Knight—did you say something?" Amber had a mild voice, nearly accentless, American Ivy League. It got under his skin. Everything about her did. A sharp, ambitious mind in a simmeringly curved body. From the shining fall of her waist-length honey-brown hair to her Alice-in-Wonderland blue eyes, alert, wide with inquiry. A bit startled, as if he'd caught her off guard. "Can I do something for you?" she asked, a faint line between her brows.

Firmly he pushed away the sudden fantasy of ordering her to kneel and open that blouse. "No, sorry—was talking to my email."

"I don't think it can answer," she replied in a wry tone. "Unless you've got voice-activation that us plebes don't."

"Heh. I apologize for disturbing you—carry on."

"Yes, sir!" She nodded crisply and gave him a cheery smile, completely oblivious to what that phrase did to him. How he'd relish hearing her say it under other circumstances. Yet another completely inappropriate thought. He scowled as three more emails pinged in.

"The bloody things never stop arriving." Ill-timed again, as his muttered comment stopped the lovely Amber from leaving.

She turned back. Tilted her head thoughtfully. "You have it sorting by conversation threads, right? So the stuff for me to deal with goes in a folder you don't have to look at?"

"I know how to use email, Ms. Dolors." He sounded more irritated than he should have. Not that it daunted her at all. In fact, she took several steps into his office.

"It's just that—" She paused, not hesitating, but clearly deciding how to put it to him. "See, as Joe's assistant, with him on vacation this week, I get his inbox along with Jean's email. We all get the same company-wide stuff. But I'm not getting yours. I check your spam folder for anything that shouldn't be there. I should be seeing the unimportant stuff too. Unless Jean is sorting it? As your admin, I'd think she'd be too busy. That's something I could be handling for you, if they aren't. I'd be happy to."

"Is that so?"

She flushed a little, a flustered rose. "I apologize if I'm overstepping. I'd wondered about this before. You have better things to do with your time than delete emails about the company picnic or the vending machine policy. I could be doing that for you." She raised her eyebrows significantly. "I would be doing that, if your inbox was organized by conversation threads."

Despite himself—uncertain whether his frustration was sexual or technological—he huffed out a laugh. "You're waiting for me to tell you I have no idea what you're talking about, right? And then you'll go post on some forum for Millennials about how your stuffy old boss can't handle his own email."

"Never." She gave him a solemn, serious look. "Millennials don't use forums. Too archaic. I'd tweet about it."

He really laughed then and waved a hand at the screen beneath the glass-topped desk. "Show me then."

A bright light flared in her eyes and she set down her water bottle and came round the desk. Tucking a long, shining strand of hair behind her ear, she leaned over, apparently unaware that her hip brushed his arm, nudging his hands away from the keyboard on its recessed tray. Her fingers flew over the keys and she explained as she reordered the lists. "See, the company server sends things by topic. You don't need to look at the standard-topic stuff, the aforementioned vending machine policy and all the griping about it. I can sort through it for you, then bullet-point what you need to know."

Her scent—something essentially fresh, like green leaves—hit him hard. A mistake to let her get so close, bent over his desk as she was. What the hell had he been thinking? So easy to tell her to grasp the far edge of the desk. To stay perfectly still while he worked her black skirt up over her tight little bum. Or to simply brush the back of her knee, where the skirt slit revealed it, the darling tender crease of it. From there, short work to slide his hand up the inner curve of her thigh. She'd be wearing tights, not stockings, but they'd rip easily and—

"Mr. Knight?"

She'd turned her head, looking at him quizzically, as he'd lost track of her explanation, failed to reply to some question. His gaze locked with hers—and her lips parted, the blue of her eyes deepening. The tension sizzled and, had they been anywhere else, anyone else, he'd have taken her up on the implicit invitation. Closed the scant inches between them and taken that mouth, ripped open her pink blouse—

Enough already.

"Looks splendid." He wheeled his chair back a few inches. "Do you need to do more or—?"

"No, it's, um, all set up now." She straightened, smoothed her skirt and picked up the water bottle. "I'll go take a look and flag anything that looks important. Of course, you'll still have total control of it all. You're the final word."

"Thank you." Was the minx baiting him on purpose? Likely had no idea what fire she was playing with. "Now, if you'd leave me be, I'll attempt to get some work done. As should you."

"Of course. Sir." She gave him a little smile and walked back across the office. He stared at the reconfigured email so as not to watch that enticing bottom swinging pertly under her short jacket. "Mr. Knight?"

"What is it?" He snapped it out, wishing she would leave, let him clear his mind.

"I want to do a good job here." She stood in the doorway, hands demurely folded around her water bottle. "If you have any feedback on my performance, or…corrections. I'd be grateful."

Helpless to do otherwise, he watched her until she went out of sight, dark fantasies crowding into his brain.

TITLES BY JEFFE KENNEDY

FANTASY ROMANCES

BONDS OF MAGIC
Dark Wizard
Bright Familiar
Grey Magic
Familiar Winter Magic
(Also Available in Fire of the Frost)

RENEGADES OF MAGIC
Shadow Wizard
Rogue Familiar

HEIRS OF MAGIC
The Long Night of the Crystalline Moon
(also available in *Under a Winter Sky*)
The Golden Gryphon and the Bear Prince
The Sorceress Queen and the Pirate Rogue
The Dragon's Daughter and the Winter Mage
The Storm Princess and the Raven King
The Long Night of the Radiant Star

THE FORGOTTEN EMPIRES
The Orchid Throne
The Fiery Crown
The Promised Queen

THE TWELVE KINGDOMS
Negotiation
The Mark of the Tala
The Tears of the Rose
The Talon of the Hawk
Heart's Blood
The Crown of the Queen

THE UNCHARTED REALMS
The Pages of the Mind
The Edge of the Blade
The Snows of Windroven
The Shift of the Tide
The Arrows of the Heart
The Dragons of Summer
The Fate of the Tala
The Lost Princess Returns

THE CHRONICLES OF DASNARIA
Prisoner of the Crown
Exile of the Seas
Warrior of the World

SORCEROUS MOONS
Lonen's War
Oria's Gambit
The Tides of Bára
The Forests of Dru
Oria's Enchantment
Lonen's Reign

A COVENANT OF THORNS

Rogue's Pawn
Rogue's Possession
Rogue's Paradise

CONTEMPORARY ROMANCES

Shooting Star

MISSED CONNECTIONS

Last Dance
With a Prince
Since Last Christmas

CONTEMPORARY EROTIC ROMANCES

Exact Warm Unholy
The Devil's Doorbell

FACETS OF PASSION

Sapphire
Platinum
Ruby
Five Golden Rings

FALLING UNDER

Going Under
Under His Touch
Under Contract

EROTIC PARANORMAL

MASTER OF THE OPERA E-SERIAL
Master of the Opera, Act 1: Passionate Overture
Master of the Opera, Act 2: Ghost Aria
Master of the Opera, Act 3: Phantom Serenade
Master of the Opera, Act 4: Dark Interlude
Master of the Opera, Act 5: A Haunting Duet
Master of the Opera, Act 6: Crescendo
Master of the Opera

BLOOD CURRENCY
Blood Currency

BDSM FAIRYTALE ROMANCE
Petals and Thorns

Thank you for reading!

ABOUT JEFFE KENNEDY

Jeffe Kennedy is a multi-award-winning and best-selling author of epic fantasy romance. She is the current president of the Science Fiction and Fantasy Writers Association (SFWA) and is a member of Romance Writers of America (RWA), and Novelists, Inc. (NINC). She is best known for her RITA® Award-winning novel, *The Pages of the Mind*, the recent trilogy, *The Forgotten Empires*, and the wildly popular, *Dark Wizard*. Jeffe lives in Santa Fe, New Mexico.

Jeffe can be found online at her website: JeffeKennedy.com, on her podcast First Cup of Coffee, every Sunday at the popular SFF Seven blog, on Facebook, on Goodreads, on BookBub, and pretty much constantly on Twitter @jeffekennedy. She is represented by Sarah Younger of Nancy Yost Literary Agency.

jeffekennedy.com

facebook.com/Author.Jeffe.Kennedy

twitter.com/jeffekennedy

goodreads.com/author/show/1014374.Jeffe_Kennedy

bookbub.com/profile/jeffe-kennedy

Sign up for her newsletter here.

jeffekennedy.com/sign-up-for-my-newsletter